MW01152139

Persian Letters

Montesquieu

Table of contents

Introduction by John Davidson
Introduction
Letter 1
Letter 2
Letter 3
Letter 4
Letter 5
Letter 6
Letter 7
Letter 8
Letter 9
Letter 10
Letter 11
Letter 12
Letter 13
Letter 14
Letter 15
Letter 16
Letter 17
Letter 18
Letter 19
Letter 20
Letter 21
Letter 22
Letter 23
Letter 24
Letter 25
Letter 26
Letter 27
Letter 28
Letter 29
Letter 30
Letter 31
Letter 32
Letter 33
Letter 34
Letter 35
Letter 36
Letter 37
Letter 38
Letter 39
Letter 40
Letter 41
Letter 42

Letter 43

Letter 44

Letter 45

Letter 46

Letter 47

Letter 48

Letter 49

Letter 50

Letter 51

Letter 52

Letter 53

Letter 54

Letter 55

Letter 56

Letter 57

Letter 58

Letter 59

Letter 60

Letter 61

Letter 62

Letter 63

Letter 64

Letter 65

Letter 66

Letter 67

Letter 68

Letter 69

Letter 70

Letter 71

Letter 72

Letter 73

Letter 74

Letter 75

Letter 76

Letter 77

Letter 78

Letter 79

Letter 80

Letter 81

Letter 82

Letter 83

Letter 84

Letter 85

Letter 86

Letter 87

Letter 88

Letter 89
Letter 90
Letter 91
Letter 92
Letter 93
Letter 94
Letter 95
Letter 96
Letter 97
Letter 98
Letter 99
Letter 100
Letter 101
Letter 102
Letter 103
Letter 104
Letter 105
Letter 106
Letter 107
Letter 108
Letter 109
Letter 110
Letter 111
Letter 112
Letter 113
Letter 114
Letter 115
Letter 116
Letter 117
Letter 118
Letter 119
Letter 120
Letter 121
Letter 122
Letter 123
Letter 124
Letter 125
Letter 126
Letter 127
Letter 128
Letter 129
Letter 130
Letter 131
Letter 132
Letter 133
Letter 134

Letter 135
Letter 136
Letter 137
Letter 138
Letter 139
Letter 140
Letter 141
Letter 142
Letter 143
Letter 144
Letter 145
Letter 146
Letter 147
Letter 148
Letter 149
Letter 150
Letter 151
Letter 152
Letter 153
Letter 154
Letter 155
Letter 156
Letter 157
Letter 158
Letter 159
Letter 160
Letter 161
Footnotes

Charles-Louis de Secondat, Baron de La Brède et de Montesquieu (18 January 1689 – 10 February 1755), generally referred to as simply Montesquieu, was a French judge, man of letters, and political philosopher.He is famous for his articulation of the theory of separation of powers, which is implemented in many constitutions throughout the world. He is also known for doing more than any other author to secure the place of the word "despotism" in the political lexicon.

Biography:

Montesquieu was born at the Château de la Brède in southwest France, 25 kilometres (16 mi) south of Bordeaux. His father, Jacques de Secondat, was a soldier with a long noble ancestry. His mother, Marie Françoise de Pesnel, who died when Charles was seven, was an heiress who brought the title of Barony of La Brède to the Secondat family. After the death of his mother he was sent to the Catholic College of Juilly, a prominent school for the children of French nobility, where he remained from 1700 to 1711. His father died in 1713 and he became a ward of his uncle, the Baron de Montesquieu. He became a counselor of the Bordeaux Parliament in 1714. In 1715 he married Jeanne de Lartigue, a Protestant, who eventually bore him three children. The Baron died in 1716, leaving him his fortune as well as his title, and the office of Président à Mortier in the Bordeaux Parliament.

Montesquieu's early life occurred at a time of significant governmental change. England had declared itself a constitutional monarchy in the wake of its Glorious Revolution (1688–89), and had joined with Scotland in the Union of 1707 to form the Kingdom of Great Britain. In France the long-reigning Louis XIV died in 1715 and was succeeded by the five-year-old Louis XV. These national transformations had a great impact on Montesquieu; he would refer to them repeatedly in his work.Montesquieu withdrew from the practice of law to devote himself to study and writing. He achieved literary success with the publication of his Lettres persanes (Persian Letters, 1721), a satire representing society as seen through the eyes of two imaginary Persian visitors to Paris and Europe, cleverly criticizing the absurdities of contemporary French society. He next published Considérations sur les causes de la grandeur des Romains et de leur décadence (Considerations on the Causes of the Grandeur and Decadence of the Romans, 1734), considered by some scholars, among his three best known books, as a transition from The Persian Letters to his master work. De l'Esprit des Lois (The Spirit of the Laws) was originally published anonymously in 1748. The book quickly rose to influence political thought profoundly in Europe and America. In France, the book met with an unfriendly reception from both supporters and opponents of the regime. The Catholic Church banned l'Esprit – along with many of Montesquieu's other works – in 1751 and included it on the Index of Prohibited Books. It received the highest praise from the rest of Europe, especially Britain.

Montesquieu was also highly regarded in the British colonies in North America as a champion of liberty (though not of American independence). Political scientist Donald Lutz found that Montesquieu was the most frequently quoted authority on government and politics in colonial pre-revolutionary British America, cited more by the American founders than any source except for the Bible.Following the American revolution, Montesquieu's work remained a powerful influence on many of the American founders, most notably James Madison of Virginia, the "Father of the Constitution". Montesquieu's philosophy that "government should be set up so that no man need be afraid of another"reminded Madison and others that a free and stable foundation for their new national government required a clearly defined and balanced separation of powers.Besides composing additional works on society and politics, Montesquieu traveled for a number of years through Europe including Austria and Hungary, spending a year in Italy and 18 months in England where he became a freemason, admitted to the Horn Tavern Lodge in Westminster,before resettling in France. He was troubled by poor eyesight, and was completely blind by the time he died from a high fever in 1755. He was buried in the Église Saint-Sulpice, Paris.

John Davidson's Introduction

I

Of all the great French authors perhaps Montesquieu is the least known in this country. It is more than a hundred years since any work of his was translated into English, and no greater sign of the neglect which has befallen him could be instanced than the infrequency of the appearance of his name in our periodical and journalistic literature, at a time when our ideas of government are once more in the crucible. The greater fame of Voltaire and Rousseau, and the absorbing interest of the French Revolution, are the principal causes of this neglect; at the same time, had there been anything in the shape of a true biography of Montesquieu, a living picture of the man, the operation of these causes might have been in some degree obviated.

It was the custom under the ancien régime in the great law-families for the eldest son to compose a life of his father: a document designed to hide the actual man behind a mask of the domestic and legal virtues so effectually that his friends and colleagues should be unable to recognize him. Such a mémoire pour servir in the highest style of the art, Montesquieu's son prepared and published in 1755. The eulogies of D'Alembert, Maupertuis, and the Chevalier de Solignac, founded, all of them, so far as they refer to Montesquieu's life, upon this filial effigy, represent only a mask with the conventional air proper to a great and good man.

This lack of a truthful picture has, of course, had a bad effect on Montesquieu's fame in France as well as in England. Least known, until recently, as regards his life, of all the great Frenchmen of the eighteenth century, he has had perhaps the most varied fortune of all writers of that or any other age. For about fifty years after his death, his reputation was unrivalled; but from 1789 till 1814, the alterations of feeling towards him in France were as extravagant as if he had been a living agent in the Revolution and its sequel, "now extolled to the clouds as the master of political science, as the man of genius who had rediscovered the title-deeds of the human race; now denounced as laudator temporis acti, the apostle of privilege, and the defender of abuses." Abandoned and condemned in evil times, he has always reappeared when France has recognized its truest interests. Under the Consulate and the First Empire he is intentionally forgotten, but in 1814 he comes to the front once more. Publishers and editors were seized about that time with a "sort of fury" for the works of Montesquieu, and from 1819 till 1834 numerous annotated editions appeared. Then again there came a period of eclipse, and it was not until the close of the Second Empire that France, once more free, resumed the study of him who first tried to show it what freedom meant.

In 1875 M. Edouard Laboulaye's edition of Montesquieu's works, perhaps the best, was published in seven volumes; and in 1878 M. Louis Vian issued his "Histoire de Montesquieu," the most important work on Montesquieu that has yet appeared. M. Vian had access to much unpublished matter; and his book, which is the result of fifteen years of study and research, supplies that biography for want of which Montesquieu's personality has hitherto been as vague as a spectre. In short, they seem at last in France in a fair way to get something like the true focus of Montesquieu, to have him placed in his proper niche: to understand him, even to label him, for he is not one of the very greatest whom it is criminal, and indeed impossible, to docket and define until one can look at them through the thought of many generations.

It is from M. Vian's biography that the material for this introduction is mainly drawn. The writer is also indebted to M. Albert Sorel's monograph on Montesquieu, and to the prefaces of M. Laboulaye. For the translation, the editions used were those of M. Laboulaye and M. Tourneux, the text of the former having been followed as a rule: the notes in both have been found very serviceable.

II

Like Montaigne, Montesquieu was a Gascon. His father, Jacques de Secondat, married Marie-Françoise de Penel, the desendant of an English family which had remained in France after the English rule had ceased there. She was an only child, and her husband received with her the title and barony of La Brède, an estate in Gascony, with a fantastic old Gothic donjon built in the thirteenth century. Montesquieu was the second of six children. The date of his birth is not known, but he was baptized on the 18th of January, 1689. His godfather, like the godfathers of Montaigne in 1553, of the lord of Beauvais in 1644, and of the Comte de Buffon in 1742, was a beggar belonging to the district, chosen "in order that his godchild might remember all his life that the poor are his brothers." He was christened Charles-Louis, and bore, according to a curious custom of the time, the surname of De la Brède, the patronymic, De Secondat, being reserved for the head of the house.

His nurse was a miller's wife, and the first three years of his life were spent with her. Most of those who have written of Montesquieu have attributed his constant use of the Gascon accent, and of certain idioms and solecisms, to these three years. Is it likely, if he had not heard the Gascon accent in his father's household, and probably from his father's lips, that the effect of his lisping in a patois in his earliest infancy would have remained with him all his life? If, however, he heard nothing in his father's house but the best "French of Paris," his close and lasting friendship with his foster-brother, Jean Demarennes, is a sufficient cause for the perpetuation of his Gasconisms. But the point is of small moment.

Montesquieu's mother died when he was seven years old, and four years after, in 1700, he was sent to the college of the Oratorian Fathers at Juilly, near Meaux, in the department of Seine-et-Marne. There he remained till 1711. He was docile and diligent, and the solid foundation laid in Juilly enabled him to become the best informed writer of his time in France. In the year in which he left Juilly he wrote his first non-scholastic piece – the first, at least, of which we known anything. It was a refutation, in the form of a letter, of the doctrine of the eternal damnation of idolaters: the substance of it he afterwards incorporated in the "Persian Letters."[1]

III

On leaving college Montesquieu began to study law. It was natural, as both his grandfathers had been presidents of the Parliament of Guienne, and his uncle occupied a similar position. Methodical in all things, he studied jurisprudence according to a plan of his own, the draft of which still exists; and found plenty of time to frequent the best salons in Bordeaux, in which the rank of his family and his own reputation as a young man of talent secured him a welcome. The chief figure in Bordeaux society was the Duke of Berwick,[1] the son of James II. And Marlborough's sister. This careful soldier and upright man, the only cool-headed and thoroughly sensible scion of the House of Stuart, perceived the merit of Montesquieu, and a friendship sprang up between them which ended only with the Duke's death. Montesquieu cherished his memory, and among his papers was found a warm and eloquent eulogy of the victor of Almanza.

In 1713 Montesquieu's father died, and his uncle, the Baron de Montesquieu, took upon himself the duties of guardian. Two months after his nephew had reached his twenty-fifth year, he caused him to be appointed a lay-councillor of the Parliament of Guienne; and a year later, on the 30th of April 1715, Montesquieu married the girl of his uncle's choice, the Demoiselle Jeanne Lartigue, a plain-looking Calvinist, inclined to limp,[2] but frank, good-natured, and with a dowry of a hundred thousand livres. Love had nothing to do with the marriage: Montesquieu's wife was his housekeeper, and the mother of his heir.

In the beginning of 1716 his uncle died, leaving him sole legatee on condition that he should call himself Montesquieu. Besides the name, which he had already adopted on the day of his marriage, he inherited a house in Bordeaux, lands in Agénois, and the position of *President à mortier* in the Parliament of Guienne. His installation took place in July, 1716, and he retained his presidentship till 1728.

Of the twelve provincial parliaments of France, that of Guienne, which sat at Bordeaux, ranked third with regard to the extent of its jurisdiction. It was directed by *six presidents à mortier*,[3] and as it possessed political, religious, administrative, and judicial attributes, the proper performance of the duties of a president entailed considerable study, and were in themselves by no means light. Montesquieu is believed to have given them sufficient attention, although on his own showing, he did not understand legal procedure; but no trace remains of his judicial functions.

His official duties did not by any means occupy him exclusively. After the Academies of Caen and Paris, that of Bordeaux, having been established in 1712, is the most ancient. Three years after its constitution, Montesquieu was admitted, and became one of its most enthusiastic members. Wherever he was, and in whatever me might be engaged, he had always time to attend to its interests. More than once in acknowledgment of his many services he was appointed president. Much of the work he prepared for the Academy has been lost; of the dissertation which was considered the most remarkable, only the title remains – "The Religious Policy of the Romans." Medicine, physics, natural history, were all studied, and numerous discourses written. The effect of these studies is to be found throughout all his works, the principal definitions in "L'Esprit des Lois" itself being, not those of a lawyer or metaphysician, but rather of a geometer and naturalist.

IV

In all likelihood the idea of the "Persian Letters" occurred to Montesquieu before he left college. The first of them, dated the 21st of the moon of Muharram (January), 1711, was written in his twenty-second year; the last in his thirty-second. Reflections of his favourite reading are to be found in their framework, and critics have pointed out the many resemblances to Dufresney's "Amusements," "The Turkish Spy," "The Spectator," the "Decameron," with borrowings from Erasmus and other less-known writers. But Montesquieu has at least spoiled nothing that he has used. The "Letters" were printed in Amsterdam, and published anonymously in 1721; and at once, as a friend of Montesquieu's had predicted, "they sold like loaves." No French writer had ever before said so perfectly what all felt and were trying to say; and it was done so skillfully, so pleasantly, like a man telling a story after supper.

At the time they appeared the social order of the ancien régime was beginning to crumble about the monarchy. The revocation of the Edict of Nantes in 1685, by exiling the Huguenots, had deprived the country of many of its most industrious subjects, and struck a disastrous blow at its trade; the power of France, build up peacefully by Mazarin and Colbert, had been shattered at Ramilies and Malplaquet; and Louis XIV.'s acceptance of the Bull Unigenitus, directed against the Jansenists, had destroyed the last remnant of religious liberty. As for the parliaments, they were only able to mumble and grumble, endless edicts having pulled their teeth, as it were, one by one; and the condition of the people was desperate in the extreme. It is no wonder that when Louis XIV. Died, the middle and lower classes thanked God with "scandalous frankness" as for a long-expected and certain deliverance. The upper classes were delighted also, although they hardly returned thanks in the same quarter, nor for the same reason. It was not a lightening of taxation, some liberty of conscience, more equal laws, that the latter anticipated, but the old licence, the "unchained libertinage," the idea of which had never disappeared, but had been handed down, as Sainte-Beuve says, in direct and uninterrupted descent from the Renaissance to the Fronde, from the Fronde to the Regency, through De Retz, Saint-Evremond, Vendome, Bayle, to the Epicureans, Pyrrhonists, professors of an imperturbable impiety, the unbelievers, as full and certain in their unbelief as Bossuet was in his faith, who made a byword of the eight years from the death of Louis XIV. To his successor's assumption of power. Grown sanctimonious in his old age, Louis XIV. Had made his subjects hypocrites. At his death the boast of vice succeeded to ostentatious devotion; the court like one man changed from Tartuffe into Don Juan. All things were discussed, examined, and torn to shreds. The intestine quarrels of the Church gave scoffers the opportunity they would have made. Dubois debauched politics; Law, finance; and the populace debauched themselves: for gaming, which had before been confined to people of quality, became the common amusement. Incest, too, was quite à la mode; and those who could not be in the height of the fashion had to be satisfied with lesser vices. The autocratic rule of the Grand Monarque gave place to the laissez-aller of Philip of Orleans, the "unbelieving Regent." Hope, desire, speculation, knew no bounds, all things in heaven above and in the earth beneath having become common and unclean. It is this period that is reflected and criticized in the "Persian Letters."

V

The "Persian Letters" are the correspondence of several Persians, on a visit to Europe, with each other and their friends in Ispahan. Rica, the younger of the two principal writers, is good-humoured, sarcastic, and represents the lighter side of Montesqiueu's nature. His lively intellect makes him a keen observer; his youth and health enable him to go everywhere, see everybody, and experience everything. He describes the surface of society with a quick glance that sometimes pierces deep enough, too. The King of France, although he has no mines of gold and silver, like the King of Spain, is much wealthier, deriving supplies from an inexhaustible source, the vanity of his subjects. He is likewise a magician, for his dominion extends to the minds of his subjects. If he has a costly war on hand, and is short of money, he simply suggests that a piece of paper is a coin of the realm, and his people are straightway convinced of it. But this is a small matter. There is a much more powerful magician, the Pope, to wit, who sometimes makes the King believe that three are no more than one; that the bread he eats is not bread, and the wine he drinks not wine. It is Rica who makes the discovery that the Christian religion practically consists in the non-fulfilment of an immense number of tedious duties; and it is he who quotes the epitaph on the diner-out which recalls by its numerical exactness Teufelsdröck's epitaph on Philippus Zaehdarm. "Here," it runs, "rests one who never rested before. He assisted at five hundred and thirty funerals. He made merry at the births of two thousand six hundred and eighty children. He wished his friends joy, always varying the phrase, upon pensions amounting to two millions six hundred thousand livres; in town he walked nine thousand six hundred furlongs, in the country thirty-six furlongs. His conversation was pleasing; he made a ready-made stock of three hundred and sixty-five stories; he was acquainted also from his youth with a hundred and eighteen apophthegms derived from the ancients, which he employed on special occasions. He died at last in the sixtieth year of his age. I say no more, stranger; for how could I ever have done telling you all that he did and all that he saw."[1] It is Rica who sketches the alchemist in his garret, praying fatuously that God would enable him to make a good use of his wealth; the people whose conversation is a mirror which relects only their own impertinent faces; the professional wits planning a conversation of an hour's length to consist entirely of bons-mots; the compilers who produce masterpieces by shifting the books in a library from one shelf to another; the universal "decider," who knew more about Ispahan than his Persian interlocutor; the French Academy, a body with a chokeful of tropes, metaphors, and antitheses; the geometer, a martyr to his own accuracy, who was offended by a witty remark, as weak eyes are annoyed by too strong a light; the quidnuncs, petits-maîtres, lazy magistrates, financiers, bankrupts, and opera-dancers.

Usbek is older, graver, given to meditation and reflection. Although from his earliest youth a courtier, he has remained uncorrupted. As he could not flatter, his sincerity made him enemies, and brought upon him the jealousy of the ministers. His life being in danger, he forsook the court, and retired to his country-house. Even there persecution followed him, and he determined on the journey to Europe. Rica went as his companion.

The opening paragraph of Letter XLVIII., in which Usbek characterizes himself, is undoubtedly descriptive of Montesquieu. "Although I am not employed in any business of importance, I am yet constantly occupied. I spend my time observing, and at night I write down what I have noticed, what I have seen, what I have heard during the day. I am interested in everything, astonished at everything: I am like a child, whose organs, still over-sensitive, are vividly impressed by the merest trifles." Usbek can be as brilliant and satirical on occasion as his younger companion, but his aim is to probe to the heart of things, and he knows that truth will only reveal itself to a reverent search. To him all religions are worthy of respect, and their ministers also, for "God has chosen for Himself, in every corner of the earth, souls purer than the rest, whom He has separated from the impious world that their mortification and their fervent prayers may suspend His wrath." He thinks that the surest way to please God is to obey the laws of society, and to do our duty towards men. Every religion assumes that God loves men, since He establishes a religion for their happiness; and since He loves men we are certain of pleasing Him in loving them, too. Usbek's prayer in Letter XLVI. Is not yet out of date. "Lord, I do not understand any of those discussions that are carried on without end regarding Thee: I would serve Thee according to Thy will; but each man whom I consult would have me serve Thee according to his." He insists that religion is intended for man's happiness; and that, in order to love it and fulfil its behests, it is not necessary to hate and persecute those who are opposed to our beliefs – not necessary even to attempt to convert them. Indeed, he holds that variety of belief is beneficial to the state. A new sect is always the surest means of correcting the abuses of an old faith; and those who profess tolerated creeds usually prove more useful to their country than those who profess the established religion, because, being excluded from all honours, their endeavour to distinguish themselves by becoming wealthy improves trade and commerce. Proselytism, with its intolerance, its affliction of the consciences of others, its wars and inquisitions, is an epidemic disease which the Jews caught from the Egyptians, and which passed from them to the Christians and Mohammedans, a capricious mood which can be compared only to a total eclipse of human reason. "He who would have me change my religion is led to that, without doubt, because he would not change his own, although force were employed; and yet he finds it strange that I will not do a thing which he himself will not do, perhaps for the empire of the world."[2] Usbek is a sophist, but it is quite evident that he is no bigot; he even goes further than Montesquieu himself, a wit of the Regency, felt to be right; and when he praises suicide as being no more a disturbance of the order of Providence than the making a round stone square, he is rapped over the knuckles with the reminder that the preservation of the union of body and soul is the chief sign of submission to the decrees of the Creator.

Usbek has his character-sketches as well as Rica. He gives a lively description of those geniuses who frequent the coffee-houses, and on quitting them believe themselves four times wittier than when they entered. The savage king sitting on his block of wood, dressed in his own skin, and inquiring of the sailors if they talked much of him in France, is an illustration of his. One letter, the forty-eighth, is quite a picture-gallery. Usbek is in the country at the house of a man of some note; and he describes to his friend Rhedi various members of the company he meets. There are vulgar farmers-general who brag of their cooks; jaunty confessors, necessities of female existence, who can cure a headache better than any medicine; poets, the grotesquest of humankind, declaring that they are born so; the old soldier, who cannot endure the thought that France has gained any battles without him; and last, but not least, the lady-killer who has a talk with Usbek. "'It is fine weather,' he said. 'Will you take a turn with me in the garden?' I replied as civilly as I could, and we went out together. 'I have come to the country,' said he, 'to please the mistress of the house, with whom I am not on the worst of terms. There is a certain woman in the world who will be rather out of humour; but what can one do? I visit the finest women in Paris; but I do not confine my attentions to one; they have plenty to do to look after me, for, between you and me, I am a sad dog.' 'In that case, sir,' said I, 'you doubtless have some office or employment which prevents you from waiting on them more assiduously?' 'No, sir; I have no other business than to provoke husbands, and drive fathers mad; I delight in alarming a woman who thinks me hers, and in bringing her within an ace of losing me. A set of us young fellows divide up Paris among us in this pursuit, and keep it wondering at everything we do.' 'From what I understand,' said I, 'you make more stir than the most valorous warrior, and are more regarded than a grave magistrate. If you were in Persia you would not enjoy all these advantages; you would be held fitter to guard our women than to please them.' The blood mounted to my face; and I believe had I gone on speaking, I could not have refrained from affronting him." Then there are casuists, great lords, men of sense and men of none, bishops, philosophers and philosophasters, all pricked off as deftly as any of Rica's acquaintances, and with less exaggeration, if with more sobriety. One brief dramatic sketch must not be omitted. Has any one failed to meet the gentleman who says, "I believe in the immortality of the soul for six months at a time; my opinions depend entirely on my bodily condition: I am a Spinozist, a Socinian, a Catholic, ungodly or devout, according to the state of my animal spirits, the quality of my digestion, the rarity or heaviness of the air I breathe, the lightness or solidity of the food I eat?"[3]

Montesquieu has distinguished the characters of Rica and Usbek with care; and during the first months of their stay in Europe, he succeeds with fair success in depicting their state of mind in the midst of, what was to them, a new world. Soon, however, they become in all except their domestic matters merely mouthpieces for the author's satire and criticism, and expounders of his theories. It is Usbek who in several letters explains those ideas which Montesquieu afterwards developed in "L'Esprit des Lois." On this subject he writes as a legislator, with the well-balanced judgment, the restraint and reserve which always temper Montesquieu's enthusiasm and control his expressions of opinion. Here in one sentence is the policy of "L'Esprit des Lois": "I have often inquired which form of government is most conformable to reason. It seems to me that the most perfect is that which obtains its object with the least friction;

so that the government which leads men by following their propensities and inclinations is the most perfect."[4] And in the following has been detected the philosophy of Montesquieu's great book: "Nature always works tardily, and, as it were, thriftily; her operations are never violent; even in her productions she requires temperance; she never works but by rule and measure; if she be hurried she soon falls into decline."[5] In fact, the latter portion of the "Persian Letters" is edited from Montesquieu's commonplace-book. It reveals his ideas on international law, on the advancement of science, and on the origin of liberty; and states those problems which were to be the study of his life.

From the travels of Chardin and Tavernier, Montesquieu derived his knowledge of Persia. To Chardin he is particularly indebted, not only for the background, but for his theory of despotism [6] and his theory of climates.[7] The story of the revolt of Usbek's harem, though belonging to a style long out of fashion, is skillfully told, and will be found to interest the most prudish reader in spite of some disgust. The forsaken wives, the long-winded pedantic eunuchs, are all French, of course, French people of the Regency; and Usbek himself is as jealous as a petit-maître. As for the story of Anais, and the sexual love of brother and sister in "Apheridon and Astarte," all that need be said of them is that they are characteristic of the mood of the Regency. The translator gave a passing thought to the propriety of omitting the former; but the author did not omit it, so it appears. One word more on this subject, and it shall be a word from Montesquieu himself. He found his daughter one day with the "Persian Letters" in her hand. "Let it alone, my child, he said. "It is a work of my youth unsuited to yours."

VI

Soon after the publication of the "Persian Letters" Montesquieu went to the capital to enjoy his reputation. There he found society more agreeable in Paris than in Versailles, because in the small world of the latter intrigue was the rule, whereas in the former people amused themselves. He became a member of the informal Club de l'Entre-sol, which met on Saturdays in the house of President Hénault. Bolingbroke was the founder of this club, and its most distinguished member. Among those who frequented it were the Abbé de Saint-Pierre, D'Argenson, "secretary to the Republic of Plato," and Ramsai. Probably the principal benefit which Montesquieu derived from his attendance at the Entre-sol was his introduction to Lord Chesterfield; but he continued a member until Cardinal Fleury interdicted the club in 1730, on account of the active part it began to take in politics.

With the aid of Mademoiselle de Clermont, Louis XIV.'s unspeakable tenth muse, Montesquieu was elected to the Academy in 1725; but his election was invalidated on account of his non-residence in Paris. He then returned to Bordeaux, sold his presidentship, acquired the necessary qualification, and, not without a questionable intrigue, was elected in 1728 to the chair rendered vacant by the death of De Sacy, a forgotten translator.

In the spring of the same year Montesquieu set out on his travels with a nephew of the Duke of Berwick, whose affairs called him to Vienna. It was during this journey that he applied for nomination to some diplomatic post. In urging his claim he pointed out that he was not duller than other men; that, being of independent means, honour was the only reward he sought; that he was accustomed to society, and had toiled (beaucoup travaillé) to make himself capable. The powers that then were, however, elected to dispense with his services.

Montesquieu was much disappointed with his reception at the hands of the great. On his first entrance into society he had been announced as a man of genius, and had been looked on favourably by people in place; but when the success of the "Persian Letters" proved that he actually had ability, and brought him the esteem of the public, people in place began to be shy of him. It was no consolation for him to tell himself that officialdom, secretly wounded by the reputation of a celebrated man, takes vengeance by humiliating him, and that he who can endure to hear another praised must merit much praise himself.[1] He was deeply disappointed. In his youth he had written, "Cicero, of all the ancients, is he whom I should most wish to be like." A public career was denied him and he suffered, having set his heart on it; but he was more of an ancient Roman than Cicero, if that was his ambition; and it is surely better to be famous as the author of "L'Esprit des Lois," than to be infamous as one of Louis XV.'s ministers.

In Italy he found Lord Chesterfield. The two men had already tested each other in the Entre-sol, and they were now glad to travel together. Journeying to Venice, they met Law, the creator of credit, who, having preserved his taste for speculation and a fine diamond, passed his time in staking the latter at the gaming-table. Montesquieu had dealt severely with him in the "Persian Letters," but that did not prevent Law from receiving him pleasantly; nor did the ruined financier's complaisance prevent Montesquieu from applying the lash again in "L'Esprit des Lois."

From Venice they went to Rome. Montesquieu frequented the salon of Cardinal Polignac, the French ambassador; and the city, both ancient and modern, had its due effect. Before leaving it, he paid a visit to the Pope, Benedict XIII., who said to him, "My dear president, I wish you to carry away some souvenir of my friendship. To you and yours I grant permission to eat meat every day for the term of your natural lives." Montesquieu thanked the Pope and withdrew. Next day they brought him the dispensation with a note of charges. "The Pope," said Montesquieu, returning the papers, "is an honest man; I will not doubt his word; and I hope God has no reason to doubt it either." An answer becoming a shrewd economic Gascon. After visiting Naples, Pisa, Florence, Turin, and the Rhine country, they arrived at the Hague, where Chesterfield was English ambassador. From the Hague they sailed to England, reaching London in November, 1729.

VII

Although Montesquieu lived in England for eighteen months, there is but little to tell of his visit. According to his custom he went everywhere, and saw, if not everybody, certainly Walpole, Pope, and Swift. Montesquieu derived immense benefit from his travels, because he was always pliant to the manners of the country in which he sojourned. "When I am in France," he said, "I swear friendship with everybody; in England, with nobody; in Italy, I do the agreeable all round; in Germany, I drink with the whole world." He found England the most useful country to visit. Germany, he thought, was made to travel in, Italy to rest in, England to think in, and France to live in.

Montesquieu left behind him a set of notes on England, from which we can gather and condense his impressions.

In London the people eat much fleshmeat, with the result that they become very stout, and collapse at forty or forty-five.

The streets of London are so bad, that it is advisable to make one's will before taking a hackney-coach.

The young English noblemen are divided into two classes: those who, having been to the University, have some learning, and are consequently shamefaced and constrained; and the shameless ones who know nothing, and are the petits-maîtres of the nation. But the English in general are modest.

Paris is a handsome city where there are ugly corners; London is a villainous place containing some very beautiful things.

The complaints of foreigners, especially of the French, in London, are lamentable. They say that they cannot make a friend; and that their overtures are received as injuries. But how can the Kinski, the Broglies, and La Vilette, with their profuse French manners, expect the English to be like them? How should the English, who do not love each other, love strangers?

I look on the King of England simply as a man who has a pretty wife, a hundred servants, a handsome equipage, and a good table. People think him fortunate; but when he is left alone, and his door closed, and he has to quarrel with his wife and his servant, and swear at his butler, he is not so much to be envied after all.

By dint of suspecting everybody, people grow hard-hearted here.

There are some Scotch members of parliament who can get only two hundred pounds for their votes, and who sell them at that price.

A minister thinks only of defeating the opposition; and to that end he would sell England – the whole world.

Extraordinary things are done in England for money. The English do not even know the meaning of honor and virtue.

I do not know what will be the upshot of European emigration to Africa and the West Indies; but I am certain that England will be the first nation to be deserted by its colonies.

The English make little effort at politeness, but are never impolite.

Women in England are reserved because they see little of the men. If a foreigner speaks to them, they suspect his intentions. "'Je ne veux pas,' disent-elles, 'give to him encouragement.'"

There is no religion in England. If religion is spoken of everybody laughs.

England is at present the freest country in the world, not excepting any republic. I call it free, because unlimited power is in the hands of the King and the Parliament. A good English citizen will therefore endeavour to protect liberty as much against the Commons as against the King.

Montesquieu's impressions of England were written on his lands as well as in his books; for when he returned to France he had his ancestral estate of La Brède laid out in the English style.

VIII

The rest of Montesquieu's life was spent at his estates in the country and at Paris.

He made great improvements in his land, and increased his revenues largely. At his death his income is said to have been sixty thousand francs. He was not ambitious to be rich; but in all that he took in hand he wished to feel and to see signs of his ability. He has been accused of parsimony, but that is one of the commonest charges the weak have to bring against the strong. Order was the law of his being, and prodigality and dissipation as repugnant to him as anything else chaotic. Indeed there was always too little chaos about Montesquieu.[1] He saw life steadily and saw it whole, too soon, too easily; and he took a part for the whole. But, to return, he was certainly not avaricious. His enlightened benevolence appeared in the moderate rents he charged; and there are several specific acts of generosity recorded.

Henry Sully, an English astronomer of note, being at Bordeaux pursuing experiments in horology, received much attention at the hands of Montesquieu, then President of the Bordeaux Academy. One day Sully, reduced to his last sou, "no uncommon thing with inventors," wrote

Montesquieu a brief note, "very English and very artless"—"I am in the mood to hang myself, but I don't think I should do so if I had a hundred crowns." "I send you a hundred crowns," replied Montesquieu, "don't hang yourself, and come and see me."

In the winter of 1747-48, Guienne, on account of the war with England, had been unable to import a sufficient quantity of grain. On the 7th of December, Montesquieu, being at La Brède, was told that the tenants on an estate of his fifty leagues away were almost famine-stricken. He drove to the place at once with hardly a halt; summoned the curés of "the four villages," and while waiting for them examined the state of provisions. On their arrival, he said, "Gentlemen, I beg you to assist me in procuring some help for your parishioners. You know those who are in need of corn, or of money to buy it. I wish all the grain in my barns to be distributed gratuitously. My steward will hand it out in quantities to be fixed in proportion to the needs of those who are in want of it. It is not right that any one should lack the necessaries of life on my lands as long as I have a superabundance. Gentlemen, you are good fellows. I trust to you entirely to make this distribution. You will oblige me by carrying out my intentions promptly; and by keeping the thing a secret."

Montesquieu then went away at once, to escape the thanks of his tenants. According to the friend—of a scenic turn of mind evidently—who accompanied him, wheat to the value of 6400 livres was distributed by the curés. To prevent the recurrence of the distress which he had so munificently relieved, Montesquieu established on his estates granaries for the poor (greniers de charité).

Montesquieu was, indeed, one of the best of landlords and country gentlemen. He was looked upon in France as a species of "Milord Anglais," as interested in men as in books; and he was so—in the peasants of La Brède, who were "not learned enough to make the worse appear the better reason," as well as in the wits of Paris. His habits and manners were as simple as could be. He would go about La Brède all day long with a white cotton cap on his head and a vine-pole over his shoulder; in which guise he was, of course, mistaken more than once for a vine-dresser, and asked by those who came to offer him "les hommages de l'Europe," if that "was the chateau of Montesquieu."[2] A Genevese naturalist, Trembley,[3] whom he had met in England, wrote to a friend, after having passed several days at La Brède in the autumn of 1752, "I cannot describe the pleasure I enjoyed during my stay. How beautiful, how charming the things I heard! What do you think of conversations which begin at one o'clock in the day and last till eleven at night? Now there was talk of the loftiest subjects; anon full bodied laughter over some delightful story. . . I talked much of agriculture with M. de Montesquieu. In a conversation on that subject he exclaimed:

' O fortunatos nimium sua si bona norint Agricolas!'   adding, 'I have often thought of putting these words on the front of my house.'"

The Earl of Charlemont wrote requesting an audience.[4] The reply was favourable, and he and his companion, so excited were they at the prospect of seeing the great man, arrived at his house before he was up. The servant put them into the library, where "the first thing we saw was an open book lying on a table at which he had probably sat on the preceding evening: the extinguished lamp was still in position. Impatient to know the night reading of the great philosopher, we stepped at once to the volume: it was the Elegies of Ovid, open at one of the most gallant pages. We had not recovered from our surprise, when it was increased by the entrance of the president, whose appearance and manners were entirely opposed to the idea which we had formed of him. Instead of a grave and austere philosopher, whose very presence would have intimidated young folk like us, the person who addressed us was a Frenchman"—

even the French philosophers are French! – "gay, polished, full of vivacity, who, after a thousand agreeable greetings, and a thousand thanks for the honour which we did him, invited us to breakfast; but". . . in short, we went to walk instead. "At the skirt of a fine wood, cut in alleys, surrounded by a paling, and entered by a gate three feet high and fastened with a chain, 'Come on,' said he, after having searched in his pocket, 'it is not worth while waiting for the key. You can jump as well as I, I am sure, and it's not a gate like that I'm afraid of.' So saying, he ran at the gate and leapt over it as light as you like. He had noticed our embarrassment on first meeting him—for we were much moved—and so he set to work, out of pure good-nature, to put us at our ease. Little by little his age and his genius disappeared so completely that the conversation became as free and easy as if we had been his equals in every respect. We spoke of the arts and sciences. He questioned us on our travels, and as I had visited the east he addressed himself particularly to me, interesting himself in the smallest details of the lands through which I had traveled. I heard him say more than once that he regretted not having seen these countries. . . After having made the tour of his estate, laid out in the English style, we returned and were received by Madame la Baronne and her daughter. . . . The meal was simple and abundant. After dinner Montesquieu insisted that we should stay, and he kept us for three days, during which his conversation was equally amusing and instructive." This, though of the gushing order, is evidently a true picture of the man who said, "He who writes well does not write as people write, but as he writes; very often in talking badly such a one writes well." To himself may be applied what he said of Montaigne: "In most authors I see a writing man; in Montaigne, a thinking man." He was always saying, "The misfortune of certain books is the killing work one has to do in condensing what the author took so much trouble to expand."

IX

This simplicity was the great charm of the man, as it is that of the writer. He never lectures the reader, he talks with him; "he makes him assist him in his composition." In Paris he was, as in the country, as in his books, even-tempered, simple, and pleasantly merry. In the very heat of conversation he never lost his equanimity. Simple, profound, sublime, he charmed, instructed, without offence: was even more marvelous in conversation than in his works:[1] "and always that same energy when his hatred of despotism lighted his face."[2] Without bitterness, without satire, full of wit and brilliant sallies, no one could tell a better story, promptly, vividly, without premeditation.[3] And he was always more willing to listen than to talk; he learnt as much from conversation as from books. The Duchess de Chaulnes said of him, "That man makes his book in society: he remembers everything that is said to him, and only talks with those who have something to tell him worth remembering.: Such a man requires the company of the best brains to bring him out; with commonplace people he will be commonplace: and yet he could find wit in those who were called dull.[4] It was possible, however, to bore him. On one occasion, when disputing with some portentous councilor who got warm and cried, "M. le Président, if it is not as I say, I will give you my head, " he replied, coolly, "I accept; little gifts are the cement of friendship."[5] A certain young lady, un peu galante, annoyed him with a torrent of questions one evening. His opportunity came when she asked him in what happiness consisted. "Happiness," he replied, "means for queens, fertility; for maidens, sterility; and for those who are near you, deafness."[6] Still he delighted in the company and conversation of women, and in his younger days did not object be in their best graces. He tells that he attached himself to such as he thought loved him, and detached himself as soon as he thought they didn't:[7] the manners of the Regency being somewhat different from ours.

X

The eighteenth century was in France the age of the "monstrous regiment of women." The divine right of kings, as it had done in England half a century before, resolved itself into the divine right of mistresses. One legacy bequeathed by them was the French Revolution; modern conversation was the other. In England conversation remained among men, and produced clubs; in France women invaded it, and the salon was the result: the heyday past, the Regent's mistress, the minister's mistress, opened a salon, where Montesquieu and all celebrities might meet to talk. Claudine Guérin de Tencin, saddened by the suicide of a lover and the arrival of her forty-fifth year; Madame Geoffrin, "whimsical and cross-grained," citizen's daughter, millionaire's widow, who had the excellent talent of drawing every one out in his own subject, and called her salon "a shop;" Marie de Vichy, Marquise du Deffand, whom Massillon could not convert, who was interested in nothing, and had neither temperament nor romance; and the Duchess de Chaulnes, the "intimate enemy" of Madame du Deffand, "a typical woman of the eighteenth century," delighting only in wit, bons-mots, and gallantry, and made piercingly sagacious by her wicked life: these and others like them kept salons, primarily for their own amusement. Earnest talk on momentous matters was the one thing forbidden. Clear analysis of questions of finance, of morality, of legislation, clear mockery of the problems of human destiny, the facile, brilliant, and winged talk, "on everything à propos of nothing," was the order of the day.

Madame du Deffand was Montesquieu's favourite among these. She gathered about her in her own phrase "les trompeurs, le trompés, et les trompettes"—everybody connected with diplomacy, in fact. In her salon the author of "L'Esprit des Lois" learned much. "I like that woman," he said, "with all my heart; she pleases me, amuses me; it is impossible to weary in her company." It was in this society that Montesquieu "talked out" his books; and the reader should remember that it was for this society they were written.

Montesquieu was often glad to retire from the "official centers of conversation" to quieter houses, where he could be more at home, and where he could meet such marvels of the age as the two sisters of Madame de Rochefort, "the Marquise de Boufflers, who was faithful to her lover, and the Duchesse de Mirepoix, who was faithful to her husband." But of all salons he preferred that the Duchesse d'Aiguillon. There he met the most interesting men of the day of all nationalities, attracted by the impartiality of the duchess, her abundant and original wit, her refined talk, her obligating manners, and her ability to speak four languages. Gustavus III. called her the "living journal of the Academy." But she had judgment also; and authors consulted her about their works. Montesquieu liked her for herself and also because in her house he could meet Madame Dupré de Saint-Maur, wife of the Intendant of Bordeaux, who was "equally charming as mistress, as wife, and as friend." It was in the arms of Madame Dupré de Saint-Maur that Montesquieu died on the 10th of February, 1755, in his sixty-sixth year.

XI

Of "L'Esprit de Lois," perhaps the greatest French book of the eighteenth century, "La Grandeur des Romains et leur décadence," and Montesquieu's minor works, it is not necessary to speak here. It has been said that Montesquieu only wrote one book, the "Persian Letters" and the "Grandeur and Decadence of the Romans" being studies for "L'Esprit des Lois;" but with a master the sketch is as perfect a work of art as the completed picture. "Timidity"—Montesquieu was a severe judge of himself—"timidity has been the curse of my life," he said; but his very dread of being weak—which he never was—helped to make his first work a masterpiece.

Quesnay, the elder Mirabeau, Raynal, Morelly, Servan, Malesherbes, Voltaire, Beccaria, Filangieri, Blackstone, Ferguson, all descend from Montesquieu; and Gibbon found "the strong ray of philosophic light," which "broke from Scotland in our times" upon political economy, only a reflection, though with a far steadier and more concentrated force, from the scattered but brilliant sparks kindled by the genius of Montesquieu. Chateaubriand and Benjamin Constant imitated him; Talleyrand, the best servant France ever had , was his disciple. Catherine of Russia said, "His 'Esprit de Lois' is the breviary of sovereigns." The men of the French Revolution swore by him. Robespierre was parodying him when he said, "The principle of democratic government is virtue; the means of its establishment, terror;" and Napoleon honoured him by discarding him as an ideologist.

France never had a wiser counselor, "his blood and judgment were so well commingled;" but he could not prevent the Revolution any more than Horatio could have saved Hamlet.

JOHN DAVIDSON

London

September 1891

== Some Reflections on the Persian Letters == [1] Nothing in the Persian Letters has been found more attractive than the unexpected discovered of a sort of story, which can be followed easily from beginning to end. A chain of circumstance connects the various characters. In proportion as their stay in Europe is extended, the morals and manners of that part of the world appear to them less wonderful and odd; and the degree in which they are affected by the marvelous and the eccentric depends upon the difference in their dispositions. On the other hand, the Asiatic *seraglio*[2] becomes more disorderly the long Usbek remains away—that is to say, in proportion as frenzy increases and love abates.

Another cause of the success of romances of this kind lies in the fact that events are described by the characters themselves as actually happening. This produces a sensational effect unattainable in the narrative of an outsider; and it is to this that the popularity of certain works which have appeared since the publication of the "Persian Letters" is mainly due.

Although in the regular novel, digressions are inadmissible unless they themselves constitute a fresh romance, and argumentative discussion is altogether beside the mark, since the characters are not brought together for the purpose of chopping logic; yet, in the epistolary form, where accident selects the characters, and the subjects dealt with are independent of any design or preconceived plan, the author is enabled to mingle philosophy, politics, and morality with a romance, and to connect the whole by a hidden, and somewhat novel, bond.

So great was the sale of the "Persian Letters" when they came out that publishers did their utmost to obtain sequels. They button-holed every author they met, and entreated him to write "Persian Letters.

What I have just stated, however, should convince the reader that they do not admit of a sequel 3, still less of any admixture from the hand of another. [4]

Some remarks have been found by many people sufficiently audacious; but I beg them to consider the nature of the work. The Persians, who were to play so important a part in it, found themselves, transported, to all intents and purposes, into another world. It was therefore necessary for some time to represent them as ignorant and full of prejudices: attention was bestowed exclusively on the formation and development of their ideas. Their first thoughts must have been exceptional. [5] It seemed to the author that all he had to do was to endow them with singularity in as spirited a manner as he could; and to this end what was more necessary than to depict their state of mind in presence of whatever appeared to them extraordinary? Nothing was further from his thoughts than the idea of compromising any principle of our religion—he did not even suspect himself of the simplest indiscretion. What questionable remarks there are on religion will always be found united with feelings of surprise and astonishment, and not with any critical intention, still less with that of censure. Why should these Persians appear better informed when speaking of our religion, than when they discuss our manners and customs? And if they do sometimes find our dogmas singular, it is always a proof of their entire ignorance of the connection between those dogmas and other religious truths.

The author advances this justification out of his love for these great truths, independently of his respect for the human race, whose tenderest feelings he certainly did not intend to wound. The reader is, therefore, requested not for one moment to regard the remarks referred to as other than the result of amazement in people who could not fail to be amazed, or as the paradoxes of men who were in no condition to be paradoxical. The reader should also observe that the whole charm of the work lies in the continuous contrast between the existing state of things and the remarkable, artless, or odd manner in which they are regarded. Beyond a doubt, the nature and design of the "Persian Letters" are so obvious that they can only deceive those who are inclined to deceive themselves.

Introduction (1721)

I am not about to write a dedication, nor do I solicit protection for this work. It will be read, if it is good; and if it is bad, I am not anxious that it should be read.

I have issued these first letters in order to gauge the public taste; in my portfolio I have a goodly number more which I may hereafter publish. [1]

This, however, depends upon my remaining unknown: let my name once be published and I cease to write. I know a lady who walks well enough, but who limps if she is watched. [2] Surely the blemishes of my book are sufficient to make it needless that I should submit those of my person to the critics. Were I known, it would be said, "His book is at odds with his character; he might have employed his time to better purpose; it is not worthy of a serious man." Critics are never at a loss for such remarks, because there goes no great expense of brains to the making of them.

The Persians who wrote those letters lodged at my house, and we spent our time together: they looked upon me as a man belonging to another world, and so they concealed nothing from me. Indeed, people so far from home could hardly be said to have secrets. They showed me most of their letters, and I copied them. I also intercepted some, mortifying to Persian vanity and jealously, which they had been particularly careful to conceal from me.

I am therefore nothing more than a translator: all my endeavor has been to adapt the work to our taste and manners. I have relieved the reader as much as possible of Asiatic phraseology, and have spared him an infinitude of sublime expressions which would have driven him wild,

Nor does my service to him end there. I have curtailed those tedious compliments of which the Orientals are lavish as ourselves; and I have omitted a great many trifling matters which barely survive exposure to the light, and ought never to emerge from the obscurity proper to "small beer."

Had most of those who have given the world collections of letters done likewise, their words would have disappeared in the editing. One thing has often astonished me, and that is, that these Persians seemed often to have as intimate an acquaintance as I myself with the manners and customs of our nation, an acquaintance extending to the most minute particulars and not un-possessed of many points which have escaped the observation of more than one German traveler in France. This I attribute to the long stay which they made, without taking it into consideration how much easier it is for an Asiatic to become acquainted with the manners and customs of The French in one year, than it would be for a Frenchman to become acquainted with the manners and customs of the Asiatics in four, the former being as communicative as the latter are reserved.

Use and wont permits every translator, and even the most illiterate commentator, to adorn the beginning of his version, or of his parody, with a panegyric on the original, and to extol its usefulness, its merit, and its excellence. It should not be very difficult to divine why I have not done so. One very excellent reason may be given: it would simply be adding tediousness to what is in itself necessarily tedious, namely, a preface.

Letter 1

Usbek to his friend Rustan, at Isfahan

We stayed only one day at Qom. After having said our prayers before the tomb of the virgin who brought forth twelve prophets, [1] we resumed our journey, and yesterday, the twenty-sixth day since our departure from Ispahan, we came to Tauris.

Rica and myself are perhaps the first Persians who have left their native country urged by the thirst for knowledge; who have abandoned the amenities of a tranquil life for the laborious search after wisdom.

Although born in a prosperous realm, we did not believe that its boundaries should limit our knowledge, and that the lore of the East should alone enlighten us.

Tell me, without flattery, what is said of our journey: I do not expect that is will be generally commended. Address your letter to Erzeroum, where I shall stay for some time. Farewell, my dear Rustan. Rest assured that in whatever part of the world I may be, you have in me a faithful friend.

Tauris, the 15th of the moon of Saphar [2], 1711.

Letter 2

Usbek to the chief black Eunuch, at his Seraglio in Ispahan

You are the faithful keeper of the most loveliest women in Persia; I have entrusted you with what in this world is most dear to me; you bear the keys of those fatal doors which are opened only for me. Whilst you watch over this precious storehouse of my affections, my heart, at rest, enjoys an absolute freedom from care. You guard it in the silence of the night as well as in the bustle of the day. Your un-relaxing care sustains virtue when it wavers. Should the women whom you guard incline to swerve from their duty, you would destroy their hopes in the bud. You are the scourge of vice, and the very monument of fidelity.

You command them and they obey. You fulfill implicitly all their desires, and exact from them a like obedience to the laws of the seraglio; you take a pride in rendering them the meanest services; you submit to their lawful commands with reverence and in dread; you serve them like the slave of their slaves. But, resuming your power, you command imperiously, as my representative, whenever you apprehend any slackening of the laws of chastity and modesty.

Never forget that I raised you from the lowest position among my slaves, to set you in your present place as the trusted guardian of the delights of my heart. Maintain the most humble bearing in the presence of those who partake my love; but, at the same time, make them deeply conscious of their own powerlessness. Provide for them all innocent pleasures; beguile them of their anxiety; entertain them with music, dancing, and delicious drinks; persuade them to meet together frequently. If they wish to go into the country, you may escort them thither; but lay hands on every man who dares to enter their presence. Exhort them to that cleanliness which is the symbol of the soul's purity; speak sometimes of me. I long to see them again in that delightful place which they adorn. Farewell.

Tauris, the 18th of the moon of Saphar, 1711.

Letter 3

We instructed the chief of the eunuchs to take us into the country; he will inform you that we arrived there without accident. When we had to leave our litters in order to cross the river, we went, as usual, into boxes: two slaves carried us on their shoulders, and we were seen by nobody.

Dear Usbek, how I can endure existence in your seraglio at Ispahan! It recalls everlastingly my past happiness, provoking daily my desires with renewed vehemence.

I wander from room to room, always searching for you; mocked at my every turn by the cruel memory of my vanished bliss. Sometimes I behold you in that spot where I first received you in my arms; again I see you in the room where you decided that famous quarrel among your women. Each of us asserted a superiority in beauty. We came just before you, after having exhausted our fancy in decking ourselves with jewelry and adornments. You noted with pleasure the marvels of our art; you were astonished at the height to which we had carried our desire to please you. But you soon made those borrowed graces give way to more natural charms; you destroyed the result of our labours: we were compelled to despoil ourselves of those ornaments, now become tiresome to you, and to appear before you in the simplicity of nature. For me, modesty counted as nothing; I thought only of conquest. Happy Usbek! What charms did you then behold. Long you wandered from enchantment to enchantment, unable to control your roving fancy; each new grace required your willing tribute; in an instant you covered us all with your kisses; your eager looks strayed into the recesses of our charms; you made us vary our attitudes a thousand times; and new commands brought forth new obedience. I avow it, Usbek, a passion stronger even than ambition filled me with a desire to please you. Gradually I saw myself become your heart's mistress; you chose me, left me, returned your love to me, and I knew now to keep your love: my triumph was the despair of my rivals. You and I felt as it we were the sole inhabitants of the world: nothing but ourselves deserved a moment's thought. Would to Heaven my rivals had been brave enough to witness all the proofs of love you gave me! Had they watched well my transports they would have felt the difference between their love and mine; it would have been plain to them that, though they might dispute the palm of beauty, they could not vie with me in tenderness…But what is this? Where has this vain rehearsal led me? It is a misfortunate not to be loved, but to have love withdrawn from one is an outrage. You abandon us, Usbek, to wander in barbarous climes. What! Do you count it as nothing to be loved? Alas! You do not even know what it is you lose! The sighs I heave there is none to hear; my falling tears are not by to pity. Your insensibility takes you further and further from the love that throbs for your in your seraglio. Ah! My beloved Usbek, if you only knew your happiness!

The Seraglio at Fatme, the 21st of the moon of Maharram, [1] 1711.

Letter 4

Zephis to Usbek, at Erzeroum

At length the black monster has resolved to drive me to despair. He is absolutely determined to deprive me of my slave, Zelida--Zelida, who serves me with such affection, and at whose magical touch new charms appear. Nor is he satisfied with the pangs this separation causes me; he is bent on my dishonour. The wretch pretends to treat as criminal the motives of my confidence, and because he was weary of standing behind the door, where I always tell him to wait, he dares to imagine that he heard or saw things which my fancy cannot even conceive. I am very unhappy! Neither my isolation nor my virtue can secure me from his preposterous suspicions. A vile slave would drive me from your heart, and I am called on to defend myself even in your bosom!--But no; I am too proud to justify myself: you alone shall vouch for my behaviour--your love and my love, and--need I say it, dear Usbek?--my tears.

The Seraglio at Fatme, the 29th of the moon of Maharram, 1711.

Letter 5

Rustan to Usbek, at Erzeroum

You are the one subject of conversation at Ispahan; nothing is talked of but your departure: some ascribe it to a giddy spirit, others to some heavy affliction; your friends are your only defenders, and they make no converts. People fail to understand why you should forsake your wives, your relations, your friends, and your native country, to visit lands of which Persians know nothing. Rica's mother is inconsolable; she wants her son again, whom, she declares, you have decoyed away. As for me, my dear Usbek, I am, of course, anxious to approve of all your actions; but I do not see how I am to pardon your absence, and, however good your reasons may be, my heart will never appreciate them.

Ispahan, the 28th of the first moon of Rebiab[1], 1711.

Letter 6

Usbek to his friend Nessir, at Ispahan

At the distance of a day's journey from Erivan we left Persian ground, and entered Turkish territory. Twelve days after, we reached Erzeroum, where we stayed three or four months.

I own, Nessir, I felt sorry, though I did not show it, when I lost sight of Persia and found myself among the treacherous Osmanli. It seems to me that I become more and more of a pagan the further I advance into this heathenish country.1

My fatherland, my family, and my friends came vividly before me; my affections revived; and, to crown all, an indefinable uneasiness laid hold of me, warning me that I had ventured on too great an undertaking for my peace of mind.

But that which afflicts me most is the memory of my wives. I have only to think of them to be consumed with grief.

Do not imagine that I love them: insensibility in that matter, Nessir, has left me without desires. Living with so many wives, I have forestalled love--it has indeed been its own destruction; but from this very callousness there springs a secret jealousy which devours me. I behold a band of women left almost entirely to themselves; except some low-minded wretches, no one is answerable for their conduct. I would hardly feel safe, if my slaves were faithful: how would it be if they were not so? What doleful tidings may I not receive in those far-off lands which I am about to visit! The mischief of this is, that my friends are unable to help me; they are forbidden to inquire into the sources of my misery; and what could they do after all? I would prefer a thousand times that such faults should remain unknown because uncorrected, than that they should become notorious through some condign punishment! I unbosom myself to you, my dear Nessir: it is the only consolation left me in my misery.

Erzeroum, the 10th of the second moon of Rebiab, 1711.

Letter 7

You have been gone for two months, my dear Usbek, and I am so dejected that I cannot yet persuade myself you have been so long away. I wander through every corner of the seraglio as if you were there; I cherish that sweet delusion. What is there left to do for a woman who loves you; who has been accustomed to clasp you in her arms; whose only desire was to give you new proofs of her affection; who was born to the blessings of freedom, but became a slave through the ardour of her passion?

When I married you, my eyes had not yet seen the face of man; and you are still the only man whom I have been permitted to look on:[1] for I do not count as men those frightful eunuchs whose least imperfection is that they are not men. When I compare the beauty of your countenance with the deformity of theirs, I cannot forbear esteeming myself a happy woman: my imagination can conceive no more ravishing idea than the bewitching charms of your person. I pledge you my word, Usbek, that were I allowed to leave this place in which the necessity of my condition detains me; could I escape from the guards who hem me in on all sides--even if I were allowed to choose among all the men who dwell in this capital of nations--Usbek, I swear to you, I would choose none but you: there is no man else in the wide world worthy a woman's love.

Do not think that your absence has led me to neglect those charms which have endeared me to you: although I may not be seen by any one, and the ornaments with which I deck myself do not affect your happiness, I strive notwithstanding to omit no art that can arouse delight; I never go to rest until I am all perfumed with the sweetest essences. I recall that happy time when you came to my arms; a flattering dream deceives me, and shows me the dear object of my love; my fond imagination is whelmed in its desires; sometime I think that, disgusted with the trials of your journey, you are hurrying home: between waking and sleeping the night is spent in such vague dreams; I seek for you at my side, and you seem to flee from me; until at last the very fire which burns me disperses these unsubstantial joys, and I am broad awake. Then my agitation knows no bounds....You will not believe me, Usbek, but it is impossible to live like this; liquid fire courses in my veins: why cannot I find words to tell you all I feel, and why do I feel so deeply what I cannot utter? In such moments, Usbek, I would give the world for a single kiss. What an unhappy woman is she who, having such passionate desires as these, is deprived of the company of him who alone can satisfy them! Abandoned to herself, with nothing to divert her, her whole life is spent in sighs and in the frenzy of a goading passion. Instead of being happy, she has not even the privilege of ministering to the happiness of another: a useless ornament of a seraglio, she is kept for her husband's credit merely, and not for his enjoyment! You men are the cruellest creatures! Delighted when we have desires that we cannot gratify, you treat us as if we had no emotions--though you would be very sorry if that were so: you imagine that our long repressed love will be quickened when we behold you. It is very difficult for man to make himself beloved; the easiest plan is to obtain from our constitutional weakness what you dare not hope to obtain through your own merit.

Farewell, my dear Usbek, farewell. Believe that I live only to adore you: the thought of you fills my soul; and your absence, far from making me forget you, would make my love more vehement, if that were possible.

The Seraglio at Ispahan, the 12th of the first moon of Rebiab, 1711.

Letter 8

Usbek to his friend Rustan, at Ispahan

I got your letter at Erzeroum, where I am now. I was quite certain that my departure would cause some stir, but that gives me no trouble: which would you have me obey--the petty maxims that guide my enemies, or the dictates of my own free soul?

From my earliest youth I have been a courtier; and yet I make bold to say that my heart has remained uncorrupted: indeed, I conceived the grand idea of daring to be virtuous even at court. From the moment I recognised vice, I withdrew from it; afterwards, when I approached it, it was only to unmask it. I carried my veracity even to the foot of the throne, and spoke a language never heard there before; I disconcerted flattery, amazing at the same time the idol and its worshippers.

But when I saw that my sincerity had made me enemies, and had brought upon me the jealousy of the ministers, I determined to forsake a corrupt court in which my unseconded virtue could no longer maintain me. I feigned a mighty interest in science; and, by dint of pretending, soon became really attached to it. I ceased to be a man of affairs, and retired to a house in the country. But even here persecution followed me: the malice of my enemies almost deprived me of the means of protecting myself. Information received in secret led me to consider my position seriously: I resolved to leave my native land, and my withdrawal from court supplied a plausible excuse. I waited on the king; I emphasised the great desire I had to acquaint myself with the sciences of the west, and hinted that my travels might even be of service to him. I found favour in the king's sight; I set out, and snatched from my enemies their expected victim.

Here, Rustan, you have the true motive of my journey. Let them talk in Ispahan; say nothing in my defence except to my friends. Leave the evil-disposed to their misconstructions; I would be too happy if that were the only harm they could do me.

They discuss me at present; perhaps I shall soon be forgotten, and my friends...But no, I will not, Rustan, resign myself to these sad thoughts: I will always be dear to them; I rely upon their faithfulness as upon yours.

Erzeroum, the 20th of the second moon of Gemmadi,[1] 1711.

Letter 9

The Chief Eunuch to Ibbi,[1] at Erzeroum

You follow your old master on his travels; you wander through provinces and kingdoms; no grief can make any impression on you; you see new sights all day long; everything you behold entertains you, and you are unconscious of the flight of time.

It is not so with me. Shut up in a hideous prison, I am always surrounded by the same objects; there is no change even in what vexes me. Weighed down by fifty years of care and annoyance, I lament my wretched case: all my life long I have never passed a single untroubled day, or known a peaceful moment.

When my first master formed the cruel design of entrusting his wives to my care, and induced me by flattering promises, supplemented by a thousand threats, to separate myself forever from my manhood, tired of the toilsome service in which I was engaged, I calculated that the sacrifice of my passions would be more than repaid by ease and wealth. How unfortunate was I! Preoccupied with the thought of the ills I would escape, I had no idea of the others to which I fled: I expected that the inability to satisfy love would secure me from its assaults. Alas! although passion had been rendered inefficient, its force remained unabated; and, far from being relieved, I found myself surrounded by objects which continually whetted my desires. When I entered the seraglio, where everything filled me with regret for what I lost, my agitation increased each moment; a thousand natural charms seemed to unfold themselves to my sight only to tantalise me; and to crown my misery, I had constantly before me their fortunate possessor. While this wretched time lasted, I never led a woman to my master's bed without feeling wild rage in my heart, and despair unutterable in my soul.

And thus I passed my miserable youth, with no confidant but my own bosom. Wearied with longing and sad as night, there was nothing left but to endure in silence. I was forced to turn the sternest glances on those very women whom I would fain have regarded with looks of love. It would have undone me had they read my thoughts: how they would have tyrannised over me! I remember one day, as I attended a lady at the bath, I was so carried away that I lost command of myself, and dared to lay my hand where I should not. My first thought was that my last day had come. I was, however, fortunate enough to escape a dreadful death; but the fair one, whom I had made the witness of my weakness, extorted a heavy price for her silence: I entirely lost command of her, and she forced me, each time at the risk of my life, to comply with a thousand caprices.

At length, the fire of youth burnt out, I grow old and become, in that particular, at peace with myself. Women I regard with indifference, I pay them back for all their contempt, and all the torments which I suffered through them. I never forget that I was born to command them, and in the exercise of my authority I feel as if I had recovered my lost manhood. I hate women now that I can regard them without passion, and detect and discuss all their weaknesses. Although I guard them for another, I experience a secret joy in making myself obeyed. When I take all their pleasures from them, I feel as if it were at my behest alone; and that always gives me satisfaction more or less direct. The seraglio is my empire; and my ambition, the only passion left me, finds no small gratification. I mark with pleasure that all depends on me, and that my presence is required at all times: I willingly incur the hatred of these women, because that establishes me more firmly in my post. And they do not hate me for nothing, I can tell you: I interfere with their most innocent pleasures; I am always in the way, an insurmountable obstacle; before they know where they are they find their schemes frustrated; I am armed with refusals, I bristle with scruples; not a word is heard from me but duty, virtue, chastity, modesty. I make them desperate by dinning them with the weakness of their sex, and the authority of our master. Then I lament the necessity which requires me to be so severe, and lead them to believe that my only motives are their truest interests and my profound attachment to them.

Do not suppose that in my turn I have not to suffer endless unpleasantness. Every day these women seek occasions to repay me with interest, and their reprisals[2] are often terrible. Between us there goes on a constant interchange of ascendancy and obedience. They are always putting upon me the meanest services; they affect a sublime contempt; and, regardless of my age, they force me to rise ten times during the night for the merest trifle. I am worn off my feet with endless commissions, orders, employments, and caprices; one would think that they take turn about in inventing occupations for me. They often amuse themselves by making me doubly vigilant; they give me imaginary confidences. Sometimes I am told that a young man has been seen prowling round the walls, or a startling noise has been heard, or some one is about to receive a letter. All this bothers me, and amuses them; they are delighted when they see me tormenting myself. Sometimes they station me behind the door, and keep me standing there night and day. They well know how to pretend to be ill, to swoon away, to be frightened out of their wits: they are never at a loss for some pretext to work their will on me. When they are in this mood, implicit obedience, unquestioning compliance are my only resources: a refusal from such a man as I am would be a thing unheard of; and if I were to hesitate in obeying them, they could punish me at their discretion. I would sooner die, my dear Ibbi, than submit to such humiliation.

But this is not all. I am never for an instant sure of my master's favour; for each of his wives is an enemy who never ceases to hope for my ruin. They take advantage of certain snatches of time when I cannot be heard, when he can refuse them nothing, and when I am always in the wrong. I conduct to my master's bed women whose spite is roused against me: do you imagine that they will move a finger in my behalf, or say a single word in my favour? I have everything to fear from their tears, their sighs, their embraces, from their very pleasures; it is their time of triumph; their charms are arrayed against me: their present services obliterate in a moment all those rendered by me in the past; and nothing can plead for me with a master who is no longer himself.

Many a time I lie down high in my master's favour, and awake to find myself disgraced. The day on which they whipped me so ignominiously round the seraglio, what had I done? I leave a woman in my master's arms: when she sees him impassioned she bursts into a torrent of tears, and pours out complaints so skilfully that they become more anguished in proportion as the love she causes grows vehement. What could I do to defend myself at a crisis of that kind? When I least expected it, ruin overtook me; I was the victim of an amorous intrigue, of a treaty sealed with sighs. Behold, dear Ibbi, the wretched plight in which I have always lived.

What happiness is yours! Your duties are confined to attendance on Usbek. It is easy for you to please him, and to retain his favour to your dying day.

The Seraglio at Ispahan, the last day of the moon of Saphar, 1711.

Letter 10

Mirza to his friend Usbek, at Erzeroum

You alone could recompense me for the absence of Rica, and it is only Rica who could console me for yours. We miss you, Usbek; you were the very life of our circle. How hard it is to break away from those attachments in which both the heart and the mind are engaged!

We have great debates here; our talk turns principally on morality. We disputed yesterday whether true happiness consists in pleasure and sensual gratification, or in the practice of virtue.

I have heard you often affirm that men were made to be virtuous, and that justice is as indispensable to existence as life itself. I beg you to explain to me what you mean by this.

I have spoken of this to the mollahs[1], but they exasperate me with their quotations from the Koran; for I do not consult them as a true believer, but as a man, a citizen, and the father of a family. Farewell.

Isaphan, the last day of the moon of Saphar, 1711.

Letter 11

Usbek to Mirza, at Ispahan

You waive your own judgment in deference to mine;[1] you even deign to consult me; you to profess your belief in my ability to instruct you. My dear, Mirza if there is one thing which flatters me more than your good opinion of me, it is the friendship which prompts it.

In the fulfillment of the task you have prescribed me, I do not think there is any necessity for argument of an abstruse order. There are certain truths which it is not sufficient to know, but which must be realized: such are the great commonplaces of morality. Probably the following fable will affect you more than the most subtle argument:

One upon a time there dwelt in Arabia a small tribe called Troglodites, descendents of the ancient Troglodites, who, if historians are to be believed,[2] were liker beasts than men. They were not, however, counterfeit presentments of the lower animals. They had not fur like bears; they did not hiss like serpents; and they did possess two eyes:[3] but they were so malicious, so brutish, that they lacked all notion of justice and equity.

A king of foreign origin reigned over them. Wishing to correct their natural wickedness, he treated them with severity; but they conspired against him, slew him, and exterminated his line.

They then assembled to appoint a governing body. After many dissensions, they elected magistrates. These had not been long in office, when they found them intolerable, and killed them also.

Freed from this new yoke, the people were swayed only by their savage instincts. Every man determined to do what was right in his own eyes; and in attending to his own interests, the general welfare was forgotten.

The unanimous decision gave universal satisfaction. They said: "Why should I kill myself with work for those in whom I have no interest? I will only think of myself: how should the welfare of others affect me: I will provide for my own necessities; and, if these are satisfied, it is not concern of mine though all the other Troglodites live in misery."

Each man said to himself in seed-time, "I shall till no more land than will supply me with corn enough for my wants. What use have I for any more? I am not going to bother myself for nothing."

The land in this little kingdom was not all of the same quality: some of it was barren and mountainous; and other portions, lying low, were well-watered. One year a drought occurred, so severe, that the uplands bore no crop at all, whilst those that were well-watered brought forth abundantly. In consequence of this, the highlanders almost all died of hungered, because the people of the lowlands had no mercy on them, and refused to share the harvest.

The year after, the weather being very wet, the higher grounds produced extraordinary crops, whilst the lowlands were flooded. Again half the people were famine-stricken; but the wretched sufferers found the mountaineers as hard as they themselves had been.

One of the chief men of the country had a very lovely wife. A neighbour of his fell in love with her, and carried her off. This gave rise to a bitter quarrel; and after many words and blows, the parties agreed to submit their case to the judgment of a Troglodite, who had been well esteemed during the republic. Having gone to him, they were about to argue the case before him, when he cried, "What does it matter whose wife she is? My land waits to be tilled; and I am not going to waste my time settling your quarrels and doing your business, when I might be attending to my own; be kind enough to leave me alone, and trouble me no more with your disputes." With that he left them, and went to work in his fields. The ravisher, who was the stronger man, swore he would sooner die than give up the woman. The other, smarting under his neighbour's ill-treatment and the unfeeling conduct of the umpire, was going home in despair, when he met a fine young woman returning from the well. Having no longer a wife of his own, he was attracted towards her; and she pleased him all the more when he learnt she was the wife of him whom he had solicited to judge his case, and who had proved so pitiless to him. He therefore seized the woman and carried her to his house.

Another man, the owner of some fairly productive ground, took great pains in its cultivation. Two of his neighbors conspired to drive him from his house, and seize his lands. They entered into a compact to oppose all who should try to oust them, and they actually succeeded for several months. One of the two, however, disgusted at having to share what might be his own exclusively, killed the other, and became sole master of the ground. But his reign was soon over: two other Troglodites attacked him, and as he was no match for them, they killed him.

Still another Troglodite, seeing some wool exposed for sale, asked the price of it. The seller argued thus with himself: "At the market price I should receive for my wool as much money as would buy two measures of corn; but I will sell it for four times that sum, and then I can buy eight measures." As the other wanted the wool, he paid the price demanded. "Many thanks," said the vendor, "I shall now buy some corn." "What rejoined the buyer, "you want corn? I have some to sell; but the price will rather astonish you. You must know that, as there is a famine in the land, corn is extremely dear. If you return me my money, I will give you on measure of corn: I would not give you a grain more for the price, though you were to die of hunger."

Meantime a dreadful malady was ravaging the land. An able physician came from a neighboring country, and prescribed with such success that he cured all his patients. When the plague ceased, he called for his fees, but was refused by one and all. There was nothing for it but to return to his own country, which he reached worn to a skeleton by the fatigues of a long journey. Soon after he heard that the same disease had broken out afresh among these thankless people, and with more virulence than before. This time they did not wait for him, but sent to entreat his presence. "Begone," he cried, "unrighteous men! In your souls there is a poison more deadly than that which you wish me to cure; you are unworthy to live, for you are inhuman monsters, unacquainted with the first principles of justice. I will not offend the gods who punish you by opposing their just wrath."

Erzeroum, the 3rd of the second moon of Gemmadi[4], 1711.

Letter 12

You have seen, my dear Mirza, how the Troglodites perished in their sins, the victims of their own righteousness. Only two families escaped the doom which befell the nation.

In that country there lived just two very remarkable men, humane, just, lovers of virtue. United by their uprightness as much as by the corruption of their fellows, they regarded the general desolation with hearts from which pity expelled every other feeling; and their compassion united them in a new bond. Together they laboured for their mutual benefit; no dissensions arose between them except such as may spring from the tenderest friendship. In a secluded part of the country, far removed from those who were unworthy of their companionship, they led a calm and happy life. The earth, glad to be tilled by such virtuous hands, seemed to yield her fruits of her own accord.

They loved their wives, and were beloved most tenderly. Their utmost care was given to the virtuous training of their children. They kept before their young minds the misfortunes of their countrymen, and held them up as a most melancholy example. Above all, they led them to see that the interest of the individual was bound up in that of the community; that to isolate oneself was to court ruin; that the sot of virtue should never be counted, nor the practice of it regarded as troublesome; and that in acting justly by others, we bestow blessings on ourselves.

They soon enjoyed the reward of virtuous parents, which consists in having children like themselves. Happy marriages increased the number of the young people who grew up under their guidance. Although the community increased, there was still but one interest; and virtue, instead of losing its force in the crowd, grew stronger by reason of more numerous examples.

It is impossible to depict the happiness of these Troglodites! So upright a people could not fail to be the special objects of divine care. They were taught to reverence the Gods with the first dawning of intellect; and religion refined manners that nature had left untutored. They established feasts in honour of the Gods. Young men and maidens, decked with flowers, worshipped them with dances and rural minstrelsy. Banquets followed, in which they struck a happy mean between mirth and frugality. At these gatherings nature spoke its artless language; there the young folks learned how to make love's bargain of hearts: trembling girls blushed to find on their lips a promise which the blessing of their parents soon ratified; tender mothers delighted themselves in forecasting happy marriages.

When they visited the temple it was not to ask of the Gods wealth and overflowing plenty; these fortunate Troglodites regarded such requests as unworthy of them; if they made them at all, it was not for themselves, but for their countrymen. They approached the altar only to pray for the health of their parents, for the unity of their brethren, for the love of their wives, the affection and obedience of their children. Thither the maidens came to offer up the sweet sacrifice of their hearts, asking in return only the right to make a Troglodite happy.

In the evening, when the flocks had left the fields, and the weary oxen had returned from ploughing, these people met together. During a frugal meal they sang of the crimes of the first Troglodites, and their sad fate; of the revival of virtue with a new race, and of its happiness. Then they celebrated the greatness of the Gods, abounding in mercy to those who seek them, and visiting with inevitable judgments those who reverence them not. These would be followed by a description of the delights of a country life, and the happiness that springs from a state of innocence. Soon after they retired to rest, and their slumbers were unbroken by care or anxiety.

The provision of nature was sufficient for both their pleasures and their wants. A covetous man was unknown in this happy country. When they made presents, the giver always felt himself more blessed than the receiver. The whole race looked upon themselves as one single family; their flocks were almost always intermixed, and the only trouble which they usually shirked was that of separating them.

Erzeroum, the 6th of the second moon of Gemmadi, 1711

Letter 13

Usbek to the Same

I cannot say half I wish to say about the virtue of the Troglodites. One of them once said, "Tomorrow it is my father's turn to work in the fields; I shall rise two hours before him, and when he comes to his work he will find it all done."

Another said to himself, "I think my sister has taken a fancy for a young cousin of mine. I must talk to my father about it, and get him to arrange a marriage."[1]

Another, being told that robbers had carried off his herd, replied, "I am very sorry, because it contained a white heifer which I meant to offer to the Gods."

One was heard telling another that he was bound for the temple to return thanks to Heaven for the recovery from sickness of this brother, who was so dear to his father, and whom he himself loved so much.

This also was once said: "In a field adjoining my father's, the workers are all day long exposed to the heat of the sun. I shall plant some trees there that these poor folks may sometimes rest in their shade."

Their unexpected prosperity was not regarded without envy. A neighbouring nation gathered together and on some paltry context determined to carry off their cattle. As soon as they heard this, the Troglodites dispatched ambassadors, who addressed their enemies in the following terms, "What evil have the Troglodites done you? Have they carried off your wives, stolen your cattle, or ravaged your lands? No; we are just men, and fear the Gods. What, then, do your require of us? Would you have wool to make clothes? Do you wish the milk of our cows, or the products of our fields? Lay down your arms, then; come with us and we will give you all you demand. But we swear by all we hold most sacred, that if you enter our territories in enmity, we will regard you as dishonest men, and deal with you as we would with wild beasts."

This speech was received with contempt; and, believing that the Troglodites had no means of defence except their innocence, the barbarians invaded their territory in warlike array.

But the Troglodites were well prepared to defend themselves. They had placed their wives and children in their midst. Astonished they certainly were at the injustice of their enemies, but were not dismayed by their number. Their hearts burned within them with an ardour before unknown. One longed to lay down his life for his father, another for his wife and children, this one for his brothers, that one for his friends, and all for each other. When one fell in fight, he who immediately took his place, besides fighting for the common cause, had the death of his comrade to avenge.

And so the battle raged between right and wrong. Those wretched creatures, whose sole aim was plunder, felt no shame when they were forced to fight. They were forced to yield to the prowess of that virtue, whose worth they were unable to appreciate.

Erzeroum, the 9th of the second moon of Gemmadi, 1711

Letter 14

Usbek to the Same

As their numbers increased every day, the Troglodites thought it behoved them to elect a king. They judged it wise to confer the crown upon the justest man among them; and their thoughts turned to one, venerable by reason of his age and his long career of virtue. He, however, had refused to attend the meeting, and withdrew to his house, oppressed with grief.

When deputies were sent to him to announce his election, "The Gods forbid," cried he, "that I should wrong the Troglodites by permitting them to believe that there is one man among them more just than I! You offer me the crown; and if you insist upon it absolutely, I cannot but take it. Remember, however, that I shall die of sorrow, having known the Troglodites freemen, to behold them subjected to a ruler." Having said this, he burst into a torrent of tears. "Unhappy day!" he exclaimed. "Why have I lived to see it?" Then he upbraided them. "I see," he cried, "O Troglodites, what moves you to this; uprightness becomes a burden to you. In your present condition, having no head, you are constrained in your own despite to be virtuous; otherwise your very existence would be at stake, and you would relapse into the wretched state of your ancestors. But this seems to you too heavy a yoke; you would rather become the subjects of a king, and submit to laws of his framing-laws less exacting than your present customs. You know that then you would be able to satisfy your ambition, and while away the time in slothful luxury; and that, provided you avoided the graver crimes, there would be no necessity for virtue." He ceased speaking for a little, and his tears fell faster than ever. "And what do you expect of me? How can I lay commands upon a Troglodite? Would one act more nobly because I ordered him? You forget that a Troglodite without any command does what is right from natural inclination?"

"O Troglodites, my days are nearly done, my blood is frozen in my veins, I shall soon join your blessed ancestors; why would you have me carry them the sad news that you have submitted to another law than that of virtue?"

Erzeroum, the 10th of the second moon of Gemmadi, 1711.

Letter 15

May Heaven restore you to this country, and deliver you from all danger!

Although friendship is a bond almost unknown to me, and although I am wrapped up in myself, yet you have made me feel that I have a heart; and while I was as a bronze statue to the rest of the slaves who lived under my rule, it was with pleasure that I watched your growth from infancy.

The time came when my master threw his eyes on you. Nature had not yet whispered her secrets, when the knife separated you from her for ever. I will not say whether I pitied you, or whether I was glad to see you brought into my own condition. I dried your tears and stilled your cries. I imagined that I saw you born again, issuing from a state of thraldom in which you would always have had to obey, to enter into a service in which you would exercise authority. I charged myself with your education. That severity, without which instruction is impossible, kept you long in ignorance of my love. You were dear to me, however; and I assure you that I loved you as a father loves his son, if the names of father and son can be applied to such as you and I.

Since you are to travel in countries inhabited by unbelieving Christians, it is impossible that you should escape defilement. How shall the prophet look on you with favour in the midst of so many millions of his enemies? I hope my master, on his return, will perform the pilgrimage to Mecca: you would be purified in that blessed place.

The Seraglio at Ispahan, the 10th of the second moon of Gemmadi, 1711.

Letter 16

Usbek to the Mollah Mehemet Ali, Guardian of The Three Tombs[1] at Koum

Why, divine Mollah, do you live in the tombs? You are better fitted to dwell among the stars. Doubtless you hide yourself lest you should eclipse the sun: unlike the day-star you have no spots; but you resemble him in your cloudy concealment.

Your knowledge is more abysmal that the ocean; your intellect, keener than Zufagar,[2] the twin-pointed sword of Hali. You know the secrets of the nine orders of celestial powers; you read the Koran on the breast of our holy Prophet, and when you come to an obscure passage, an angel, by his order, spreads his rapid wings, and descends from the throne to reveal you its meaning.

I may, with your help, conduct a private correspondence with the seraphim; for, in short, O thirteenth Iman,[3] are you not the centre where earth and heaven meet, the point of communication between the abyss and the empyrean?

In the midst of a profane people, permit me to purify myself through you. Suffer me to turn my face towards the holy place in which you dwell; mark me off from among the wicked, as one distinguishes night from day;[4] aid me with your counsels; be my soul's guardian; feed me with divine knowledge; and let me humbly expose to you the wounds of my spirit. Address your inspired letters to Erzeroum, where I shall stay for a month or two.

Erzeroum, the 11th of the second moon of Gemmadi, 1711.

Letter 17

Usbek to the Same

I am powerless, divine Mollah, to calm my impatience; I do not know how I am to wait for your sublime answer. I have doubts, which must be resolved; I feel that my reason has gone astray; restore it to the right path. Illumine my darkness, O source of light! Annihilate with the lightning of your divine pen the difficulties I am about to propose to you; enable me to commiserate myself, make me ashamed of the questions I ask you.

Whence comes it that our lawgiver forbids the use of swine's flesh, and of all those meats which he denominates unclean? Why are we forbidden to touch a corpse, and why for the purification of our souls is this endless washing of the body ordained? To me it seems that things in themselves are neither clean nor unclean: I can conceive of no inherent quality which makes them the one or the other. The filthiness of filth consists in its offending our sight or some other sense; but in itself it is no dirtier than gold or diamonds. The idea of uncleanness, resulting from contact with a dead body, proceeds from a natural repugnance with which it fills us. If the bodies of those who do not wash offended neither the smell nor the sight, how could we tell that they were unclean? Should not, therefore, the senses, divine Mollah, be the only judges of what is clean or unclean? Yet, since the same objects do not affect all men alike, that which is agreeable to one producing disgust in another, it follows that the witness of the senses is no sure guide in this matter, unless we are permitted to decide the point, each according to his fancy, and to separate for our own behoof things that are clean from those that are not.

But would not this, reverend Mollah, confound the distinctions established by our holy Prophet, and overturn the foundations of that law which was written by angelic hands?

Erzeroum, the 20th of the second moon of Gemmadi, 1711.

Letter 18

Mollah Mehemet Ali, Servant of the Prophets, to Usbek, at Erzeroum

You are always propounding questions that have been laid before our holy Prophet thousands of times. Why do you not read the traditions of the doctors? Why not go to that pure fountain-head of all intelligence? There you would find all your doubts resolved.

Unhappy man! Constantly troubled about earthly things, you have never looked with a single eye on those of heaven. You reverence the life of the Mollahs, but you have not the courage to embrace and follow it.

O profane ones who never enter into the secrets of the Eternal, your light is as the darkness of the pit, and the reasoning of your minds are no more that the dust which rises as you walk, when the sun is at the highest pitch of noon in the scorching month of Chahban.[1]

The very zenith of your understanding does not attain to the nadir of that of the least of the Imans: your vain philosophy is but as the lightning which heralds storm and darkness: in the midst of the tempest, you are driven by the wind and tossed.

Nothing is easier than the solution of your difficulty. For that purpose it is sufficient to narrate what happened once when our holy Prophet, tempted by the Christians and pestered by the Jews, effectually silenced both parties.

The Jew, Abdias Ibesalon,[2] asked him why God had prohibited the eating of swine's flesh. "There is good reason for it," answered Mohammed. "The creature is unclean, and of that I will convince you." He took some earth and shaped it into the figure of a man. Then he threw it on the ground, and cried, "Arise." Immediately a man stood up, and said, "I am Japhet, the son of Noah." "Was your hair as white at your death as it is now?" asked the holy Prophet. "No," replied he, "but when you roused me I thought the day of judgment had come; and such fear laid hold of me that my hair turned white on the instant."

"Now tell me," said the messenger of God, "the whole history of Noah's ark." Japhet obeyed, and after having minutely recounted all that passed during the first months, he continued as follows: "All the excrement of the animals we cast on one side of the ark, which made it lean so much that we were all in mortal terror, especially our wives, who made a terrible outcry. Our father Noah sought divine aid, and God commanded him to take the elephant and place him with his head towards the side that was overweighted. The excrement of the huge animal was so plentiful that there came forth from it a pig." Do you wonder, Usbek, that since then we have abstained from swine's flesh, and have regarded that animal as unclean?

"But, as the pig wallowed every day among the filth, he caused such a stench in the ark that he was himself compelled to sneeze; and from his nose there dropped a rat, which began to gnaw everything that came in his way. This became so intolerable to Noah, that he once more sought God's help in prayer. God commanded him to strike the lion a heavy blow on the forehead, which made him sneeze too, and from his nose there leapt a cat." Are you yet persuaded that these animals are unclean? How does it strike you?

When, therefore, you fail to understand the reason of the uncleanness of certain things, it is because you are ignorant of much else, and have no acquaintance with what has passed between God, the angels, and men. You know not the history of eternity; you have not read the writings that were penned in heaven; what has been revealed to you is but an insignificant part of the divine library: nay, those who, like us, have approached so near that they may be said to live the heavenly life, are still in obscurity and darkness. Farewell. May Mohammed be in your heart!

Koum, the last day of the moon of Chahban, 1711.

Letter 19

Usbek to his friend Rustan, at Ispahan

We stayed only eight days at Tocat. After a journey of thirty-five days, we are now at Smyrna. Between Tocat and Smyrna we did not see a single place worthy the name of town. I have marked with astonishment the weakness of the empire of the Osmanli: a diseased body, it is not supported by a plain and temperate diet, but by violent remedies, which exhaust and waste it away continually.

The pashas, who obtain office only by purchase, bankrupt when they enter their provinces, ravage them like conquered countries. The insolent militia are governed only by their own caprices. The towns are dismantled, the cities deserted, the country desolate, agriculture and commerce entirely neglected.

Impunity is the order of the day under this ruthless government. The Christians who till the land, and the Jews who collect the taxes, are exposed to a thousand outrages.

Property in land is uncertain; and consequently the desire to increase its value has diminished: neither title nor possession is of any avail against the caprice of those in power.

These barbarians have abandoned all the arts, even that of war. While the nations of Europe become more refined every day, these people remain in a state of primitive ignorance; and rarely think of employing new inventions[1] in war, until they have been used against them a thousand times.

They have no experience of the sea, nor skill in naval affairs. They say that a mere handful of Christians, descending from a barren[2] rock, terrify the Ottomans, and shake their ascendancy.

Although they are themselves unfit for commerce, it is with great reluctance that they allow the Europeans, always industrious and enterprising, to conduct their trade: they think they are conferring a favour on these strangers in permitting them to enrich themselves.

Throughout the wide stretch of country which I have crossed, Smyrna is the only town which can be regarded as rich and powerful; and Smyrna owes its prosperity to the Europeans: it is no fault of the Turks that it is not like all the others.

Here you have, my dear Rustan, a correct idea of this empire, which will be within two centuries the scene of some conqueror's exploits.

Smyrna, the 2nd of the moon of Rhamazan, 1711.

Letter 20

Usbek to his wife Zachi, at the Seraglio at Ispahan

You have offended me, Zachi; and my emotions are such as you should dread, did not my distance from you afford you time to change your conduct, and set at rest the fierce jealousy with which I am tormented.

I learn that you have been found alone with Nadir, the white eunuch, who will pay with his head for his infidelity and treachery. How could you forget yourself so far as not to feel that it is forbidden you to receive a white eunuch in your chamber, as long as you have black ones at your service? You have been careful to tell me that eunuchs are not men, and that your virtue raises you above those thoughts which an imperfect likeness might arouse. That is not enough either for you or for me: not enough for you, because you have done that which the laws of the seraglio forbid; not enough for me, inasmuch as you have robbed me of honour, in exposing yourself to the gaze—what do I say?—perhaps to the attempts of a traitor who would have defiled you by his misdeeds, and still more by his repining and his impotent despair. You will doubtless tell me that you have always been faithful. Yes, but how could you fail to be? Could you possible deceive the vigilance of the black eunuchs, who are so amazed at the life you lead? Do you think you could force the doors that keep you from the world? You boast of a virtue which is not free; and perhaps your impure desires have robbed you again and again of the merit and the worth of your vaunted fidelity.

I am persuaded that you are not guilty of all that might be laid to your charge: that the traitor did not lay his sacrilegious hands upon you; that you were not so prodigal as to expose to him the delights of his master; that, covered with your garments, you allowed at least that barrier to remain between you; that he, struck with reverent awe, cast down his eyes; and that, his hardihood forsaking him, he trembled at the prospect of the punishment he had incurred. All this granted, it is none the less true that you have failed in you duty. And, since you have done a gratuitous wrong, without accomplishing your sinful desires, what would you not do to satisfy then? Still more, what would you do if you could escape from that sacred place which seems to you a melancholy prison, but which your companions find a happy asylum against the attacks of vice, a consecrated temple where their sex loses its weakness, and becomes invincible in spite of all its natural disadvantages? What would you do if, left to yourself, you had no other defence than your love for me, which is so sadly shaken, and your duty, against which you have so unworthily sinned? How immaculate are the manners of the country in which you live! They protect you from the attempts of the vilest slaves! You ought to be grateful to me even for the constraint in which you live, since it is that alone which make you worthy of life.

You cannot endure the chief of the eunuchs, because he is for ever watching you behaviour, and giving you good advice. His ugliness, you say, is so horrible that you cannot look at him without suffering. As if one would place in posts of that kind, miracles of manly beauty! No; what annoys you is that you have not in his place the white eunuch who dishonours you.

But what has your chief slave done to you? He has told you that the familiarities which you have taken with the youthful Zelida were unbecoming: that is the cause of your hatred.

Duty requires me, Zachi, to be an impartial judge; I am, however, only a kind husband who seeks to find you innocent. The love which I bear Roxana, my new wife, has not deprived me of the tenderness which is so rightly due to you, as being not less beautiful that she. I share my love among you all; and the only advantage possessed by Roxana is that which virtue adds to beauty.

Smyrna, the 12th of the moon of Zilcade,[1] 1711.

Letter 21

Usbek to the chief white Eunuch

When you open this letter you ought to tremble; or rather you should have trembled when you permitted the treachery of Nadir. You who, even in the dullness and frigidity of old age, may not without guilt raise your eyes towards the dread objects of my love; you, to whom it is for ever forbidden to set a sacrilegious foot across the threshold of that awful place which conceals them from every eye: it is you who permit in those, for whose conduct you are responsible, liberties which you would not yourself dare to take; and do you not quake at the anticipation of the thunderbolt about to fall upon them and you?

And what are you, but vile instruments whom I may destroy at my pleasure; whose existence depends upon obedience; who have been sent into the world to live under my laws, or to die when I require it; who will cease to breathe as soon as my happiness, my love, my jealousy, has no more need of your ignoble service; who, in fine, can have no other lot that submission, whose soul is my will, whose only hope begins and ends in pleasing me?

I am aware that some of my wives are very fretful under the strict laws of duty; that the constant presence of a black eunuch annoys them; that they are weary of those hideous objects, which are appointed to keep them spotless for their husband; I know it well. As for you, who have abetted this disorder, you shall be punished in a manner to strike terror into all those who abuse my confidence.

I swear by all the prophets in heaven[1], and by Hali, the greatest of them, that if you swerve from your duty, I will hold your life of no more account that that of the insects which I tread upon.

Smyrna, the 12th of the moon of Zilcade, 1711.

Letter 22

[1]*Jaron to the first Eunuch*

The further Usbek journeys from the seraglio, the more he thinks of these devoted women: he sighs; he weeps; his grief becomes embittered, and his suspicions grow stronger. He wishes to increase the number of their guardians. He intends to send me back, with all the blacks who accompany him. It is not for himself he fears, but for that which is to him a thousand times dearer.

I return then to live under your laws, and to share your cares. Great God! What a world of things is necessary for one man's happiness!

Nature, which seems originally to have placed women in a state of dependence, afterwards withdrew them from it, with the result that dissensions arose between the sexes because of their mutual rights. The sexes now live in a new kind of unity: hatred is the link between women and men, love is the bond.

My brow begins to wear a constant frown. My eyes dart forth somber glances, and joy forsakes my lips. Outwardly I appear calm; within unrest reigns. Grief will furrow my face long before wrinkles of old age appear.

I should have greatly enjoyed accompanying my master in his western journey, but my will belongs to him. He wishes me to guard his wives; I shall watch over them faithfully. I know how to behave towards that sex, which, when not allowed to be vain, turns haughty, and which it is easier to break than to bend. I prostrate myself before you.

Smyrna, the 12th moon of Zilcade, 1711.

Letter 23

Usbek to his friend Ibben, at Smyrna

We have now arrived at Leghorn after a forty days' voyage. It is a new town and bears witness to the genius of the dukes of Tuscany, who, from a marshy village, have made it the most flourishing town in Italy.

The women here enjoy much liberty: they are allowed to look at men through a species of window called *jalousie*: they have permission to go out every day in the company of some old women: they wear only one veil.[1] Their brothers-in-law, their uncles, and their nephews, are allowed to visit them, and this hardly ever troubles their husbands.

The first sight of a Christian town is, for a Mohammedan, a wonderful spectacle. I do not mean only those things that strike the eye at once, such as the difference in the buildings, the dresses, and the chief customs: there is, even in the merest trifles, a singularity, which I feel, but cannot describe.

We set out to-morrow for Marseilles, where our sojourn will be brief. Rica's intention and mine is to get at once to Paris, the capital of the European empire. Travelers are always anxious to visit great cities, because they are a sort of common country to all strangers. Farewell, Rest assured that I shall never cease to love you.

Leghorn, the 12th of the moon of Saphar, 1712.

Letter 24

Rica to Ibben, at Smyrna

We have now been a month at Paris, and all the time constantly moving about. There is much to do before one can get settled, find out the people with whom one has business, and procure the many requisites which are all wanted at the same time.

Paris is quite as large as Ispahan. The houses are so high that you would swear they must be inhabited by astrologers. You can easily imagine that a city built in the air, with six or seven houses one above the other, is densely peopled; and that when everybody is abroad, there is a mighty bustle.

You will scarcely believe that during the month I have been here I have not yet seen any one walking. There is no people in the world who hold more by their vehicles than the French: they run; they fly: the slow carriages of Asia, the measured step of our camels, would put them into a state of coma, As for me, who am not made for such hurry, and who often go a-foot without changing my pace, I am sometimes as mad a Christian; for, passing over splashing from head to foot, I cannot pardon the elbowings I meet with regularly and periodically. A man, coming up behind me, passes me, and turns half round; then another, crossing me on the opposite side, spins me suddenly round to my first position. Before I have walked a hundred paces, I am more bruised than if I had gone ten leagues.

You must not yet expect from me an exhaustive account of the manners and customs of the Europeans: I have myself but a faint notion of them yet, and have hardly had time to recover from my astonishment.

The king of France[1] is the most powerful of European potentates. He has no mines of gold like his neighbour, the King of Spain; but he is much wealthier than that prince; because his riches are drawn from a more inexhaustible source, the vanity of his subjects. He has undertaken and carried on great wars, without any other supplies than those derived from the sale of titles of honour; and it is by a prodigy of human pride that his troops are paid, his towns fortified, and his fleets equipped.

Then again, the king is a great magician, for his dominion extends to the minds of his subjects; he makes them think what he wishes. If he has only a million crowns in his exchequer, and has need of two millions, he has only to persuade them that one crown is worth two, and they believe it.[2] If he has a costly war on hand, and is short of money, he simply suggests to his subjects that a piece of paper is coin of the realm, and they are straightway convinced of it. He has even succeeded in persuading them that his touch is a sovereign cure for all sorts of diseases, so great is the power and influence he has over their minds.

What I have told you of this prince need not astonish you: there is another magician more powerful still, who is master of the king's mind, as absolutely as the king is master of the minds of his subjects. This magician is called the Pope. Sometimes he makes the king believe that three are no more than one; that the bread which he eats is not bread; the wine which he drinks not wine; and a thousand things of a like nature.

And, to keep him in practice, and prevent him form losing the habit of belief, he gives him, now and again, as an exercise, certain articles of faith. Some two years ago he sent him a large document which he called *Constitution*,[3] and wished to enforce belief in all that it contained upon this prince and his subjects under heavy penalties. He succeeded in the case of the king,[4] who set the example of immediate submission; but some of his subjects revolted, and declared that they would not believe a single word of what was contained in this document. The women are the prime movers in this rebellion, which divides the court, the kingdom, and every family in the land, because the document prohibits them from reading a book which all the Christians assert is of divine origin: it is, indeed, their Koran. The women, enraged at this affront to their sex, exert all their power against the *Constitution*; and they have brought over to their side all the men who are not anxious about their privilege in the matter. And truly, the Mufti does not reason amiss. By the great Hali! he must have been instructed in the principles of our holy religion, because, since women are inferior creatures compared to us, and may not, according to our prophets, enter into Paradise, why should they meddle with a book which is only designed to teach the way thither?

Some things of a miraculous nature have been told me of the king, which I am certain will appear to you hardly credible.

It is said, that, while making war against such of his neighbours as had leagued against him, there were in his kingdom an infinite number of invisible foes surrounding him on all sides.[5] They add, that, during a thirty years' search, in spite of the indefatigable exertions of certain dervishes who are in his confidence,[6] not one of these have ever been discovered. The live with him, in his court and in his capital, among his troops, among his legislators; and yet it is believed that he will have the mortification of dying without having discovered them. They exist, as it were, in general, but not in particular: they constitute a body without members. Beyond a doubt, heaven wishes to punish this prince for his severity to the vanquished, in afflicting him with invisible enemies of a spirit and a destiny superior to his own.

I will continue to write you, and acquaint you with matters differing widely from the Persian character and genius. We tread, indeed, the same earth; but it seems incredible, remembering in the presence of the men of this country those of the country in which you are.

Paris, the 4th of the second moon of Rebiab,[7] 1712.

Letter 25

Usbek to Ibben, at Smyrna

I HAVE received a letter from your nephew, Rhedi, in which he informs me that he has left Smyrna intending to visit Italy; and that the sole object of his voyage is to improve himself, and so render himself worthier of you. I congratulate you on having a nephew who will some day be the consolation of your old age.

Rica tells me he wrote you a long letter full of details about this country. The liveliness of his intellect makes him a keen observer: I, whose mind moves slowly, am in no case to write of anything.

We often speak of you with warm affection; and are never done recalling the welcome you gave us in Smyrna, and the services your friendship rendered us daily. May you, generous Ibben, find friends everywhere as grateful and as faithful as we are!

I hope to see you soon again, and to enjoy once more those happy days which pass so pleasantly between two friends. Farewell.

Paris, the 4th of the second moon of Rebiab, 1712.

Letter 26

Usbek to Roxana, at the Seraglio at Ispahan

HOW happy you are, Roxana, to be in the delightful country of Persia, and not in these poisoned regions, where shame and virtue are alike unknown! How happy, indeed! In my seraglio you live as in the abode of innocence, inaccessible to the attacks of all mankind; you rejoice in the good fortune which makes it impossible for you to fall; no man has ever sullied you with a lascivious look; your father-in-law himself, even during the licence of the festivals, has never beheld your lovely mouth, for you have never neglected to conceal it with a sacred veil. Happy Roxana! In your visits to the country, eunuchs have always walked before you to deal out death to all those who dared to look at you. As for me, who received you as a gift from heaven to increase my happiness, what trouble did I not have in entering upon the possession of that treasure which you defended with such constancy! How I was mortified, during the first days of our marriage, when you withheld yourself from my sight! How impatient I was, when I did see you! You refused to satisfy my eager longing; on the contrary, you increased it by the obstinate refusals of an alarmed modesty; you failed to distinguish between me and all other men from whom you always conceal yourself. Do you remember that day when I lost you among your slaves, who betrayed me, and baffled me in my search? Or that other time, when, finding your tears powerless, you employed your mother's authority to stay the eagerness of my love? Do you remember when all your resources failed, except those which your courage supplied? Seeing a dagger, you threatened to destroy a husband who loved you, if he continued to demand the sacrifice of what was dearer to you than your husband himself. Two months passed in this combat between love and modesty; and you carried your chaste scruples so far, that you did not submit even after you were conquered, but defended to the last gasp a dying virginity. You regarded me as an enemy who had outraged you, and not as a husband who loved you. It was more than three months before you could look at me without blushing; your bashful glance seemed to reproach me for the advantage I had taken. I did not even enjoy a quiet possession; to the best of your ability you robbed me of your charms and graces; and without having received the least favours, I was ravished with the greatest.

If you had been brought up in this country, you would not have been so put about. The women here have lost all reserve: they appear before the men with their faces uncovered, as if they sought their overthrow; they watch for their glances; they accompany them to their mosques, on their promenades, even to their rooms; the service of eunuchs is quite unknown to them. In place of that noble simplicity, that amiable modesty which reigns among you, a brute-like impudence prevails, to which one can never grow accustomed.

Yes, Roxana, were you here, you would feel yourself outraged at the dreadful ignominy in which your sex is plunged; you would fly from this abominable land, sighing for that sweet retreat, where you find innocence and self-security, where no danger makes you afraid; where, in short, you can love me, without fear of ever losing that love which it is your duty to feel for me.

When you heighten the brilliance of your complexion with the loveliest colour, when you perfume your whole body with the most precious essences, when you clothe yourself in your most beautiful garments, when you seek to distinguish yourself from your companions by your gracefulness in the dance, and the sweetness of your song, as you gently dispute with them in beauty, in tenderness, in vivacity, I cannot imagine that you have any other aim than to please me; and, when I see you blushing modestly as your eyes seek mine, as you wind yourself into my heart with soft and flattering words, I cannot, Roxana, suspect your love.

But what am I to think of the women of Europe? The artful composition of their complexion, the ornaments with which they deck themselves, the care they have of their bodies, the desire to please which occupies them continually, are so many stains on their virtue, and affronts to their husbands.

It is not, Roxana, that I believe they carry their encroachment on virtue as far as such conduct might be expected to lead them, or that their debauchery extends to such horrible excess as the absolute violation of their conjugal vow – a thought to make one tremble. There are very few women so abandoned as to go to that length: the hearts of all of them are engraved from their birth with an impression of virtue, which education weakens, but cannot destroy. Though they may be lax in the observation of the external duties which modesty requires; yet, when it is a question of the last step, their better nature revolts. And so, when we imprison you so closely, and have you watched by crowds of slaves, when we restrain your desires so forcibly lest they break beyond bounds; it is not because we fear the final deed of infidelity, but because we know that purity cannot be too immaculate, and that the slightest stain would soil it.

I pity you, Roxana. Your long-tried chastity deserves a husband who would never have left you, and who would himself have restrained those desires which without him your virtue must subdue.

Paris, the 7th of the moon of Regeb,[1] 1712.

Letter 27

Usbek to Nessir, at Ispahan

We are now at Paris, that proud rival of the city of the sun.[1]

When I left Smyrna, I commissioned my friend Ibben to forward to you a box, containing some presents for you, which you will receive along with this letter. Although I am five or six hundred leagues distant from him, we exchange news as easily as if he were at Ispahan and I at Koum. I send my letters to Marseilles, whence vessels are constantly sailing for Smyrna: from Smyrna he despatches those destined for Persia by the Armenian caravans which start every day for Ispahan.

Rica enjoys the best of health: the strength of his constitution, his youth, and his natural gaiety enable him to pass unhurt through every ordeal.

I, however, am far from well; depressed both in body and mind, I surrender myself to reflections which become daily more melancholy. My impaired health makes me long for my own land, and adds to the strangeness of this one.

But I conjure you, dear Nessir, on no account to let my wives know how depressed I am. If they love me, I would spare their tears; and if not, I have no desire to increase their frowardness.

If my eunuchs believed me in danger, if they dared hope that a base compliance would pass unpunished, they would soon cease to be deaf to the seductive voice of that sex, which can melt rocks, and move inanimate things.

Farewell, Nessir. It is a great happiness to me that I can confide in you.

Paris, the 5th of the moon of Chahban, 1712.

Letter 28

*Rica to * * ***

YESTERDAY I witnessed a most remarkable thing, although it is of daily occurrence in Paris.

In the evening, after dinner, all the people gather together and play at a sort of dramatic game, which I have heard them call comedy. The main performance takes place upon a platform which is called the theatre.[1] On both sides may be seen little nooks called boxes, men and women who perform in dumb show, something after our own style in Persia.

Here you see a languishing love-sick lady; there, a more animated dame exchanges burning glances with her lover: their faces portray every passion, and express them with an eloquence, none the less fervid because it is mute. The actresses here display only half their bodies, and usually wear a modest muff to hide their arms. In the lower part of the theatre there stands a crowd of people who ridicule those who are seated on high; the latter, in their turn, laugh at those who are below.

But the most zealous and active of all are certain people whose youth enables them to support fatigue. They are obliged to appear everywhere; they move through passages known only to them, mounting with surprising agility from storey to storey; now above, now below, they visit every box. They dive, so to speak; are lost, and reappear; often they leave the place of performance, and carry on the game in another. And there are some who, by a miracle one would hardly have expected from the fact that they carry crutches, perform prodigies similar to those I have described. Lastly, there are the rooms where a private comedy is played. Commencing with salutations, the performers proceed to embrace each other: I am told that the slightest acquaintance gives a man a right to squeeze another to death. The place seems to inspire tenderness. Indeed, it is said that the princesses who reign here are far from cruel, and, with the exception of two or three hours during the day in which they are sufficiently hard-hearted, it must be admitted that they are uniformly very tractable, their hard-heartedness being a species of frenzy, which goes as easily as it comes.

All this that I have described goes on in much the same style at another place called the Opera: the sole difference being, that they speak at the one, and sing at the other. One of my friends took me the other day to a box where one of the principal actresses was undressing. We became so well acquainted, that next morning I received the following letter from her:

"SIR, - I, who have always been the most virtuous actress at the Opera, am yet the most miserable woman in the world. About seven or eight months ago, while I was in the box where you saw me yesterday, and in the act of undressing myself as priestess of Diana, a young Abbé broke in upon me. Undismayed by my white robe, my veil, and my frontlet, he stole from me my innocence. I have tried to persuade him of the greatness of the sacrifice I made; but he mocks me, and maintains that he found me very profane. In the meantime, my pregnancy is so apparent, that I dare not show myself upon the stage; for I am, in the matter of honour, extremely delicate, and always insist that it is easier for a well-born woman to lose her virtue than her modesty. You will readily believe that the young Abbé would never have overcome such exquisite modesty, had he not given me a promise of marriage. Having such a good reason to do so, I overlooked the usual petty formalities, and began where I should have ended. But, since I am dishonoured by his faithlessness, I do not wish to remain longer at the Opera, where, between you and me, they scarcely give me enough for a livelihood; because now, as I grow older, and, on the one hand, begin to lose my charms, on the other, my salary, which remains stationary, seems to grow less and less every day. I have learned from a member of your suite, that, in your country, they cannot make enough of a good dancer; and that, if I were once at Ispahan, I would quickly realize a fortune. If you would deign to take me under your protection, and carry me with you to your country, you would do yourself the credit of aiding a woman, whose virtuous behaviour renders her not altogether unworthy of your good offices. I am…"

Paris, the 2nd of the moon of Chalval[2], 1712.

Letter 29

Rica to Ibben, at Smyrna

The Pope is the head of the Christians: an old idol, kept venerable by custom. Formerly he was feared even by princes; for he deposed them as easily as our glorious sultans depose the kings of Irimetta and Georgia. He is, however, no longer dreaded. He declares himself to be the successor of one of the first Christians, called Saint Peter: and it is certainly a rich succession; for he possesses immense treasures, and a large territory owns his sway.

The bishops are the administrators under his rule, and they exercise, as his subordinates, two very different functions. In their corporate capacity they have, like him, the right to make articles of faith. Individually, their sole duty is to dispense with the observance of these articles. For you must know that the Christian religion is burdened with an immense number of very tedious duties: and, as it is universally considered less easy to fulfil these than to have bishops who can dispense with their fulfillment, the latter method has been chosen for the benefit of the public. Thus, if any one wishes to escape the fast of Rhamazan[1], or is unwilling to submit to the formalities of marriage, or wishes to break his vows, or to marry within the prescribed degrees, or even to forswear himself, all he has to do is to apply or a bishop, or to the Pope, who will at once grant a dispensation.

The bishops do not make articles of faith for their own government. There are a very great number of learned men, for the most part dervishes[2], who raise new questions in religion among themselves: they are left to discuss them for a long time, and the dispute lasts until a decision terminates it.

I can also assure you that there never was a realm in which so many civil wars have broken out, as in the kingdom of Christ.

Those who first propound some new doctrine, are immediately called heretics. Each heresy receives a name which is the rallying cry of those who support it. But no one need be a heretic against his will: he only requires to split the difference, and allege some scholastic subtlety to those who accuse him of heresy; and, whether it be intelligible or not, that renders him as pure as the snow, and he may insist upon his being called orthodox.

What I have told you holds good only in France and Germany: for I have heard it affirmed that in Spain and Portugal there are certain dervishes who do not understand raillery, and who cause men to be burned as they would burn straw. Happy the man, who, when he falls into the hands of these people, has been accustomed to finger little balls of wood[3] while saying his prayers, who has carried on his person two pieces of cloth attached to two ribbons[4], and who has paid a visit to a province called Galicia[5]. Without that, a poor devil is in a wretched plight. Although he should swear like a Pagan that he is orthodox, they may very likely decline to admit his plea, and burn him for a heretic. Much good his scholastic subtlety will do him! They will none of it; he will be burned to ashes before they would dream of even giving him a hearing.

Other judges assume the innocence of the accused; these always deem them guilty. In dubious cases, their rule is to lean to the side of severity, apparently because they think mankind desperately wicked. And yet, when it suits them, they have such a high opinion of mankind, that they think them incapable of lying; for they accept as witnesses, mortal enemies, loose women, and people whose trade is infamous. In sentencing culprits, they pay them a little compliment. Having dressed them in brimstone shirts, they assure them that they are much grieved to see them in such sorry attire; that they are tender-hearted, abhorring bloodshed, and are quite overcome at having to condemn them. Then these heart-broken judges console themselves by confiscating to their own use all the goods of their miserable victims.

Oh, happy land, inhabited by the children of the prophets! There such woeful sights as these are unknown[6]. There, the holy religion which angels brought protects itself by innate truth; it can maintain itself without recourse to violent means like these.

Paris, the 4th of the moon of Chalval, 1712.

Letter 30

Rica to the Same, at Smyrna

The curiosity of the people of Paris exceeds all bounds. When I arrived, they stared at me as if a I had dropped form the sky: old and young, men, women, and children, were all agog to see me. If I went abroad, everybody flew to the window. If I visited the Tuileries, I was immediately surrounded by a circle of gazers, the women forming a rainbow woven of a thousand colours. When I went sight-seeing, a hundred lorgnettes were speedily leveled at me: in fact, never was a man so stared at as I have been. I smiled frequently when I heard people who had never traveled beyond their own door, saying to each other, "He certainly looks very like a Persian." One thing struck me: I found my portraits everywhere-in all the shops, on every mantelpiece-so fearful were they lest they should not see enough of me.

So much distinction could not fail to be burdensome. I do not consider myself such a rare and wonderful specimen of humanity; and although I have a very good opinion of myself, I would never have dreamt that I could have disturbed the peace of a great city, where I was quite unknown. I therefore resolved to change my Persian dress for a European one, in order to see if my countenance would still strike people as wonderful. This experiment made me acquainted with my true value. Divested of everything foreign in my garb, I found myself estimated at my proper rate. I had reason to complain of my tailor, who had made me lose so suddenly the attention and good opinion of the public; for I sank immediately into the merest nonentity. Sometimes I would be as much as an hour in a given company, without attracting the least notice, or having an opportunity given me to speak; but, if any one chanced to inform the company that I was a Persian I soon overheard a murmur all round me, "Oh! ah! A Persian, is he? Most amazing! However can anybody be a Persian?"

Paris, the 6th of the moon of Chalval, 1712.

Letter 31

Rhedi to Usbek, at Paris

I am at present, my dear Usbek, at Venice. Although one had seen all the cities of the world, there would still be a surprise in store for him here. The sight of a town whose towers and mosques rise out of the water, and of an innumerable throng of people where one would expect to find only fish, will always excite astonishment.

But this heathenish city lacks the most precious treasure the world holds, pure water, to wit; it is impossible to accomplish a single lawful ablution. The place is held in abomination by our holy Prophet; he never beholds it from on high but with indignation. With that exception, my dear Usbek, I would be delighted to live in a town where my mind is developed every day. I am gaining an understanding of the secrets of commerce, of the affairs of princes, and of their form of government. Nor do I neglect European superstitions; I apply myself to medicine, physics, and astronomy; I study the arts: in short, I am couching my eyes of the film which covered them in my native land.

Venice, the 16th of the moon of Chalval, 1712.

Letter 32

Rica to ***

I went the other day to look through a house where a meagre provision is made for some three hundred people.[1] I was not long about it; for the church and the buildings do not deserve much attention. Those who live in this establishment were quite cheerful; many of them played at cards, or other games of which I knew nothing. As I left, one of the residents left also; and having heard me ask the way to the Marais, the remotest district of Paris, "I am going there," said he, "and will conduct you; follow me." He guided me wonderfully, steered me through the crowds, and protected me dexterously from carriages and coaches. We had almost arrived, when curiosity got the better of me. "My good friend," I said, "may I not know who you are?" "I am blind, sir," he answered. "What!" I cried; "blind? Then why did you not ask the good fellow who was playing at cards with you to be our guide?" "He is blind, too," was the answer: "for four hundred years there have been three hundred blind folks in the house where you met me. But I must leave you. Here is the street you want. I am going with the crowd into that church, where, I promise you, people will be less in my way than I will be in theirs."

Paris, the 17th of the moon of Chalval, 1712.

Letter 33

Usbek to Rhedi, at Venice

Wine is so very dear in Paris, on account of the duties laid on it, that it seems as if there were an intention to fulfil the injunctions of the divine Koran, which prohibits the use of strong drink.

When I consider the disastrous effects of that liquor, I cannot help regarding it as the most baleful of nature's gifts to men. If there is one good thing that has soiled the lives and the good fame of our monarchs, it has been intemperance; that is the chief and vilest source of their injustice and cruelty.

To the shame of these men it must be said, that, though the law prohibits them from using wine, they drink it to an excess which degrades them beneath the lowest of mankind. Here, however, the princes are allowed to use it, and no one has ever observed that it has caused them to do wrong. The human mind is inconsistency itself. In a drunken debauch, men break out madly against all precept; and the law, intended to make for our righteousness, often serves only to increase our guilt.

But, when I disapprove of the use of this liquor which deprives men of their reason, I do not also condemn those beverages which exhilarate the mind. The wisdom of the Orientals shows itself in their search for remedies against melancholy, which they prosecute with as much solicitude as in the case of the most dangerous maladies. When a misfortune happens to a European, his only resource is to read a philosopher called Seneca; but we Asiatics, more sensible, and better physicians in this matter, drink an infusion which cheers the heart and charms away the memory of its sufferings.

There is no greater affliction than those consolations which are drawn from the necessity of evil, the inefficacy of remedies, the inevitableness of destiny, the dispensations of Providence, and the wretched state of mankind generally. It is mockery to think of lightening misfortune, by remembering that we are born to misery; it is much wiser to raise the mind above these reflections, to treat man as a being capable of feeling, and not as a mere reasoner.

The soul, while united to the body, is a slave under a tyrant. If the blood moves sluggishly, if our spirits are not light enough, or high enough, we fall into dejection, and grow melancholy; but, if we drink what has the power to change the disposition of our body, our soul becomes capable of receiving delightful impressions, and experiences an inward joy as its machine recovers, so to speak, life and motion.

Paris the 25th of the moon of Zilcade, 1713.

Letter 34

Usbek to Ibben, at Smyrna

The Persian women are finer than the French women; but those of France are prettier. It is as difficult not to love the former, as it is to be displeased with the latter: these attract by their tenderness and modesty, while those conquer us with their sprightly humor.

That which preserves the beauty of the women in Persia is the regular life they lead: they neither gamble, nor sit up late; they drink no wine, and are never exposed to the air. It must indeed be admitted that the life of the seraglio is more conducive to health than to happiness, it is so dull and uniform. Everything turns upon discipline and duty; the very pleasures are solemn, and mirth itself is sad; enjoyment is hardly ever tasted except as an indication of authority and dependence.

Even the men are not so cheerful in Persia as in France: one never sees that freedom of spirit, and that air of contentment, which I find here among all sorts and conditions of men.

It is still worse in Turkey. There, families may be found, in which, from father to son, no soul has laughed since the foundation of the monarchy.

This Asiatic gravity is the result of the unsocial life which people lead: they never see each other except on ceremonial occasions. Friendship, that dear solace of the heart, the sweetener of our life below, is almost unknown to them; they withdraw into their houses, where they always have the same companions; and in this way each family is, as it were, isolated.

One day, when I was discussing the subject with a young man of this country, he said, "That which offends me most among your customs is the necessity you are under of living with slaves, whose thoughts and inclinations are always subdued to the vileness of their condition. These wretched creatures, by whom you have been beset from infancy, weaken in you, and ultimately destroy, those virtuous feelings which nature implants.

"For, in short, when you have cleared your mind from prejudice, what is to be expected from an upbringing at the hands of a wretch, who makes his honour consistent with the guardianship of another's wives, and prides himself upon the most loathsome employment which society affords; whose only virtue, his fidelity, is utterly despicable, because it is prompted by envy, jealousy, and despair; who, belonging to neither sex, burns to be avenged on both, and yet submits to the tyranny of the stronger, in order that he may afflict the weaker; who, deriving from his imperfection, his ugliness, and his deformity, all the éclat of his position, is esteemed only because he is unworthy; who, finally riveted for ever to the gate which he guards, harder than the bolts and bars which secure it, brags of fifty years in this ignoble station, where, as the minister of his master's jealousy, he has given the rein to all his own vileness?"

Paris, the 14th of the moon of Zilhage, 1713.[1]

Letter 35

Usbek to Gemchid, his Cousin, Dervish of the glorious Monastary of Tauris

What is your opinion, sublime dervish, of the Christians? Do you think that at the day of judgment, like the unbelieving Turks, who are to serve the Jews for asses, they will be hurried off at the gallop into hell? I am well aware that their abode will not be with the prophets, and that the great Hali's mission was not to them. But, do you think they will be condemned to everlasting punishment because they have not been fortunate enough to find mosques in their country? Will God chastise them for failing to practise a religion which He has withheld from their knowledge? I may tell you, I have often examined these Christians; I have questioned them to find out if they had any ideas about the great Hali, who was the most perfect of all men, and it is certain that they have never even heard of him.

They are not like those infidels whom our holy prophets put to the sword, because they refused to believe in the miracles of Heaven: they are like those unfortunates who lived in the darkness of idolatry, before the divine light illuminated the face of our great prophet.

Besides, an examination of their religion reveals the presence of some rudiments of our doctrines. I have often admired the secret workings of Providence, which seems in this way to have prepared them for a general conversion. One book of their learned men, entitled "Polygamy Triumphant,"[1] of which I have heard, proves that polygamy is enjoined upon Christians. Their baptism is an emblem of our ablutions; and their only error consists in ascribing to that first ablution an efficacy which enables them to omit all others. Their priests and friars pray, like ours, seven times a day. They hope to inherit a paradise where, by means of the resurrection of the body, they will enjoy a thousand delights. Like us also, they have appointed fasts, and times of mortification, by which they hope to move the divine clemency. They worship good angels, and are in dread of evil ones. They believe in miracles which God works by means of His servants. They recognise, as we do, their own unworthiness, and the need they have for an intercessor with God. Throughout their religion I find traces of Mohammedanism, although there is no word of Mohammed. It has been well said, that truth will break through the darkest clouds. The day is hastening when the Eternal will behold upon the earth none but true believers. Time, which devours all, will make away even with error. Men will be astonished to find themselves all under the same standard: everything, the law itself, will be accomplished; and the godly will be taken from the earth, and carried to the mansions of the blest.

Paris, the 20th of the moon of Zilhage, 1713.

Letter 36

Usbek to Rhedi, at Venice

Coffee is very much used in Paris, there are a great many public houses where it may be had. In some of these they meet to gossip, in others to play at chess. There is one[1] where the coffee is prepared in such a way that it makes those who drink it witty: at least, there is not a single soul who on quitting the house does not believe himself four times wittier than when he entered it.

But that which shocks me most in these geniuses, is, that they are quite useless to their country, and amuse their talents with puerilities. For example, when I arrived at Paris I found them warm to dispute over the most trifling matter imaginable.[2] It was all about an old Greek poet, whose birthplace and time of dying no one has known for two thousand years. Both sides agreed that he was a most excellent poet: it was only a question of the degree of merit to be ascribed to him. Each wished to fix his rank; but among those apportioners of praise, some carried more weight than others. Here you have the whole dispute. It was a lively quarrel; for both sides abused each other most heartily with such gross aspersions, and such bitter raillery, that I admired the conduct of the quarrel, as much as the subject of it. "If any one," said I to myself, "were fool enough to attack, in the presence of the defenders of the Greek poet, the reputation of some honest citizen, he would surely find a warm reception; and, indeed, I believe that this extreme zeal for the reputation of the dead, would blaze up to some purpose in defence of the living. But, however that may be," added I, "God keep me from ever drawing on myself the enmity of these censors of this poet, who has not been saved from their implacable hate even after having lain two thousand years in his grave! At present they fight the air; but how would it be, if their rage were animated by the presence of an enemy?"

Those of whom I have told you dispute in the vulgar tongue; and must be distinguished from another set of disputants, who employ a barbarous language,[3] which seems to increase the fury and the obstinacy of the combatants. There are places[4] where these people are to be seen struggling as in a battle, dismal and confused; they are fed upon subtleties, they live upon obscure arguments and false inferences. This profession, although one would think its followers would die of hunger, must pay in some way. A whole nation, driven from their own country,[5] has been seen to cross the sea and establish itself in France, carrying with it no other means of providing for the necessities of life, than a notable talent for debate. Farewell.

Paris, the last day of the moon of Zilhage, 1713.

Letter 37

Usbek to Ibben at Smyrna

The King of France is old.[1] We have no examples in our histories of such a long reign as his. It is said that he possesses in a very high degree the faculty of making himself obeyed: he governs with equal ability his family, his court, and his kingdom: he has often been heard to say, that, of all existing governments, that of the Turks, or that of our august Sultan, pleased him best: such is his high opinion of Oriental statecraft.[2]

I have studied his character, and I have found certain contradictions which I cannot reconcile. For example, he has a minister who is only eighteen years old,[3] and a mistress who is fourscore;[4] he loves his religion, and yet he cannot abide those who assert that it ought to be strictly observed;[5] although he flies from the noise of cities, and is inclined to be reticent, from morning till night he is engaged in getting himself talked about; he is fond of trophies and victories, but he has a great a dread of seeing a good general at the head of his own troops, as at the head of an army of his enemies. It has never I believe happened to any one by himself, to be burdened with more wealth than even a prince could hope for, and yet at the same time steeped in such poverty as a private person could ill brook.

He delights to reward those who serve him; but he pays as liberally the assiduous indolence of his courtiers, as the labours in the field of his captains; often the man who undresses him, or who hands him his serviette at table, is preferred before him who has taken cities and gained battles; he does not believe that the greatness of a monarch is compatible with restriction in the distribution of favours; and, without examining into the merit of a man, he will heap benefits upon him, believing that his selection makes the recipient worthy; accordingly he has been known to bestow a small pension upon a man who had run off two leagues from the enemy, and a good government on another who had gone four.

Above all, he is magnificent in his buildings; there are more statues in his palace gardens[6] than there are citizens in a large town. His bodyguard is as strong as that of the prince before whom all the thrones of the earth tremble;[7] his armies are as numerous, his resources as great, and his finances as inexhaustible.

Paris, the 7th of the moon of Maharram, 1713.

Letter 38

Rica to Ibben, at Smyrna

It is an all-important question among men, whether it is better to deprive women of their liberty, or to leave them free. It seems to me that much is to be said on both sides. When Europeans declare that it is most ungenerous to keep those whom we love in misery, we Asiatics reply that men lower themselves by renouncing the dominion which nature has given them over women. If we are told how troublesome it must be to have a crowd of women shut up together, our reply is, that ten women who obey are less bother than one who does not. If we object, in our turn, that Europeans cannot be happy with women who are unfaithful to them; they answer that the fidelity we boast of does not prevent that disgust, which always follows a surfeit of desire; that our women belong to us too absolutely; that possession obtained so easily leaves no scope for hope or fear; that a little coquetry, like salt, stimulates the appetite, and prevents corruption. Perhaps even a wiser man than I would find this question difficult to decide; for, if the Asiatics do well in seeking due means to quiet their uneasiness, the Europeans do equally well in not being uneasy.

After all, they say, though we should be unfortunate as husbands, we can always find compensation as lovers. A man could have just reason to complain of the infidelity of his wife only if there were no more than three people in the world; odd may be made even, as long as a fourth can be found.

Another much-discussed question is, whether women are intended by nature to be subject to men. "No," said a very gallant philosopher to me the other day; "nature never dictated any such law. The dominion which we exercise over them is tyrannical; they yield themselves to men only because they are more tender-hearted, and consequently more human and more rational. These advantages, which, had we been reasonable, would, without doubt, have been the cause of their subordination, because we are irrational.

"Now, if it is true that it is a tyrannical power which we have over women, it is none the less true that they exercise over us a natural dominion- that of beauty, which nothing can resist. Our power does not extend to all countries, but that of beauty is universal. Why, then, should we have any privilege? Is it because we are stronger than they? But that would be the height of injustice. We use every possible means to discourage them. Our powers would be found equal if we were educated alike. Try women in those gifts which education has not weakened, and we soon will see which is the abler sex."

It must be admitted, although shocking to our ideas of propriety, that, amongst the most polite people, women have always borne sway over their husbands; their authority was established by law among the Egyptians in honour of Isis, and among the Babylonians in honour of Semiramis. It was said of the Romans that they, who ruled all the world, were ruled by their wives. I say nothing of the Sauromates[1], who were held in a state of slavery by their women; they were too barbarous to be cited as an example.

You see, my dear Ibben, that I have fallen in with the fashion of this country, where they are fond of defending extra-ordinary opinions, and of reducing everything to a paradox. The prophet has decided this question, and has settled the rights of both sexes. "Women," he says, "ought to honor their husbands; and husbands, their wives: but men are a degree higher in the scale of creation than women."

Paris, the 26th of the second moon of Gemmadi, 1713.

Letter 39

Hagi[1] Ibbi to the Jew Ben Joshua, Mohammedan Proselyte, at Smyrna

It always seems to me, Ben Joshua, that prodigies always accompany the birth of extraordinary men, as if nature suffered a convulsion, and the celestial power could not bring forth without travail.

There is no birth so marvelous as that of Mohammed.God, who, by the decrees of his providence, has determined from the beginning to send to men that great prophet for the overthrow of Satan, created a light two thousand years before Adam, which, passing from elect to elect through the ancestors of Mohammed, reached him at last, as an authentic sign of his descent from the patriarchs.

It was because of this very prophet that God willed that no child should be conceived, that women should cease to be unclean, and that man should be circumcised.

He came into the world circumcised already, and joy shone upon his face from birth. The earth shook three times, as if she herself had brought forth; all the idols fell forward, and the thrones of kings were overturned.Lucifer was cast into the depths of the sea, and it was only after forty days' immersion that he swam up from the abyss, and took refuge on Mount Cabes, whence, with a terrible voice, he cried to the angels.

That night, God placed a barrier between the man and the woman, which neither of them could pass. The art of the magicians and of the necromancers cease to avail.A voice from heaven was heard crying, "I have sent into the world my faithful friend."

According to the testimony of Isben Aben, all the birds, the clouds, the winds, and the hosts of angels, met together to bring up this child, and disputed who should have preference.The birds said in their warblings that it was proper for them to have his upbringing, because they could so easily gather a variety of fruits from many places.The winds murmured and said, "To us rather he should be committed, because we can bear him from all quarters the sweetest odours.""No, no, " cried the clouds; "no; it is we who should have charge of him, because we can refresh him at any moment with our showers."From on high the angels indignantly exclaimed, "What will there be left for us to do?"But a voice from heaven silenced their disputes and said, "He will not be withdrawn from mortal hands, because blessed shall be the breasts that suckle him, the hands that touch him, the house wherein he lives, and the bed on which he lies."

After so many striking testimonies, my dear Joshua, only a heart of iron could refuse to believe the holy law.What more could heaven itself have done to authorize his divine mission, unless it had overturned nature, and destroyed the very men whose salvation it desired.

Paris, the 20th moon of Rhegeb, 1713.

Letter 40

Usbek to Ibben, at Smyrna

When a great man dies, people assemble in a mosque to hear his funeral oration pronounced- a discourse in his praise from which it would be very difficult to gather a true estimate of the deceased.

I would abolish all funeral pomp. Men should be bewailed at their birth and not their death. What good purpose do these ceremonies serve, with all the doleful shows that are paraded before a dying man in his last moments: the very tears of his family and the grief of his friends exaggerate for him the loss he is about to sustain.

We are so blind that we know neither when to mourn, nor when to rejoice; our mirth and our sadness are nearly always false.

When I see the Great Mogul foolishly place himself once a year in a balance to be weighed like an ox; when I see his people applaud the increase in weight of their prince, that is to say, the decrease in his capacity to govern them, my heart, Ibben, bleeds for the extravagance of humanity.

Paris, the 20th of the moon of Rhegeb, 1713.

Letter 41

The chief black Eunuch to Usbek

Ishmael, one of your black eunuchs, O magnificent master, has just died; and I tried to avoid any delay in filling up his place. As eunuchs are very scarce at present, I thought of making use of a black slave whom you have in country; but I have not yet succeeded in persuading him to undergo the sacrifice necessary for his consecration to that office. Knowing that this change would in the end work for his advantage, I wished the other day to employ towards him a little violence; and, in company with the superintendent of your gardens, I commanded that, in spite of himself, he should be put into a fit state to render you those services which most appeal to your heart, and to live with me in those sacred quarters, which, at present, he durst not even look at; but he fell a-roaring, as if we had wanted to flay him, and made such a to-do that he escaped from our hands, and so avoided the fatal knife. I have only now learned that he intends to write you begging for his mercy, and that he will urge in his defense that this design had been conceived by me, only in satisfaction of a relentless desire to be avenged for some cutting sarcasms which he says he vented against me. However, I swear to you by the hundred thousand prophets, that in this matter I have acted entirely for the benefit of your service, the only thing which is dear to me, beyond which I have not a single thought. I prostrate myself at your feet.

The Seraglio at Fatme, the 7th of the moon of Maharram, 1713.

Pharan to Usbek, his Sovereign Lord

If you were here, magnificent lord, I would appear to you clad from head to foot in white paper;[1] and even that would not be enough to contain a description of all the insults which your first black eunuch, the most malignant of men, has heaped upon me since your departure.

Under the pretext of some sarcasms which he pretends I aimed at his unfortunate lot, he makes me the victim of an insatiable vengeance. He has stirred up against me the cruel superintendent of your gardens, who, ever since you left, has laid upon me impossible tasks, in attempting which I have a thousand times taken leave of life, although I never for an instant lost my ardour in your service. Many a time have I said to myself, "I who have the gentlest of masters, am yet the most miserable slave on the face of the earth!"

I confess, most generous lord, that I did not believe myself destined to still greater miseries, but this felonious eunuch had yet to fill up some measure of his wickedness. Some days ago, on his unsupported authority, he destined me to the guardianship of your sacred wives; that is to say, to a punishment which to me would be a thousand times more cruel than death. Those, who, at their birth, have had the misfortune to undergo such treatment at the hands of their cruel parents, may perhaps comfort themselves with the thought that they have never known any other condition; but were I to lose my place among men, and be deprived of that which makes me human, I should die of grief, if I survived the barbarous knife.

I kiss your feet, sublime lord, in the deepest humility. Grant that I may feel the effects of your revered virtue. Let it not be said that, at your command, there is upon the earth one more unhappy being.

The Gardens of Fatme, the 7th of the moon of Maharram, 1713.

Letter 43

Usbek to Pharan, at the Gardens of Fatme

Rejoice in your heart, and acknowledge these sacred characters. Let the chief eunuch and the superintendent of my gardens kiss this letter. I prohibit them from attempting anything against you: tell them to purchase the eunuch they require. Do your duty, as if you had me always before you; for know, that my bounty is great, so, if you abuse it, will the measure of your punishment be.

Paris, the 25th of the moon of Rhegeb, 1713.

Letter 44

Usbek to Rhedi, at Venice

There are in France three privileged classes: the church, the sword, and the gown.Each has such sovereign contempt for the other two, that sometimes a man who deserves to be looked down upon because he is a fool, is despised only because he is a lawyer.

All classes, including the meanest workmen, contend for the excellence of the craft they have chosen; each man exalts himself at the expense of some other of a different profession, according to the idea which he has formed of the superiority of his own.

They all resemble, more or less, a certain woman of the province of Erivan, who, having received some favor from one of our monarchs, wished a thousand times, in the blessings she showered upon him, that heaven would make him governor of Erivan.

I have read in a history, how some men belonging to the crew of a French vessel which had anchored off the coast of Guinea, went ashore in order to buy some sheep.They were led before the king, who was administering justice to his subjects under a tree.He sat upon his throne, that is to say, upon a block of wood, as proudly as if it had been the seat of the Great Mogul.His guard consisted of three or four men armed with armed with pointed staves; an umbrella served as canopy to protect him from the heat of the sun; for ornaments, he and his consort wore nothing but their own black skins and some rings.This prince, whose vanity was greater even than his poverty, asked the strangers if they talked much of him in France.He imagined that his fame must have gone forth to the ends of the earth, he for his part believed that he put the whole world chattering.

When the Khan of Tartary has eaten, a herald announces that all the princes of the earth may now go to dinner if they wish; that barbarian, whose food is milk, who has no house, and who lives only by brigandage, looks upon all the kings of the world as his slaves, and insults them regularly twice a day.

Paris, the 28th of the moon of Rhegeb, 1713.

Letter 45

*Rica to Usbeck, at * * * *

YESTERDAY morning, as I lay in bed, I heard a violent knocking at my door, which was suddenly opened, or driven in, by a man with whom I have some slight acquaintance, and who appeared to me to be quite beside himself.[1]

His dress was, to say the least, very homely; his wig, all askew, had not even been combed; he had not had time to mend his black waistcoat; and he had, for that day, omitted the wise precautions with which he was in the habit of concealing the dilapidation of his attire.

"Rise," he said; "I shall want you all day. I have a thousand purchases to make, and it will be a great convenience to me to have you with me. First of all, we have to go to the Rue Saint Honoré to see a notary, who is commissioned to sell an estate worth five hundred thousand livres. On my way here, I stopped a moment in the Faubourg Saint Germain, where I hired a house at two thousand crowns; I hope to sign the contract today."

As soon as, or rather before, I was dressed, my gentleman hurried me downstairs. "Let us start," said he, "by buying and setting up a coach." As a matter of fact, we bought, not only a coach, but—and that in less than an hour—a hundred thousand francs' worth of goods: all this was done with promptitude, because my gentleman haggled about nothing, kept no account, and paid no money. I reflected upon it all; and, when I examined this man, I found in him such an extraordinary mixture of indications of both wealth and poverty, that I knew not what to think. But at last I broke silence, and taking him aside, I said, "Sir, who is to pay for all this?" "Myself," said he. "Come to my room, and I will show you immense treasures, and riches envied by the greatest kings—but not by you, because you will always share with me." I followed him. We climbed up to his fifth storey, and by means of a ladder hoisted ourselves to a sixth, which was a closet open to all the winds, and contained nothing but two or three dozen earthenware basins filled with different liquors. "I rose very early," he said, "and, as I have done every morning for the last twenty-five years, I paid a visit to my work. I saw that the great day had come, the day which would make me the richest man in the whole world. Do you see this ruddy liquor? It possesses at present all the qualities required by philosophers for the transmutation of metals. I have collected those grains which you see, and which are, as their colour shows, pure gold, although they are a little deficient in weight. This secret, which Nicholas Flamel discovered, but which Raymond Lully[2] and a million others have sought in vain, has been revealed at last to me; and to-day I find myself a happy adept. May God grant that with the treasures which He has committed to me I may do nothing but for His glory!"

Transported with anger, I left the room, and descended, or rather threw myself down the stairs, and left this man of boundless wealth in his garret. Farewell, my dear Usbek, I will visit you to-morrow, and, if you wish, we can return to Paris together.

Paris, the last day of the moon of Rhegeb, 1713.

Letter 46

I MEET here certain people who are never done discussing religion, but who seem at the same time to contend as to who shall observe it least.

These disputants are, however, no better Christians, nor even better citizens, than others; and that it is that moves me: for the principal part of any religion consists in obedience to the laws, in loving mankind, and in revering one's parents.

Indeed, ought it not to be the chief aim of a religious man to please the Deity who has founded the religion which he professes? But the surest way to please God is, without doubt, to obey the laws of society, and do our duty towards men. For, whatever religion we may profess, as soon as we grant its existence, it becomes at once necessary to assume that God loves men, since He establishes a religion for their happiness: then, since He loves men, we are certain of pleasing Him in loving them too—in other words, in fulfilling all the duties of charity and humanity, and in breaking none of the laws under which men live.

We are much more certain of pleasing God in this way, than in the observance of this or that ceremony; for ceremonies have no goodness in themselves; they are only relatively good, and on the supposition that God has commanded them. But this is a subject which might be discussed endlessly; and one could easily deceive oneself regarding it, because it is necessary to choose the rites of one religion from among those of two thousand.

A man prayed to God daily in the following terms: "Lord, I do not understand any of those discussions that are carried on without end regarding Thee: I would serve Thee according to Thy will; but each man whom I consult would have me serve Thee according to his. When I desire to pray, I know not in which language to address Thee. Nor do I know what posture to adopt: one bids me pray standing; another, sitting; and another requires me to kneel. That is not all: there are some who insist that I ought to wash every morning in cold water; others maintain that Thou regardest me with horror if I do not remove a certain small portion of my flesh. I happened the other day to eat of a rabbit in a caravansary: three men who were present made me tremble: all three maintained that I had grievously offended Thee; one,[1] because that animal was unclean; another,[2] because it had been strangled; and the third,[3] because it was not a fish. A Brahmin who was passing by, and whom I asked to be our judge, said to me, 'They are all wrong, for it appears that you did not kill the animal yourself.' 'I did, though,' said I. 'Ah, then, you have committed an abominable act, which God will never pardon,' said he to me, in a severe tone. 'How do you know that the soul of your father had not passed into that beast?' All these things, O Lord, trouble me beyond expression. I cannot move my head but I am threatened with Thy wrath. Nevertheless I would please Thee, and devote to that end the life which Thou hast given me. I may be deceiving myself; but I think that the best means to accomplish this aim is to live as a good citizen in the society where Thou hast placed me, and as a good father in the family which Thou hast given me."

Paris, the 8th of the moon of Chahban, 1713.

Letter 47

Zachi to Usbek, at Paris

I HAVE great news for you. Zephis and I are reconciled, and the seraglio, which had taken sides in our quarrel, is reunited. I need nothing now in this abode of peace but you. Come, my dear Usbek, come to me, and let love be triumphant.

I made a great feast in honour of Zephis, to which your mother, your wives, and your principal concubines were invited; your aunts and some of your female cousins also came; they arrived on horseback, covered by the dark cloud of their veils and garments.

Next day we set out for the country, where we hope to have greater liberty. We mounted our camels, four in each palanquin. As the party had been improvised, we had not time to send round the *courouc*,[1] but the chief eunuch, always attentive, took another precaution: to the cloth which hid us from sight, he attached a curtain so thick, that we could positively see nobody.

When we reached that river which we have to cross, each of us went, in the usual way, into a box which was transported in the ferry boat; for we were told that there were a great many people on the river. One inquisitive person who approached too near the place where we were shut up, received a mortal blow, which cut him off for ever from the light of day; another, who was found bathing naked on the bank, met the same fate: those two wretches were sacrificed by your faithful eunuchs to your honour and to ours.

But listen to the rest of our adventures. When we had reached the middle of the river, so violent a wind arose, and such a dense cloud covered the sky, that our sailors began to lose hope. Terrified at the danger, we nearly all swooned away. I remember that I heard the voices of our eunuchs in dispute. Some of them said that, to save us from danger, we must be set at liberty; but their chief insisted, unfalteringly, that he would sooner die than permit his master to be so dishonoured, and that he would plunge a dagger into the breast of any one who should dare to make such proposals. One of my slaves, quite beside herself and all undressed, came running to my assistance; but a black eunuch seized her brutally, and thrust her back whence she had come. Then I swooned away, and returned to myself only after the danger was past.

How distressing journeys are for us poor women! Men are exposed only to those dangers which threaten their lives; but we are in constant terror of losing either life or virtue. Farewell, my dear Usbek, whom I shall always adore.

The Seraglio at Fatme, the 2nd of the moon of Rhamazan, 1713.

Letter 48

Usbek to Rhedi, at Venice

Those who take pleasure in their own instruction are never idle. Although I am not employed on any business of importance, I am yet constantly occupied. I spend my time observing, and at night I write down what I have noticed, what I have seen, what I have heard, during the day. I am interested in everything, astonished at everything; I am like a child, whose organs, still over-sensitive, are vividly impressed by the merest trifles.[1]

You would scarcely believe it, but we have been well received in all circles, and among all classes. This is largely owing to the quick wit and natural gaiety of Rica, which lead him to seek out everybody, and make him equally sought after. Our foreign aspect offends nobody; indeed, we are delighted at the surprise which people show on finding us not altogether without manners; for the French imagine that men are not among the products of our country. Nevertheless, I must admit that they are well worth undeceiving.

I spent some days in the country near Paris at the house of a man of some note, who delights in having company with him. He has a very amiable wife, who, along with great modesty, possesses what the secluded life they lead stifles in our Persian women, a charming gaiety.

Stranger as I was, I had nothing better to do than to study the crowd of people who came and went without ceasing, affording me a constant change of subject for contemplation. I noticed at once one man, whose simplicity pleased me; I allied myself with him, and he with me, in such a manner that we were always together.

One day, as we were talking quietly in a large company, leaving the general conversation to the others, I said, "You will perhaps find in me more inquisitiveness than good manners; but I beg you to let me ask some questions, for I am wearied to death doing nothing, and of living with people with whom I have nothing in common. My thoughts have been busy these two days; there is not one among these men who has not put me to the torture two hundred times; in a thousand years I would never understand them; they are more invisible to me than the wives of our great king." "You have only to ask," replied he, "and I will tell you all you desire – the more willingly because I think you a discreet man, who will not abuse my confidence."

"Who is that man," said I, "who has told us so much about the banquets at which he has entertained the great, who is so familiar with your dukes, and who talks so often to your ministers, who, they tell me, are so difficult of access? He ought surely to be a man of quality; but his aspect is so mean that he is hardly an honour to the aristocracy; and, besides, I find him deficient in education. I am a stranger; but it seems to me that there is, generally speaking, a certain tone of good-breeding common to all nations, and I do not find it in him. Can it be that your upper classes are not so well trained as those of other nations?" "That man," answered he, laughing, "is a farmer-general; he is as much above others in wealth, as he is inferior to us all by birth. He might have the best people in Paris at his table, if he could make up his mind never to eat in his own house. He is very impertinent, as you see; but he excels in his cook, and is not ungrateful, for you heard how he praised him to-day."

"And that big man dressed in black," said I, "whom that lady has placed next her? How comes he to wear a dress so solemn, with so jaunty an air, and such a florid complexion? He smiles benignly when he is addressed; his attire is more modest, but not less carefully adjusted than that of your women." "That," answered he, "is a preacher, and, which is worse, a confessor. Such as he is, he knows more of their own affairs than the husbands; he is acquainted with the women's weak side, and they also know his." "Ha!" cried I, "he talks for ever of something he calls Grace?" "No, not always," was the reply; "in the ear of a pretty woman he speaks more willingly of the Fall: in public, he is a son of thunder; in private, as gentle as a lamb." "It seems to me," said I, "that he receives much attention, and is held in great respect." "In great respect! Why! he is a necessity; he is the sweetener of solitude; then there are little lessons, officious cares, set visits; he cures a headache better than any man in the world; he is incomparable."

"But, if I may trouble you again, tell me who that ill-dressed person is opposite us? He makes occasional grimaces, and does not speak like the others; and without wit enough to talk, he talks that he may have wit." "That," answered he, "is a poet, the grotesquest of human kind. These sort of people declare that they are born what they are; and, I may add, what they will be all their lives, namely, almost always, the most ridiculous of men; and so nobody spares them; contempt is cast upon them from every quarter. Hunger has driven that one into this house. He is well received by its master and mistress, as their good-nature and courtesy are always the same to everybody. He wrote their epithalamium when they were married, and it is the best thing he has done, for the marriage has been as fortunate as he prophesied it would be.

"You will not believe, perhaps," added he, "prepossessed as you are in favour of the East, that there are among us happy marriages, and wives whose virtue is a sufficient guard. This couple, here, enjoy untroubled peace; everybody loves and esteems them; only one thing is amiss: in their good-nature they receive all kinds of people, which makes the company at their house sometimes not altogether unexceptionable. I, of course, have nothing to say against it; we must live with people as we find them; those who are said to be well-bred are often only those who are exquisite in their vices; and perhaps it is with them as with poisons, the more subtle, the more dangerous."

"And that old man," I whispered, "who looks so morose? I took him at first for a foreigner; because, in addition to being dressed differently from the rest, he condemns everything that is done in France, and disapproves of your government." "He is an old soldier," said he, "who makes himself memorable to all his hearers by the tedious story of his exploits. He cannot endure the thought that France has gained any battles without him, nor hear a siege bragged of at which he did not mount the breach. He believes himself so essential to our history that he imagines it came to an end when he retired; some wounds he has received mean, simply, the dissolution of the monarchy; and, unlike the philosophers who maintain that enjoyment is only in the present, and that the past is as if it had not been, he, on the contrary, delights in nothing but the past, and exists only in his old campaigns; he breathes the air of the age that has gone by, just as heroes ought to live in that which is to come." "But why," I asked, "has he quitted the service?" "He has not quitted it, but it has quitted him. He has been employed in a small post, where he will retail his adventures for the rest of his days; but he will never get any further; the path of honour is closed to him." "And why?" asked I. "It is a maxim in France," replied he, "never to advance officers whose patience has been worn out as subalterns; we look upon them as men whose minds have been narrowed by detail; and who, through a constant application to small things, are become incapable of great ones. We believe that a man who, at thirty, has not the qualities of a general, will never have them; that he, whose glance cannot take in at once a tract of several leagues as if from every point of view, who is not possessed of that presence of mind which in victory leaves no advantage unimproved, and in defeat employs every resource, will never acquire such capacity. Therefore we employ in brilliant services those great, those sublime men, on whom Heaven has bestowed not only the courage, but the genius of the hero; and in inferior services those whose talents are inferior. Of this number are such as have grown old in obscure warfare; they can succeed only at what they have been doing all their lives;

and it would be ill-advised to start them on fresh employment when age has weakened their powers."

A moment after, curiosity again seized me, and I said, "I promise not to ask another question if you will only answer this one. Who is that tall young man who wears his own hair, and has more impertinence than wit? How comes it that he speaks louder than the others, and is so charmed with himself for being in the world?" "That is a great lady-killer," he replied. With these words some people entered, others left, and all rose. Some one came to speak to my acquaintance, and I remained in my ignorance. But shortly after, I know not by what chance, the young man in question found himself beside me, and began to talk. "It is fine weather," he said. "Will you take a turn with me in the garden? I replied as civilly as I could, and we went out together. "I have come to the country," said he, "to please the mistress of the house, with whom I am not on the worst of terms. There is a certain woman in the world who will be rather out of humour; but what can one do? I visit the finest women in Paris; but I do not confine my attentions to one; they have plenty to do to look after me, for, between you and me, I am a sad dog." "In that case, sir," said I, "you doubtless have some office or employment which prevents you from waiting on them more assiduously?" "No, sir; I have no other business than to provoke husbands, and drive fathers to despair; I delight in alarming a woman who thinks me hers, and in bringing her within an ace of losing me. A set of us young fellows divide up Paris among us in this pursuit, and keep it wondering at everything we do." "From what I understand," said I, "you make more stir than the most valorous warrior, and are more regarded than a grave magistrate. If you were in Persia, you would not enjoy all these advantages; you would be held fitter to guard our women than to please them." "The blood mounted to my face; and I believe, had I gone on speaking, I could not have refrained from affronting him.

What say you to a country where such people are tolerated, and where a man who follows such a profession is allowed to live? Where faithlessness, treachery, rape, deceit, and injustice lead to distinction? Where a man is esteemed because he has bereaved a father of his daughter, a husband of his wife, and distresses the happiest and purest homes? Happy the children of Hali who protect their families from outrage and seduction! Heaven's light is not purer than the fire that burns in the hearts of our wives; our daughters think only with dread of the day when they will be deprived of that purity, in virtue of which they rank with the angels and the spiritual powers. My beloved land, on which the morning sun looks first, thou art unsoiled by those horrible crimes which compel that star to hide his beams as he approaches the dark West!

Paris, the 5th of the moon of Rhamazan, 1713.

Letter 49

Rica to Usbek, at ***

As I was in my room the other day, there came to me a dervish amazingly dressed. His beard descended to his rope-girdle; his feet were naked; his gown grey, coarse and peaked in places. The whole appeared to me so odd that my first idea was to send for a painter to make a sketch of it.

First of all he paid me a prolonged compliment, in which he informed me that he was a man of merit, and a Capuchin to boot. "They tell me, sir," continued he, "that you return soon to the court of Persia, where you hold high rank. I have come to ask your protection, and to beg you to obtain for us from the king a small establishment in the neighbourhood of Casbin for two or three friars." "Father," said I, "do you then wish to go to Persia?" "Me, sir," cried he; "I shall take better care of myself. I am Provincial here, and I would not exchange my place for that of all the Capuchins in the world." "Then why the devil do you make this request?" "Because, said he, "if we had this monastery, our Italian fathers would send out two or three friars." "You know those friars, of course," said I. "No, sir, I do not." "'Sdeath!" cried I, "of what consequence is it to you that they should go to Persia then? A charming project, indeed, to send two Capuchins to take the air in Casbin! How useful that will be to Europe and to Asia! and how important it is to interest monarchs in it! So, this is what is meant by your admirable colonies! Begone; you and your fellows were not made to be transplanted; and you had best to continue to crawl about the places in which you were engendered."

Paris, the 15th of the moon of Rhamazan, 1713.

Letter 50

*Rica to * * **

I HAVE met some people to whom virtue was so natural, that they were not even conscious of it; they applied themselves to their duty without any compulsion, and were led to it instinctively; far from making their own admirable qualities a subject of conversation, it seemed as if they were quite ignorant of their existence. Such people I love; not those men who seem to be astonished at their own virtue, and who look upon a good deed as a marvel the relation of which should excite wonder.

If modesty is a necessary virtue in those to whom Heaven has given great talents, what is to be said of those insects who dare to exhibit a pride which would dishonour the greatest men?

On every hand I meet people who talk constantly about themselves; their conversation is a mirror which reflects only their own impertinent faces; they will tell you of the merest trifles that happen to them, and expect the interest they take in them to magnify their importance in your eyes; they have done everything, seen everything, said everything, thought everything; they are a pattern of mankind, a subject of inexhaustible comparisons, a source of precedents which never dries up. Oh! how insipid is self-praise!

Some days ago a man of this type worried us for two hours, about himself, his worth, his talents; but, since there is no such thing as perpetual motion, he had to cease. It was then our turn to talk and we took it.

A man, who seemed sufficiently splenetic, commenced to grumble at the tediousness of conversation. "What! are there none but fools, who describe their own character and bring everything home to themselves?" "You are right," replied our tattling friend abruptly. "Nobody does as I do; I never praise myself; I have means, am well-born, spend freely, and my friends say that I have some wit; but I never talk of all that; if I have any good qualities, that which I set most store by, is my modesty."

I wondered at this malapert; and while he was talking very loudly, I whispered, "Happy is he who has enough of vanity never to boast of his own qualities, who dreads the ridicule of his audience, and never hurts the pride of others by exalting himself!"

Paris, the 20th of the moon of Rhamazan, 1713.

Letter 51

Nargum, Persian Envoy in Muscovy, to Usbek, at Paris

THE news has come from Ispahan, that you have left Persia, and are actually in Paris. Why was I left to learn these tidings from another than yourself?

By order of the king of kings I have now been five years in this country, where I have concluded several important transactions.

You know that the Czar is the only Christian prince whose interests are allied to those of Persia, because, like us, he is the enemy of the Turks.

His empire is larger than ours, for the distance between Moscow and the extremities of his dominions on the Chinese frontier measures a thousand leagues.

He is absolute master of the lives and goods of his subjects, who are all slaves, with the exception of four families. The vicar of the prophets, the king of kings, whose footstool is the sky, does not wield a scepter more puissant.

In view of the frightful climate of this country, one would never think that exile could be a punishment for a Muscovite: nevertheless, when a man of consequence is disgraced, he is banished to Siberia.

It is the law of our prophet which forbids us to drink wine, it is that of their prince which forbids the Muscovites.

They receive their guests in a style very unlike the Persians. When a stranger enters a house, the husband presents his wife to him, and he kisses her: this is counted an act of courtesy to the husband.

Although fathers, in arranging their daughters' marriages, usually stipulate that the husband shall not whip them, yet you would hardly believe how dearly the Muscovite women like to be beaten;[1] they are unable to understand how they can possess their husband's love, if he does not thrash them in proper style. If he is slack in this matter, it is an unpardonable indication of coldness. Here is a letter which a Muscovite wife recently wrote to her mother: –

"MY DEAR MOTHER, – I am the most wretched woman in the world. I have left nothing undone to make my husband love me, and I have never been able to succeed. Yesterday, having a thousand things to attend to in the house, I went out, and stayed away all day. I expected on my return he would beat me severely, but he did not say a single word. My sister fares much better; her husband beats her every day; he knocks her down at once if she only looks at a man: they are very affectionate, and there is between them the best understanding in the world.

"It is that which makes her so proud, but I will not allow her to triumph over me any longer. I am resolved to make my husband love me, whatever it may cost: I will so anger him that we will be forced to give me marks of affection. No one shall say that I am not beaten, and that I am of no consequence in my own house. I will cry with all my might at the least touch, so that people may think that all goes well; and if any of my neighbours shall come to my aid, I feel as if I would strangle them. I wish, my dear mother, you would point out to my husband how unworthily he treats me. My father is a gentleman, and behaved differently; indeed, if I remember rightly, when I was a little girl he used to love you too much. I embrace you dear mother."

The Muscovites may not leave their country, even in order to travel; and so, separated from other nations by the law of the land, they have become attached to their ancient customs, all the more warmly, that they do not think it possible to have others.

But the reigning prince[2] wishes to change everything; he had a great quarrel with his subjects about their beards; the clergy and the monks defended their ignorance with equal obstinacy.

He is bent on the improvement of the arts, and leaves nothing undone to spread throughout Europe and Asia the fame of his nation, till now forgotten, and hardly even known to itself.

Restless, and always occupied, he wanders about his vast dominions, leaving everywhere tokens of his savage nature. Then he quits them, as if they were too small to contain him, and goes to Europe exploring other provinces and new kingdoms.

I embrace you, my dear Usbek, and beg you to send me your news.

Moscow, the 2nd of the moon of Chalval, 1713.

*Rica to Usbek, at * * ***

I WAS much amused in a certain house the other day. There were present women of all ages; one of eighty years, one of sixty, and one of forty; the last had with her a niece of from twenty to twenty-two. Instinct led me to choose the company of the youngest. She whispered to me, "What do you think of my aunt? Old as she is, she still tries to pass for a beauty, and wishes to have lovers." She is wrong," said I; "such an intention is becoming only in you." A moment after I found myself beside her aunt, who said to me, "What do you think of that woman? Although she is at least sixty years old she has spent hours to-day over her toilet." "It was a waste of time," said I, "which only such charms as yours could have exhausted." I crossed over to the unfortunate dame of threescore, and was pitying her in my heart, when she whispered to me, "Did you ever see anything so ridiculous? Fancy a woman of eighty wearing flame-coloured ribbons! She would like to be young, and she succeeds, for that is childish."

"Good Heavens!" I exclaimed to myself; "must we be for ever blind to our own folly? Perhaps, after all," I argued, "it is a blessing that we should find consolation in the absurdities of others." However, I was bent on being amused, and I said, still to myself, "This is surely high enough; let us descend, beginning at the summit." So, I addressed the lady of fourscore. "Madam," I said, "you are so wonderfully like that lady, whom I have just left to speak to you, that I am certain you must be sisters – I should say about the same age." "Indeed, sir," she rejoined, "when one of us dies, the other will not have long to live; I do not believe there is two days' difference between us." Having left my decrepit dame, I went again to her of sixty. "Madam, you must decide a bet I have made. I have wagered that you and that lady," indicating her of forty, "are of the same age." "Well," she said, "I believe there is not six months' difference." Good, so far; let us get on. Still descending, I returned to the lady of forty. "Madam, have the goodness to tell me if you were jesting when you called that young lady at the other table, your niece. You are as young as she; there is even a touch of age in her face, which you certainly have not; and the brilliancy of your complexion…" "Listen, she said; "I am her aunt; but her mother was at least twenty-five years older than me. We are not even children of the same marriage; I have heard my departed sister say that her daughter and I were born the same year?" "I was right, then, madam, and you cannot blame me for being astonished."

My dear Usbek, women who feel that the loss of their charms is ageing them before their time, long ardently to be young again; and why should we blame them for deceiving others, since they take such trouble to deceive themselves, and to dispossess their minds of the most painful of all thoughts?

Paris, the 3rd of the moon of Chalval, 1713.

Letter 53

Zelis to Usbek, at Paris

NO passion was ever stronger or more vehement than that of Cosrou, the white eunuch, for my slave Zelida; he has asked her in marriage with such persistence, that I can no longer refuse him. And why should I object when her mother does not, and since Zelida herself seems satisfied with the idea of this mock union, and the empty shadow which it offers her?

What does she want with this wretched creature? She is marrying jealously personified, a husband who is no husband; who will only exchange his coldness for an impotent despair; who, by perpetually recalling the memory of what he was, will but remind her of what he no longer is; who, always ready to possess, but never possessing, will for ever deceive himself and her, keeping constantly alive to the wretchedness of her condition.

And then! to be always in dreams and fancies; to live only in imagination; to be always on the threshold, and never in the abode, of pleasure; languishing in the arms of impotence, responding, not to happy sighs, but to vain regrets!

How one ought to despise a man of that kind, made only to guard and not to own! I seek love, and cannot find it!

I speak to you freely, because you love my artlessness, and prefer my frankness and amorous disposition to the affected modesty of my companions.

I have heard you say a thousand times that eunuchs do enjoy a certain pleasure with women, which we know nothing of; that nature compensates them for their loss, having means with which to amend their unfortunate condition; that one may cease to be a man, but not to feel desire; and that in that state one acquires a third sense, and exchanges, as it were, one pleasure for another.

If that be so, Zelida, will have less to complain of. It is something to live with people who are not, after all, so miserable. Send me your instructions in the matter, and let me know if you wish the marriage to take place in the seraglio. Farewell.

The Seraglio at Ispahan, the 5th of the moon of Chalval, 1713.

Letter 54

MY room is, as you know, separated from the others only by a slim partition, which is broken here and there, so that one can hear what is said next door. This morning I overheard a man, pacing rapidly up and down, and saying to another, "I don't know how it is, but everything seems to go against me. For more than three days I have said nothing which can do me honour; and I find myself entirely lost among the crowd of talkers; no one pays the least attention to me, no one speaks to me twice. I had prepared some brilliant passages to lighten my conversation; not once was I allowed to get them off. I had a charming story to tell; but always when I found an opportunity for it, people evaded it, as if on purpose. I have nursed some witticisms in my head for four days without being able to make the least use of them. If this continues, it will end in my becoming a fool; I cannot avoid it; it seems to be my fate. Yesterday I had hoped to shine in the company of four old ladies, who certainly had no idea of imposing on me. I had some of the most charming things to say imaginable; but it took me more than a quarter of an hour to bring the conversation round, and even then they failed to follow me; like the fatal sisters, they cut the thread of my discourse. Shall I tell you? It is most difficult to support the character of a man of wit. I fail to comprehend how you obtained it."

"I have an idea," replied the other. "Let us help each other to gain this reputation: suppose we form a partnership for the purpose. Every day we shall tell each other what we intend to say; and we shall help each other so well, that if anyone attempts to interrupt the flow of our ideas, we shall inspire him with admiration; and if he refuses to be fascinated, then he will be coerced. We shall have the points fixed at which to approve; and where to smile, and where to burst out into a roar of laughter, will all be arranged beforehand. You will see that we shall give the tone to conversation, and that everybody will admire the nimbleness of our wit, and the felicity of our repartees; and we shall have a code of head-shakes for our mutial protection. To-day you will shine, to-morrow you will be my foil. We shall go together to a house, and I shall exclaim, indicating you, 'I must tell you the delightful reply my friend made just now to a man we met in the street.' I shall then turn towards you, and say, 'He did not expect this. You see how astonished he is.' I shall repeat some of my verses, and you will say, 'I was present when he made them; at a supper, it was; he turned them off in an instant.' Sometimes we shall rally each other, and then people will exclaim, 'Look, how they attack each other, how they defend themselves; this is no child's play; let us see how he will come out of that. Wonderful, what presence of mind! Why, this is a downright battle!' But no one will dream how we practised it all beforehand. We shall have to buy certain books, repositories of wit composed for the use of those who, having none, would fain appear as if they had: all depends on the pattern. I should say, that before six months are out we should be able to keep up a conversation of an hour's length, entirely consisting of bon-mots . But we shall have to be careful of one thing, and that is, the fate of our witticisms: it is not enough to make a brilliant remark, it must be sown broadcast; without that, it is as good as lost; and I confess there is nothing so heartrending as to see a smart thing that one has said die in the ear of the fool who hears it. For misfortunes of that kind we have often, it is true, a sort of compassion in the speedy oblivion which overtakes the foolish things we say. Here, my dear sir, is the part we must play. Do as I have suggested, and I promise you, before six months, a place in the Academy. You see the time of toil will not be long; and then you can abandon your art as soon as you like; but you will always be a man of wit, no matter what you do. They say, that in France, when a man enters any circle of society, he catches at once what is called l'esprit du corps: this you will do, and the only thing I dread is, that you will be overwhelmed with applause."

Paris, the 6th of the moon of Zilcade, 1714.

Letter 55

Rica to Ibben, at Smyrna

AMONG the Europeans, the first quarter of any hour of marriage settles all difficulties; the last favors are always contemporary with the marriage blessing. The women here are not like those of Persia, who sometimes dispute the ground for months together. They give themselves at once; and if they lose nothing, it is because they have nothing to lose. One shameful result of this is, that one can always tell the moment of their defeat; and, without consulting the stars, it is possible to predict to the very hour the birth of their children.

The French seldom speak of their wives:[1] they are afraid to do so before people who may know them better than themselves.

There are, among the French, a set of most miserable men, whom nobody comforts--jealous husbands, to wit; there are among them those whom everybody hates--namely, jealous husbands; there are men whom the whole world despises--once more, jealous husbands.

And so, there is no country where there are so few of them as in France. Their peace of mind is not based upon the confidence which they have in their wives; but on the bad opinion which they have of them. All the wise precautions of the Asiatics; the veils which cover them, the prisons in which they are kept, the eunuchs who guard them, seem to the French only so many obstacles better fitted to exercise than to tire the ingenuity of women. Here, husbands accept their lot with a good grace, and the infidelities of their wives seem to them as inevitable as fate. A husband, who would wish to monopolise his wife, would be looked upon as a disturber of the pleasure of the public, as a lunatic who wanted to enjoy the light of the sun to the exclusion of everybody else.

Here, a husband who loves his wife is a man who has not enough merit to engage the affections of some other woman; who makes a bad use of the power given to him by the law to supply those pleasures which he can obtain no other way; who claims all his rights to the prejudice of the whole community; who appreciates to his own use that which he only holds in pawn; and who tries, as far as he can, to overturn the tacit agreement, in which the happiness of both sexes consists. The fame, so little desired in Asia, of being married to a beautiful woman, is here the source of no uneasiness. No one has ever to seek far for entertainment. A prince consoles himeslf for the loss of one place by taking another: when Baghdad fell to the Turks, were we not taking from the Mogul the fortress of Candahar?

Generally speaking, a man who winks at his wife's infidelities, does not lose respect; on the contrary, he is praised for his prudence: dishonour only attaches to special cases.

Not that there are no virtuous women; there are, and they may be said to be distinguished too. My conductor always took care to point them out; but they were all so ugly that one would require to be a saint not to hate virtue.

After what I have told you of the morals and manners of this country, you will easily imagine that the French do not altogether plume themselves upon their constancy. They believe that it is as ridiculous to swear eternal love to a woman, as to insist that one will always be in the best of health, or always as happy as the day is long. When they promise a woman to love her all their lives, they suppose that she on her side undertakes to be always lovable; and if she breaks her word, they think that they are no longer bound by theirs.

Paris, the 7th of the moon of Zilcade, 1714.

Letter 56

Usbek to Ibben, at Smyrna

GAMING is very common in Europe. To be a gamester is to have a position in society, although one is neither well-born, wealthy, nor a man of integrity: it entitles one, without any inquiry, to rank as a gentleman. All know that it is often a most untrustworthy credential, but people have made up their minds to be deceived.

Above all, the women follow it. It is true that the attractions of a dearer passion prevent them from giving it much attention in their youth; but as they grow old, their love of gaming seems to grow young, and when all others are decayed, that passion fills up the void.

Their desire is to ruin their husbands; and for that purpose, they have means suitable to all ages, from the tenderest youth to the most decrepit age; dress and luxury begin the disorder, which gallantry increases, and gaming completes.

I have often seen nine or ten women, or rather, nine or ten centuries, seated round a table; I have watched them hoping, fearing, rejoicing--above all, in their transports of anger: you would have said that they would never grow calm again, and that life would leave them before their despair; you would have been in doubt whether they were paying their creditors or their legatees.

It seems to have been the chief aim of our holy Prophet to restrain us from everything that might disturb the reason: he has prohibited the use of wine, which steals away man's brains; by a special law he has forbidden games of chance; and where the cause of passion could not be removed he has subdued it. Love among us brings with it no trouble, no frenzy: it is a languid passion which leaves our souls serene: plurality of wives saves us from the dominion of women, and tempers the violence of our desires.

Paris, the 18th of the moon of Zilhage, 1714.

Letter 57

Usbek to Rhedi, at Venice

AN immense number of courtesans are maintained by the libertines of Paris, and a great crowd of dervishes by its bigots. These dervishes take three oaths: of obedience, of poverty, and of chastity. They say that the first is the best observed of the three, as to the second, it is not observed at all; you can form your own opinion with regard to the third.

But whatever the wealth of these dervishes may be, they always profess poverty, just as our glorious Sultan would never dream of renouncing his magnificence and sublimity; and they are right, for their reputation as paupers prevents them from being poor.

The physicians and some of these dervishes, called confessors, are always treated with contumely: yet it is said that heirs, on the whole, prefer physicians to confessors.

The other day, I visited a convent of dervishes. One of them, whose white hair made him venerable, received me very courteously. He showed me over the whole house, and then we went into the garden, and had some talk. "Father," said I, "what is your employment in the community?" "Sir," replied he, evidently well pleased with my question, "I am a casuist." "A casuist," exclaimed I. "During my stay in France I have not heard of this profession till now." "What!" You do not know what a casuist is? Very well, listen; I will give you an explanation which will leave nothing to be desired. There are two descriptions of sin: that called mortal, which excludes the sinner for ever from Paradise; and venial sin, which certainly offends God, but does not excite Him to that pitch of wrath which can be satisfied only by depriving the sinner of felicity. Now, all our art consists in carefully distinguishing these two descriptions of sin; for, with the exception of some libertines, all Christians wish to go to heaven; but there is hardly one among them who would not prefer to get there at as cheap a rate as possible. When they thoroughly understand which sins are mortal, they try not to commit them; and their business is done. There are some who do not aspire to such a high degree of perfection; and, having no ambition, they do not care for the first place: accordingly they would enter Paraside as easily as possible; provided they get there, they are satisfied: that is their aim, neither more nor less. There are people who would take heaven by storm rather than not obtain it, and who would say to God, 'Lord, I have fulfilled the conditions exactly; you cannot refuse to keep your word: as I have done no more than you have required, I expect no more from you than you have promised.'

"Therefore, sir, we casuists are a necessity. This is not all, however; you shall learn something further. The deed does not constitute the crime, but the knowledge of him who commits it: he who does what is wrong, so long as he can believe that it is not so, has a safe conscience; and, as there are an immense number of ambiguous actions, a casuist can endue them with a degree of goodness which they have not, simply by pronouncing them good; and, provided he can convince people of their harmlessness, such sins lose their deadliness entirely.

"This is the secret of the craft in which I have grown old; I have shown you its nicety: all things, even such as may seem most refractory, are susceptible of the required twist."

"Father," said I, "this is admirable; but how do you reconcile yourself with Heaven? If the Sophy had at his court a man who dealt with him as you deal with God, who played fast and loose with his commandments, and taught his subjects when they ought to obey them, and when they might break them, he would have him impaled at once. I salute you, master dervish," and I left him without waiting for his reply.

Paris, the 23rd of the moon of Maharram, 1714.

Letter 58

Rica to Rhedi, at Venice

My dear Rhedi, there are in Paris a great many trades. Some good-natured creature will offer you for a little money the secret of making gold. Another promises you the love of the spirits of the air, if you will see no women for a small trifle of thirty years.

Then you will meet with wizards so skilful, that they can tell you all your life, with the simple proviso of a quarter of an hour's conversation with your servants.

Adroit women turn virginity into a flower, which withers and blooms again every day, and is gathered for the hundredth time with more anguish than the first.

There are other women as skilful, who, repairing by the force of their art all the ravages of time, know how to restore to a face beauty enough to strike one blind, and even to summon a woman from the very end of life's journey back to its tender youthful opening.

All these people live, or seek a livelihood, in this great city, the mother of invention.

The incomes of citizens cannot be farmed: they consist only in skill and industry: each has his own, and makes the best of it.

He who would wish to count the dervishes who run after the revenue of some mosque, might as well attempt to number the sands of the sea, or the slaves of our monarch.

An infinite number of professors of languages, of arts, and of sciences, teach what they do not know; and their talent is not by any means despicable; for much less wit is required to exhibit one's knowledge, than to teach what one knows nothing of.

One cannot die here, except suddenly: death is left no other method of exercising his power; because, in every hole and corner, people are ready with infallible cures for every imaginable disease.

All the shops are hung with invisible nets, in which the customers are snared. Sometimes, however, one gets off with a good bargain. A shopgirl will wheedle a man for a stricken hour, and all to make him buy a packet of tooth-picks.

Every one who goes from this city, leaves it a warier man than when he entered: by dint of throwing away his means on others, he learns how to keep it to himself – the only benefit a stranger carries away from this sorceress of a city.

Paris, the 10th of the moon of Saphar, 1714.

Letter 59

*Rica to Usbek, at ****

The other day I visited a house, where the company was of the most miscellaneous description. I found the conversation monopolized by two old women, who had laboured in vain all morning to rejuvenate themselves. "I must say," remarked one of them, "that the men of to-day are very different from those we knew in our youth: they were refined, courteous, obliging; but now, I find their coarseness intolerable." "All is altered," said a man, who appeared to be crippled with gout. "Things are not as they used to be forty years ago. People are healthier; affairs went well; and everybody was cheerful; nobody asked for anything better than to dance and sing. Now, you won't see a single cheerful face." A moment after, the conversation turned to politics. "'Sdeath!" said an old lord; "the state is no longer governed. Where will you find now a minister like M. Colbert? I knew him well, M. Colbert; he was a friend of mine; he always made them pay me my pension before it was due: he was such a capital financier! Everybody was comfortable; but now I am ruined." "Sir," said an ecclesiastic, "you are speaking of the most wonderful period of our invincible monarch's reign: could anything be more magnificent than what he then did to extirpate heresy?" "And does the abolition of dueling count for nothing?" asked a self-satisfied man who had not yet spoken. "A most judicious remark," whispered some one in my ear. "That man is delighted with the dueling law; and he observes it so faithfully, that six months ago he took a sound drubbing, rather than violate it."

It seems to me, Usbek, that our opinions are always influenced by a secret application to ourselves. I am not surprised that Negroes paint the devil with a complexion of dazzling whiteness, and their gods as black as coal; that the Venus of certain races has breasts that hang down to her thighs; and finally, that all idolaters have represented their gods in the likeness of men, and have ascribed to them all their own passions. It has been very well said, that if triangles were to make to themselves gods, they would give them three sides.

My dear Usbek, when I behold men, mere crawlers on this atom, the earth,, which is but a point in the universe, proposing themselves as exact models for Providence, I know not how to harmonise such extravagance with such littleness.

Paris, the 14th of the moon of Saphar, 1714.

Letter 60

Usbek to Ibben, at Smyrna

You ask me if there are Jews in France. Know that wherever there is money, there are Jews. You ask me what they do. Exactly what they do in Persia: nothing is liker an Asiatic Jew than a European one.

They exhibit among the Christians, as among ourselves, an invincible attachment to their religion, amounting to folly.

The Jewish religion is like the trunk of an old tree which has produced two branches that cover the whole earth – I mean Mohammedanism and Christianity: or rather, she is the mother of two daughters that have loaded her with a thousand bruises;[1] for, in religious matters, the nearest relations are the bitterest foes. But however badly her daughters have treated her, she ceases not to glory in having brought them forth: she has made use of both of them to encircle the whole earth, just as her venerable age embraces all time.

The Jews therefore regard themselves as the fountain of all holiness, the source of all religion: us they look upon as heretics who have changed the law, or rather as rebel Jews.

If the change had been made gradually, they imagine that they might have been easily led away; but as it took place suddenly, and with violence, and as they can mark the day and the hour of the birth of both daughters, they mock at religions that have had beginnings, and cling to one that is older than the world itself.

They have never been freer from molestation in Europe than they are now. Christians are beginning to lose the spirit of intolerance which animated them: experience has shown the error of the expulsion of the Jews from Spain, and of the persecution of those Christians in France whose belief differed a little from that of the king. They have realized that zeal for the advancement of religion is different from a due attachment to it; and that in order to love it and fulfil its behests, it is not necessary to hate and persecute those who are opposed to it.

It is much to be desired that our Mussulmans regarded this matter as rationally as the Christians, and that peace were established in all good faith between Hali and Abubeker,[2] leaving God to decide the merits of these holy prophets. I would have them honoured by acts of veneration and respect, and not by foolish preferences. Let us seek to merit their favour, whatever place God has given them; whether it be at His right hand, or beneath the footstool of His throne.

Paris, the 18th of the moon of Saphar, 1714.

Letter 61

Usbek to Rhedi, at Venice

I went the other day into a famous church called Notre Dame. While I was admiring this magnificent building I had an opportunity of conversing with an ecclesiastic, led there, like myself, by curiosity. The conversation turned upon the peaceful life enjoyed by those of his profession. "Most people," said he, "envy the happiness of our condition, and they are right. However, it has its disadvantages: although we are in a measure separated from the world, yet a thousand things require our presence in it; and in this way we have a very difficult part to fill.

"Worldly people are truly astonishing: they can endure neither our praise nor our blame: if we desire to admonish them, they think us ridiculous; if to commend them, they regard us as undignified. Nothing can be more humiliating than the thought that one has offended even the wicked. We are therefore compelled to adopt an ambiguous method, and to influence libertines, not by a direct appeal, but by the uncertainty in which our manner of receiving their remarks leaves them. This requires abundance of talent, it is so difficult to maintain a neutral attitude: men of the world who risk everything, who give themselves up to all their fancies, dropping them or pursuing them, according to their felicity, succeed much better.

"This is not all. We cannot preserve in the world that happy peaceful state which is so loudly praised. As soon as we appear there, we are forced into argument: for example, we have to undertake to prove to a man who does not believe in God, the efficacy of prayer; or the necessity of fasting, to another who all his life has denied the immortality of the soul: the task is heavy, and the laughter is not on our side. Besides this, a desire to convert others to our own opinions, which belongs, as it were, to our profession, torments us endlessly; and is as ridiculous as if Europeans, anxious to improve human nature, were to try to change the Ethiopian's skin. We disturb the state, and torment ourselves to enforce points of religion which are not fundamental: we are like that conqueror of China, who drove his subjects to a general revolt, by insisting that they should cut their hair or their nails.

"The zeal which we have to secure the fulfilment of the duties of our holy religion on the part of those over whom we are placed, is often dangerous, and cannot be accompanied by too much prudence. An emperor, called Theodosius, put to the sword all the inhabitants of a certain town, even to the women and children. Immediately afterwards, as he was about to enter a church, a bishop, Ambrose by name, shut the doors against him as a sacrilegious murderer: in doing so he performed an heroic action. This emperor, having shortly done the penance which such a crime required, and being admitted into the church, the same bishop made him come from among the priests with whom he had seated himself: that was the action of a fanatic. Thus you see how true it is, that one should not be over-zealous. Of what importance was it to religion or to the state, whether this prince had, or had not, a place among the priests?"

Paris, the 1st of the first moon of Rebiab, 1714.

Letter 62

Zelis to Usbek, at Paris

Your daughter having attained her seventh year, I have judged it time to remove her to the inner apartments of the seraglio, and not to wait till she should be ten to entrust her to the care of the black eunuchs. It is impossible to deprive a young girl too soon of the liberty of childhood, and to give her a holy upbringing within those walls sacred to modesty.

For I am not of the opinion of those mothers who only sequester their daughters when they are about to bestow them in marriage, who sentence, rather than consecrate them, to the seraglio, and force them to embrace a manner of life which they ought to have taught them to love. Must we expect everything from the compulsion of reason, and leave nothing to the gentle influences of habit?

We are in vain told of the state of subjection in which nature has placed us. It is not enough to make us realize this; we must be made to practise submission, in order that we may be upheld at that critical time when the passions begin to awaken, and that we may learn voluntary subordination.

Were we only attached to you by duty, we might sometimes forget it; or if it were inclination alone that bound us, a more potent feeling might perhaps weaken it. But, when the laws bestow us on one man they withdraw us from all others, and place us as far from them as if a hundred thousand leagues intervened.

Nature, diligent in the service of men, has been no niggard in her dowry of desire; to women also she has not been unkind, and has destined us to be the living instruments of the enjoyment of our masters; she has set us on fire with passion in order that they may live at ease; should they quit their insensibility, she has provided us to restore them to it, without our ever being able to taste the happiness of the condition into which we put them.

Yet, Usbek, do not think that your situation is happier than mine; I have experienced here a thousand pleasures unknown to you. My imagination has laboured without ceasing to make me conscious of their worth; I have lived, and you have only languished.

Even in this prison where you keep me I am freer than you. You can only redouble your care in guarding me, that I may rejoice at your uneasiness; and your suspicions, your jealousy, your annoyance, are so many marks of your dependence.

Continue, dear Usbek, to have me watched night and day; take no ordinary precautions; increase my happiness in assuring your own; and know, that I dread nothing except your indifference.

The Seraglio at Ispahan, the 2nd of the first moon of Rebiab, 1714.

Letter 63

*Rica to Usbek, at * * **

DO you mean to spend your whole life in the country? At first I was to lose you only for a day or two, but now fifteen have passed since I last saw you. I know that you are living in a delightful house where the company suits you, where you can speculate at your ease: nothing more is required to make you forget the whole universe.

For myself, my life moves on pretty much as it did when we were together. I go into society and try to understand it; my thought loses gradually all that remained of its Asiatic cast, and conforms without effort to European manners. I am no longer amazed to find in one house half-a-dozen women with as many men; indeed, I begin to think it not altogether a bad idea.

This I will say: I knew nothing of women until I came here; I have learnt more about them in one month of Paris, than I could have done in thirty years of a seraglio.

With us, character is uniform, because it is constrained; we do not see people as they are, but as they are obliged to be; in that slavery of heart and mind, it is only fear that utters a dull routine of words, very different from the language of nature which expresses itself so variously.

Dissimulation, that art so practised and so necessary with us, is here unknown: they say everything, see everything, and hear everything; hearts are as open as faces; in manners, in virtue, even in vice, one detects always a certain artlessness.

In order to gratify women a talent is necessary different from that other gift which pleases them still more; it consists in a sort of playfulness of mind, which entertains them, as it seems to promise them every moment what one cannot perform except occasionally.

The gaiety of mind naturally adapted to the dressing-room[1] seems to be forming the general character of the nation: they trifle in council, at the head of the army, with an ambassador. Professions appear ridiculous only in proportion to the professional gravity adopted: a doctor would be less absurd if his dress were more cheerful, and if, while killing his patients, he jested pleasantly.

Paris, the 10th of the first moon of Rebiab, 1714.

Letter 64

The Chief of the black Eunuchs to Usbek, at Paris

I CANNOT tell you, magnificent lord, how deeply perplexed I am. Appalling disorder and confusion prevail in the seraglio: war reigns among your wives; your eunuchs are divided; nothing is heard bur murmurs, complaints, reproaches; my remonstrances are despised: everything seems to be permitted in this time of licence, and I am nothing but a name in the seraglio.

There is not one of your wives who does not deem herself superior to the others by her birth, her beauty, her wealth, her intellect, or her love; and who does not claim every preference on the score of the value she sets upon one or other of these titles to respect. I lose every moment that long-suffering patience, with which, nevertheless, I have had the misfortune to displease them all: my prudence, even my kindness, so rare and strange a virtue in the post which I occupy, have been useless.

Is it your pleasure that I should disclose to you, magnificent lord, the cause of all these disorders? It is in your heart alone, in the tender affection which you have for them. If you did not withhold my hand; if, instead of remonstrating, you would allow me to punish; if, rather than suffer them to soften you by their complaints and tears, you would send them to weep before me, whom nothing can move, I would soon fashion them to the yoke they ought to bear, and weary out this proud and independent temper.

Stolen, at the age of fifteen years, out of the heart of Africa, my native country, I was at first sold to a master, who had more than twenty wives, or concubines. Judging from my grave and taciturn air, that I would be an acquisition in the seraglio, he ordered that I should be prepared for it, and made me undergo an operation, painful at first, but fortunate in its results, because it has given me the ear and the confidence of my masters. I entered the seraglio, to me a new world. The first eunuch, the sternest man I have ever known, governed there with undisputed sway. Nothing was ever heard of divisions or of quarrels: profound silence reigned everywhere: all these women were put to bed at the same hour, and wakened a the same hour, from one year's end to the other: they entered the bath in turn, and left it at the slightest sign made by us: the rest of the time they were almost always shut up in their rooms. He had one rule, which exacted the observance of the greatest neatness, and he was in this matter inexpressibly careful: the least refusal of obedience was punished without mercy. "I am," said he, "a slave; but the slave of a man who is your master and mine; and I use the power which he has given me over you: it is he who chastises you, not I; I only lend my hand." These women never entered my master's chamber but when they were summoned; that favour they welcomed gladly, and saw themselves deprived of it without a murmur. As for myself, the least of the blacks in that peaceful seraglio, I was a thousand times more respected than I am in yours, where I command all.

As soon as the chief eunuch had recognised my genius, he regarded me with favour, and spoke of me to his master as of one able to carry out his views, and to succeed him in the post which he filled: he was not afraid of my great youth, believing that my application would make up for my want of experience. Shall I tell you? I advanced so rapidly in his confidence that he went the length of entrusting me with the keys of those dreadful places, which he had guarded for so long a time. It was under this great master that I learnt the difficult art of commanding, and that I was formed according to the maxims of an inflexible government: I studied under him the heart of women: he taught me to take advantage of their weaknesses, and not to be dismayed by their arrogance. Often he amused himself by watching me drive their obedience to the very last verge; he then made them return gradually, and required that I for some time should appear to yield. But he should have been seen at those times when, now beseeching, now reproaching, they were driven almost to despair: he beheld their tears unmoved, rejoicing in his triumph. "See," said he, with a satisfied air, "how women must be governed: their number does not trouble me; I could manage in the same way all those of our great king. How can a man hope to win their hearts, if his faithful eunuchs have not begun by breaking their spirits?"

He was not only a man of resolution, but also of penetration. He read their thoughts and their dissemblings: their studied gestures, their made-up looks, concealed nothing from him. He knew all their most hidden actions, their most secret words. He obtained information by making them tell on each other; and it was his pleasure to reward the most insignificant confidence. As they never approached their husband except when they were ordered, the eunuch summoned whom he liked, and directed the attention of his master to those whom he wished to please; and this distinction was the reward for the revelation of some secret. He had persuaded his master that it was of the first importance that the choice should be left to him, as it would give his authority much greater weight. That was the method of government, magnificent lord, in a seraglio, which was, I believe, the best regulated in Persia.

Give me a free hand, allow me to make myself obeyed, and eight days will see order take the place of confusion: this, your glory demands, and your safety requires.

Your Seraglio at Ispahan, the 9th of the first moon of Rebiab, 1714.

Letter 65

Usbek to his Wives, at the Seraglio at Ispahan

I UNDERSTAND that the seraglio at Ispahan is in disorder, that it is full of quarrels, and intestine divisions. At my departure did I not recommend you to be at peace and maintain a good understanding?

You promised this; was it to deceive me?

It is you who will be deceived, if I choose to follow the counsels of the chief eunuch; if I choose to employ my authority to make you live as I exhorted you to do.

I do not, however, see why I should make use of those violent means until I have tried all others. Do, then, for your own sakes, what you have not cared to do for mine.

The first eunuch has a great subject of complaint: he says that you pay no attention to him. How can you harmonise that behaviour with the modesty which should belong to your condition? Is not your virtue confided to him during my absence? It is a sacred treasure, of which he is the guardian. But the contempt with which you treat him, makes it apparent that those who are charged to lead you in the paths of honour are irksome to you.

Change your behavior then, I beg you; and see to it that I may be able still to reject the proposals which have been made to me against your freedom and your tranquility.

For I wish you to forget that I am your master, and to be remembered only as your husband.

Paris, the 5th of the moon of Chahban, 1714.

Letter 66

*Rica to * * **

PEOPLE are very much devoted to the sciences here, but I question if they are very learned. He who, as a philosopher, doubts of all, dare deny nothing as a theologian: the inconsistent man is always well pleased with himself provided you agree with him.

The passion of nearly every Frenchman, is to pass for a wit; and the passion of those who wish to be thought wits, is to write books.

There never was such an erroneous idea: it seems to be a wise provision of nature that the follies of men should be short-lived; but books interfere and immortalize them. A fool, not content with having bored all those who have lived with him, insists on tormenting generations to come; he would have his folly triumph over oblivion, which should have been as welcome to him as death; he wishes posterity to be informed of his existence, and he would have it remember for ever that he was fool.

Of all the authors, there are none whom I despise more than compilers. They crowd from all quarters to pick up the shreds of other men's works; these they fit into their own, as one would patch the turf of a lawn: they are not one whit superior to the compositor, whose type-setting may be called book-making if manual labor is all. I would have original books respected; and it seems to me a species of profanation, to take from them the matter of which they are composed, as if from a sanctuary, and expose it to an undeserved contempt.

When a man has nothing new to say, why can't he be quiet? Why should one be troubled with these useless repetitions? But I will give you a new illustration. You are a man of ability! You come into my library; and you shift the books from the lower shelves to the upper ones, and from the upper to the lower: you have produced a masterpiece!

I write you, * * *, because I am exasperated with a book which I have just laid down—a book so big that it seems to contain all science: but it has only split my head without putting anything into it. Farewell.

Paris, the 8th of the moon of Chahban, 1714.

Ibben to Usbek, at Paris

Three vessels have arrived here without bringing any news from you. Are you ill, or does it amuse you to make me uneasy?

If you do not love me in a country where you are quite unfettered, how will it be in the middle of Persia, and in the bosom of your family? But perhaps I am wrong: you are charming enough to find friends everywhere; the heart is a native of all lands: what should hinder a generous nature from forming attachments? I confess, I respect old friendships; but I am quite pleased to make new ones everywhere.

In whatever country I have been, I have lived as if I were to spend the rest of my days there: I have had the same strong liking for virtuous people, the same pity, or should I say the same love, for the wretched and the same esteem for those whom prosperity has not blinded. That is my character, Usbek: wherever I find men, I choose friends.

There is here a Guebre[1] who I believe, after you, holds the chief place in my heart: he is the very soul of honour. Special reasons have obliged him to retire to this town, where, with his beloved wife, he lives peacefully on the earnings of an honest trade. A generous temper has distinguished him all his life; and although he prefers obscurity, there is more of true heroism in him than in many of the greatest monarchs.

I have often spoken to him of you, and I show him all your letters. I note that this gives him great pleasure, and I perceive already that you have a friend, who is unknown to you.

Here you will find his principal adventures. Although he was very reluctant to write them, he can refuse nothing to my friendship, and I confide them to yours.

THE HISTORY OF APHERIDON AND ASTARTE.

I was born among the Guebres, whose religion is perhaps the oldest in the world. My misfortunes began, when, at the age of six, love dawned in me before reason, and I could not live without my sister. My eyes were always fixed on her, and if she left me for a moment, she found me, on returning, bathed in tears: each new day added not more to my age than to my love. My father, astonished at such strength of feeling, was quite willing that we should be married, according to the ancient custom of the Guebres, introduced by Cambyses[2]; but fear of the Mohammedans, under whose yoke we lived, prevented our people from thinking of those holy alliances, which our religion orders rather than permits, and which are such innocent reflections of a union already formed by nature.

My father, seeing how dangerous it would be to follow my inclination, which was also his, determined to extinguish a flame, believed by him to be newly lit, but which was already at its height. Under pretext of a voyage, he took me away, leaving my sister in the hands of a relative; for my mother had been dead for two years. I cannot describe the misery of that separation: I embraced my sister, she all bathed in tears, but I, dry-eyed; for grief had made me callous. We arrived at Tiflis; my father, having entrusted my education to one of our relatives, left me, and returned home.

Some time after, I learned that, through the influence of one of his friends, he had placed my sister in the harem of the king to wait upon a sultana. Had I been told of her death, I could not have been more overcome; for, apart from the fact that I could never hope to see her again, her entrance into the harem had made her a Mohammedan, and according to the superstition of that religion she could only regard me with horror. Nevertheless, unable to live longer at Tiflis, tired of myself and of life, I returned to Ispahan. My first words to my father were acrimonious; I reproached him with having placed his daughter in a place which could not be entered without a change in religion. "You have drawn upon your family," said I to him, "the anger of God and of the Sun which lights you: you have done more wrong than if you had polluted the elements, inasmuch as you have polluted the soul of your daughter, which is not less pure: I shall die of grief and of love; and may my death be the only calamity which God will make you suffer!" With these words I went away; and for two years I spent my life staring at the walls of the harem, and wondering in which part of it my sister might be, in danger every day of having my throat cut by the eunuchs, who walk their rounds about that dread place.

At last my father died; and the sultana whom my sister served, seeing that she grew in beauty every day, became jealous, and married her to a eunuch who was passionately in love with her. In this way my sister left the seraglio, and occupied with her eunuch a house in Ispahan.

It was three months before I was able to get speech of her, the eunuch, the most jealous of men, always putting me off with various excuses. But at last I was admitted to his harem, where I had to talk to my sister through lattice. She was so closely wrapped in robes and veils that the eyes of a lynx could not have discovered anything, and I could recognise her only by the sound of her voice. My emotion was overpowering when I found myself so close to her, and yet so far away. I restrained myself, however, for I was watched. As for her, she seemed to shed a few tears. Her husband offered some kind of halting apology; but I treated him like the least of his slaves. He was very much annoyed when he heard me speak to my sister in a tongue unknown to him. It was ancient Persian I used, the language of our religion. "What, my sister!" cried I, "is it true that you have renounced the worship of your fathers? I know that, in entering a harem, you must perforce profess Mohammedanism; but, tell me, did your heart agree with your lips in renouncing the religion which permits me to love you? And for whom have you renounced that religion which should be so dear to us? For a wretch still branded with the marks of slavery; who, if he were a man, would be the basest of his kind." "Brother," said she, "this man of whom you speak is my husband; it is my duty to honour him, all unworthy as he may appear to you; and it is I who would be the basest of women, if . . ." "Ah! My sister," said I, "you are a Guebre: this man is not, and can never be, your husband. Had you kept the faith like your fathers, you would regard him only as a monster." "Alas!" said she, "how far removed from me that religion seems now! I had hardly learned its precepts when I was obliged to forget them. You hear that this language which I speak to you is no longer familiar to me, and that I have the greatest difficulty in expressing myself. But remember that I cherish always the exquisite memory of our childhood; that since then I have known only the mockery of happiness; that not a day has passed in which I have not thought of you; that you have had a greater share in my marriage than you imagine, for it was the hope of seeing you again that won my consent to it. But this day, which has cost me so much, will cost me more yet! I see you beside yourself with passion, and my husband quivers with rage and jealousy. I will never see you more; I speak to you without a doubt for the last time in my life; and if that be so, my brother, I know it will not be a long one." She melted at these words; and finding herself unable to continue the conversation, she left me, the most disconsolate of men.

Three or four days afterwards I asked to see my sister. The brutish eunuch would have been very glad to prevent me; but, besides the fact that husbands of that kind have not so much power over their wives as others, he loved my sister so frantically, that he could refuse her nothing. I saw her again in the same place, veiled as before, and accompanied by two slaves, and was compelled to resort to our own language. "My sister," said I, "how is it that I cannot see you except in these horrible circumstances? The walls which keep you imprisoned, these bolts and gratings, these miserable guards who watch you, drive me mad. How have you lost the sweet freedom in which your ancestors rejoiced? Your mother, who was so chaste, gave to her husband, as the sole pledge of her virtue, that virtue itself: they lived happy in each other, and in their mutual confidence; and the simplicity of their manners was to them a thousand times more precious than the false splendor which you seem to enjoy in this sumptuous house. In losing your religion, you have lost your liberty, your happiness, and that precious equality which is the honour of your sex. But there is something much worse behind; and that is, the thing which you are – not the wife, for that you cannot be, but the slave of a slave, who has been degraded from humanity!" "Ah, my brother!" said she, "have respect for my husband, for the religion which I have embraced: according to that religion, I cannot listen, I cannot speak, to you without sin." "What, my sister!" said I, trembling with emotion, "then you believe that religion, you think it true!" "Ah!" said she, "how much better it would be for me if it were not true! I have made too great a sacrifice for it, not to believe in it; and if my doubts. . . ." At these words she became silent. "Yes, my sister, your doubts! They are well founded, whatever they may be. What can you expect from a religion which makes you miserable in this world, and leaves you no hope for the next? Remember that our religion is the most ancient in the world; that it has always flourished in Persia, and that it originated with the Persian empire, the beginnings of which are beyond human ken; that it is only chance that has introduced Mohammedanism here; that that sect has been established, not by the power of persuasion, but by conquest. If our native princes had not been weak, you would have beheld the worship of these ancient Magi[3] reigning still. Transport yourself into those remote ages: everything will speak to you of Magism, and nothing of the Mohammedan sect which, many thousands of years after, was not even in its infancy." "But," said she, "although my religion may be more modern than yours, it is at least purer, since it adores but one God; while you still worship the sun, the stars, fire, and even the elements." "I perceive, my sister, that you have learned among the Mussulmans to slander our holy religion. We adore neither the stars nor the elements; and our fathers did not adore them: they never built temples to them, nor offered sacrifices in their honour: they yielded only such inferior reverence as is due to the works and manifestations of the Deity. But, my sister, in the name of God who is our light, accept this sacred volume which I have brought you: it is the book of our lawgiver, Zoroaster: read it without prejudice, and receive into your heart the light which will shine upon you: remember your fathers, who for so long a time honoured the sun in the holy city of Balk;[4] and, finally, do not forget me, whose hopes of peace, of fortune, and of life, depend upon your conversion." Transported by my feelings, I went away, and left her to decide alone the most momentous event of my life.

I returned to her in two days. I did not speak; I waited in silence the sentence of life or death. "You are loved, my brother," she said, "and by a Guebre. I have resisted long; but, ye Gods! what difficulties love can overcome! A load had fallen from me! I am no longer afraid that I may love you too much; there is no limit to my passion now that excess itself is lawful. Ah! how sweetly that thought chimes with my happy heart! But you, who have found a way to break the chains which my soul had forged for itself, when will you break those which fetter my hands? From this moment I give myself to you: show by the speed with which you take me how dear the gift is. My brother, when I shall embrace you for the first time, I think I shall die in your arms." I can never fully express the joy which I felt at these words; I believed myself, and actually saw myself, in one instant, the happiest of men: I beheld almost fulfilled all the desires which I had formed in my twenty-five years of life, and the disappearance of all misery which had made it so hard. But, when I had grown somewhat accustomed to these delightful thoughts, I perceived that I was not so near my happiness, as I had on the first blush imagined, although I had overcome the chief obstacle in my path. It would be necessary to evade the watchfulness of her guards; I dared not confide to any one the secret of my life; I had only my sister, and she had only me: if my attempt failed, I ran the risk of being impaled; but no torture seemed so cruel as to be without her. We arranged that she should send to me for a time-piece which her father had left her; and that I should put inside it a file to cut the lattice of the window which opened on the street, and a knotted rope by which to descend; that thereafter I should cease to visit her, but should wait every night under her window until she could execute her design. I passed fifteen entire nights without seeing any one, because she had not found a favourable opportunity. At length, on the sixteenth, I heard the rasping of the file: from time to time the work was interrupted, and in the intervals my dread was inexpressible. After an hour's labour, I saw her fasten the rope; she let herself go, and slid into my arms. All danger was forgotten, and for a long time we stood there motionless. Then I led her out of the city to a spot where I had a horse all ready: I lifted her to the croup behind me, and fled with all imaginable speed from a neighbourhood which might have been so disastrous to us. We arrived before morning at the house of a Guebre, in a lonely place to which he had retired, living frugally on the produce of his own labour. We did not think it wise to stay with him, and by his advice we entered a dense forest, where we lodged in the hollow of an old oak, until the rumour of our flight had died away. We lived together in this out-of-the-way abode, unseen of any, telling our love over and over again to each other, and waiting until the ceremony of marriage, prescribed by our religion, could be performed by a Guebre priest. "My sister," said I, "how holy is that union! Nature has joined us, and our holy law will join us in another bond." At last a priest came to quiet the impatience of our love. In the house of the peasant he performed all the ceremonies of marriage; he blessed us, and wished us a thousand times the vigour of Gustaspes, and the holiness of Hohoraspes. Soon after we left Persia, where we were not safe, and retired into Georgia. We lived there a year, and every day increased the pleasure we found in each other's company. But when my money was nearly done, fearing misery for my sister, not for myself, I left her to seek help from our relatives. Never was a parting more tender. My journey, however, was not only useless, but disastrous. For, having found all our goods confiscated, and my relatives almost powerless to aid me, I brought away with me no more money than sufficed for my return. But imagine my despair! My sister was not to be found. Some days before my arrival the Tartars had invaded the city where she was, and finding her beautiful, had seized her, and sold her to some Jews who were bound for Turkey, leaving me only a little daughter born some months before. I followed these Jews, and overtook them three leagues off. In vain I besought them with tears, they persisted in demanding thirty tomans[5], and would not bate a single coin.

Having gone to everybody, and having begged the aid of both the Christian and the Turkish priests, I applied to an Armenian merchant: to him I sold my daughter and myself for thirty-five tomans. I went to the Jews, gave them their thirty tomans, and carried the other five to my sister, whom I had not yet seen. "You are free," said I, "my sister; and I can embrace you. Here are five tomans I have brought; I am sorry that they would not buy me for more." "What!" cried she, "you have sold yourself?" "Yes," replied I. "Ah! wretched man, what have you done? Was I not miserable enough, that should make me more so? Your freedom was my comfort; your bondage will bring me to the grave. Ah! my brother, how cruel your love is! And my daughter? I do not see her!" "I have sold her too," said I. We both burst into tears, and were unable to utter a single word. At last I had to return to my master. My sister was with him almost as soon as I. She threw herself at his feet saying, "I beg from you slavery as others as for freedom: take me, you can sell me for a greater sum than my husband." Then there took place a struggle which drew tears from my master's eyes. "Unhappy man!" said she, "did you think that I would accept my liberty at the cost of yours? Master, you behold two unfortunates who will die if you separate them. I give myself to you; pay me: perhaps that money and my services will some day obtain from you what I dare not ask. It is for your own interest not to separate us: remember his life depends on me." The Armenian, a humane man, was touched by our woes: "Serve me, both of you, with fidelity and zeal, and I promise you that in a year I will give you your freedom. I see that neither of you deserve the wretchedness of your lot. If, when you become free, your happiness is as great as your merit, and fortune smiles upon you, I am certain that you will repay me that which I shall lose." We both embraced his knees, and attended him on his journey. We comforted each other in our servile tasks; and I was delighted when I could do the work which fell to my sister's share.

The end of the year arrived; our master kept his word and set us free. We returned to Tiflis. There I found an old friend of my father's, who practised successfully as a physician in that city. He lent me some money, with which I traded. Some business called me shortly after to Smyrna, where I established myself. I have lived there for six years in the enjoyment of the most amiable and agreeable society in the world. Unity reigns in my family, and I would not change my lot for that of all the kings of the earth. I have been fortunate enough to meet again the Armenian merchant, to whom I owe all; and I have been able to render him some important services.

Smyrna, the 27th of the second moon of Gemmadi, 1714.

Letter 68

Rica to Usbek, at ***

The other day I dined at the house of a magistrate, who had often invited me. After we had talked of a variety of things, I said to him, "Sir, it appears to me that your profession is very laborious." "Not so much as you imagine," he rejoined;

"As we prosecute it, it is only an amusement." "But how! Is your head not always full of other people's business? Are you not always occupied with matters that do not interest you?" "You are right; these matters do not interest us, because we take not the least interest in them; and that is how our profession is not so fatiguing as you supposed." When I saw that he took the matter so carelessly, I continued, and said, "Sir, I have not seen your study." "I believe you; for I have none. When I took this post, lacking the money to pay for it, I sold my library. The bookseller who bought it, out of a vast number of volumes, left me only my account book. Nor do I regret them: we judges have no need to stuff our heads with useless knowledge. What have we to do with all these legal volumes? Almost all of the cases are questions of fact, and outside the general rule." "But, sir, may it not be because you make them so? For, in short, why should all the peoples of the world have laws, if these laws are not to be applied? And how can one who does not know them, apply them?" "If you were acquainted with the courts of justice," replied the magistrate, "you would not speak as you do. We have living books, the advocates: they work for us, and take upon themselves the task of instructing us." " And do they not also sometimes take upon themselves the task of deceiving you?" I retorted. "It would not be a bad thing to guard yourself against their wiles. They have weapons with which to attack your justice: it would be well if you were in a condition to defend it: you ought not to rush into the midst of the fight, thinly clad, among people armed to the teeth."

Paris, the 13th of the moon of Chahban, 1714.

Letter 69

Usbek to Rhedi, at Venice

You would never have dreamed that I could become a greater metaphysician than I was. Such is the case, however; and you will be convinced of it, when you have waded through this flood of my philosophy.

The most sensible of those philosophies, who have considered the nature of God, have declared that He is a being supremely perfect; bit they have sadly abused this idea. They have tabulated all of the various perfections which man is capable of possessing and of imagining, and with these they have clad the idea of God, not thinking that these attributes are often contradictory, and, being mutually destructive, cannot subsist in the same individual.

The western poets tell how a painter [1], wishing to make a likeness of the goddess of beauty, gathered together the most beautiful Greek women, and, having taken from each that grace in which she most excelled, combined their selective charms into a picture of the loveliest of the goddesses. If, on that account, a man should think that she was both fair and dark, that her eyes were black and blue, and that she was, at one and the same time, sweet tempered and haughty, he would pass for a fool.

God often falls short of a perfection which would make Him very imperfect: He is His own law. Thus, although God is all-powerful, He can neither break His promises, nor deceive men. Often too, His importance is not subjective, but objective; and that is the reason why He cannot change the nature of things.

So, also, it is not so very wonderful that some of our learned men should have denied the infinite foreknowledge of God, upon the principle that it is incompatible with His justice.

However bold this idea may be, it is countenanced remarkably by metaphysics. According to metaphysical principles, it is impossible that God should foresee such things as depend upon the determination of free causes; because that which has not happened does not exist, and consequently, cannot be known; for nothing, having no properties, cannot be perceived: God cannot read a will which does not exist, nor discern in the mind what it does not contain, for, until the mind is made up, the thing determined on is not in it.

The mind is the author of its determination; but there are occasions when it is so irresolute, that it does not even know for which side to determine. Often indeed it makes a selection only to use its liberty; in such a manner that God cannot foresee its choice, neither in its own action, nor in the operation of objects upon it.

How could God foresee things which depend upon the determination of free causes? He could only see them in two ways: by the conjecture, which is incompatible with His infinite foreknowledge; or He could see them as necessary effects proceeding infallibly-a method even more at variance with divine foreknowledge, for it supposes that the mind is free, with a freedom, however, no greater than that of a billiard ball, which is at liberty to move when it is struck by another.

Do not think, however, that I wish to limit God's knowledge. Since He directs the actions of His creatures according to His pleasure, He knows all that He wishes to know. But although He can see everything, He does not always make use of that power: He generally leaves man the power to do a thing or to leave it alone, in order that he may be able to choose between right and wrong; and this is why God renounces the absolute authority which He has over the mind. But, when he desires to know anything, He always knows it, because He has only to will that a thing shall happen from the number of the mere possibilities, fixing by His decrees the future determinations of men's minds, and depriving them of the power which He gave them to do or not to do.

Let me employ a comparison in a matter which transcends all comparisons:-A monarch, ignorant of what his ambassador will do in an important affair, if he wishes to know, has only to command him to conduct the negotiation in such or such an manner, and he will be certain that the thing will happen as he planned.

The Koran and the Hebrew books are constant witnesses against the dogma of absolute foreknowledge: God appears throughout these writings as ignorant of the future determinations of men's minds: and it seems that this was the first truth that Moses taught mankind.

God placed Adam in the terrestrial paradise, on condition that he should not eat of a certain fruit: an absurd command to be given by a being acquainted with the future determinations of men's minds; for, in short, could such a being make His favor depend on such conditions, without rendering it ridiculous? It is as if a man who was aware of the capture of Bagdad should say to another, "I will give you a hundred tomans if Bagdad is not taken."[2] Would that not be a very sorry jest?

My dear Rhedi, why all this philosophy? God is so far above us that we cannot perceive even His clouds. We have no knowledge of Him except in His commandments. He is a spirit, immense and infinite. May His greatness make us conscious of our own weakness. To humble ourselves continually, is to adore Him continually.

Paris, the last day of the moon of Chahban, 1714.

Letter 70

Zelis to Usbek, at Paris

Soliman, whom you love, has been driven desperate by an affront which he has just received. Three months ago a young giddypate, named Suphis, sought his daughter in marriage; he seemed satisfied with the girl's appearance from the report and description given him by the women who had been with her during her childhood; the dowry had been agreed upon, and all was going well. Yesterday, after the first ceremonies, the girl set out on horseback, accompanied by her eunuch, and veiled, according to custom, from head to foot. But when she arrived at the house of her intended husband, he caused the door to be shut in her face, and swore that he would never receive her unless her dowry were increased. Her relatives hastened from quarters to arrange the matter; and after a deal of resistance, Soliman agreed to make a small present to his son-in-law. The marriage ceremonies were complete, and the girl conducted to her husband's bed with sufficient violence; but, an hour after, this giddypate rose in a rage, cut her face in several places, and, declaring that she was not a virgin, sent her back to her father. No one could be more afflicted then he is by the injury. Many people maintain that the girl is innocent. Fathers are most unfortunate in being exposed to such affronts. If my daughter were to receive similar treatment, I believe I should die of grief. Farewell.

The Seraglio at Fatme, the 9th of the first moon of Gemmadi, 1714.

Letter 71

Usbek to Zelis

I am sorry for Soliman, especially as his misfortune is without remedy, since his son-in-law has done no more than law allows him. I think it a very harsh law, which exposes in this way the honour of a family to the caprice of a fool. It has been lightly said that here are sure signs whereby to know the truth: it is an old error from which we have now departed; and our physicians have supplied invincible reasons for the uncertainty of these proofs. Even among the Christians there are none who do not regard them as imaginary, although they are plainly established in their sacred writings, and although their ancient lawgiver[1] has made the innocence or condemnation of all their daughters depend on them.

I am pleased to know that you are giving great care to the education of yours. God grant that her husband may find her as lovely and as pure as Fatima;[2] may she have ten eunuchs guard her; may she be the honour and the ornament of the seraglio to which she is destined; may she have overhead none but gilded ceilings, and underfoot the richest carpets! And, to crown these wishes, may my eyes see her in all her glory!

Paris, the 3rd of the moon of Chalval, 1714.

Letter 72

Rica to Ibben, at ***

I found myself recently in a company where I met am man very well satisfied with himself. In a quarter of an hour, he decided three questions in morals, four historical problems, and five points in physics. I have never seen so universal a decider[1]; his mind was not once troubled with the least doubt. We left science, and talked of the current news: he decided upon the current news. I wished to catch him, so I said to myself, "I must get to my strong point; I will betake me to my own country." I spoke to him of Persia; but hardly had I opened my mouth, when he contradicted me twice, basing his objections upon the authority of Tavernier and Chardin [2] "Ah! Good heavens!" said I to myself, "what kind of man is this? He will know next all the streets in Ispahan better than I do!" I soon knew what part to play-to be silent, and let him talk; and he is still laying down the law.

Paris, the 8th of the moon of Zilcade, 1715.

Letter 73

Rica to ***

I have heard much talk of a sort of court called the French Academy. There is no tribunal in the world which is less respected; for they say that no sooner does it issue a decree than the people break it, and substitute laws which the Academy is bound to follow.

Some time ago, in order to establish its authority, it issued a code of its decisions.[1] This child of so many fathers may be said to have been old when it was born; and although it was legitimate, a bastard [2],born before it, nearly strangled it at its birth.

Those who compose this court have no other function that to jabber perpetually: eulogy suggests itself as the one subject of their incessant babble; and as soon as they are initiated into its mysteries, a frenzy of panegyric lays hold of them, and will not be shaken off.

This body had forty heads, all of them chokeful of tropes, of metaphors, and of antitheses; so that their lips scarcely ever open without an exclamation, and their ears are always waiting to be touched with rhythm and harmony. As for their eyes, they are out of the question; the Academy seems to be intended to talk and not to see. It is not firm on its legs; for time, which is its scourge, smites it incessantly and destroys all it does. It is said that at one time its hands were grasping; I have nothing to say on the subject, and will leave those to decide it who know more about it than I do.

Such eccentricities, ***, are unknown in our Persia. We have no bent towards what is odd and extravagant; we endeavor to shape our simple customs and artless manners in the mould of nature.

Paris, the 27th of the moon of Zilhage, 1715.

Letter 74

Usbek to Rica, at ***

Some days ago a man of my acquaintance said to me, "I promised to introduce you to the best houses in Paris. I will take you now to that of a great lord who supports his rank as well as any man in France."

"What do you mean by that, sir? Is he more refined, more polite than others?" "No," said he. "Ah! I understand: he makes his superiority felt on all occasions by those who approach him. If that is it, I shall have nothing to do with him; I give up the whole case, and accept my inferiority."

I had, however, to go; and I saw a little man, supercilious to a degree. He took a pinch of snuff with such a haughty air, he blew his nose so mercilessly, he spat with such indifference, and caressed his dogs in a style so offensive to the onlookers, that I could not but marvel at him. "Ah! Sweet Heaven!" said I to myself; "if, when I was at the court of Persia, I behaved in this way, I behaved like a great fool!" We would have been the very inferior creatures, Rica, had we offered a hundred little insults to those people who waited upon us daily in token of their goodwill. They knew well that we were above them; and if they had not, our favors would have made them daily conscious of it. There being no need to secure their respect, we did our utmost to win their affection: we were accessible to the humblest; in the midst of our greatness, usually so hardening, they found we had feelings; only our hearts appeared to belong to a higher order; we descended to their wants. But, when it was necessary to support the dignity of our sovereign in public ceremonies, to make the nation worthy of respect in the eyes of strangers; and lastly, when, in times of danger, we required to animate our soldiers, our bearing became more lofty a hundred times than it had been before lowly; we resumed our haughty looks; and not seldom we were found to play our part at least adequately.

Paris, the 10th of the moon of Saphar, 1715.

Letter 75

Usbek to Rhedi, at Venice

I must confess that I have not noticed in the Christians that lively faith in their religion which prevails among Mussulmans. With them there is a vast difference between profession and belief, between belief and conviction, between conviction and practice. Religion is not so much a matter of holiness as it is the subject of a debate, in which everybody has a right to join. Courtiers, warriors, women even, array themselves against the ecclesiastics, and insist upon their proving what they have made up their minds not to believe. Not that, willing to be guided by reason, they have taken the trouble to examine the falseness of that religion which they reject: they are rebels who have felt the yoke, and have shaken it off before knowing what it is. Nor are they any securer in their incredulity than in their faith: their life is a constant ebb and flow between belief and unbelief.[1] One of them said to me once, "I believe in the immortality of the soul for six months at a time; my opinions depend entirely upon my bodily condition: I am a Spinozist, a Socinian, a Catholic, ungodly or devout, according to the state of my animal spirits, the quality of my digestion, the rarity or heaviness of the air I breathe, the lightness or solidity of the food I eat. When the doctor is at my bedside, the confessor has me at a disadvantage. I know very well how to prevent religion from annoying me when I am in good health; but I allow myself to be consoled by it when I am ill: when I have nothing more to hope for here below, religion offers itself, and gains me by its promises; I am glad to give myself up to it, and to die with hope on my side."

A long time ago the Christian princes enfranchised all the slaves in their dominions; because, said they, Christianity makes all men equal. It is true that this religious action was of great service to them, for by its means they diminished the power which the great lords exercised over the lower classes. Afterwards, having made conquests in countries where they found it to their advantage to keep slaves,[2] they permitted them to be bought and sold, forgetting that religious principle which had moved them so strongly. What can one say? Truth at one time, error at another. Why should we not do like the Christians? We were very simple-minded to reject settlements and easy conquests in pleasant climates,[3] because we could not find water pure enough to wash us according to the principles of our holy Koran. I give thanks to Almighty God, Who sent His great prophet Hali, whence it is that I profess a religion which requires to be preferred before all human interest, and which is as pure as the sky from which it came.

Paris, the 13th of the moon of Saphar, 1715.

Letter 76

Usbek to his friend Ibben, at Smyrna

European law is dead against suicide. Those who kill themselves suffer, as it were, a second death: they are dragged with ignominy through the streets: their infamy is published, and their goods confiscated.

It seems to me, Ibben, that this law is very unjust. When I am loaded with grief, misery, and contumely, why should I be hindered from putting an end to my sufferings, and cruelly deprived of a remedy which is in my hands?

Why should I be forced to labour for a society to which I refuse to belong? Why in spite of myself, should I be held to an agreement made without my consent? Society is founded upon mutual advantage; but, when it becomes burdensome to me, what hinders me from leaving it? Life was given me as a blessing; when it ceases to be so I can give it up: the cause ceasing, the effect ought also to cease.

Will any prince require me to be his subject, if I reap none of the benefits of subjection? Can my fellow-citizens require our lots to be so unequal; theirs, usefulness—mine, despair? Will God, unlike other benefactors, condemn me to receive favours which are a burden to me?

I am obliged to obey the laws while I live under them; but, if I cease to live, can they still bind me?

"But," some one may say, "you disturb the order of Providence. God has joined your soul to your body; in separating them, you oppose His designs and resist His will."

What force is there in this argument? Do I disturb the order of Providence, when I alter the qualities of matter, and square a ball which the first laws of motion, that is to say the laws of creation and preservation, made round? Certainly not; I only exercise a right which has been given me; and, in that sense, I can disturb, as my fancy dictates, the whole order of Nature, without any one being able to say that I oppose Providence.

When my soul shall be separated from my body, will there be less order, less harmony, in the universe? Do you think that that new combination will be less perfect, and less dependent upon general laws; that the world would lose anything by it; that the works of God would be less great, or rather less immense?

Do you think that my body, become a blade of grass, a worm, a grass-green turf, will be changed into a work of nature less worthy of her; and that my soul, freed from all its earthly trammels, will become less sublime?

All these ideas, my dear Ibben, have their only source in our pride. We do not feel our littleness; and, however small we may be, we wish to count for something in the universe, to cut a figure there, and to be of some consequence in it. We imagine that the annihilation of such a perfect being would degrade all nature: and we cannot conceive that one man more or less in the world—what do I say?—that the whole world, that a hundred millions of worlds[1] like ours, can be more than one small frail atom, which God perceives only because His knowledge is all-embracing.

Paris, the 15th of the moon of Saphar, 1715.

Letter 77

[1]Ibben to Usbek, at Paris

My dear Usbek, it seems to me that, in the eyes of a true Mussulman, misfortunes are not so much punishments as warnings. Those are priceless days upon which we are led to atone for our offences. It is the time of prosperity that ought to be curtailed. To what end is all our impatience, but to show us that we are seeking happiness, independently of Him who gives it, because He is happiness itself?

If a human creature is composed of two beings, and if the acknowledgment of the necessity of preserving their union is the chief mark of submission to the decrees of our Creator, that necessity should be made a religious law; and if the enforced preservation of this union will make men more responsible for their actions, it should be made a civil law.

Smyrna, the last day of the moon of Saphar, 1715.

Letter 78

*Rica to Usbek, at * * **

I send you a copy of a letter, written by a Frenchman who is in Spain: I believe that you will be glad to see it.

I have travelled for six months in Spain and Portugal, where I lived among people despising all nations except the French, whom they honour with their hate. Gravity is the distinctive characteristic of both nations: it has two chief methods of manifestation—spectacles and moustaches.

Spectacles demonstrate clearly that the wearer of them is an accomplished man of science, who has injured his sight by the extent and profundity of his reading; and every nose which they adorn or burden, may pass, without contradiction, for the nose of a savant.[1]

As regards the moustache, in itself it is respectable, independently of results; although sometimes it has been of great use in the service of the king, and in the maintenance of national honour, as appears from the case of a famous Portuguese general in the Indies:[2] for, being in want of money, he cut off one of his moustaches, and offered it to the inhabitants of Goa as a pledge for the loan of twenty thousand pistoles, and the money was advanced at once; afterwards he redeemed his moustache with honour.

One can easily understand how such a grave and phlegmatic people might very well be haughty; and so they are. They usually base their pride upon two matters of sufficient importance. Of those who live in Spain and Portugal, the most uplifted are such as are called old Christians; that is to say such as are not descended form the converts to Christianity made by the Inquisition in later times. Those who dwell in the Indies are not less elated by the consideration that they have the sublime merit to be, as they say, white-skinned men. There was never in the seraglio of the Grand Seigneur, a sultana so proud of her beauty, as the oldest and ugliest rascal among them is of his complexion of pale olive, when in a Mexican town he sits at his own door with his arms folded. A man of such importance, a creature so prefect, would not work for all the wealth of the world; and could never persuade himself to compromise the honour and the dignity of his colour by vile mechanic industry.

For you must know, that, when a man possesses some special merit in Spain, as, for example, when he can add to the qualities which I have already described, that of owning a long sword, or that of having learnt from his father to strum a jangling guitar, he works no more: his honour is concerned in the repose of his limbs. He who remains seated ten hours a day obtains exactly double the respect paid to one who rests only five, because nobility is acquired by sitting still.

But, although these invincible foes of work make a great show of philosophic calm, they have nothing of the sort in their hearts; for they are always in love. In dying of languor under their mistress's windows they have not their match in the world; no Spaniard is esteemed gallant who is without a cold.

They are, firstly, bigots—secondly, jealous. They are particularly careful not to expose their wives to the attempts of a soldier riddled with wounds, or of some decrepit magistrate; but they will shut them up with a fervent novice who casts down his eyes, or a robust Franciscan with a bold glance.

They allow their wives to appear with uncovered bosoms; but they would not have any one see their heels, lest hearts should be ensnared by a glimpse of their feet.[3] They say all the world over that love is cruelly rigorous: in Spain it is especially so. The women cure love, but only with the substitution of other suffering: there often remains a long and disagreeable memorial of an extinguished passion.

They have certain little courtesies which in France would appear out of place; for example, an officer never strikes a soldier without asking his permission; and the Inquisition always apologizes to a Jew before burning him.

Spaniards who are not burned seem so fond of the Inquisition, that it would be ill-natured to deprive them of it. Indeed, I should like to see another established; not for heretics, but for heresiarchs who ascribe to paltry monkish practices the same efficacy as to the seven sacraments; who worship what they should only respect; and who are so devout that they are hardly Christians.

Wit and common sense are to be found among the Spaniards; but let no one seek for them in their books. Glance at one of their libraries, with romances on the one side, and the schoolmen on the other; and you would say that the arrangement had been made, and the whole collected by some secret foe of human reason.

Their only good book is one which was written to expose the absurdity of all the others.[4]

They have made immense discoveries in the New World, and yet they do not know thoroughly their own country: there are upon their rivers an undiscovered bridge or two, and among their mountains races unknown to them.[5]

They say that the sun rises and sets within their dominions; but it must also be said that in making his journey he encounters only ruined fields and desolate countries.

It would not grieve me, Usbek, to see a letter written to Madrid by a Spaniard who was travelling in France: I think he would have little difficulty in avenging his nation. What a grand opportunity for an even-tempered, thoughtful man! I imagine he would begin his description of Paris in this way:

There is a house here in which they place mad people: one would at first expect it to be the largest in the city; but no, the remedy is much too insignificant for the disease. Without doubt, the French, being held in very slight esteem by their neighbours, shut up some madmen in this house, to create the impression that those who are at large are sane.

There I leave my Spaniard. Farewell, my dear Usbek.

Paris, the 17th moon of Saphar, 1715.

Letter 79

Usbek to Rhedi, at Venice

MOST legislators have been men of inferior capacity whom chance exalted over their fellows, and who took counsel almost exclusively of their own prejudices and whims.

It would seem that they had not even a sense of the greatness and dignity of their work: they amused themselves by framing childish institutions, well devised indeed to please small minds, but discrediting their authors with people of sense.

They flung themselves into useless details; and gave their attention to individual interests: the sign of the narrow genius, which grasps things piecemeal and cannot take a general view.

Some of them have been so affected as to employ another language than the vernacular-a ridiculous thing in a framer of laws; for how can they be obeyed if they are not known?

They have often abolished needlessly those which were already established-that is to say, they have plunged nations into the confusion which always accompanies change.

It is true that, by reason of some extravagance springing rather from the nature than from the mind of man, it is sometimes necessary to change certain laws. But the case is rare; and when it happens it requires the most delicate handling; much solemnity ought to be observed, and endless precautions taken, in order to lead the people to the natural conclusion that the laws are most sacred, since so many formalities are necessary to their abrogation.

Often they have made them too subtle, following logical instead of natural equity. As a consequence such laws have been found too severe; and a spirit of justice required that they should be set aside; but the cure was as bad as the disease. Whatever the laws may be, obedience to them is necessary; they are to be regarded as the public conscience, with which all private consciences ought to be in conformity.

It must, however, be admitted that some legislators in their attention to one matter have shown sufficient wisdom; and that is, in giving fathers so much power over their children: nothing is a better lightener of the magistrate's labours, nothing tends more to keep the courts of justice empty, in short, nothing is more conducive to tranquillity in a state, for morality always makes better citizens than law.

Of all the powers it is that which is least abused; it is the most sacred of all magistracies-the only one which does not spring from a contract, which, indeed, precedes all contracts.

It has been noticed that families are best ruled in those countries where there is a large paternal discretion in matter of reward and punishment; fathers represent the Creator of the universe, who, although able to lead men by His love, does not refrain from binding them to Himself still more closely by motives of hope and fear.

I cannot finish this letter without pointing out the capricious turn of mind of the French. It is said that they have retained many things in the Roman laws which are useless, and even worse than useless; from them, however, they have not derived the paternal power, which they have established as the source of all lawful authority.

Paris, the 18th of the moon of Saphar, 1715.

Letter 80

The chief black Eunuch to Usbek, at Paris

YESTERDAY some Armenians brought to the seraglio a young Circassian slave whom they wished to sell. I made her enter the secret apartments; I undressed her, I examined her with eyes of a judge; and the more I examined, the more beauties I found. A virginal shame seemed anxious to hide them from my view: I saw how much it cost her to obey: she blushed upon beholding herself naked, even before me, exempt, as I am from the passions which can alarm decency, and entirely delivered from the dominion of the sex—the servant of modesty in the freest actions, looking only with the chastest glance, and capable of inspiring nothing but innocence.

From the moment I judged her worthy of you, I cast down my eyes, and threw over her a scarlet cloak; I placed a ring of gold upon her finger, I prostrated myself at her feet, I adored her as the queen of your heart. I paid the Armenians, and hid her from every eye. Happy Usbek! You possess more beauties than all the palaces of the east enclose. What a pleasure to find on your return whatever Persia has that is most ravishing, and to see in your seraglio all the graces reborn as fast as time and possession work their destruction!

The Seraglio at Fatme, the 1st of the first moon of Rebiab, 1715.

Letter 81

[1]*Usbek to Rhedi, at Venice*

SINCE I have been in Europe, my dear Rhedi, I have seen many forms of government. It is not here as in Asia, where the rules of policy are everywhere the same.

I have often inquired which form of government is most conformable to reason. It seems to me that the most perfect is that which attains its object with the least friction; so that the government which leads men by following their propensities and inclinations is the most perfect.

If under a mild government the people are as submissive as under a severe one, the former is to be preferred, since it is more rational, severity being a motive foreign to reason.

Remember, my dear Rhedi, that obedience to the laws in a state is not measured by the degree of cruelty in the punishments. In countries where penalties are moderate, they are dreaded as much as in those where they are atrocious and tyrannical.

Whether a government be mild or cruel, there must be degrees of punishment; the gravity of the chastisement must always be in proportion to the gravity of the crime. Our imagination adapts itself to the customs of the county in which we live. Eight days' imprisonment, or a lighter punishment, has a greater effect on the mind of a European brought up in a mild-mannered country, than the loss of an arm had upon an Asiatic. A certain degree of dread attaches to a certain degree of punishment, and each feels it in his own way: a punishment which would not rob a Turk of a single quarter of an hour's sleep, would overwhelm a Frenchman with infamy and despair.

Besides, I do not see that police regulations, justice, and equity, are better observed in Turkey, in Persia, or in the dominions of the Mogul, than in the Republics of Holland, and of Venice, and even in England: it does not appear that fewer crimes are committed there, and that men, intimidated by the greatness of punishments, are more obedient to the laws.

On the contrary, I note a source of injustice and vexation in the midst of these very states.

I find even the prince, who is himself the law, less master there than anywhere else.

I observe that, at times when severe punishments are inflicted, there are always tumults, which nobody commands, and that when once authority depending upon violence is set at nought, there remains with no one sufficient power to restore it;

That the certainty of punishment itself strengthens and increases the disorder;

That in these states a petty revolt never takes place; and that an uprising follows the first murmur of sedition without a moment's interval;

That in them great events are not necessarily prepared by great causes: on the contrary, the least accident produced a great revolution, often as unforeseen by those who cause it as by those who suffer from it.

When Osman, Emperor of the Turks, was deposed[2], none of those who committed that crime had any intention of doing so: they simply asked, as suppliants, that justice should be done for some wrong: a voice, which no one knew, issued from the crowd by chance; it pronounced the name of Mustapha, and suddenly Mustapha was Emperor.

Paris, the 2nd of the first moon of Rebiab, 1715.

Letter 82

Nargum, Persian Envoy in Muscovy, to Usbek, at Paris

OF all the nations of the world, my dear Usbek, none has excelled that of the Tartars in the splendour and magnitude of its conquests. This people is the veritable ruler of the earth: all the others seem to be intended for its service; it is alike that founder and the destroyer of empires; in all times, it has afforded the world signs of its prowess; in every age it has been the scourge of the nations.

Twice the Tartars conquered China, and they still keep it in subjection.

They rule over those vast territories which form the Mogul's empire.

Masters of Persia, they sit upon the throne of Cyrus and Hystaspes. They have subdued Muscovy. Under the name of Turks, they have made immense conquests in Europe, Asia, and Africa; and they are the dominant power in these three quarters of the earth.

In more remote times, from them issued forth some of those races who overthrew the Roman Empire[1].

What are the conquests of Alexander compared with those of Zenghis Khan?

Nothing is wanted to this victorious nation except historians to celebrate its achievements.

What immortal deeds have been buried in oblivion! Of how many empires founded by them is the origin unknown to us! This warlike nation, occupied exclusively with its immediate glory, and certain of conquest in every age, gave no thought to the commemoration of its fame.

Moscow, the 4th of the first moon of Rebiab, 1715.

Letter 83

Rica to Ibben, at Smyrna

ALTHOUGH the French are great talkers, there is nevertheless among them a sort of silent dervishes, called Carthusians. They are said to cut out their tongues on entering the convent; and it is much to be desired that all other dervishes would deprive themselves in the same way of that which their profession renders useless to them.

Talking of these taciturn people reminds me that there are others who excel them in taciturnity, and who have a very remarkable gift. These are they who know how to talk without saying anything; and who carry on a conversation for two whole hours without its being possible to discover their meaning, to rehearse their talk, or to remember a word of what they have said.

This class of people are adored by the women; but not so much as some others who have received from nature the charming gift of smiling at the proper time, that is to say, every moment; and who receive with delighted approbation everything the ladies say.

But these people carry wit to its highest pitch; for they can detect subtlety in everything, and perceive a thousand little ingenious touches in the merest commonplaces.

I know others of them who are fortunate enough to be able to introduce into conversation inanimate things, and to make a long story about an embroidered coat, a white peruke, a snuff-box, a cane, a pair of gloves. It is well to begin in the street to make oneself heard by the noise of a coach and a thundering rap at the door: such a prologue paves the way for the rest of the discourse; and when the exordium is good, it secures toleration for all the nonsense which follows, but which fortunately, arrives too late to be detected.

I assure you that these little gifts, which with us are of no account, are of great advantage here to those who are happy enough to possess them; and that a sensible man has no chance of shining where they are displayed.

Paris, the 6th of the second moon of Rebiab, 1715.

Usbek to Rhedi, at Venice

IF there is a God, my dear Rhedi, HE must of necessity be just; because, if He were not so, He would be the worst and most imperfect of all beings.

Justice is a true relation existing between two things; a relation which is always the same, whoever contemplates it, whether it be God, or an angel, or lastly, man himself.

It is true that men do not always perceive these relations: often indeed, when they do perceive them, they turn aside from them, their own interest being always that which they perceive most clearly. Justice cries aloud; but her voice is hardly heard in the tumult of the passions.

Men act unjustly, because it is their interest to do so, and because they prefer their own satisfaction to that of others. They act always to secure some advantage to themselves: no one is a villain gratis; there is always a determining motive, and that motive is always an interested one.

But it is not possible that God should ever commit an injustice. As soon as we grant that He perceives what is right, it becomes necessary that He should follow it: were it no so, as He has no need of anything and is sufficient to Himself, He would be the most wicked of all beings, having no motive for wickedness.

And so, even if there were no God, we ought to love righteousness; that is to say, we should endeavour to resemble that Being of whom we have so lofty an idea, and who, if He did exist, would of necessity be righteous. Freed as we would be from the yoke of religion, we would still be bound by that of justice.

Here you have, Rhedi, that which makes me believe that justice is eternal and independent of human conditions. And, if it were dependent on them, it would be a truth so terrible that we would be compelled to hide it from ourselves.

We are surrounded by men stronger than ourselves; they can injure us in a thousand different ways, and with impunity three times out of four: what a satisfaction it is for us to know that there is in the heart of all men, an innate principle which fights in our favour, and shields us from their attempts!

Without that we would be in continual terror; we would move among men as among lions; and we would never feel sure for an instant of our property, our honour, and our lives.

All these considerations incense me against those doctors who represent God as a being who makes a tyrannical use of His power; who make Him act in a manner which we would ourselves eschew for fear of offending Him; who charge Him with all the imperfections which He punishes in us; and who, in their inconsistency, represent Him, now as a malicious being, and now as a being who hates evil and punishes it.

When a man examines himself, what a satisfaction for him it is to find that he has a righteous heart! That delight, austere as it is, should ravish him: he perceives that he is a being as far above those who have it not, as he is above tigers and bears. Yes, Rhedi, were I sure of following always and inviolably that idea of righteousness which I have before my eyes, I would believe myself the best of men.

Paris, the 1st of the first moon of Gemmadi, 1715.

Letter 85

Rica to * * *

YESTERDAY I was at the Hotel des Invalides: if I were a king I would rather have founded that establishment than have gained three battles. Throughout it the hand of a great monarch appears. I think it is worthier of respect than any other institution in the world.

What a sight to see assembled within the same walls all those who have suffered for their country, who lived only to defend it; and who, high-hearted as ever, but lacking their old vigour, complain only of their inability to sacrifice themselves again!

What could be worthier of admiration than the sight of these disabled warriors in their retirement, observing a discipline as strict as if they were constrained by the presence of an enemy, seeking their last satisfaction in that semblance of war, and dividing their thoughts and emotions between the duties of religion and those of their profession.

I would have the names of those who die for their country preserved in the temples, and inscribed in registers which should be the fountain-head of glory and honour.

Paris, the 15th of the first moon of Gemmadi, 1715.

Letter 86

[1]Usbek to Mirza, at Ispahan

YOU know, Mirza, that some ministers of Shah Soliman formed the design of obliging all the Armenians of Persia to quit the kingdom or become Mohammedans, in the belief that our empire will continue polluted, as long as it retains within its bosom these infidels.

If, on that occasion, bigotry had carried the day, there would have been an end to the greatness of Persia.

It is not known how the matter dropped. Neither those who made the proposition, nor those who rejected it, realised the consequences of their acts: chance performed the office of reason and of policy, and saved the empire from jeopardy greater than that which would have been entailed by a defeat in the field, and the loss of two cities.

It is understood that the proscription of the Armenians would have extirpated in a single day all the merchants and almost all the artisans in the kingdom. I am sure that the great Shah Abbas would rather have lost both his arms than have signed such an order; in sending to the Mogul and to the other kings of Ind the most industrious of his subjects, he would have felt that he was giving away the half of his dominions.

The persecution of the Guebres by our zealous Mohammedans, has obliged them to fly in crowds into the Indies, and has deprived Persia of that nation,[2] which laboured so heartily, that it alone, by its toil, was in a fair way to overcome the sterility of our land.

Only one thing remained for bigotry to do, and that was, to destroy industry; with the result that the empire fell of itself, carrying along with it as a necessary consequence, that very religion which they wished to advance.

If unbiased discussion were possible, I am not sure, Mirza, that it would not be a good thing for a state to have several religions.

It is worthy of note that those who profess tolerated creeds usually prove more useful to their country than those who profess the established faith; because, being excluded from all honours, and unable to distinguish themselves except by wealth and its shows, they are led to acquire riches by their labour, and to embrace the most toilsome of occupations.

Besides, as all religions contain some precepts advantageous to society, it is well that they should be zealously observed. Now, could there be a greater incitement to zeal than a multiplicity of religions?

They are rivals who never forgive anything. Jealousy descends to individuals: each one stands upon his guard, afraid of doing anything that may dishonour his party, and of exposing it to the contempt and unpardonable censures of the opposite side.

It has also been remarked that a new sect introduced into a state, was always the surest means of correcting the abuses of the old faith.

It is sophistry to say that it is against the interest of the prince to tolerate many religions in his kingdom: though all the sects in the world were to gather together into one state, it would not be in the least detrimental to it, because there is no creed which does not ordain obedience and preach submission.

I acknowledge that history is full of religious wars: but we must distinguish; it is not the multiplicity of religions which has produced wars; it is the intolerant spirit animating that which believed itself in the ascendant.

This is the spirit of proselytism which the Jews caught from the Egyptians, and which passed from them like an epidemic disease to the Mohammedans and the Christians.

It is, in short, that capricious mood, which in its progress can be compared only to a total eclipse of human reason.

In conclusion, even if there were no inhumanity in distressing the consciences of others, even if there did not result from such a course any of the evil effects which do spring from it in thousands, it would still be foolish to advise it. He who would have me change my religion is led to that, without doubt, because he would not change his own although force were employed; and yet he finds it strange that I will not do a thing which he himself would not do, perhaps for the empire of the world.

Paris, the 26th of the first moon of Gemmadi, 1715.

Letter 87

*Rica to * * **

IT seems that every member of a family in this country controls his own actions. The authority exercised by a husband over his wife, a father over his children, a master over his slaves, is merely nominal. The law interferes in all differences; and you may be certain that it is always against the jealous husband, the sorrowing father, the exasperated master.

The other day I visited the place where justice is administered. Before getting there, I had to run the gauntlet of a crowd of young shopwomen who press you to buy in a most seductive manner. At first, the sight is sufficiently amusing; but it becomes dismal when one enters the great halls, where all the people wear dresses even more solemn than their faces. At last one comes to the sacred place where all the secrets of families are revealed and the most hidden actions brought to light.

Here a modest girl comes to confess the torments of a virginity too long preserved, her struggles and her painful resistance; she is so little proud of her victory that she is always on the verge of accepting defeat; and, in order that her father may no longer be ignorant of her wants, she exposes them to everybody.[1]

Then some shameless woman appears to publish the injuries she has done her husband, as a reason for a separation.

With equal modesty another comes to declare that she is tired of wearing the title, without enjoying the rights of a wife; she reveals the hidden mysteries of the marriage night; she wishes to be examined by the most skilful experts, and prays for a decision re-establishing her in all the rights of virginity. Some even dare to challenge their husbands, and demand from them a public contest which the presence of witnesses renders so difficult; a test as disgraceful for the wife who passes it, as for the husband who fails to stand it.

A great number of young women, ravished or seduced, represent the men as being much worse than they are. This court resounds with love; nothing is talked of but enraged fathers, deluded daughters, faithless lovers, afflicted husbands.

According to the law which here holds sway, every infant born in wedlock is considered the husband's; should he have good reasons to believe it not his, the law believes it for him, and relieves him of his scruples and of the necessity for inquiry.

In this tribunal judgment goes by the majority; but it is said that experience teaches that it would be wiser to follow the decision of the minority; which is natural enough, for there are very few just minds, and plenty of ill-balanced ones, as all the world knows.

Paris, the 1st of the second moon of Gemmadi, 1715.

Letter 88

MAN, they say, is a social animal. In this matter a Frenchman appears to me to be more of a man than any other; he is the man par excellence, for he seems to be intended solely for society.

But I have noticed among them some who are not only sociable, but are themselves society itself. They multiply themselves at every corner; they people in an instant the four quarters of a city; a hundred such men make more appearance than two thousand citizens; a stranger would think that they might repair the ravages of plague and famine. It is debated in the schools whether a body can be in more than one place at once; they are a proof of that which philosophers call in question.

They are always in a hurry, because they are engaged in the important business of asking every one they meet whither they are going, and whence they come.

It can never be driven out of their heads that it is a part of good breeding to visit the public every day individually, without counting the wholesale visits which they make to places of general resort, which being much too brief a method is reckoned as nothing in the rules of their etiquette.

Their knocking harasses the doors of the houses more than the winds and the storms. If one were to examine the lists of all the porters, their names would be found daily mutilated in a thousand different ways in Swiss writing. They pass their lives in going to funerals, in expressions of condolence, or in marriage congratulations. The king never confers a favour on any of his subjects, without putting these gentry to the expense of a carriage to go and express their delight. At last, tired out, they return home, and rest themselves to be able to resume next day their laborious functions.

The other day one of them died of weariness; and they put this epitaph on his tomb: "Here rests one who never rested before. He assisted at five hundred and thirty funerals. He made merry at the births of two thousand six hundred and eighty children. He wished his friends joy, always varying the phrase, upon pensions amounting to two million six hundred thousand lives; in town he walked nine thousand six hundred furlongs, in the country thirty-six furlongs. His conversation was pleasing; he had a ready-made stock of three hundred and sixty-five stories; he was acquainted also from his youth with a hundred and eighteen apophthegms derived from the ancients, which he employed on special occasions. He died at last in the sixtieth year of his age. I say no more, stranger; for how could I ever have done telling you all that he did and all that he saw?"

Paris, the 3rd of the second moon of Gemmadi, 1715.

Letter 89

Usbek to Rhedi, at Venice

LIBERTY and equality reign in Paris. Birth, worth, even military fame, however brilliant it may be, fail to distinguish a man from the crowd in which he is lost. Jealousy about rank is unknown here. They say that the chief man in Paris is he who has the best horses in his coach.

A great lord is a man who sees the king, who speaks with ministers, who has ancestors, debts, and pensions. If he can, in addition to this, veil his indolence under an appearance of business, or by a feigned attachment to pleasure, he considers himself the happiest of men.

In Persia, we count none great except those on whom the monarch bestows some share in the government. Here there are people who are great by their birth, but they are not esteemed. The kings act like those skilful craftsmen who in executing their works employ always the simplest tools.

Favor is the great goddess of the French; and the Minister is the high-priest who offers her many victims. Those who surround her are not dressed in white; sometimes those who sacrifice, and sometimes the sacrifices offer themselves up to their idol along with the whole people.

Paris, the 9th of the second moon of Gemmadi, 1715.

Letter 90

[1]Usbek to Ibben, at Smyrna

THE desire of glory is in no sense different from the instinct of self-preservation common to all creatures. We seem to enlarge our existence when we are enabled to extend it to the memory of others; it is a new life which we acquire, and which becomes as precious to us as that which we receive from heaven.

But men are as unlike in their attachment to life as they are in their sensibility to fame. This noble passion is always deeply engraved in their hearts; but imagination and education modifies it in a thousand ways.

This difference which exists between man and man, is even more marked among nations.

It may be laid down as a maxim that in each state the desire of glory increases and diminishes with the liberty of the subject: glory is never the companion of slavery.

A sensible man said to me the other day, "In most things we are much freer in France than in Persia; and so we love glory more. This happy idea causes a Frenchman to do with pleasure and inclination what your Sultan obtains from his subjects only by keeping constantly before them rewards and punishments.

"Again, among us the prince is most jealous of the honour of the meanest of his subjects. For its support there exist highly esteemed tribunals: it is the sacred treasure of the nation, and the only one which the sovereign does not control, because to do so would defeat his own interests. So that if a subject finds his honour wounded by his prince, whether by some preference, or by the slightest mark of contempt, he leaves at once his court, his employment, his service, and retires to his estate.

"The difference between the French troops and yours is this: among the latter, composed of slaves who are naturally cowards, the fear of death is overcome only by the fear of punishment, and this produces in the soul a new kind of terror which stupefies it; the former, on the other hand, go where the blows are thickest, and fear is driven out by a feeling of satisfaction which is superior to it.

"But the sanctuary of honour, of reputation, and of virtue, appears to be established in republics, and in countries where one dare pronounce the word Fatherland. In Rome, in Athens, in Lacedaemonia, honour was the sole reward for the most distinguished services. A crown of oak or of laurel, a statue, a panegyric, was a magnificent recompense for a battle gained or a city taken.

"There a man who had performed a brave deed thought the deed itself sufficient recompense. He could not behold one of his countrymen without a feeling of pleasure at having been his benefactor; he reckoned the number of his services by that of his fellow-citizens. Every man is capable of benefiting another, but he who contributes to the happiness of a whole community resembles the gods.

"Now, must not this noble emulation be quite extinct in the hearts of you Persians, with whom office and honour are derived only from the caprice of the sovereign? Reputation and virtue are looked upon as imaginary, if unaccompanied by the favour of the prince with whom is their sole beginning and end. A man who enjoys the public esteem is never sure that the morrow may not bring forth dishonour. To-day he is a general of the army; to-morrow, perhaps, the prince makes him his cook, and leaves him with no hope of any other eulogy than that of having made a good ragout."

Paris, the 15th of the second moon of Gemmadi, 1715.

Letter 91

Usbek to the Same, at Smyrna

FROM the general passion which the French have for glory, there has been developed in the minds of individuals a certain something which they call "the point of honour;" it is properly the characteristic of every profession, but most marked in military men—theirs, indeed, is the point of honour par excellence. It would be very difficult to make you understand what this is, because the idea is so foreign to us.

Formerly the French, especially the aristocracy, obeyed no other laws than those of this point of honour, and by them they regulated the whole conduct of their lives. These laws were so severe, that without incurring a penalty more cruel than death, one might not, I do not say infringe them, but even evade their slightest punctilio.

When they had occasion to arrange their differences, almost the only method of decision prescribed was the duel, which resolved all difficulties. The worst part of it, however, was that frequently the trial took place between other parties than those immediately concerned.

However little one man might know another, he had to enter into the quarrel, and pay with his person as if he himself had been enraged. He always felt himself honoured by such a choice, and a distinction so flattering; and one who would have been unwilling to give four pistols to a man to save him and all his family from the gallows, would make no difficulty in risking his life for him a thousand times.

This method of decision was badly enough conceived; for although a man might be more dexterous and stronger than another, it did not follow that he had more right on his side.

Accordingly the kings prohibited it under very severe penalties, but in vain;[1] honour which wishes always to reign, revolts, and regards not the laws.

On this account violence prevails amongst the French; for these laws of honour require a gentleman to avenge himself when he has been insulted; but, on the other hand, justice punishes him unmercifully when he does so. If one follows the laws of honour, one dies upon the scaffold; if one follows those of justice, one is banished for ever from the society of men: this, then, is the barbarous alternative, either to die, or to be unworthy to live.

Paris, the 18th of the second moon of Gemmadi, 1715.

Letter 92

[1]*Usbek to Rustan, at Ispahan*

THERE has appeared here a person who burlesques the part of Persian ambassador, and insolently makes sport of the two greatest kings in the world. He bears to the French monarch presents which ours would not offer to a king of Irimetta or of Georgia; and by his wretched avarice, he has disgraced the majesty of two empires.

He has brought ridicule upon himself before a people who pretend to be the most polished in Europe; and he has caused it to be said in the west that the king of kings reigns over none but savages.

He has received honours which he would apparently have been glad to decline; and, as if the court of French had had the grandeur of the court of Persia more at heart than he, it forced him to appear with dignity before a people who scorn him.

Say nothing of this at Ispahan: spare the head of an unhappy wretch. I would not have our ministers punish him for their own imprudence, and for the unworthy choice which they made.[2]

Paris, the last day of the second moon of Gemmadi, 1715.

Letter 93

Usbek to Rhedi, at Venice

THE monarch who reigned so long is no more.[1] He made people talk much about him during his life; everybody is silent at his death. Firm and courageous at the last moment, he seemed to yield only to destiny. Thus died the great Shah Abbas after filling the whole earth with his name.

Do not imagine that this great event has given rise to none but moral reflections. Every one considered his own affairs and how to take advantage of the change. The king, great-grandson of the late monarch, being only five years old, a prince, his uncle, has been declared regent of the kingdom.[2]

The late king left a will which limits the power of the regent. This clever prince went to the Parliament, and having laid before them all the rights he has by birth, made them break the arrangements of the late monarch, who, wishing to survive himself, seemed to lay claim to govern after his death.

Parliaments are like those ruins which are trampled under foot, but which always recall the idea of some temple famous on account of the ancient religion of the people. They hardly interfere now except in matters of law; and their authority will continue to decrease unless some unforeseen event restores them to life and strength. The common fate has overtaken these great bodies; they have yielded to time which destroys everything, to moral corruption which weakens everything, and to absolute power which overbears everything.

But the regent, anxious to secure the favour of the people, appeared at first to respect this shadow of public freedom; and, as if he had intended to lift from the ground the temple and the idol, he was willing that the parliament should be regarded as the prop of the monarchy, and the foundation of all legitimate authority.[3]

Paris, the 4th of the moon of Rhegeb, 1715.

Letter 94

Usbek to his brother, Santon[1] at the Monastery of Casbin

I HUMBLE myself in the dust before you, holy Santon; your footprints are to me as the apple of my eye. Your holiness is so great that it seems as if you had the heart of our sacred Prophet: your austerities astonish Heaven itself; the highest angels have watched you from the skies, and have said, "How is he still on earth, since his spirit is with us, and flies about the throne which the clouds bear up?"

How then should I not honour you, I who have learned from our doctors that dervishes, even though infidels, have always a character of holiness which makes them venerable in the eyes of true believers; and that God has chosen for Himself, in every corner of the earth, souls purer than the rest, whom He has separated from the impious world, that their mortifications and their fervent prayers may suspend His wrath, ready to fall upon so many rebel nations?

Christians narrate wonders of their first santons who took refuge by thousands in the dreadful desert of the Thebaid, and whose chiefs were Paul, Antony, and Pacomus. If what is told of them be true, their lives are as full of marvels as those of our most sacred Imans. They sometimes spent ten whole years without seeing a single soul; but they dwelt night and day with demons; they were ceaselessly tormented by these evil spirits, who haunted their bed, and sat down with them at meat; there was no refuge from them. If all this is true, reverend Santon, it must be confessed that nobody ever lived in more disagreeable company.

The more sensible Christians regard all these stories as a very natural allegory, which may be of use in making us realise the wretchedness of our condition as human beings. We search in vain for a state of repose in the desert; temptations follow us everywhere: our passions, symbolised by the demons, never quit us altogether; those monsters of the heart, those illusions of the mind, those vain phantoms of error and falsehood, haunt us continually to mislead us, and attack us even in our fasts and our hair-cloths, that is to say, even in our strongholds.

As for me, reverend Santon, I know that God's messenger has chained Satan, and flung him headlong into the abyss; He has purified the earth, formerly filled with his power, and has made it worthy of the abode of angels and prophets.

Paris, the 9th of the moon of Chahban, 1715.

Letter 95

Usbek to Rhedi, at Venice

I HAVE never heard public law discussed, without a preliminary careful inquiry into the origin of society, which seems to me absurd. If men did not unite, if they avoided and fled from each other, it would be necessary to ask the reason, and to inquire why they kept apart; but we are all born with relations; a son comes into the world beside his father, and stays there: that is society, and the cause of society.

International law is better understood in Europe than in Asia; and yet it must be said that the passions of princes, the patience of the people, and the flattery of authors, have corrupted all its principles.

At the present time this law is a science which teaches princes to what length they may carry the violation of justice without injuring their own interests. What a design, Rhedi, to wish to harden the conscience by reducing iniquity to a system, by giving it rules, by settling its principles, and drawing inferences from it!

The absolute power of our sublime Sultans, which is a law to itself, produces no greater monstrosities than this unworthy art, which would bend justice, inflexible as it is.

One would say, Rhedi, that there are two species of justice wholly different from each other: one which regulates the affairs of individuals, and rules in civil law; another which settles the differences arising between peoples, and tyrannizes over international law; as if international law were not itself a civil law, not indeed of a particular country, but of the world.

I will explain to you in another letter my thoughts on this subject.

Paris, the 1st of the moon of Zilhage, 1716.

Letter 96

Usbek to the Same

MAGISTRATES ought to do justice between citizen and citizen; and each nation between itself and other nations. In this second administration of justice, no other maxims should be employed than in the first.

There is rarely need for a third party to act as umpire between nation and nation, because the subjects in dispute are almost always clearly defined and easily decided. The interests of two nations are usually so distinct, that it is only necessary to love justice to discover where it lies; one can hardly be prejudiced in one's own cause.

It is not the same with the differences which happen among individuals. As they live together, their interests are so intermingled and so confused, and also so various that it is necessary for a third party to clear that which the covetousness of the other two endeavours to obscure.

There are only two kinds of just wars: those which are waged to repel an attacking enemy, or to aid an ally who is attacked.

There would be no justice in making war for the private quarrels of a prince, unless the crime were so grave as to require the death of the prince or of the people who committed it. Thus, a prince ought not to make war because he has been refused an honour which is his due, or because his ambassadors have been treated with scant courtesy, or for any such reason; any more than a private person should kill him who refuses him precedence. The reason of this is, that, since a declaration of war ought to be an act of justice, which always requires the punishment to be proportioned to the crime, it is necessary to make sure that he upon whom war is declared merits death: for to wage war on any one is to pronounce against him the death penalty.

In international law the severest act of justice is war, since it may have the effect of destroying society.

Reprisals are next in severity. No tribunal has been able to avoid the law which proportions the punishment to the crime.

A third act of justice is to deprive a prince of the advantages which he may derive from us, always measuring the penalty by the offence.

The fourth act of justice, which ought to be the most frequent, is to renounce the alliance of a people which gives cause of complaint. This penalty corresponds to that of banishment, which has been established by tribunals to remove criminals from the community. In this way, the prince whose alliance we renounce is cut off from our community, and is no longer one of the members which compose it.

No greater insult can be offered a prince, than to renounce his alliance, and no greater honour can be conferred upon him, than to enter into one with him. Nothing on earth adds more to our honour, and is really more useful, than to see others always careful of our preservation.

But, in order that the alliance may be binding, it must be just: thus an alliance contracted between two nations to oppress a third is not lawful; and there would be no guilt in breaking it.

It is by no means honourable or dignified in a prince to ally himself with a tyrant. They say that an Egyptian monarch once remonstrated with the king of Samos upon his cruelty and tyranny, and called upon him for amendment; and when he would not amend, he sent to him renouncing his friendship and alliance.

Conquest in itself does not establish a right. As long as a community holds together, it is a pledge of peace, and of the reparation of wrong; if it is destroyed or dispersed, it is a monument of tyranny.

Treaties of peace are so sacred among men, that they seem to be the voice of nature reclaiming her rights. They are quite legitimate, when the conditions are such that both nations can preserve themselves; without that, the nation which would perish, deprived of its natural defence by peace, may seek safety in war.

For nature, although she has fixed different degrees of strength and weakness among men, has often by means of despair made the weak equal to the strong.

This, my dear Rhedi, is what I call international law, the law of peoples, or rather, the law of right.

Paris, the 4th of the moon of Zilhage, 1716.

Letter 97

The Chief Eunuch to Usbek, at Paris

A GREAT number of yellow women from the kingdom of Visapour have arrived here. I have bought one for your brother, the governor of Mazenderan, who sent me a month ago his sublime commands and a hundred tomans.

I am skilled in women, especially as they can no longer delude me, and as my heart does not interfere with my understanding.

I have never seen beauty so regular, so perfect: her dazzling eyes lighten up her countenance, and heighten the lustre of a complexion which might eclipse all the charms of Circassia.

The chief eunuch of a merchant of Ispahan bade for her against me: but she withdrew herself disdainfully from his gaze, and seemed to invite mine; as if to tell me that a wretched merchant was unworthy of her, and that she was destined for a more illustrious husband.

I confess to you, that I feel within me a sacred joy, when I think of the charms of this lovely person. I fancy I see her entering the seraglio of your brother: I delight myself with a foresight of the astonishment of all his wives; the haughty grief of some; the silent but heavier sorrow of others; the malicious pleasure of those who have nothing to hope for, and the enraged ambition of those whose hope is not yet dead.

I travel from one end of the kingdom to the other, to change the entire face of a seraglio. What passions shall I excite! What terrors and punishments am I preparing!

Nevertheless, in spite of this internal disturbance, outward tranquility will be undisturbed: great revolutions will be hidden in the depths of the heart; grief will be repressed and joy will be restrained; obedience will be no less prompt, nor discipline less inflexible: amiability, which is always exacted, will spring from the depths of despair itself.

We have noticed that the more women we have under our care, the less trouble they give us. A greater necessity to be agreeable, less opportunity for conspiring, more examples of submission; all this increases their fetters. They are constantly watchful of the doings of their neighbours: they seem to unite themselves with us to render themselves more dependent: they take part in our labour, and open our eyes when they are closed. What do I say? They continually incite their master against their rivals, unaware how close at hand their own punishment may be.

But all this, magnificent lord, all this is nothing without the master's presence. What can we do with this vain show of an authority which can never be entirely imparted? We represent, and that but feebly, only the half of yourself: we can only show them a hateful severity; whereas you can temper fear with hope, and are more absolute when you caress than when you threaten.

Return then, magnificent lord, return to this abode, and impress throughout it your authority. Come and alleviate despairing passions: come and remove every pretext to go astray: come to pacify complaining love, and to make duty itself pleasant: come, lastly, to relieve your faithful eunuchs of a burden which grows heavier every day.

The Seraglio at Ispahan, the 8th of the Moon of Zilhage, 1716.

Letter 98

Usbek to Hassim, Dervish of the Mountain of Jaron

OH, wise dervish! whose inquisitive mind excels in learning, give ear to what I am about to tell you.

There are philosophers here, who, it is true, have not attained to the perfection to oriental wisdom: they have not been carried up to the throne of light: neither have they heard the unutterable words, nor felt the awful approach of divine frenzy; but left to themselves, and deprived of these sacred miracles, they follow silently the footprints of human reason.

You would not believe how far this guide has led them. They have cleared up chaos, and have explained, by a simple mechanism, the order of divine architecture. The creator of nature gave motion to matter: nothing more was required to produce the prodigious variety of effects in the universe.

Ordinary law-givers offer us laws to regulate society--laws, subject to change like the minds of those who make them, and of the people who obey them: those talk only of general, immutable, and eternal laws, which, without exception, are obeyed with order, regularity, and absolute exactness in the immensity of space.

And what think you, most holy man, these laws may be? You imagine, perhaps, that entering into the counsels of the Eternal, you are about to be astonished by sublime mysteries: you give up in advance all idea of understanding, and propose only to admire.

But you will soon change your opinion: they do not dazzle us by a pretended profundity: their simplicity has made them long misunderstood; and it is only after much reflection, that people have seen how fruitful they are, and how far they reach.

The first is, that every body tends to describe a straight line, unless it meets with some obstacle which diverts its course; and the second, which is but a consequence of the first, is, that every body which moves round a centre, tends to fly from it; because the further off it is, the nearer the course it describes approaches a straight line.

Here, sublime dervish, you have the key of nature: here are the fruitful principles, from which consequences are drawn which pass beyond our ken.

The knowledge of five or six truths has filled their philosophy with wonders, and has enabled them to perform almost as many prodigies and marvels as those which are told of our holy prophets.

For, in short, I am persuaded that we have no doctor who would not have been sorely troubled, if he had been told to weigh in a balance all the air which surrounds the earth, or to measure all the water which falls each year upon its surface; and who would not have thought many times before telling how many leagues sound travels in an hour; what time a ray of light occupies in journeying from the sun to us; how many fathoms it is from here to Saturn; or according to what curve a ship should be cut to make it the best sailer possible.

Perhaps if some holy man had adorned the works of these philosophers with lofty and sublime expressions; if he had introduced bold figures and mysterious allegories, he might have made a great work, which would have ranked next to the Koran.

However, if I must tell you what I think, I never cared greatly for the figurative style. In our Koran there are a great number of trifles which always appear to me as such, although they receive distinction from the strength and liveliness of the style. At first these inspired books seemed to be only divine ideas stated in the language of mankind: on the contrary, however, one often finds in the Koran the language of God and the ideas of men; as if by some astonishing caprice, God had dictated the words, and man had supplied the thought.

You will say, perhaps, that I speak too freely of that which is held most sacred among us; regard it as the outcome of the independence which distinguishes this country. No; thanks to Heaven, my mind has not corrupted my heart, and while I live Hali shall be my prophet.

Paris, the 15th of the moon of Chahban, 1716.

Letter 99

Usbek to Ibben, at Smyrna

THERE is no country in the world where fortune is more inconstant than in this. Every ten years a revolution happens which plunges the wealthy into misery, and raises the poor on rapid wings to the summit of affluence. The one is astonished at his poverty; the other at his riches. The new-made rich man admires the wisdom of providence; the pauper, the mischance of a blind fate.

Those who gather the taxes swim in wealth; and there are few Tantaluses among them. It is the extremity of misery, however, that drives them into this employment. They are despised like dirt while they are poor; when they become rich, they are sufficiently respected, as they neglect nothing to acquire esteem.

They are at present in a dreadful situation. They are about to establish a chamber of justice, so called because it is to strip them of all their wealth. They can neither transfer, nor hide their effects; for they are compelled to render an exact account, upon pain of death; thus they have to pass through a very narrow strait, I mean between their lives and their money. To fill up the cup of their misfortune, there is a minister, remarkable for his wit, who honours them with his jokes, and makes fun of all the deliberations of the council. It is not every day that ministers are to be found disposed to make the people laugh; and they ought to be much beholden to him for having undertaken to do so.

The body of footmen is more respectable in France than anywhere else; it is a nursery of great lords; it fills up the vacancies in other ranks. The members of it take the places of the unfortunate great, of ruined magistrates, of gentlemen killed in the fury of war; and when they are unable to find supply among themselves, they re-establish all the great families by means of their daughters, which are like a kind of manure enriching barren and mountainous soil.

I find, Ibben, the ways of providence in the distribution of wealth admirable. If riches had been granted only to good people, they would not have been sufficiently distinguished from virtue, and their insignificance would not have been fully recognised. But when we consider who are the people most loaded with them, by dint of despising the rich, we come to despise riches.

Paris, the 26th of the moon of Maharram, 1717.

Letter 100

Rica to Rhedi, at Venice

THE caprices of fashion among the French are amazing. They have forgotten how they were dressed this summer; they know as little how they will be dressed in the winter; but, above all, you would never believe how much it costs a husband to dress his wife in the fashion. Where is the use of my giving you a full description of their dress and ornaments? A new fashion would destroy all my labour as it does that of the dressmakers; and before you could receive my letter all would be changed.

A woman who leaves Paris to spend six months in the country, returns from it as out of date as if she had been forgotten for thirty years. The son does not know the portrait of his mother, so strange does the dress in which she was painted appear to him; he imagines that it represents some American, or that the painter wished to express a fancy of his own.

Sometimes the headdresses grow gradually to a great height, until a revolution brings them down suddenly. They grew so lofty once that a woman's face seemed to be in the centre of her anatomy; at another time it was the feet that occupied that place, the heels forming a pedestal which raised them into the air. Would you believe it? Architects have often been obliged to raise, to lower, or to widen their doors, according to the change in the women's dresses; and the rules of their art have had to yield to such caprices. Sometimes one sees upon a face an immense quantity of patches, which are all gone next day. Formerly women had figures and teeth; now these are of no consequence. In this changeable nation, whatever ill-natured wags may say, the daughters are differently made from the mothers.

As with their fashions, so is it with their customs and style of living: French manners change with the age of the king. The monarch could even succeed in making his people solemn if he chose to try. He impresses his own characteristics upon the court, the court upon the city, and the city on the provinces. The soul of the sovereign is a mould in which all the others are formed.

Paris, the 8th of the moon of Saphar, 1717.

Letter 101

Rica to the Same

I told you the other day of the extra-ordinary inconstancy of the French in their fashions. Yet it is inconceivable to what an extent they are infatuated about them; everything is swayed by them: fashion is the rule by which they judge what is done in other nations; whatever is foreign always seems to them ridiculous. I confess that I hardly know how to reconcile this bigoted devotion to their customs with the inconstancy which changes them every day.

When I say that they despise everything foreign, I mean only trifles; for in importent matter they are so diffident as almost to degrade themselves. They confess with the greatest goodwill that the other nations are wiser, if you grant that they are better dressed; they are willing to submit themselves to the laws of a rival nation, provided French wig-makers may decide, like legislators, the form of foreign Perukes. Nothing seems to them more glorious than to see the taste of their cooks reigning from north to south, and the decrees of their tire-women obeyed in every boudoir of Europe.

With these noble advantages, what does it matter to them that their wisdom comes from others, and that they have derived from their neighbours everything relating to political and civil government?

Who would imagine that the most ancient and powerful kingdom in Europe has been governed for ten centuries by laws which were not made for it? If the French had been conquered, it would not be difficult to understand, but they are the conquerors.

They have abandoned the old laws made by their first kings in the general assemblies of the nations; and, singularly enough, the Roman laws which have been substituted, were partly made and partly digested by emperors contemporary with their own legislators.

And, to make the borrowing complete, and in order that all their wisdom might come from others, they have adopted all the constitutions of the Popes, and have made them a new part of their law: a new kind of slavery.

Latterly, it is true, they have drawn up some provincial statutes and by-laws; but they are nearly all taken from the Roman law.

So great is the multitude of adopted, and, so to speak, naturalized laws, that it oppresses alike justice and judges. But these volumes of law are nothing in comparison with the appalling army of glossers, commentators, and compilers, a tribe as feeble by inferiority of their minds, as they are strong by their immense numbers.

This is not all : these foreign laws have introduced formalities so excessive as to be a disgrace to human reason. It would be very difficult to decide whether pedantry has been more hurtful in jurisprudence or in medicine; whether it has played more mischief under the cloak of a lawyer, or the broad brim of a physician; and whether the one has ruined more people than the other has killed.

Paris, the 17th of the moon of Saphar, 1717.

Letter 102

They are always talking here of the Constutution.[1] The other day I went into a certain house, where the first person I saw was a fat man with a red face, who said in a loud voice, "I have issued my charge; I shall make no further reply to anything you may say; but read my charge, and you will see that I have solved all your doubts. I sweated over it," he continued, pressing his brow with his hand; "I have need of all my learning, and was obliged to read many Latin authors." "I believe it," said a man who was standing by, "for it is an admirable work; and I altogether defy that Jesuit who comes so often to see you to write a better. "Read it, then," replied he, "and you will know more of these matters in a quarter of an hour than if I had talked to you about them for a whole day." In this way he avoided engaging in conversation and the exposure of his own incompetence. But finding himself pressed, he was obliged to leave his entrenchment, and began to utter a mass of theological nonsense, supported by a dervish who received his remarks with the utmost respect. When two men who were present denied any of his principles, he said at once, "It is true; we have so decided it, and we are infallible judges." "But how," said I, "are you infallible judges?" "Do you not see," he replied, "that the Holy Ghost enlightens us?" "That is fortunate," I rejoined, "for from the style of your talk to-day, I perceive how much you need to be enlightened."

Paris, the 18th of the first moon of Rebiab, 1717.

Letter 103

Usbek to Ibben, at Smyrna

The most powerful states in Europe are those of the Emperor, and of the kings of France, Spain, and England. Italy, and a large part of Germany, are divided into a great number of small states, the princes of which are, properly speaking, martyrs to sovereignty. Our glorious sultans have more wives than some of these princes have subjects. Those of Italy, being less united, are most to be pitied; their states are as open as caravansaries, in which they are forced to accommodate the first comer: they therefore require to join themselves to great princes, and share their fears with them rather than their friendship. Most European governments are monarchial, or rather are called so; for I do not know whether there was a government truly monarchial; at least they cannot have continued very long in their original purity. It is a state in which might is right, and which degenerates always into a despotism or a republic. Authority can never be equally divided between the people and the prince; it is too difficult to maintain an equilibrium; power must diminish on one side while it increases on the other; but the advantage is usually with the prince, as he commands the army.

Accordingly, the power of the kind of Spain is very great; one may say that they have as much as they desire, but they do not exercise it to such a degree as our sultans: firstly, because they are not willing to offend the manners and the religion of the people; secondly, because it is not in their own interests to carry things with so high a hand.

Nothing brings our princes nearer the condition of their subjects than the immense power which they wield over them; nothing makes them more subject to reverses and caprices of fortune.

The custom which princes have of putting to death all those who displease them upon the slightest pretence, destroys the proportion which ought to exist between crime and punishment; and that proportion, scrupulously preserved by the Christian princes, gives them an immeasurable advantage over our sultans.

A Persian who, imprudently or by mischance, draws upon himself the displeasure of his prince, is sure to die; the slightest fault or the slightest caprice reduces him to that necessity. But if he had attempted the life of his sovereign, if he had intended to betray his towns to the enemy, he would have atoned as before by losing his life; he runs no greater risk in the latter case than in the former.

And so, under the least disgrace, death being certain and nothing worse to fear, he naturally applies himself to disturb the state, and to conspire against the sovereign —his only remaining resource.

It is not the same with the grandees of Europe, who, when in disgrace, lose only the royal favour and goodwill. They withdraw from the courts and give themselves up to enjoy a quiet life and the privileges of their birth; as they are seldom done to death except for high treason, they dread to commit that crime, remembering what they may lose, and how little they are likely to gain; this is why one sees here few rebellions, and few princes who die a violent death.

If, with that unlimited power which our princes have, they did not take every precaution for the safety of their lives, they would not live a single day; and if they had not in their pay innumerable troops to coerce their other subjects, their rule would not last for a month.

It is only some four or five centuries since a king of France[1], contrary to the custom of the times, levied guards to secure himself from the assassins which a petty prince of Asia[2] had sent to kill him; till that time kings had lived peacefully among their subjects, like fathers with their children.

Although the kings of France are quite unable, of their own motion, to take away the life of one of their subjects like our sultans, yet they carry about with them always mercy for all criminals; that he should have been fortunate enough to behold the august countenance of his prince, is sufficient to make a man once more worthy to live. These monarchs are like the sun, which sheds everywhere heat and life.

Paris, the 8th of the second moon of Rebiab, 1717.

Letter 104

Usbek to the Same

Here you have as nearly as I can, continuing the subject of my last letter, what a sensible European said to me recently.

"The worst course which the princes of Asia could have adopted, is to shut themselves up as they do. They desire to render themselves more venerable; but it is royalty which they cause to be respected, and not the king; they attach the minds of their subjects to a certain throne, and not to a certain person.

"When the power that governs is invisible it is always the same to the people. Although ten kings, known only by name, should have their throats cut one after the other, the public are sensible of no difference: it is as if they were governed by a succession of spirits.

"If the detestable murderer of our great king, Henry IV, had assassinated one of the kings of Ind, master of the royal seal, and of an immense treasure which would seem to have been amassed for him, he would peacefully have seized the reins of power, without its entering into any one's mind to inquire after the king, his relations, and children.

"We are astonished that there is hardly ever any change in the government of eastern princes: how could it be otherwise, when we bear in mind their terrible tyranny?

"Changes cannot be effected except by the prince or by the people: but there the princes take care to alter nothing, because, possessed of such absolute power, they have all they can have: were they to make any change it could only be to their own injury.

As to the subjects, should one of them form any design, he cannot execute it upon the state; it would be necessary to overturn at one blow a most formidable and unchanging power; for this he lacks time and means: but he has only to attack the source of that power, for which all he needs is an arm and a moment of time.

"The murderer mounts the throne, as the monarch leaves it and falls expiring at his feet.

"In Europe a malcontent thinks of carrying on a secret correspondence, of going over to the enemy, of seizing some town, or of exciting foolish complaints among the people. A malcontent in Asia goes straight to the prince, amazes, strikes, overthrows: he obliterates all memory of his existence: in one moment slave and master, usurper and lawful sovereign.

"Unfortunate is the king who has only one head! In guarding it with all his power he only shows the first upstart where to strike."

Paris, the 17th of the second moon of Rebiab, 1717.

Letter 105

Usbek to the Same

All the nations of Europe are not equally submissive to their princes: the impatient humour of the English, for instance, leaves their king hardly any time to make his authority felt. Submission and obedience are virtues upon which they flatter themselves but little. On this subject they say most amazing things. According to them there is only one tie which can bind men, and that is gratitude: husband and wife, father and son, are only bound to each other by their mutual affection, or by the services they do each other : and these various motives of obligation are the origin of all kingdoms and communities.

But if a prince, instead of making the lives of his subjects happy, attempts to oppress and ruin them, the basis of obedience is destroyed; nothing binds them, nothing attaches them to him; and they return to their natural liberty. They maintain that all unlimited power must be unlawful, because it cannot have had a lawful origin. For, we cannot, say they, give to another more power over us than we ourselves have : now, we have not unlimited power over ourselves ; for example, we have no right to take our own lives: no one upon earth then, they conclude, had such a power.

The crime of high treason is nothing else, according to them, than the crime of the weaker against the stronger, simply disobedience, no matter what form the disobedience may take. Thus the people of England, finding themselves stronger than one of their kings,[1] pronounced it high treason in a prince to make war upon his subjects. They have therefore good reason to say that the precept of their Koran,[2] which requires submission to the powers that be, is not a very difficult one to follow, seeing that it is impossible not to do so, inasmuch as they are not enjoined to submit to the most virtuous, but to the strongest.

The English tell how one of their kings, having conquered and taken prisoner a prince who disputed his right to the crown, began to reproach him with his faithlessness and treachery, when the unfortunate prince replied, "It was decided only a moment ago which of us two is the traitor."

A usurper declares all those rebels who have not, like him, oppressed their country; and believing that where there are no judges there are no laws, he chases the caprices of chance and fortune to be reverenced like the decrees of Heaven.

Paris, the 20th of the second moon of Rebiab, 1717.

Rhedi to Usbek, at Paris

In one of your letters you said much to me about the arts and sciences cultivated in the west. You are inclined to regard me as a barbarian; but I am not certain that the profit derived from them recompenses men for the bad use to which they are put every day. I have heard it said that the invention of bombs alone has deprived all the nations of Europe of freedom. The princes being no longer able to trust the guardianship of towns to the citizens, who would surrender them at the first bomb, have made it a pretext for keeping large bodies of regular troops, whom they have since used to oppress their subjects.

You know that since the invention of gunpowder no place is impregnable; that is to say, Usbek, that there is no longer upon the earth a refuge from injustice and violence.

I dread always lest they should at last discover some secret which will furnish them with a briefer method of destroying men, by killing them off wholesale in tribes and nations.

You have read the historians: think of them seriously; almost all monarchies have been founded upon ignorance of the arts, and have been destroyed by their overcultivation. The ancient empire of Persia may furnish us with an example at our own doors.

I have not been long in Europe; yet I have heard sensible people talk of the ravages of alchemy. It seems to be a fourth plague, which ruins men, destroying them one by one, but continually; while war, pestilence, and famine destroy them in the mass, but at intervals.

Of what advantage has the invention of the mariner's compass been to us, and the discovery of so many nations who have given us more diseases than wealth? Gold and silver have been established by a general agreement as the means of purchasing all goods, and as a pledge of their value, because these metals are rare, and useless for any other purpose: of what consequence was it to us, then, that they should become more common, and that to mark the value of commodity, we should have two or three signs in place of one? This was only more inconvenient.

But, on the other hand, this invention has been hurtful to the countries of the New World. Entire nations have been destroyed; and those who have escaped death have been reduced to a slavery so dreadful, that the description of it makes even a Mussulman shudder.

Happy in their ignorance are the children of Mohammed! Their amiable simplicity, so dear to our holy Prophet, perpetually recalls to me the artlessness of the olden time, and the peace which reigned in the hearts of our first fathers.

Venice, the 5th of the moon of Rhamazan, 1717.

Letter 107

Usbek to Rhedi, at Venice

You do not think as you say, or else your actions are better than your thoughts. You left your country to acquire knowledge, and you despise all knowledge; you go to form yourself in a country where the fine arts are cultivated, and you regard them as hurtful. May I say it, Rhedi? –I am more of your mind than you are yourself.

Have you properly considered the barbarous and unhappy condition which the loss of the arts[1] would entail upon us? There is no need to imagine it; it can be seen. There are still people upon the earth, among whom a tolerably trained monkey could live with credit; he would be almost on a level with the other inhabitants; and they would not think him a curious creature, or an odd character; he would pass as well as another, and would even be distinguished by his elegance.

You say that the founders of empires have almost all been ignorant of the arts. I do not deny that barbarians have poured over the earth like impetuous torrents, and covered with their wild armies the most civilised kingdoms; but, observe this, they learnt the arts, or made the conquered races exercise them; without that, their power would have passed away like the noise of a thunderstorm.

You fear, you say, that some more dreadful method of destruction than that at present in use will be invented. No; if a fatal invention were to be brought out, it would soon be prohibited by the law of nations, and suppressed by unanimous consent. It is not in the interest of princes to make conquests by such means; they wish to gain subjects, not soil.

You complain of the invention of gunpowders and bombs; you think it strange that no place should now be impregnable- that is to say, you think it strange that wars should be brought to an end sooner to-day than they were formerly.

You must have remarked in reading history, that since the invention of gunpowder, battles are much less bloody than they used to be, because the armies are seldom intermingled.

Why, because an art is found injurious in some particular instance, should it be rejected entirely? Do you think, Rhedi, that the religion which our holy Prophet brought from heaven is harmful, because one day it will serve to confound the unbelieving Christians?

You think that the arts enervate people, and are therefore the cause of the fall of empires. You speak of the fall of that of the ancient Persians, which was the result of their effeminacy; but this example is not by any means decisive, since the Greeks, who defeated them so often, and conquered them, were much more assiduous than they in the cultivation of the arts.

When they talk of the arts making men effeminate, they are not referring at all to the people that work at them, since they know nothing of indolence, which of all vices weakens courage the most.

It is, then, those who enjoy the fruits of labour who are intended. But, as in a civilised country those who enjoy the products of one art are obliged to cultivate another on pain of being reduced to a shameful poverty, it follows that indolence and effeminacy are incompatible with the arts.

Paris is perhaps the most luxurious city in the world; in it pleasure is carried to the highest pitch of refinement; yet life there is perhaps harder than in any other city. That one man may live delicately, a hundred must labour without intermission. It comes into a lady's head that she ought to appear at an assembly in a certain dress; from that moment fifty workmen must go without sleep, and without time to eat or drink; she commands, and is obeyed as promptly as our monarch would be, because interest is the greatest monarch in the world.

This ardour for work, this passion for wealth, runs through every rank, from the workmen up to the highest in the land. Nobody likes to be poorer than he who is his immediate inferior. You may see at Paris a man with sufficient to live on till the end of the world, labouring constantly, and running the risk of shortening his days, to scrape together, as he says, a livelihood.

The same spirit prevails throughout the nation; nothing is to be seen but toil and industry. Where, then, is this effeminate people of which you talk so much?

I will suppose a kingdom, Rhedi, in which only those arts absolutely necessary for the cultivation of the land are allowed, which amount after all to a goodly number; and that all those which minister only to pleasure or to fancy are banished; I maintain that that state would be one of the most miserable in the whole world.

Though the inhabitants might have sufficient hardihood to do without so many things which their needs require, the people would decay daily; and the state would become so feeble, that there would be no force too petty to overcome it.

It would be easy to discuss this in detail, and to show you that the incomes of the subjects would cease almost entirely, and consequently that of the prince. There would hardly be any exchange of goods among the citizens, and there would be an end of that circulation of wealth, and of that increase of revenue, which arises from the dependence of the arts upon each other; each person would live upon his land, and would take from it only just enough to keep him from dying of hunger. But as this is sometimes not a twentieth part of the revenue of a state, the number of the inhabitants would diminish in proportion, until there remained of them also only a twentieth.

Consider attentively how much the revenue of industry amounts to. Land produces annually to its owner only a twentieth part of its value; but with one pistoleworth of colour a painter will make a picture which will be worth fifty. The like may be said of goldsmiths, of workers in wool and silk, and of all kinds of artisans.

From all this, one may conclude, Rhedi, that if a prince is to be powerful, it is necessary that his subjects should live in luxury; he ought to labour to procure all sorts of superfluities with as much care as the necessities of life.

Paris, the 14th of the moon of Chalval, 1717.

Letter 108

Rica to Ibben, at Smyrna

I have seen the young king.[1] His life is very precious to his people: it is not less so to the whole of Europe. But kings are like gods; and as long as they live must be considered immortal. His face is majestic, but pleasing; a good education in conjunction with a happy disposition, already give promise of a great prince.

They say that one can never tell the character of the kings of the west until they have passed through the two great ordeals of selecting their mistress and their confessor. We shall shortly see the one and the other labouring to possess the mind of this one: and on that account he will become the subject of great contentions. For under a young prince these two powers are always rivals; but they are reconciled and leagued together under an old one. Under a young prince a dervish has a very difficult part to play; the king's strength is his weakness; but the other triumphs alike in both his strength and his weakness.

When I arrived in France, I found the late king altogether governed by women, although at his age I believe him to have been the one monarch in the world who had least need of them. I heard a woman say one day, "Something must be done for that young colonel; I know his worth; I will speak to the minister for him." Another said, "It is surprising that that young abbé should have been overlooked; he must be made a bishop; he is well-born, and I can answer for his morals." You must not however suppose that the women who talked in this way were favourites of the prince: they had perhaps not spoken to him twice all their lives; which is nevertheless a very easy thing to do with European princes. But there is not a single person employed in any way at the court, in Paris, or in the provinces, who is not acquainted with some woman through whose hands pass all the favours and sometimes all the wrongs which he may wish done. These women are all in each other's secrets, and form a sort of republic, the members of which are always busy aiding and serving each other; it is like a state within a state; and anyone at court, in Paris, or in the provinces who sees the activity of the ministers, the magistrates, and the prelates, if he does not know the women who govern them, is like a man who sees a machine at work, but who is ignorant of the springs that move it.

Do you think, Ibben, that a woman consents to be the mistress of a minister for love of him? What an idea! It is in order that she may lay before him every morning five or six petitions; and the goodness of these women appears in the zeal with which they serve an infinite number of unfortunate people, who obtain for them an income of a hundred thousands livres.

They complain in Persia that the kingdom is governed by two or three women: it is much worse in France, where the women govern generally, and not only usurp all authority wholesale, but retail it among themselves.

Paris, the last day of the moon of Chalval, 1717.

Letter 109

*Usbek to * * **

There is a species of book unknown to us in Persia, and which seems to me to be very fashionable here: these are the journals.[1] Idleness feels flattered in reading them; it is so delightful to be able to run through thirty volumes in a quarter of an hour.

In most of these books, the author has not made the ordinary compliments, before the reader is in despair: he is made to enter half dead upon a subject drowned in the midst of a sea of words. This one would immortalise himself in duodecimo, that one in quarto; another with loftier propensities aims at a folio; he must therefore extend his subject to proportion; which he does without mercy, counting as nothing the trouble of the poor reader, who worries himself to death reducing what the author took such pains to amplify.

I cannot see, * * *, what merit there is in making such works; I could do it myself quite well, if I chose to ruin my health and a publisher.

The chief faults of these journalists is, that they talk only of new books; as if truth were always new. It seems to me that until a man has read all the old books, he has no right to prefer the new ones.

But when they lay it down as a law that they must never speak except of works hot from the press, they impose upon themselves another-which is, to be very tedious. They are very chary of criticising the works from which they make extracts, whatever their reason may be: and, indeed, what man is bold enough to wish to make ten or twelve enemies every month?

Most authors are like poets, who will take a caning without a murmur; but who, indifferent as to their shoulders, are so very jealous of their works, that they cannot endure the least criticism. It is necessary then to be very careful not to attack them in so sensitive a spot; and the journalists know it well. They therefore do just the contrary: they begin by praising the matter treated of; from this their first ineptitude they pass to the praise of the author, forced praise, for they have to do with people who are always on the alert, ever ready to see justice done themselves, and to attack with trenchant pen a foolhardy journalist.

Paris, the 5th of the moon of Zilcade, 1718.

Letter 110

*Rica to * * **

The University of Paris is the first-born daughter of the kings of France, and very aged; for she is more than nine hundred years old; and so she dotes now and again.

I have been told that she had at one time a great dispute with some doctors about the letter Q,[1] which they wanted to pronounce like K. The quarrel grew so warm that some of the disputants were despoiled of their substance. It became necessary for parliament to put an end to it; which it did by permitting, in a solemn decree, all the subjects of the king of France to pronounce that letter according to their fancy. It was very amusing to see the two most venerable institutions in Europe occupied in deciding the fate of a letter of the alphabet!

It seems, my dear * * *, that the ablest men grow stupid when they get together; and that, where you have the greatest number of wise men, there you have the least wisdom. Great bodies always pay so much attention to minor details, and idle customs, that essentials are never considered till afterwards. I have heard it said that a king of Arragon,[2] having assembled the states of Arragon and Catalonia, the first sessions were spent in deciding in what language the deliberations should be held: the dispute was lively, and the states would have broken up a thousand times, if they had not hit upon the expedient of putting the question in the Catalonian tongue, and the reply in that of Arragon.

Paris, the 25th of the moon of Zilhage, 1718.

Letter 111

*Rica to * * **

THE rôle of a fine lady is much more serious than one would imagine. Nothing could be more important than what takes place in the morning at her toilette among her servants: a general of an army devotes no more attention to the disposition of his right or of his reserve corps, than she gives to placing a patch which may fail, but from which she hopes or foresees success.

What mental worry, what care, to be continually reconciling the interests of two rivals; to appear neutral to both, while she is giving herself to them; and to act the part of peacemaker in all the strife she makes between them!

How she is occupied with the success and the renewal of pleasure parties, and in the prevention of all accidents that might interrupt them!

And with it all, the greatest trouble is taken, not to amuse oneself, but to appear to be amused. Bore them as much as you like, they will forgive you, so long as it is understood that they have been very merry.

Some days ago I was at a supper given by some ladies in the country. All the way they kept saying, "We must at least enjoy ourselves immensely."

We happened to be very ill paired, and were consequently very dull. "I must confess," said one of these ladies, "that we are very merry; there is not in Paris to-day a party so gay as ours." As the wearisomeness of it all began to overpower me, a lady rallied me, and said, "Well, are we not getting on charmingly?" "Yes," I replied, yawning; "I believe I shall split my sides laughing." Melancholy, however, invaded all our thoughts; and as for me, I felt myself fall from yawn to yawn into a lethargic sleep, which put an end to all my mirth.

Paris, the 11th of the moon of Maharram, 1718.

Letter 112

[1]*Usbek to * * **

THE reign of the late king was so long that the end of it had caused the beginning to be forgotten. Now it is the fashion to occupy oneself with the events that happened in his minority; and nothing is read but the memoirs of these times.

Here is the speech which one of the generals of the city of Paris delivered at a council of war: I confess I do not see anything very remarkable in it:

"Gentlemen, although our troops have been repulsed with loss, I think it will be easy to retrieve this misfortune. I have six couplets all ready to publish, which I am certain will restore all matters to a proper balance. I have chosen some admirably clear voices, which issuing from the cavity of certain very powerful chests, will move the people wonderfully. They are set to an air which has hitherto produced quite a peculiar effect.

"If this is not enough, we can bring out a print representing Mazarin hanged.

"Fortunately for us, he does not speak French well; and he mutilates it in such a way, that his importance cannot fail to decline. We take care to make the people observe with what a ridiculous accent he speaks it.[2] Some days ago we made such sport of an absurd mistake in grammar, that it is now a joke in all the streets.

"I hope that before eight days have passed, the people will make the name of Mazarin a generic term to express all the beasts of burden and beasts of draught.

"Since our defeat, our songs about original sin have annoyed him so much, that, to save his party from being reduced to half, he has been forced to send away all his pages.

"Rouse yourselves then; take courage, and be sure that with our hisses we shall send him packing over the mountains."

Paris, the 4th of the moon of Chahban, 1718.

Rhedi to Usbek, at Paris

DURING my stay in Europe, I read the ancient and modern historians: I compare all times; I please myself with watching them pass before me as it were; above all, my thoughts are fixed upon those great changes which have made the ages so different from each other, and the earth so unlike itself.

You have perhaps given some attention to a matter which continually occasions my surprise. How is the world so thinly peopled in comparison with what it was once?[1] How has nature lost the wonderful fruitfulness of the first ages? Can it be that she is already old and fallen into decline?

I dwelt for more than a year in Italy, where I saw nothing but the ruins of that ancient Italy, so famous in former times. Although all the people live in the towns, they are quite deserted and empty: they seem to exist only to indicate the places where those powerful cities stood of which history says so much.

Some people here pretend that the city of Rome alone contained formerly more people than one of the great kingdoms of Europe does to-day. There were Roman citizens who had ten, and even twenty thousand slaves, without counting those employed in their country houses; and as it is calculated that there were four or five hundred thousand citizens, the imagination rebels at any attempt to fix the number of the inhabitants.

In Sicily, there were formerly powerful and densely peopled kingdoms, which have since disappeared: that island has nothing more notable now than volcanoes.

Greece is so deserted that it does not contain a hundredth part of its ancient inhabitants.

Spain, once so crowded, can now show only uninhabited lands; and France is nothing compared with that ancient Gaul of which Cæsar speaks.[2]

The countries of the north are sadly thinned; and the people no longer require, as formerly, to divide themselves, and set out in swarms, in colonies, in whole nations, to seek for new abodes.

Poland and Turkey in Europe have almost no inhabitants.

We cannot find in America the fiftieth part of the men who formed the great empires there.

Asia is hardly in a better state. Asia Minor, which contained so many powerful monarchies, and such an immense number of great cities, has now no more than two or three. As regards the greater Asia, that part which is under the Turk is not more populous; and if that part of it which is under the dominion of our kings be compared with the prosperous state in which it once was, it will be found to contain a very small part of the innumerable inhabitants which it possessed in the times of Xerxes and Darius.

As for the petty states which border these great empires, they are really deserts, such as the kingdoms of Irimetta, Circassia, and Guriel. These princes with vast territories, rule over a bare fifty thousand subjects.

Egypt is not less deficient than the other countries.

In short, I have reviewed the whole world, and found nothing but decay: I think I see the earth emerging from the ravages of pestilence and famine.

Africa has always been so little known, that one cannot speak of it so precisely as of the other parts of the world; but, dealing only with the Mediterranean shores, which have always been known, it is plain that it has fallen away sadly from what it was under the Carthaginians and the Romans. To-day, its princes are so weak that they are the most inconsiderable potentates in the world.

After a calculation as exact as may be in the circumstances, I have found that there are upon the earth hardly one tenth part of the people which there were in ancient times. And the astonishing thing is, that the depopulation goes on daily: if it continues, in ten centuries the earth will be a desert.

Here, my dear Usbek, you have the most terrible calamity that can ever happen in the world. But we have scarcely perceived it, because it has stolen upon us gradually in the course of a great many centuries, which denotes an inward defect, a secret and hidden poison, a malady of declining, afflicting human nature.

Venice, the 10th of the moon of Rhegeb, 1718.

Letter 114

Usbek to Rhedi, at Venice

THE earth, my dear Rhedi, is not incorruptible; even the heavens are not; astronomers are eye-witnesses of their changes, which are the perfectly natural effects of the universal motion of matter.

The earth is subject, like the other planets, to the laws of motion; it suffers within itself a continual strife among its elements; the sea and the land seem to be for ever at war; each moment produces new combinations.

Men, in an abode so subject to change, are likewise in an unsettled condition: a hundred thousand causes may operate against them capable of destroying them, and much more of increasing or diminishing their number.

I do not refer to those special catastrophes, so common in history, which have destroyed whole cities and kingdoms: there are general ones which many a time have brought the human race next door to destruction.

History is full of those universal plagues which have one after the other desolated the earth. They tell of one which was so violent that it blasted the very roots of plants, and made itself felt throughout the known world, as far as the empire of China; one degree more of corruption would have destroyed, perhaps in a single day, the whole human race.

It is not two centuries since the most shameful of all diseases overran Europe, Asia, and Africa; in a very short time it worked terrible havoc; had it continued its progress with unchanging fury, it would have destroyed the race. Burdened with disease from their birth, and incapable of sustaining the duties of society, men would have perished miserably.

How would it have been, had the poison possessed a little more strength, as it would certainly have done, if, fortunately there had not been found a remedy as powerful as any yet discovered![1] Perhaps that disease, which attacks the organs of generation, would have ended by attacking generation itself.

But why do I talk of destruction that might have happened to the whole human race? Has it not already taken place? Did not the Flood reduce mankind to one single family?

There are philosophers who distinguish two creations: that of things, and that of man. They cannot believe that matter and created things have been in existence only six thousand years; that during all eternity God delayed His works, and only yesterday began to use His creative power. Was it because He could not, or because He would not? But if He could not at one time, neither could He at another. It is then because He would not; but, as time does not exist for God, if it is granted that He willed a thing once, He willed it always, and from the beginning.

However, all historians speak of a first father: they show us the origin of human nature. Is it not natural to suppose that Adam was saved from some general calamity, as Noah was, from the Flood; and that such great events have been of frequent occurrence since the creation of the world? But all destructions have not been violent. We see many parts of the earth tired out with providing subsistence for men; how do we know that the whole earth has not within itself general causes of debility, slow-working and imperceptible?

It has been a satisfaction to me to give you these general ideas before replying more particularly to your letter on the decrease of mankind which has been going on for seventeen or eighteen centuries. I will show you in a succeeding letter, that moral causes, independently of physical ones, have produced this effect.

Paris, the 8th of the moon of Chahban, 1718.

Usbek to the Same

YOU ask from what cause the earth is less populous than it was formerly; if you give the question good heed you will see that this great difference is the result of a moral change.

Things are much altered since the Christian and Mohammedan religions divided the Roman world; these two religions have not been nearly so favourable to the propagation of the species as that of those masters of the world.

In it, polygamy was prohibited; and in that respect it had a great advantage over the Mohammedan religion; and it had another, and no less considerable advantage over Christianity in that it permitted divorce.

I find nothing so inconsistent as that plurality of wives permitted by the holy Koran, and the command to satisfy them in the same book. "Visit your wives," said the Prophet, "because you are as necessary to them as their garments, and they, as necessary to you as yours." Here is a precept which renders the life of a true Mussulman very laborious. He who has four wives established by law, and only as many more concubines or slaves, must he not be weighed down by so many garments?

"Your wives are your tilth," the Prophet says again; "devote yourselves therefore to your labour, work for the good of your souls; and one day you will have your reward."

I look upon a good Mussulman as an athlete, destined to strive without respite, but who, soon weakened and overcome by his first toils, languishes even in the field of victory, and finds himself, so to speak, buried under his own triumphs.

Nature always works tardily, and, as it were, thriftily; her operations are never violent; even in her productions she requires temperance; she never works but by rule and measure; if she be hurried she soon falls into decline, and employs all her remaining strength in self-preservation, losing entirely her productive faculty and productive power.

It is to this state of debility that we are always reduced by the great number of our wives, fitter to exhaust us than to satisfy us. It is quite common among us to see a man in a very large seraglio with but few children. The children themselves are for the most part weak and unhealthy, and share the languor of their father.

This is not all: these women, forced to be continent, require people to guard them, who must necessarily be eunuchs; religion, jealousy, reason itself permit the approach of no others; there must be many of these guards, both to maintain peace within doors amid the endless quarrels of the women, and to prevent attempts from without. So that a man who has ten wives or concubines, must have as many eunuchs to guard them. But what a loss for society in this great number of men practically dead from their birth! What depopulation must be the result!

The female slaves, kept in the seraglio to attend along with the eunuchs on this great number of women, almost always grow old there in a sorrowful virginity; as long as they are there they cannot marry; and their mistresses, once accustomed to them, hardly ever dismiss them.

You see how many persons of both sexes one man employs in his pleasures, causing them to die to the state, and making them useless for the propagation of the species.

Constantinople and Ispahan are the capitals of the two greatest empires of the world; every interest should converge towards them, and people, attracted in a thousand ways, should come to them from all quarters. And yet these cities are themselves decaying, and will soon be destroyed, if their rulers do not cause to repair thither almost every century whole nations to repeople them. I will discuss this subject further in another letter.

Paris, the 13th of the moon of Chahban, 1718.

Usbek to the Same

The Romans did not have fewer slaves than we; they had indeed more, but they made a better use of them.

Far from preventing by violent measures the multiplication of their slaves, they, on the contrary, favoured it to the best of their ability; they united them in marriages, of a kind, as much as they could; by this means they filled their houses with servants of both sexes and all ages; and the state with a countless people.

Children which in time became the wealth of a master were born around him without number; he alone was responsible for their upbringing and education; the fathers, freed from that burden, followed only the inclination of nature, and multiplied without the fear of too large a family.

I have told you that among us all the slaves are employed in guarding our wives, and in nothing else; that with regard to the state they are in a perpetual lethargy; with the result that industry and agriculture are necessarily confined to a few freemen and heads of families, who apply themselves as little as possible.

It was not thus among the Romans. The republic made use of this nation of slaves to its own great benefit. Each had his own savings, which he owned on conditions imposed by his master; and this hoard he employed in whatever direction his talent lay. One became a banker; another trafficked in cargoes; this one took to retail dealing; that one applied himself to some industry; or took to farming and cultivated the soil; there was not one of them who did not give himself with all his might to increase his savings, securing for himself in the meantime comfort in his present slavery, and the hope of future liberty; this made a diligent people and encouraged arts and industry.

These slaves, enriched by their thrift and toil, bought their freedom and became citizens. The republic was continually built up, and received into its bosom new families, in proportion as the old ones decayed.

In my future letters I shall perhaps take the opportunity to prove to you that the more men there are in a state, the more prosperous its commerce; I shall prove as easily, that as commerce flourishes, men increase; these two things necessarily aid and abet each other.

Since that is so, how much must this enormous number of slaves, always busy, have grown and increased? Industry and plenty produced them; and they on their side produce plenty and industry.

Paris, the 16th of the moon of Chahban, 1718.

Usbek to the Same

Hitherto we have discussed only Mohammedan countries, seeking the cause why they are less populous than those which were subject to the government of the Romans; let us now inquire what has produced this effect among the Christians.

Divorce, which was permitted in the Pagan religion, was forbidden by Christianity. This change, which appears at first of such slight importance, produced by degrees consequences so terrible, that one can hardly believe them.

This deprived marriage not only of all its sweetness, but attacked its very aim; the desire to tighten the knot, only loosened it; and instead of uniting hearts, as was pretended, it separated them for ever.

Into an action where all should be so free, and in which the heart ought to have so large a share, were introduced constraint, necessity, fate itself. Disgust, caprice, incompatibility of temper were not considered at all; the intention was to fix the heart, that is to say, to fix the most changeable and inconstant thing in nature; people, weary of one another, and almost always badly matched, were joined in an unchanging and hopeless union, as tyrants used to unite living men with dead bodies.

Nothing contributed more to a mutual attachment than the power of divorce: husband and wife were induced to endure patiently domestic troubles, knowing that they had the power to end them; and they often retained this power all their lives without using it, from the sole reflection that they were at liberty to do so.

It is not thus with the Christians, as their present troubles make them despair of the future. They see only that the discomforts of marriage are lasting, or rather everlasting; hence arise disgust, discord, contempt, and so far a loss to posterity. Three years of marriage are hardly over when its aim is neglected; then follow thirty years of coldness; private separations take place, more enduring, and probably more baneful, than if they had been public; the couple lead divided lives, and all to the prejudice of future generations. A man is soon surfeited with one everlasting woman, and betakes himself to harlots, a commerce shameful and opposed to society, which without fulfilling the object of marriage, represents at the best only its sensual pleasures.

If, of two persons thus united, one is not suited to nature's purpose and the propagation of the species, either constitutionally or on account of age, that party buries the other along with it and renders it as useless as it is itself.

It is not a matter of astonishment, then, to see among the Christians so many marriages producing such a small number of citizens. Divorce is abolished; badly assorted marriages cannot be amended; women do not pass as with the Romans through the hands of several husbands, who in turn made the best they could of them.

I dare to say that, in a republic like Lacedæmonia, where the citizens were continually plagued by peculiar and subtle laws, and in which the state was the only family, if it had been decreed that husbands could change their wives every year, an innumerable people would have been born.

It is very difficult to understand what reason led the Christians to abolish divorce. Marriage among all the nations of the world is a contract susceptible to all kinds of stipulations, and none should be banished from it, except such as would weaken its intention; but the Christians do not look at it in that light, and have taken much trouble to explain their point of view. They make out that marriage does not consist in sensual pleasure; on the contrary, as I have already told you, they seem to wish to exclude that as much as possible; with them it is a

symbol, a type, and something mysterious which I do not understand.
Paris, the 19th of the moon of Chahban, 1718.

Usbek to the Same

The prohibition of divorce is not the only cause of the depopulation of Christian countries: the great number of eunuchs which they have among them is another not less important.

I mean those priests and dervishes of both sexes who devote themselves to perpetual continence: this is with the Christians the virtue of virtues; in which I fail to understand them, not perceiving how that can be a virtue which results in nothing.

I find that their learned men distinctly contradict themselves, when they say that marriage is holy, and that celibacy, the opposite of marriage, is holier still; without considering that in matters of teaching and fundamental doctrines, the expedient is always the best.

The number of people professing celibacy is enormous. Formerly fathers condemned their children to it from the cradle; now they dedicate themselves from the age of fourteen, which amounts to pretty much the same thing.

The practice of continence has destroyed more men than plagues and the most sanguinary wars. In every religious house we see an unending family, where nobody is born, and which depends for its upkeep upon the rest of the world. These houses are always open, like so many pits, in which future generations are entombed.

This is a very different policy from that of the Romans, who instituted penal laws against those who rebelled against marriage, and wished to enjoy a liberty so opposed to the public good.

I am only referring here to Catholic countries. The Protestant religion grants the right of producing children to everybody; it permits neither priests nor dervishes; and if, in the establishment of that religion, which restored everything to an earlier order, its founders had not been constantly accused of incontinence, there can be no doubt that, after having made the practice of marriage universal, they would have lightened the yoke still further, and would have ended by removing entirely the barrier which separates, in this particular, the Nazarene and Mohammed.

But however that may be, it is certain that their religion gives the Protestants a great advantage over the Catholics.

I dare to say that, in the present state of Europe, it is not possible for the Catholic religion to exist there for five hundred years.

Before the humiliation of the power of Spain, the Catholics were much more powerful than the Protestants. Little by little the latter have arrived at an equality. The Protestants will become richer and more powerful, and the Catholics will grow weaker.

The Protestant countries ought to be, and are, in fact, more populous than the Catholic ones; from which it follows, firstly, that their revenue is greater, because it increases in proportion to the number of those who pay taxes; secondly, that their lands are better cultivated; lastly, that commerce is more prosperous, because there are more people who have fortunes to make; and that, with increased wants, there is an increase of resources to supply them. When there are only people enough to cultivate the land, trade must perish; and if there are no more than are necessary to carry on trade, agriculture must go to the wall; that is to say, both would be ruined at the same time, because devotion to the one can only be at the expense of the other.

As to Catholic countries, not only is agriculture abandoned, but industry itself is mischievous; it consists only in learning five or six words of a dead language. When a man has made this provision for himself, he need not trouble himself more about his fortune; in the cloister he finds a peaceful life, which would have cost him in the world, care and toil.

This is not all. The dervishes hold in their hand almost all the wealth of the state; they are a miserly crew, always getting, and never giving; they are continually hoarding their income to acquire capital. All this wealth falls as it were into a palsy: it is not circulated, it is not employed in trade, in industry, or in manufactures.

There is no Protestant prince who does not levy upon his people much heavier taxes than the Pope draws from his subjects; yet the latter are poor, while the former live in affluence. Commerce puts life into all ranks among the Protestants, and celibacy lays its hand of death upon all interests among the Catholics.

Paris, the 26th moon of Chahban, 1718.

Letter 119

Usbek to the Same

Having nothing further to say of Asia and Europe, let us pass on to Africa. We can really speak of nothing but its shores, as we do not know the interior.

The Barbary coast, where the Mohammedan religion is established, is not so populous as it was in the times of the Romans, for the reasons I have already given. As to the Guinea coast, it must be terribly depopulated, since for two hundred years the petty kings or village chiefs have been selling their subjects to the European princes for transportation to their American colonies.

A very remarkable thing about this America is, that while it receives every year new inhabitants, it is itself a desert, profiting nothing from the continual drain on Africa. Those slaves, transported into a foreign clime, perish there in thousands; and the work in the mines in which natives and foreigners are constantly employed, the poisonous vapours which issue from them, and the quicksilver which is continually in use, destroy them without remedy.

There is nothing more absurd than to cause countless numbers of men to perish in extracting from the bowels of the earth gold and silver, metals in themselves absolutely useless, and which constitute wealth only because they have been chosen as the symbols of it.

Paris, the last of the moon of Chahban, 1718.

Letter 120

Usbek to the Same

The fertility of a people depends sometimes on the most trifling circumstances in the world; so that often nothing more is necessary to increase its numbers than to give a new direction to its imagination.

The Jews, always being exterminated, and always increasing again, have repaired their continual losses and destruction by the single hope, shared by all their families, that from one of them shall spring a powerful king who will be the master of the world.

The ancient kings of Persia had such an immense number of subjects, simply because of that dogma of the Magian religion which declares that the deeds of men most acceptable to God are to beget a child, to till a field, and to plant a tree.

If the population of China is so enormous, it is only the result of a certain way of thinking; for since children look upon their parents as gods, reverence them as such in life, and honour them after death with sacrifices by means of which they believe that their souls, absorbed into Tyen,[1] recommence a new existence, each one is bent on increasing a family so dutiful in this life, and so necessary for the next.

On the other hand, the Mohammedan countries become daily more deserted, because of a belief, all-hallowed as it is, which fails not of most baneful effects when it is deeply rooted in the mind. We look upon ourselves as travellers, who ought to think only of another country: useful and lasting works, care to make provision for our children, projects which look beyond our own short and fleeting lives, seem to us somewhat absurd. Easy minded as regards the present, and without anxiety for the future, we trouble neither to repair public buildings, to reclaim wasted lands, nor to cultivate those which are suited for tillage; we live generally in a state of indifference, and allow Providence to do everything.

It is a spirit of vanity which established in Europe the unjust law of primogeniture, so unfavourable to propagation in that it fastens the attention of the father upon one of his children, and turns his eyes from all the others, forcing him in order to make a substantial fortune for one to prevent the settlement of several; and lastly, in that it destroys equality among citizens, which constitutes all their wealth.

Paris, the 4th of the moon of Rhamazan, 1718.

Letter 121

Usbek to the Same

Countries inhabited by savages are usually thinly peopled, on account of the dislike which they almost always have for toil and tillage. This unfortunate dislike is so strong, that when they invoke a curse against one of their enemies, they can wish him no greater evil than to be reduced to plough a field, believing that hunting and fishing are the only exercises worthy of them.

But, as there are often years in which hunting and fishing are very unproductive, they are desolated by frequent famines; without considering that game and fish are never abundant enough in any country to support a numerous people, because animals always forsake thickly-inhabited districts.

Besides, savage hordes, each numbering two or three hundred people, separated from each other, and having interests as divided as those of two empires, cannot maintain themselves, because they have not the resources of great states, whose members are all in accord, and work together for each other's good.

There is another custom not less baneful than the first; the cruel habit which the women have of procuring abortion, in order that their pregnancy may not make them disagreeable to their husbands.

There are dreadful laws against this crime, which are carried to excess. Every unmarried woman who does not declare her pregnancy before a magistrate is punished with death if her offspring dies:[1] shame and modesty, accidents even, are no excuses.

Paris, the 9th of the moon of Rhamazan, 1718.

Usbek to the Same

The ordinary effect of colonies is to weaken the countries from which they are taken, without peopling those which are colonized.[1]

Men ought to stay where they are: the change from a good climate to a bad one produces diseases, and others spring from the mere change itself.

The air, like the plants, is loaded with the particles of the soil of each country. It acts upon us in such a way as to fix our constitutions. When we are transported to a foreign country we become ill. The fluids being accustomed to a certain consistency and the solids to a certain arrangement, and both to a certain degree of motion, cannot put up with others, and resist a new order.

When a country is uninhabited, it is an indication of some particular defect in the nature of the soil or of the atmosphere: so that when men are removed from an agreeable clime to such a country, exactly the opposite of what was intended is done.

The Romans knew this by experience: they banished all their criminals to Sardinia, and sent the Jews there too. They had little difficulty in consoling themselves for their loss, on account of the contempt in which they held these wretched creatures.

The great Shah Abbas, wishing to deprive the Turks of the means of supporting large armies on the frontier, transported almost all the Armenians out of their own country, and sent more than twenty thousand families into the province of Guilan, where they nearly all perished in a very short time.

None of the transportations of people into Constantinople has ever succeeded.

The immense numbers of Negroes already mentioned have not peopled America.[2]

Since the destruction of the Jews under Adrian, Palestine has been uninhabited.

It must therefore be admitted that great depopulations are almost irreparable, because a people whose numbers are brought down to a certain point, remains there; and if by chance it recovers itself, it must be the work of ages.

If, in a state of decay, the least of the circumstances which I have mentioned comes to pass, a people not only never recovers, but falls off daily and approaches annihilation.

The expulsion of the Moors from Spain is still as much felt as at the time it happened; instead of the void being filled up, it grows greater every day.

Since the devastation of America, the Spaniards, who have taken the place of the ancient inhabitants, have not been able to repeople it: on the contrary, by a fatality, which I ought rather to call an instance of Divine justice, the destroyers are destroying themselves, and waste away daily.

Princes ought not therefore to think of peopling large countries by means of colonies. I do not say that they are not sometimes successful; there are climes so favourable, that the human race always multiplies there; witness the isles[3] which have been peopled by some sick folks abandoned by passing vessels, and who soon recovered their health there.

But, if these colonies were to succeed, in place of increasing power, they only divide it; unless they should happen to be of small extent, like those which are occupied for trading purposes.

The Carthagenians, like the Spaniards, discovered America, or, at any rate, certain large islands with which they carried on an enormous trade; but, when they beheld the number of their inhabitants decreasing, that wise republic forbade its subjects to carry on that trade, or to sail to these islands.

I dare affirm that, if in place of sending the Spaniards into the Indies, the Indians and cross-breeds had been transported to Spain; if its scattered people had been returned to it, and supposing only half of its great colonies had been preserved, Spain would have become the most formidable European power.

An empire may be compared to a tree whose branches, if too widely spread, draw all the sap from the trunk, and are of use only to give shade.

Nothing is fitter to cure in princes the rage for distant conquests than the example of the Portuguese and the Spaniards.

These two nations having conquered with inconceivable rapidity immense kingdoms, more amazed at their victories than the conquered peoples at their defeat, considered the means of preserving them, and chose each of them for that purpose a different method.

The Spaniards, despairing to keep the conquered nations faithful to them, took the plan of exterminating them, and of sending to Spain for dutiful subjects: never was a dreadful design carried out with greater thoroughness. A people, as numerous as all those of Europe together, was seen to disappear from the earth, on the arrival of these barbarians, who, in discovering the Indies, seemed only to have thought of discovering to mankind the utmost reach of cruelty.

By that barbarity, they held the country under their government. Judge from this what baleful things conquests are, since such are their effects. For, indeed, this horrible expedient was the only one.[4] How could they have kept so many millions of men in subjection? How could they have carried on a civil war at such a distance? What would have become of them, had they given these people time to recover from the consternation caused by the advent of these new gods, and from the terrors of their thunders?

As to the Portuguese, they took an entirely opposite course; they did not employ cruelty, and were consequently very soon expelled from all the countries which they had discovered. The Dutch favoured the rebellion of their foreign subjects against the Portuguese, and profited by it.

What prince would envy the lot of these conquerors? Who would wish for conquests on these conditions? One nation was soon driven out from its conquests; the other made them into deserts, and made a desert of its own country at the same time.

It is the destiny of heroes to ruin themselves by conquering countries which they suddenly lose, or by subjecting nations which they themselves are obliged to destroy; like that madman who wasted his substance in buying statues which he cast into the sea, and glasses which he broke as soon as bought.

Paris, the 18th of the moon of Rhamazan, 1718.

Letter 123

Usbek to the Same

The propagation of the species is wonderfully aided by a mild government. All republics are a standing proof of this; especially Switzerland and Holland, which, with regard to the nature of the land, are the two worst countries in Europe, and which are yet the most populous.

Nothing attracts strangers more than liberty, and its accompaniment, wealth: the latter is sought after for itself, and our necessity leads us into those countries in which we find the former.

Mankind multiplies in a country which affords abundance for the children, without diminishing in the least the parents' provision.

That very equality of the citizens which generally produces equality in their fortunes, brings plenty and vigour into all the parts of the body politic, and spreads these blessings throughout the whole state.

It is not so in countries subject to arbitrary power: the prince, the courtiers, and a few private persons, possess all the wealth, while all the rest groan in extreme poverty.

If a man is not well off, and feels that his children would be poorer than he, he will not marry; or if he does, he will be afraid of having too great a number of children, who would complete the ruin of his fortune and sink even lower than their father.

I admit that the boor or peasant, once married, will increase the race without any regard to his poverty or wealth; that consideration does not affect him: he has always a safe inheritance to leave his children, and that is his plough; so nothing withholds him from following blindly the instincts of nature.

But of what use to a state are those crowds of children which waste away in misery? They perish almost as rapidly as they are born: they never thrive: feeble and impotent, they die retail in a thousand ways, or are carried off wholesale by those frequent epidemics which poverty and bad diet always produce: those who escape attain the age of manhood without possessing its vigour, and waste away during the rest of their lives.

Men are like plants which never flourish if they are not well cultivated: among poor people, the race declines and sometimes even degenerates.

France supplies a great proof of all this. During the late wars, the dread which all the youths had of being enrolled in the militia forced them to marry, and that at too tender an age and in the bosom of poverty. A great many children were born of these numerous marriages who are not now to be found in France, because poverty, famine, and disease carried them off.

Now if, of a kingdom so well governed as France, and with such a good climate, remarks like these may be made, what shall be said of other states?

Paris, the 23rd of the moon of Rhamazan, 1718.

Letter 124

Usbek to the Mollah Mehemet Ali, Guardian of the Three Tombs, at Koum

To what end are the fasts of the imans, and the sackcloth of the mullahs? The hand of God has twice lain heavy upon the children of the law: the sun has obscured his beams and seems to shine only upon their overthrow: their armies assemble to be dispersed like dust.

The empire of the Osmanli is shaken by two defeats more disastrous than it ever experienced before. A Christian Mufti supports it with great difficulty: the grand vizier of Germany[1] is the scourge of God, sent to chastise the followers of Omar: he carries everywhere the wrath of Heaven, enraged at their rebellion and their treachery.

Holy spirit of the imans, thou weepest night and day over the children of the Prophet, whom the detestable Omar misled: thy bowels are moved at the sight of their misfortunes: thou desirest their conversion, and not their perdition: thou wouldst have them united under the standard of Hali through the tears of the saints; and not scattered among the mountains and the deserts through terror of the infidels.

Paris, the 1st of the moon of Chalval, 1718.

Letter 125

[1]Usbek to Rhedi, at Venice

What can be the motive of those immense gratuities which princes lavish upon their courtiers? Is it to attach them to themselves? They have gained them already as far as that is possible. And besides, should they gain some of their subjects by bribery, they would lose a great many others, impoverished by the very same means.

When I consider the situation of princes, always surrounded by greedy and insatiable men, I cannot but pity them; and I pity them still more, when they have not the strength to resist demands—always a task to those who need to ask for nothing.

I never hear talk of their liberality, of the favours and pensions which they grant, but I give myself up to a thousand reflections: a throng of ideas present themselves to my mind: it seems to me that I hear the following decree published:—

"The indefatigable courage of some of our subjects in suing for pensions, having taxed without intermission our royal magnificence, we have at length granted the multitude of requests presented to us, which hitherto have been the greatest anxiety of the throne. Some have represented to us that they have never failed since our accession to the crown to attend our levees; that we have always seen them in our progresses as motionless as posts; and that they have raised themselves on the highest shoulders to gaze at our serenity. We have even received several petitions on the part of some members of the fair sex, who have begged to draw attention to the notorious fact that they are very circumspect in their conversation: some very ancient dames have desired us, with shaking heads, to consider that they adorned the courts of the kings, our predecessors; and that if the generals of their armies have made the state formidable by their warlike deeds, they have made the court not less celebrated by their intrigues. And so, wishing to be bounteous to these suppliants, and to grant them all their desires, we have decreed what follows:—

"That every labourer, having five children, shall daily curtail by one fifth the bread which he gives them. We also admonish all fathers of families to decrease the share of each child in as just a proportion as possible.

"We expressly forbid all those who are engaged in the cultivation of their estates, or who rent them out in farms, to make any improvement in them of what kind soever.

"We decree that all persons engaged in base and mechanical trades, who have never attended a levee of Our Majesty, shall in future purchase clothes for themselves, their wives, and their children only once in four years: we further most strictly forbid them those little merry-makings which they have been accustomed to hold in their families on the principal festivals of the year.

"And, inasmuch as we are advised that the greater part of the citizens of our good towns are wholly occupied in providing establishments for their daughters, who have made themselves esteemed in our state only by a solemn and tedious modesty; we decree that their fathers shall delay their marriage until, having attained the age prescribed by the statutes, they can insist on being portioned. We forbid our magistrates to provide for the education of their children."

Paris, the 1st of the moon of Chalval, 1718.

*Rica to * * ***

It is a puzzling thing in all religions to give any idea of the pleasures ordained for those who live well. It is easy to terrify the wicked with a long list of the torments which await them; but who knows what to promise the virtuous. Joys seem by nature to be of short duration, the imagination can hardly picture them otherwise.

I have seen descriptions of Paradise sufficient to make all sensible people give up their hopes of it: some make the happy shades play incessantly on the flute; others condemn them to the torture of an everlasting promenade; while others, who represent them as dreaming on high of their mistresses below, are of opinion that a period of a hundred millions years is not sufficient to overcome a taste for the pains of love.

I remember, in this connection, a story which I heard told by a man who had been in the country of the Mogul; it shows that the Indian priests are as fertile as others in their ideas of the pleasure of Paradise.

A woman who had just lost her husband, went in due form to the governor of the city demanding permission to burn herself; but since, in the countries subject to the Mohammedans, they have abolished to the best of their ability that cruel custom, he refused her absolutely.

When she saw that her prayers were in vain, she flew into a transport of rage. "Look you," said she, "how you torment me! A poor woman is not even allowed to burn herself when she has a mind to! Did one ever see the like! My mother, my aunt, my sisters, were all decently burned! And, when I come to ask permission of this confounded governor, he gets angry, and begins raging like a madman."

A young bonze[1] happened to be present. "Infidel," said the governor to him, "is it you who have set on this woman to commit this folly?" "No," said he, "I never spoke to her; but if she believes as I do, she will complete her sacrifice; she will perform an action pleasing to the god Brahma: she will also be well rewarded, for she will find her husband in the other world, and begin with him a second marriage." "What do you say?" cried the woman, astonished. "I shall find my husband again? Ah! I will not burn myself then. He was jealous, peevish, and, besides, so old, that if the god Brahma has not brought about some improvement in him, assuredly he has no need of me. Burn myself for him! . . . not even the end of my finger to take him from the bottom of hell. Two old bonzes who misled me, and who knew what kind of life I led with him, took care to tell me nothing of this; if the god Brahma has no other present to make me, I renounce this felicity. Mr. Governor, I will be a Mohammedan. And for you," turning to the bonze, "you can, if you like, go and tell my husband that I am very well."

Paris, the 2nd of the moon of Chalval, 1718.

Letter 127

*Rica to Usbek, at * * ***

I expect you here to-morrow: meantime I send you your letters from Ispahan. Mine bring word that the ambassador of the Great Mogul[1] has received orders to quit the kingdom. They add that the prince, the uncle of the king,[2] who has charge of his education, has been arrested, conducted to a castle, where he is closely guarded, and deprived of all his honours. The fate of this prince moves me, and I pity him.

I own, Usbek, that I have never beheld the tears fall from the eyes of any one without deep sympathy: my humanity feels for the unhappy, as if they only were human; and great people even, towards whom my heart is hardened when they are prosperous, gain my affection in adversity.

Indeed, in the time of their prosperity what need have they of useless affection? It comes too near equality. They prefer respect, which requires no return. As soon, however, as they have fallen from their greatness, there is nothing left to recall it to them but our lamentation.

I find an admirable simplicity, and an equally admirable greatness, in the words of a prince, who, being in great danger of falling into the hands of his enemies, said to his courtiers, who stood weeping round him, "I see by your tears that I am still your king."

Paris, the 3rd of the moon of Chalval, 1718.

Letter 128

Rica to Ibben, at Smyrna

You have heard much talk of the famous king of Sweden:[1] while he was visiting the trenches, with an engineer as his sole companion, during the siege of a town in a kingdom called Norway, he received a wound in the head, of which he died. His prime minister[2] was immediately arrested, and the assembled states condemned him to lose his head.

He was accused of a very grave crime; that of having slandered the nation, and of having caused the king to lose confidence in it: an offence which, in my judgment, deserves a thousand deaths.

For, in short, if it is a villainous action to blacken the character of the meanest of his subjects in the eyes of a prince, what must it be to traduce an entire nation, and to withdraw from it the goodwill of him whom providence has set over it for its welfare?

I would have men talk with kings, as the angels talked with our holy Prophet.

You know that, in the sacred banquets, when the king of kings descends from the most sublime throne in the world to converse with his slaves, I laid a severe injunction on myself to restrain an unruly tongue: no one ever heard escape from me a single word which could be disagreeable to the meanest of his subjects. When it behoved me to cease to be sober, I never ceased to be a gentleman; and in that test of our fidelity I risked my life, but never my virtue.

I know not how it happens, but the wickedest king is hardly ever so bad as his minister; if he commits a vile action, it has nearly always been suggested to him: thus the ambition of princes is never so dangerous as the baseness of their advisers. But can you understand how a man who was yesterday made minister, and may perhaps to-morrow be disgraced, can become in a moment his own enemy, the enemy of his family, of his country, and of the people who are yet to be born of those he is about to oppress?

A prince has passions; the minister works on them: it is in that way that he manages his ministry: that is his only aim, nor does he desire another. The courtiers mislead him by their applause; and he flatters him more dangerously by his advice, by the designs with which he inspires him, and by the maxims which he proposes to him.

Paris, the 25th of the moon of Saphar, 1719.

Letter 129

*Rica to Usbek, at * * ***

As I was passing the other day over the Pont-Neuf with one of my friends, he met a man of his acquaintance, who, he said, was a geometer; and he looked it, for he was in a deep meditation: my friend had to tug at his sleeve for a long time and to shake him to bring him down to himself, he was so much occupied with a curve which had tormented him perhaps for more than a week. There was a most polite interchange of compliments, and they imparted to each other some items of literary news. Their talk continued till we came to the door of a coffee-house, which I entered with them.

I noticed that our geometer was received by everybody with marked cordiality, and that the coffee-house waiters made much more of him than of two musketeers who were in a corner. As for him, he appeared to be very well pleased with the company; for he unwrinkled his face a little, and fell a-smiling, as if there had not been the least particle of geometry in him.

However, his exact mind measured everything that was said in the conversation. He seemed like a man in a garden, who with a sword cuts off the head of every flower which rises above its neighbours. A martyr to his own accuracy, he was offended by a witty remark, as weak sight is annoyed by too strong a light. Nothing was indifferent to him provided it was true. Thus his conversation was very remarkable. He had come that day from the country with a man who had been to see a fine chateau and splendid gardens; but he himself had only seen a building sixty feet long and thirty-five wide, and a parallelogrammic grove of ten acres: he would have liked very much that the rules of perspective had been so observed that the walks of the avenues might have appeared throughout of the same width; and for that purpose he would have supplied an infallible method. He appeared to be much pleased with a dial which he had discovered there of a very peculiar make; and he became very angry with a learned man, who sat beside me, and unfortunately asked him if this dial indicated the Babylonian hours. A newsmonger spoke of the bombardment of the castle of Fontarabia; and he at once told us the properties of the line which the bombs described in the air; and, delighted with this bit of knowledge, he was quite content to be wholly ignorant of the success of the bombardment. A man complained that in the preceding winter he had been ruined by a flood. "What you say is agreeable to me," said the geometer. "I find that I am not mistaken in the observation which I made, and that there fell upon the earth two inches of water more than in the year before."

A moment after he left, and we followed him. As he walked very fast, and neglected to look before him, he ran full tilt against another man: they struck each other violently; and each rebounded from the collision in proportion to his speed and weight. When they had recovered somewhat from their dizziness, this man, pressing his hand on his forehead, said to the geometer, "I am very glad you ran against me, for I have great news to tell you: I have just published my Horace." "How!" exclaimed the geometer; "it is two thousand years since Horace was published." "You do not understand me," replied the other. "It is a translation of that ancient author which I have given to the world: I have been engaged as a translator for twenty years."

"What, sir!" rejoined the geometer; "have you been twenty years without thinking? You are only the mouthpiece of others." "Sir," replied the savant, "do you not think that I have done the public a great service in making them familiar with good authors?" "I am not so sure of that: I esteem as highly as any one the sublime geniuses whom you have travestied: but you are not as they; for though you translate for ever, you will never be translated.

"Translations are like copper money, which have quite the same value as a gold piece, and are even of greater use among the people; but they are base coin and always light.

"You wish, you say, to revive among us those illustrious dead; and I admit that you give them indeed a body; but you do not give the body life: the animating spirit is always wanting.

"Why do you not engage rather in seeking for some of those glorious truths which a simple calculation discovers for us every day?" After this piece of advice they parted, I imagine not in the best of humour with each other.

Paris, the last day of the second moon of Rebiab, 1719.

Letter 130

*Rica to * * ***

In this letter I shall tell you of a certain tribe called the Quidnuncs, who assemble in a splendid garden[1], where they are always indolently busy. They are utterly useless to the state, and half a century of their talk has no more effect than would be produced by a silence of the same length; yet they imagine themselves of consequence, because they converse about magnificent projects and discuss great interests.

The basis of their conversation is a frivolous and ridiculous curiosity: there is no cabinet, however mysterious, whose secrets they do not pretend to fathom; they will not admit that they are ignorant of anything; they know how many wives our august Sultan has, and how many children he begets every year; and, although they go to no expense for spies, they are informed of the measures he is taking to humble the Emperor of Turkey and the Great Mogul.

Hardly have they exhausted the present when they plunge into the future, and stealing a march on Providence, anticipate it in all its dealings with men. They take a general in hand, and after having praised him for a thousand follies which he has not committed, they prepare for him a thousand others which also will never come to pass.

They make armies fly like cranes, and overturn walls like a house of cards; they have bridges on all the rivers, secret paths in all the mountains, immense arsenals in burning deserts; they lack nothing but common sense.

A man with whom I lodged received a letter for a Quidnunc, which, as it seemed to me remarkable, I kept. Here it is:

"Sir,--I am seldom mistaken in my surmises on the affairs of the day. On the 1st of January 1711, I foretold that the Emperor Joseph would die in the course of a year: it is true that, as he was then quite well, I conceived that I would be derided, if I explained my meaning too clearly; which caused me to employ terms somewhat enigmatic; but rational people understood me well enough. On the 17th of April, in the same year, he died of the small-pox.

"As soon as war was declared between the Emperor and the Turks, I went through every corner of the Tuileries in search of our gentlemen: and having gathered them together near the basin, I prophesied to them that Belgrade would be besieged and taken. I was fortunate enough to have my prophecy fulfilled. It is true that towards the middle of the siege, I wagered a hundred pistoles that it would be taken on the 18th of August;[2] it was not taken till the day after: how tantalising to lose by so little!

"When I saw the Spanish fleet disembark in Sardinia, I judged that it would conquer it: I said so, and it proved true. Puffed up with this success, I added that the victorious fleet would land at Final, in order to conquer the Milanese. As this opinion encountered much opposition, I determined to support it nobly: I wagered fifty pistoles, and lost again; for that devil of an Alberoni, violating the treaty, sent his fleet to Sicily, and deceived at one and the same time two great politicians, the Duke of Savoy and myself.

"All this, sir, has disconcerted me so much, that I have resolved to continue prophesying, but never to bet. At the Tuileries formerly the practice of betting was quite unknown, and the late Count L.[3] would hardly permit it; but, since a crowd of petits-maîtres have got in among us, we don't know where we are. Hardly have we opened our mouths to report a piece of news, when one of these youngsters offers to bet against it.

"The other day, as I was opening my manuscript, and fixing my spectacles on my nose, one of those swaggering blades, catching promptly at the pause between my first and second words, said to me, 'I bet you a hundred pistoles that it's not.' I behaved as if I had not heard this piece of extravagance; and, resuming in a louder voice, I said, 'the Marshal of * * *, having learned . . .' 'That is false,' cried he. 'Yours news is always extravagant; there is an absence of common sense in all that.'

"I beg you, sir, to favour me with the loan of thirty pistoles; for I confess that these bets have almost ruined me. Herewith I send you copies of two letters which I have written to the minister. I am," &c.

Letters of a Quidnunc to the Minister

"My Lord,--I am the most loyal subject the king ever had. It was I who constrained one of my friends to undertake a scheme I had formed of a book, proving that Louis the Great was the greatest of all the princes who have deserved that title. I have been engaged for a long time on another work, which will increase the glory of our nation still further, if your highness will grant me a privilege:[4] my design is to prove that, since the beginning of the monarchy, the French have never been beaten, and that what historians have hitherto written of our defeats is the merest invention. I am obliged to correct them on many occasions; and I flatter myself that I shine above all as a critic. I am, my lord," &c.

"My Lord,--As we have lost the Count of L.,[5] we beg you to have the goodness to allow us to elect a president. Confusion reigns at all our meetings; and state affairs are not so thoroughly discussed as before: our young folks live without the slightest regard for their elders, and without any discipline among themselves: it is exactly like the council of Rehoboam, where the young overbore the old. We point out to them in vain that we were in peaceable possession of the Tuileries twenty years before they were born: I believe they will at last drive us out; and that, being forced to quit these quarters, where we have so often called up the shades of the French heroes, we will have to hold our meetings in the king's garden or in some more out-of-the-way place. I am . . ."

Paris, the 7th of the second moon of Gemmadi, 1719.

Letter 131

[1]*Rhedi to Rica, at Paris*

Nothing has interested me more since my arrival in Europe than the history and origin of republics. You know that most Asiatics have not only no notion of this form of government, but that their imagination is unable to conceive the possibility of there being any other in the world than despotism.

The first governments of which we know anything were monarchical; it was only by chance, and in the course of ages, that republics were formed.

Greece, having been destroyed by a flood, new inhabitants came to people it; it drew almost all its colonies from Egypt and the neighbouring countries of Asia; and as these countries were governed by kings, the races which came from them were governed in the same way. But the tyranny of these princes becoming intolerable, they threw off the yoke, and from the ruins of so many kingdoms sprang those republics which made Greece so prosperous, and the only cultured nation among a crowd of barbarians.

Love of liberty, and hatred of kings, preserved the independence of Greece for a long time, and extended far and wide the republican form of government. The Greek cities found allies in Asia Minor; they sent thither colonies as free as themselves, which served them as a rampart against the attacks of the kings of Persia. This is not all: Greece peopled Italy; and Italy, Spain, and perhaps Gaul. Every one knows that the wonderful Hesperia, so famous among the ancients, was at first Greece, regarded by its neighbours as an abode of bliss. The Greeks, who failed to find at home that happy country, went to Italy in search of it; the inhabitants of Italy, to Spain; and those of Spain, to Bettica or Portugal; so that all these countries bore the name of Hesperia among the ancients. These Greek colonies brought with them a spirit of liberty derived from that delightful land. It is on this account that we hardly ever hear of a monarchy in Italy, Spain, or Gaul in these remote times. It will shortly appear that the peoples of the north and of Germany were not less free; and if traces of kingly government are found among them, it is because the chiefs of armies or republics have been mistaken for monarchs.

All this took place in Europe, for Asia and Africa have always been oppressed by despots, with the exception of some cities in Asia Minor already mentioned, and the Carthagenian republic in Africa.

The world was divided between two powerful republics: that of Rome and that of Carthage. Nothing is better known than the beginnings of the Roman republic, and there is nothing of which we have less knowledge than the origin of that of Carthage. Of the African princes who succeeded Dido, and how they lost their power, we know absolutely nothing. The wonderful rise of the Roman republic would have been of immense benefit to the world, if there had not existed an unjust distinction between the Roman citizens and the conquered nations; if the governors of provinces had received less power; if the righteous laws enacted to prevent their tyranny had been observed, and if, to render these laws of no effect, the governors had not employed the very wealth amassed by their injustice.

Liberty would seem to have been intended for the genius of the European races, and slavery for that of the Asiatics. In vain the Romans offered that priceless treasure to the Cappadocians. That mean-spirited nation refused it, and rushed into slavery with the same eagerness with which other races fly to liberty.

Caesar destroyed the Roman republic, and subjected it to arbitrary power.

For a long time Europe groaned under the violence of a military government, and the gentle Roman sway was changed into cruel oppression.

Meantime an immense number of unknown races came out of the north, and poured like torrents into the Roman provinces: finding it as easy to conquer as to rob, they dismembered the empire, and founded kingdoms. These peoples were free, and they put such restrictions on the authority of their kings, that they were properly only chiefs or generals. Thus these kingdoms, although founded by force, never endured the yoke of the conqueror. When the peoples of Asia, such as the Turks and the Tartars, made conquests, being subject to the will of one person, they thought only of providing him with new subjects and of establishing by force of arms his reign of might; but the peoples of the north, free in their own countries, having seized the Roman provinces, did not give their chiefs much power. Some of these races, indeed, like the Vandals in Africa, and the Goths in Spain, deposed their kings when they ceased to please them; and, amongst others, the power of the prince was limited in a thousand different ways; a great number of lords partook it with him; a war was never undertaken without their consent; the spoils were divided between the chief and the soldiers; and the laws were made in national assemblies. Here you have the fundamental principles of all those states which were formed from the ruins of the Roman Empire.

Venice, the 20th of the moon of Rhegeb, 1719.

Letter 132

*Rica to * * **

Five or six months ago I happened to be in a coffee-house, where I observed a gentleman well enough dressed who had the ear of the company; he spoke of the pleasure which life in Paris gave him, and lamented that the state of his affairs obliged him to pine away in the country. "I have," said he, "fifteen thousand livres of income from the land, and I should think myself a happier man if I had a quarter of that property in money and portable effects. In vain I put the screw on my tenants, and burden them with the expenses of lawsuits: it only makes them less solvable; I can never manage to see a hundred pistoles at a time. If my debts amounted to ten thousand francs, all my lands would be seized, and I would be brought to the workhouse."

I left without having paid much attention to all this talk; but, finding myself yesterday in that quarter, I entered the same house, and there saw a solemn man, with a long pale face, who, in the midst of five or six chatterers, seemed sad and thoughtful, until he suddenly burst into the conversation, and said, in a loud voice, "Yes, gentlemen, I am ruined; I have nothing to live on, for I have at present at home two hundred thousand livres in bank-notes[1] , and a hundred thousand crowns in money; my situation is frightful; I thought myself rich, and here I am a beggar; if I had only a small estate to which I could retire, I would be sure at least of a livelihood, but I have not as much land as would fill this hat."

I happened to turn my head to the other side, and saw another man grimacing like one possessed. "Who can be trusted now?" cried he. "There is a traitor, whom I thought so much my friend, that I lent him my money; and he has paid it back! What abominable treachery! Whatever he may do now, in my opinion he will always be disgraced."[2]

Quite near him was a very ill-dressed man, who, raising his eyes to heaven, said, "God bless the schemes of our ministers! May stocks rise to two thousand livres, and may I see all the lacqueys of Paris richer than their masters!" I had the curiosity to ask what he was. "He is a very poor man," they said, "with a very poor profession: he is a genealogist, and he hopes that his art will become profitable if fortunes continue to be made, and that all the nouveaux riches will have need of him to improve their names, polish up their ancestors, and adorn their coaches; he imagines that he is about to make as many people of quality as he wants to, and he trembles with joy at the thought of an increased practice."

Lastly, I saw a pale thin man come in, whom I recognized for a Quidnunc before he had got seated; he was not one of those who are sure of victory in face of every reverse, and always predict triumphs and trophies; he was, on the contrary, a weak-kneed brother, whose news was always doleful. "Things have taken a very bad turn for us in Spain," he said; "we have no cavalry on the frontier, and it is feared that Prince Pio, who has a large force, will fleece the whole of Languedoc." Opposite me there sat a philosopher in shabby clothes, who held the Quidnunc in contempt, and shrugged his shoulders in proportion as the other grew loud. I approached him, and he whispered to me, "You see how this fop has plagued us for an hour with his fears for Languedoc; and I, who detected yesterday evening a spot in the sun, which, if it increase, may throw nature generally into a state of stagnation – I have not said a word about it."

Paris, the 17th of the moon of Rhamazan, 1719.

Letter 133

*Rica to * * ***

The other day I visited a great library in a convent of dervishes, to whose care it has been entrusted, and who are obliged to admit all comers at certain hours.

On entering I saw a grave-looking man, who walked up and down in the midst of a prodigious number of volumes which surrounded him. I approached him, and asked him to tell me what books those were which I saw better bound than others. "Sir," he replied, "I live here in a strange land, where I know no one. Many people ask me similar questions; but you can easily understand how I cannot read all these books to satisfy them; my librarian will tell you all you wish, for he employs himself night and day in deciphering all you see here; he is a good-for-nothing, and is a great expense to us, because he does no work for the convent. But I hear the refectory bell. Those who, like me, are at the head of a community, ought to be foremost in all its exercises." With that, the monk pushed me out, shut the door, and vanished from my sight as if he would have flown.

Paris, the 21st of the moon of Rhamazan, 1719.

Letter 134

Rica to the Same

Yesterday I returned to the same library, and met a man very different from him whom I had seen the first time. His manner was simple, his countenance intelligent, and his address most courteous. As soon as he understood my desire, he set himself to satisfy it, and even, as I was a stranger, to instruct me.

"Good father," said I, "what are those large volumes which fill all that side of the library?" "These," said he, "are interpretations of the Scriptures." "What a quantity there are!" rejoined I; "the Scriptures must have been very obscure formerly, and cannot fail to be very obvious now. Do any doubts remain? Are there any points left in dispute?" "Any, good heavens! any!" cried he; "there are almost as many as there are lines." "Indeed!" said I; "then what have all these authors done?" "These authors," he replied, "did not search the Scriptures for what ought to be believed, but for what they themselves believed; they did not regard the Scriptures as a work containing doctrines which they were bound to accept, but as a work which might sanction their own ideas; therefore it is that they have corrupted its meaning, and twisted every text. It is a country which all sects invade as if bent on pillage; it is a battlefield on which hostile nations encounter each other in endless engagements, attacking and skirmishing in every possible manner.

"Close to these you see books of asceticism and devotion; then books of morality, much more useful; theological tomes, doubly unintelligible, on account of the matter discussed, and the manner of treatment; and the works of the mystics, that is to say, of passionate-hearted devotees." "Ah, my father!" said I, "stay a moment; tell me about these mystics." "Sir," said he, "devotion warms a heart inclined to passion, and the heat mounting to the brain, produces ecstasies and raptures. This is the delirium of devotion; often it develops, or rather degenerates into quietism; you must know that a quietist is nothing else than a madman, a devotee, and a libertine, all in one.

"There are the casuists, who expose the secrets of the night; who form in their fancy all the monsters which the demon of love can produce, collect them, compare them, and make them the everlasting subject of their thoughts; happy are they, if their hearts do not become accomplices in the many debaucheries they describe with such simplicity and directness!

"You see, sir, that I think freely, and tell you all I think. I am naturally artless, and more so with you who are a stranger, desirous of information, and to know things as they are. If I wished, I could speak of all this with admiration, and be for ever saying, 'It is divine, it is worthy of all reverence, it is truly marvelous!' And there would happen one of two things: either I would deceive you, or I would lower myself in your regard."

There we stopped; some business called away the dervish, and interrupted our conversation till the morrow.

Paris, the 23rd of the moon of Rhamazan, 1719.

Letter 135

Rica to the Same

I returned at the appointed time; and my friend led me to the very spot we had left. "Here," he said, "are the grammarians, the glossers, and the commentators." "Father," said I, "have not all these people been able to dispense with common sense?" "Yes," said he, "they have; and yet it does not appear, and their works are not a penny the worse, which is very convenient for them." "True," said I; "and I know plenty of philosophers who would do well to occupy themselves with sciences of this kind."

"There," continued he, "are the orators who can convince people without employing reason; and the geometers, who compel a man to be convinced in spite of himself, and conquer him by sheer force.

"Here are metaphysical books, which deal with very lofty concerns indeed, and in which the infinite meets one at every turning; books of physics, which detect nothing more marvellous in the economy of the vast universe, than in the simplest machine of our craftsmen.

"Books of medicine, those monuments of the frailty of nature and of the power of art, which when they treat even of the slightest disorders make us tremble by bringing the idea of death home to us; but which when they discuss the power of remedies make us feel secure as if we were immortal.

"Near these are the books of anatomy, which do not so much contain descriptions of the parts of the human body, as the barbarous names which have been given them – neither likely to cure the patient of his disease nor the physician of his ignorance.

"Here are the alchemists, who inhabit now the hospital, now the madhouse, dwellings equally suitable for them.

"Here are the books of science, or rather of occult ignorance; of such are those which contain any kind of sorcery – execrable according to most people; in my opinion contemptible. Such also are the books of judicial astrology." "What do you say, father? The books of judicial astrology!" I cried with enthusiasm. "These are the books we make most of in Persia. They rule all the actions of our lives, and determine us in all our undertakings: in fact, the astrologers are our spiritual fathers, and more, for they take part in the government of the state." "If that is so," said he, "you live under a yoke much heavier than that of reason. Yours must be the strangest of all governments: I pity from my heart a family, and above all a nation, which permits the planets to have such ascendancy over them." "We make use of astrology," replied I, "just as you make use of algebra. Every nation has its proper science, according to which it guides its policy. All the astrologers together have never committed so many follies in Persia, as a single algebraist has done here. Do you think that the fortuitous concourse of the stars is not as sure a guide as all the fine reasoning of your system-monger?[1] If the votes on that subject were counted in France and in Persia, astrology would have good reason to triumph; you would see the schemers properly humbled, from which how disastrous a corollary might be deduced against them!"

Our dispute was interrupted, and I had to leave him.

Paris, the 26th of the moon of Rhamazan, 1719.

Letter 136

Rica to the Same

At our next interview, my learned instructor took me into a separate room. "Here," said he, "are the books of modern history. First of all, there are the historians of the Church, and of the Popes; books which I read for instruction, but which often produce in me an opposite effect.

"There are the works of those who have written of the decline of the great Roman Empire, which was formed from the ruins of so many monarchies, and from the destruction of which there sprang as many again. An infinite number of barbarous nations, as unknown as the countries which they inhabited, suddenly appeared, overran the Roman empire, ravaged it, cut it to pieces, and founded all the kingdoms which you now see in Europe. These races were not altogether barbarians, because they were free; but they became so afterwards, as the most part of them, having submitted to absolute power, lost that sweet freedom, so conformable to reason, to humanity, and to nature.

"There you see the historians of the German empire, which is but a shadow of the Roman one; but which is, I believe, the only power on earth unweakened by faction, and I believe also, the only one which grows stronger from its losses, and which, tardy in profiting by success, becomes invincible in defeat.

"Here are the historians of France, who show us to begin with the power of kings taking shape; then we see it perish twice, and reappear only to languish through many ages; but, insensibly gathering strength, and built up on all sides, it achieves its final stage: like those rivers which in their course lose their waters, or hide them under the earth; then reappearing again, swollen by the streams which flow into them, rapidly draw along with them all that opposes their passage.

"There you see the Spanish nation issuing from some mountains; the Mohammedan princes overcome as gradually as they had conquered quickly: many kingdoms joined in one vast monarchy, which became almost the only one; until, overborne by its own greatness and its fictitious wealth, it lost its strength and even its reputation, preserving only its original pride.

"These, again, are the historians of England. Here you may see liberty flaming up again and again from discord and sedition; the prince, always tottering up on immovable throne; a nation impatient, but prudent in its rage; and which, mistress of the sea (a thing unheard-of before), combines commerce with power.

"Near by are the historians of that other queen of the sea, the Republic of Holland, so respected in Europe, and so feared in Asia, where its merchants behold many a king bow to the dust before them.

"The historians of Italy show you a nation once mistress of the world, now the common slave; its princes disunited and weak, with no other attribute of sovereignty than an ineffectual policy.

"There are the historians of the republics: of Switzerland, which is the type of liberty; of Venice, resourceless but for its own thrift; and of Genoa, superb only because of its buildings.

"And here are those of the north—among others, of Poland, which makes such a bad use of its liberty and of the right it possesses of electing its kings, that it would seem to be its intention thereby to console its neighbours which have lost both the one and the other."

Thereupon we separated until next day.

Paris, the 2nd of the moon of Chalval, 1719.

Rica to the Same

Next morning he took me to another room. "Here," he said, "we have the poets; that is to say, those authors whose business it is to shackle common sense, and to smother reason with embellishment, as women were formerly buried under their ornaments and jewellery. You must know them; they are not uncommon in the east, where a hotter sun seems to give new heat even to the imagination."[1]

"There are the epic poems." "Ah! And what are epic poems?" Indeed," said he, "I don't know; critics say that there were never more than two, and that the others, which go by the name, are not epics: that, too, I know nothing about. They say, besides, what is still more surprising, that it is impossible to make more.[2]

"Here are the dramatic poets, which are, in my opinion, the best of all, and the masters of passion. There are two kinds: the comic dramatists, who move us so agreeably, and the tragic dramatists, who rouse our passions and shake our dispostions.

"And here are the lyric poets, whom I despise as much as I esteem the others, and who have reduced art to the production of melodious nonsense.

"Then come the authors of idylls and eclogues, which charm even courtiers, who imagine that they receive from them a feeling of serenity which they do not possess, and that they are brought face to face with the pastoral life.

"But of all the authors we have passed in review, here are the most dangerous: those, namely, who forge epigrams, little, sharp darts, which make a deep and incurable wound.

"Here you see the romances, whose authors are a sort of poets, and who are as extravagant in their wit as they are outrageous in their treatment of passion: they spend their lives seeking nature and never finding it: their heroes are about as natural as winged dragons and hippogriffs."

"I have seen," said I, "some of your romances, and if you could see ours, you would be yet more disgusted. They are as unnatural as yours, and, on account of our manners, excessively tedious; it takes ten years of devotion before a lover may be allowed as much as to see the face of his mistress. Yet the authors are compelled to conduct their readers through these wearisome preliminaries. As it is impossible that incidents should be endlessly varied, they have recourse to an artifice worse than the evil they would remedy; I mean the introduction of prodigies. I am sure you would not approve of a sorceress causing an army to spring out of the earth, or of a hero destroying single-handed a hundred thousand men. Yet such are our romances; the repetition of these dull adventures tires us out, and these absurd marvels disgust us."

Paris, the 6th of the moon of Chalval, 1719.

Letter 138

Rica to Ibben, at Smyrna

Ministers succeed and destroy each other here like the seasons; during three years I have seen the financial system change four times. To-day taxes are levied in Turkey and Persia, as they were levied by the founders of these empires; a state of affairs very different from that which exists here. It is true that we do not set about it so intelligently as the people of the west. We imagine that there is no more difference between the administration of the revenues of a prince and the fortune of a private person, than there is between counting a hundred thousand tomans and counting only a hundred; but the matter is very much more delicate and mysterious. It requires the greatest geniuses to work night and day, inventing endless new schemes with all the pains of travail; they must listen to the advice of a multitude of people, who, unasked, meddle in their affairs; they have to retire and live shut up in closets inaccessible to the great, and worshipped by the small; they must always have their heads full of important secrets, miraculous plans, and new systems; and, being absorbed in thought, it behoves them to be deprived of the use of speech, and sometimes even of the ability to be polite.

No sooner had the late king died, than they thought of setting up a new administration. They felt that things were in a bad way; but knew not how to bring about a better state. They did not believe in the unlimited authority of the preceding ministers; they wished the power to be divided. For that purpose five or six councils were created, and that ministry was perhaps the wisest of all those which have governed France; it did not last long, and neither did the good which it brought to pass.

France, at the death of the late king, was a body overcome by a thousand disorders: N***[1] took the knife in hand, cut away the useless flesh, and applied some local remedies. But there always remained an internal disease. A stranger came who undertook its cure.[2] After many violent remedies, he imagined he had put it into good condition, whereas it had only become unhealthily stout.

All who were rich six months ago are now paupers, and those who lacked bread are rolling in wealth. These two extremities never before approached so near. This foreigner has turned the state as an old-clothes man turns a coat; he causes that to appear uppermost which was under, and that which was above he places beneath. What unexpected fortunes, incredible even to those who made them! God creates men out of nothing with no greater expedition. How many valets are now waited on by their fellows, and may tomorrow be served by their former masters!

The oddest things happen as a result of all this. Lacqueys, who made their fortune in the last reign, brag to-day of their birth: they avenge themselves upon those who have just doffed their livery in a certain street,[3] for all the contempt poured out upon themselves six months before; they cry with all their might, "The nobility is ruined! What a chaotic condition the state is in! What confusion of ranks! Only nameless people now make fortunes!" And these nameless ones, you may be sure, will take their revenge on those who come after them; in thirty years as people of quality they will make sufficient noise in the world.

Paris, the 1st of the moon of Zilcade, 1720.

Letter 139

Rica to the Same

Here is an example of conjugal affection, wonderful in any woman, but much more so in a queen. The Queen of Sweden,[1] having quite made up here mind that the prince,[2] her husband, should share the government with her, in order to overcome all difficulties sent to the Assembly a declaration resigning the regency, provided they elected him.

Some sixty years ago or more another queen, called Christina, abdicated the throne in order to devote herself entirely to philosophy. I know not which of these two examples one ought to admire most.

Although I entirely approve of every one maintaining himself firmly in the station in which nature has placed him, and although I cannot praise the weakness of those who, feeling themselves inferior to their position, leave it by what is little short of desertion, yet I am much struck with the magnanimity of these two princesses, which enabled the mind of the one and the heart of the other to rise superior to their fortunes. Christina aspired to knowledge at an age when others think only of enjoyment; and the other wished to enjoy her power only that she might place her entire happiness in the hands of her noble husband.

Paris, the 27th of the moon of Maharram, 1720.

Letter 140

Rica to Usbek

The Parliament of Paris has just been banished to a little town called Pontoise.[1] The Council ordered it to register or approve a declaration dishonouring to it; and it registered it in a manner which dishonoured the Council.

Other parliaments of the kingdom are threatened with similar treatment.

These assemblies are always detested; they approach kings only to tell them disagreeable truths, and while a crowd of courtiers are never done representing to them that the people are quite happy under their rule, the parliaments come giving the lie to flattery, and carrying to the foot of the throne the tearful complaints committed to them.

When it is necessary to bear it into the presence of princes, truth, my dear Usbek, is a heavy burden! It ought therefore to be remembered that those who do so are constrained to it, and that they never would have made up their minds to a course so disagreeable and distressing for those who undertake it, if they were not compelled by their duty, their respect, and even by their affection.

Paris, the 21st of the first moon of Gemmadi, 1720.

*Rica to the Same, at * * **

I will visit you at the end of the week. How pleasantly the time will pass in your company!

Some days ago, I was presented to a lady of the court who had taken a fancy to see my foreign figure. I found her beautiful, deserving the affection of our monarch, and a high rank in the sacred place where his heart reposes.

She asked me a thousand questions about the customs and lifestyles of the Persians, and the style of life led by the Persian women. The life of the seraglio did not appear to her taste, and she displayed repugnance at the idea of one man being shared among ten or a dozen women. She could not think of the men's happiness without envy, nor of the condition of the women without compassion. As she loved reading, above all the works of the poets and romance-writers, she desired me to talk to her of ours. What I told her redoubled her curiosity; she begged me to translate for her a portion of one of those which I have with me. I did so, and sent to her, some days after, a Persian tale. Perhaps you will be amused to see it in my translation.

In the time of Sheik Ali-Khan, there lived in Persia a woman called Zulema; she knew the whole of the sacred Koran by heart; not a dervish among them understood better than she the traditions of the holy prophets; the Arab scholars never said anything so mysterious that she could not comprehend all its meaning; and she united to all this learning a cast of mind so sprightly, that those who heard her talk could hardly make out whether she meant to amuse or instruct them.

Once, while she was with her companions in a room of the seraglio, one of them asked her what she thought of the next life; and if she held to that ancient tradition of our doctors which declares that Paradise was made for men alone.

"It is the general opinion," she said; "nothing has been left undone to degrade our sex. There is even a race scattered throughout Persia, called the Jews, who maintain, by the authority of their sacred writings, that we have no souls.

"These most insulting opinions have no other origin than the vanity of men, who wish to carry their superiority even beyond this life, forgetting that at the last day all creatures will appear before God as nothing, and that no one will have any advantage over another except that which virtue gives.

"God will be impartial in His rewards: and as those men who have led a good life, and have made a good use of the power which they have over us here below, will be sent to a paradise full of beauties so celestial and ravishing, that were a mortal to see them, he would at once kill himself in his impatience to enjoy them; so virtuous women will enter into a delightful abode, where they will be surfeited with a torrent of pleasure in the arms of godlike men who will be at their beck: each of them will have a seraglio in which these men will be sequestrated, with eunuchs, even more faithful than ours, to guard them.

"I have read," she continued, "in an Arab book, of a man called Ibrahim, who was insufferably jealous. He had twelve exceedingly beautiful wives, to whom he behaved in a most barbarous fashion; he had no faith in his eunuchs, nor in the walls of his seraglio; he kept them almost always under lock and key, shut up in their rooms, and unable to see, or speak to, each other; for he was jealous even of an innocent friendship: all his actions were coloured by his brutal nature: a soft word was never heard to issue from his mouth: and he never gave them the slightest attention, except to add something to the severity of their slavery.

"One day when he had them all gathered together in an apartment of his seraglio, one, bolder than the rest, reproached him with his morose disposition. 'When one takes such strong measures to make himself feared,' she said, 'he always finds that he makes himself hated instead. We are so miserable that we cannot help wishing a change: others in my pace, would desire your death, it will be all the sweeter on that account.' This speech, which should have softened him, sent him off into a paroxysm of anger; he drew his dagger, and plunged it into her breast. 'My dear companions,' said she, with her dying breath, 'if Heaven has compassion on my virtue, you will be avenged.' With these words, she quitted this miserable life, and entered into the abode of bliss, where women who have followed virtue, enjoy a happiness which never palls.

"At first she saw a peasant meadow whose greenery was relieved with enamel of the brightest flowers: a river, the waters of which were purer than crystal, rolled through it in a labyrinth of meanders. Then she entered a delightful wood, where the silence was broken only by the sweet song of birds. Splendid gardens next opened on her view; on these nature had bestowed her simple charm as well as her magnificence. At last she came to a glorious palace prepared for her, and filled with heavenly men destined for her delight.

"Two of them advanced to her at once and undressed her: others led her to the sweetest essences: then they gave her garments infinitely richer than her old ones: after which they led her into a spacious apartment, where was a fire made of odorous woods, and a table spread with a most exquisite repast. All things seemed to unite to ravish every sense; she heard on one side a strain of lofty music, all the more so as it throbbed with passion; on the other, she beheld the dances of these godlike men, exclusively devoted to her pleasure. Yet all the pleasures were only intended to lead her by degrees to pleasures yet more entrancing. They conducted her to her bed chamber; and, having been again undressed, she was laid in a sumptuous bed, where two men of exquisite beauty received her in their arms. Then was she in a ecstasy of delight; her raptures exceeded even her desires. 'I am transported,' she said; 'I should not think of myself dying, were I not certain that I am immortal. It is too much; release me; I am overcome by excess of pleasure. Ah! you restore a little tranquility to my senses; I breathe again; I return to myself. Why have the lights been taken away? Why can I not still contemplate your godlike beauty? Why can I not see...But, what do I talk of seeing? You make me glide once more into my former transports. Sweet heavens! how soothing is this darkness! What! I shall be immortal; and immortal with you! I shall be...No; respite a moment; for I see that you are not likely to ask it.'

"After reiterated commands she was obeyed: but not until she seemed to wish it in good earnest. Drooping, she gave herself to repose, and slumbered in their arms. Two moments of sleep restored her strength, and she received two kisses which not only wakened her, but reawakened her passions. 'I am uneasy,' she said; 'I doubt you love me no longer.' It was a doubt in which she had no desire to remain long, and she soon had from them explanations as complete as she could desire. 'I see my mistake,' she cried; 'pardon me, pardon me, I will never doubt you again. You say nothing; but your actions prove it better than anything you could say; yes, yes, I own it; no one was ever loved so much. But, what is this! you contest which shall have the honor of convincing me! Ah! if you vie each other, if you join ambition to the pleasure of defeating me, I am lost; you will both be conquerors, and I, only, vanquished; but I will make you pay for your victory.'

"Day alone put an end to these delights. Her faithful and attached servants entered her chamber and caused the two young men to rise; they were reconducted by two old men to the rooms where they were kept for her pleasure. She then rose, and appeared before her devoted court, first in the charms of a simple undress, and afterwards apparelled in the most costly attire. The past night had increased her beauty; it had given greater brilliance to her complexion, and a new attraction to her charms. The entire day was spent in dances, concerts, feats, games, and promenades; and it was noticed, that Anais withdrew from time to time, and fled to her two young heroes: after some precious moments with them, she returned to the company which she had left, the expression of her face growing more and more serene. At last, towards evening, they lost sight of her altogether: she had gone to shut her self up in her seraglio, where she wished, she said, to make the acquaintances of those immortal captives who were to live with her forever and ever. She therefore visited those apartments, the most retired and the most delightful, where she counted fifty slaves, miracles of manly beauty; all night she went from room to room, receiving everywhere homage ever new, ever the same.

"Thus the immortal Anais passed her life, now in the midst of glittering throngs, now in solitary delight; admired by a brilliant company, or adored by a single ardent lover: often she would quit an enchanted palace, to pass into a rural grotto: flowers seemed to spring up at her tread, and pleasures crowded round her.

"During more than eight days she spent her time in that happy mansion, always transported, and without knowing it, and without having had a single moment of that mental repose, in which the soul, if I may say so, takes account of itself, and listens to its own discourse in the silence of the passions.

"The pleasures of the blessed are so engrossing, that they seldom enjoy this freedom of spirit: therefore it is that, being invincibly attached to present objects, they lose altogether the memory of things past, and have no longer any thought for that which they had known or loved in their other life.

"But Anais, whose spirit was truly philosophical, had passed almost all her life in meditation: she had pushed her thought much further than one would have expected from a woman left to herself. The severe seclusion in which her husband had kept her, had left her no other enjoyment.

"It was this strength of mind which had enabled her to despise the terror that had paralysed her companions, and death which was to be the end of her troubles and the beginning of her felicity.

"And so she recovered by degrees from intoxication of pleasure, and shut herself alone in a room of her palace. She gave the rein to pleasing reflection on her past condition and her present happiness; she could not help pitying the wretched lot of her companions: one can always sympathise with the miseries which one has shared. Anais did not confine herself, however, to compassion: so kindly disposed was she towards these unfortunate women, that she was constrained to aid them.

"She ordered one of the young men who were with her to assume the figure of her husband, go to his seraglio, master it, drive him out, and occupy his place until she recalled him.

"The execution was prompt: he cut through the air, and arrived at the door of the seraglio of Ibrahim, who happened to be away. He knocked; every door flew open; the eunuchs fell at his feet. He flew towards the apartments where the wives were shut up. He had in passing snatched the keys from the pocket of that jealous monster, to whom he had made himself invisible. He entered, and surprised the women first by his gentle and agreeable manner; and much more shortly after by the assiduity and the alacrity with which he embraced them. All were given cause to be astonished; and they would have taken it for a dream had there been less of reality about it.

"While these novel incidents were passing in the seraglio, Ibrahim thundered at the door, announced himself, and stormed and shouted. After having overcome many obstacles, he entered, to the great consternation of the eunuchs. He strode on, but recoiled like one dropped from the clouds when he saw the false Ibrahim, his perfect image, exercising all the liberties of a master. He called for help, and bade the eunuchs aid him to kill this impostor; but he was not obeyed. Only one weak resource remained to him; and that was, to refer the matter to the judgment of his wives. In a single hour the false Ibrahim had corrupted all his judges. He was driven away, and dragged ignominiously out of the seraglio; and he would have been killed a thousand times, if his rival had not ordered that his life should be spared. Lastly, the new Ibrahim, remaining master of the field, proved himself more and more a worthy choice, and distinguished himself by feats before unknown. 'You are not like Ibrahim,' said the women. 'Say rather that that impostor is not like me,' replied the triumphant Ibrahim. 'How could anyone deserve to be your husband, if what I do is insufficient.'

"'Ah! we shall be careful how we doubt,' said the women: 'if you are not Ibrahim, it is enough for us that you have so well deserved to be him: you are more Ibrahim, in one day, than he was in the course of ten years.' 'You promise me then,' replied he, 'that you will declare in my favour against the impostor?' 'Never doubt it,' cried they with one voice: 'we swear to be for ever faithful to you: we have been deceived quite long enough: the coward did not suspect our virtue, he suspected only his own impotence: we see clearly that men are not all made like him; it is you without a doubt whom they resemble: if you only knew how much you make us hate him!' 'Ah! I will often give you new occasions for hatred,' replied the false Ibrahim; 'you do not yet know how great a wrong he has done you.' 'We judge of his iniquity by the greatness of your revenge,' they replied. 'Yes, you are right,' said the godlike man; 'I have proportioned the punishment to the crime; and I am very glad that you are satisfied with my method of punishment.' 'But,' said these women, 'should this impostor return, what shall we do?' 'It would be, I believe, difficult for him to deceive you,' replied he: 'in the relation in which I stand to you, one could hardly maintain himself by trickery: and besides, I will send him so far away that you will hear no more of him Thereafter I shall take upon myself the care of your happiness. I will not be jealous; I know how to bind you to me without restraining you; I have a sufficiently good opinion of my own deserts to believe that you will be faithful to me; if not with me, with whom would you be virtuous?' This conversation lasted a long time between him and these women; the latter, more struck by the difference between the two Ibrahims than by their resemblance, were not specially desirous to have the mystery cleared up. At last, the desperate husband returned again to annoy them: he found his whole household rejoicing, and his wives more incredulous than ever. It was no place for a jealous man; he went away mad with rage: and the moment after, the false Ibrahim followed him, seized him, carried him through the air to a distance of two thousand leagues, and there dropped him.

"Ye gods, in what a wretched plight did these women find themselves during the absence of their dear Ibrahim! Already their eunuchs had resumed their accustomed severity; the whole household was in tears; sometimes they imagined that all that had happened was no more than a dream; they looked wistfully on each other, and recalled the slightest circumstances of these wonderful adventures. At last the heavenly Ibrahim returned more amiable than ever; it was evident to them that his journey had not put him about. The new master took a course so opposite to that of the other, that all his neighbors were amazed. He dismissed all the eunuchs, and opened his house to everybody: he would not even allow his wives to wear their veils. It was a most extraordinary thing to see them, feasting along with the men, and as free as they. Ibrahim believed, and rightly, that the customs of the country were not made for citizens such as he. Nevertheless, he spared no expense: he squandered with a lavish hand the possessions of the jealous husband, who, on his return three years after from the distant land to which he had been transported, found nothing left but his wives and thirty-six children."

Paris, the 26th of the first moon of Gemmadi, 1720.

Letter 142

Rica to Usbek, at ***

HERE is a letter which I received yesterday from a learned man: you will think it remarkable.

"SIR, -Six months ago I inherited from a very rich uncle five or six thousand livres and a magnificently furnished mansion. It is delightful to have wealth, when one knows how to make a good use of it. I have no ambition, nor any taste for pleasure: I am almost always shut up in a little room, where I lead the life of a savant. It is in such a place that the diligent antiquary is to be found.

"When my uncle died, I was very anxious to have him buried with the ceremonies observed by the ancient Greeks and Romans: but at that time I had neither lachrymatories, nor urns, nor antique lamps.

"Since then, however, I have provided myself with these precious rarities. Some days ago I sold my silver plate in order to buy an earthenware lamp which had given light to a Stoic philosopher. I have disposed of all the glass with which my uncle had covered almost all the walls of his rooms, that I might possess a little mirror, somewhat cracked, which had formerly been used by Virgil: it charms me to see my own features where those of the swan of Mantua have been reflected. That is not all: I have bought for a hundred louis-d'or five or six pieces of copper money which were current two thousand years ago. I do not think I have now in my house a single piece of furniture which was not made before the fall of the Roman empire. I have a cupboard full of the most valuable and costly manuscripts. Although it is ruining my sight, I much prefer to read them than printed copies, which are not so correct, and which are in everybody's hands. Although I hardly ever go out, that does not prevent me from having an ungovernable passion to be acquainted with all the old roads which date from the time of the Romans. There is one near my house which was made by a proconsul of Gaul about twelve hundred years ago. When I go to my place in the country, I never fail to take it, although it is very inconvenient, and leads me more than a league out of my way: but what really angers me are the wooden posts stuck up at certain intervals to indicate the distances of the neighbouring towns. I am in despair at the sight of these signposts, wretched substitutes for the military columns that stood there formerly: I have no doubt that I shall cause them to be set up again by my heirs, and that I shall be able to leave a will compelling them to do it. If, sir, you have such a thing as a Persian manuscript, you would oblige me very much by letting me have it: I will pay you your own price, and will give you into the bargain some works of mine, from which you will see that I am not a useless member of the republic of letters. Among them you will notice a dissertation in which I prove that the crown used formerly in triumphs, was of oak and not of laurel: you will admire another in which I show clearly, bylearned conjectures deduced from the weightiest Greek authors, that Cambyses was wounded, not in the right leg, but in the left; in another I demonstrate that a low forehead was a beauty much in request among the Romans. I will send you also a quarto volume, containing the explanation of a line in the sixth book of Virgil's Aeneid. All these things you will receive in a few days; and in the meantime I content myself with sending you the accompanying fragment of an ancient Greek mythologist, which has not yet been published, and which I discovered in the dust of a library.I must leave you now for an important matter which I have in hand, namely, the restoration of a beautiful passage in Pliny the naturalist, which has been strangely disfigured by the copyists of the fifth century. I am," &c.

FRAGMENT OF AN ANCIENT MYTHOLOGIST

"In an island near the Orcades, a child was born whose father was Aeolus, the god of the winds, and his mother a nymph of Caledonia.[1] They tell of him that he learned unaided to count with his fingers; and that from his fourth year he distinguished metals so well, that his mother having given him a ring of tin in exchange for one of gold, he perceived the deceit, and threw it away.

"When he had grown up, his father taught him the secret of enclosing the winds in skins, which he afterwards sold to all the travellers: but as the trade in winds was not very brisk in his country, he left it, and went up and down the world, accompanied by the blind god of chance.

"During his travels he learned that gold glittered in every part of Betica;[2] and he hurried thither at once. He was very badly received by Saturn,[3] who reigned then: but that god having quitted the earth, he judged it wise to go into all the cross-roads and cry continually in a hoarse voice, 'People of Betica, you think yourselves rich, because you have silver and gold! I pity your error. Be ruled by me: leave the land of the base metals; come into the empire of the imagination, and I promise you riches which astonish even you.' He immediately opened a great number of the skins which he had brought with him, and dealt out his merchandise to all who wished it.

"Next morning he returned to the same cross-roads, and cried, 'People of Betica, would you be rich? Imagine that I am very rich, and that you are very rich: get yourselves into the belief every morning that your fortune has been doubled during the night: rise, then, and if you have any creditors, go and pay them with what you have imagined, and tell them to imagine in their turn.'

"A few days after he appeared again, and spoke as follows: 'People of Betica, I perceive that your imagination is weaker than it was a day or two ago; try to bring it up to the strength of mine: I will place before you every morning a bill, which will be the source of wealth for you: you will see only four words,[4] but they will be of the highest significance, as they will settle the portions of your wives, the fortunes of your children, and the number of your domestics. And, as for you' –addressing those of the crowd who were nearest him –'as for you, my dear children (I may call you by that name, since you have received from me a second birth), my bill shall decide as to the magnificence of your equipages, the splendour of your feasts, and the number and pensions of your mistresses.'

"Some days later he came into the street, quite out of breath, and cried out in a violent passion, 'People of Betica, I counselled you to imagine, but you have not done so: well then, I now command you to imagine.' With that he left them abruptly; but on second thoughts retraced his steps. 'I understand that some of you are odious enough to keep your gold and silver. For the silver, let it go: but the gold…the gold…Ah! That stirs my anger!…I swear, by my sacred windbags, that if you do not bring it to me, I will inflict dire punishment upon you.'[5] Then he added, in the most seductive manner imaginable, 'Do you think it is to keep these wretched metals that I ask them from you? A proof of my good faith is, that when you brought me them some days ago, I gave you back at once one half.'[6]

"Next day, he kept at some distance, and endeavoured with soft and flattering voice to worm himself into their favour. 'People of Betica, I learn that a portion of your wealth is in foreign countries: I beg you to have it sent to me;[7] it will oblige me very much, and I will never forget your kindness.'

"The son of Aeolus was addressing people who were in no mood to be amused, yet they could not restrain their laughter; which caused him to slink away in a shame-faced manner. But, his courage having returned, he risked another little petition. 'I know that you have precious stones: in the name of Jupiter, get rid of them; nothing will so impoverish you as things of that kind; get rid of them, I tell you.[8] Should you be unable to do so yourselves, I can provide excellent agents. What wealth will pour in upon you, if you follow my advice! Yes, I promise you the very best my windbags contain.'

      "Then he got up on a platform, and, in a more resolute tone, said, 'People of Betica, I have compared the happy condition in which you now are with that in which I found you when I first came here; I behold you the richest people in the world: but, in order to crown your good fortune, allow me to deprive you of the half of your wealth.' With these words, the song of Aeolus soared away on rapid wings, and left his audience dumb with amazement, a result which brought him back next day, when he spoke as follows: 'I perceived yesterday that my speech displeased you very much. Very well! suppose that I have said nothing at all as yet. It is quite true; one half is too much. We must find some other expedient to arrive at the result which I have proposed. Let us gather all our wealth into one place; we can do so easily, because it does not occupy much space.' Immediately three-quarters of their wealth had disappeared."[9]

     Paris, the 9th moon of Chahban, 1720.

Letter 143

Rica to Nathaniel Levi, Jewish Physician at Leghorn

You ask me what I think of the virtues of amulets, and the power of talismans. Why do you address yourself to me? You are a Jew and I am a Mohammedan, that is to say, two very superstitious people.

I carry about me always two thousand passages from the holy Koran: on my arms I fasten a little slip on which are written the names of more than two hundred dervishes: the names of Hali, of Fatima, and of all the saintliest ones, are hidden in my clothes in more than twenty places.

However, I do not disapprove of those who refuse to believe in the power ascribed to certain words. We find it more difficult to reply to their arguments, than they to our experience. I carry about me all these sacred scraps through long habit, and in order to conform to a universal practice: I am certain that if they do not possess more virtue than the rings and other ornaments with which we deck ourselves, they have at least as much. You, on the other hand, place your entire confidence in some mysterious letters; and without that safeguard would be in perpetual dread.

Men are most unfortunate beings. They hover constantly between false hopes and ridiculous fears: and instead of relying on reason, make themselves monsters to terrify them, or phantoms to mislead them.

What effect do you think can be produced by an arrangement of certain letters? What evil effect can their derangement produce? What connection have they with the winds that they should calm tempests; with gunpowder, that they should overcome its force; with peccant humours, as doctors call them, and the morbific cause of diseases, that they should cure them?

What is most extraordinary is, that those who tire out their minds endeavouring to show the connection between certain events and occult powers, are forced to take as much trouble again to keep themselves from perceiving the true cause.

You will tell me that a battle was gained by means of certain spells; whereas I hold that you must be blind, not to see that the situation of the field, the number or courage of the soldiers, the experience of the captains, are sufficient to produce that effect, of which you willfully ignore the true cause.

I will grant for a moment that spells may exist: grant in your turn, for a moment, that they may not; which is far from impossible. What you grant me will not prevent two armies from encountering each other in battle: would you hold in that case that neither could defeat the other?

Do you believe that the battle will remain dubious until an invisible power comes to decide it? that every blow will be thrown away; all strategy in vain; and all courage useless?

Do you imagine that death, present on such occasions in a thousand forms, cannot produce in the minds of men those wild panics which you have such difficulty in explaining? Will you have it that in an army of a hundred thousand men there may not be a single coward? Do you think that the discouragement of such a one may not produce discouragement in another? That the second influencing a third, would soon make him produce a like effect upon a fourth? No more would be necessary to cause a whole army to be suddenly seized with despair, and the larger the army, the more sudden the seizure.

The whole world knows and feels that men, like all creatures actuated by self-preservation, are passionately attached to life: this is known to be the general rule; and yet people ask why on a particular occasion, they should fear to lose it.

Although the holy writings of all nations abound with accounts of these wild and supernatural panics, I can imagine nothing more ridiculous; because, to be certain that an effect which may be produced in a hundred thousand natural ways is supernatural, would require first of all proof positive that none of these causes had operated; which is impossible.

But I shall say no more about it, Nathaniel; it seems to me that it is not a subject deserving such serious treatment.

Paris, the 20th of the moon of Chahban, 1720.

P.S.-As I was concluding, I heard crying in the streets a letter from a country physician to one in Paris (for here every trifle is printed, published, and bought). I believe it is worth while sending it to you because it has some bearing on our subject.

Letter From a Country Physician to a Physician of Paris

"There was once in our town a sick person who had had no sleep for thirty-five days. His physician ordered him opium; but he could not make up his mind to take it, and when he had the cup in his hand he was less inclined than ever. At last, he said to his physician, 'Sir, give me only till to-morrow: I know a man who, although he does not practise medicine, has in his house an immense number of cures for insomnia; let me send for him: and if I do not sleep to-night, I promise to return to you.' The physician being dismissed, the sick man had his curtains closed, and said to his page, 'Go to M. Anis and ask him to come to me.' When M. Anis came the patient said to him, 'My dear sir, I am dying; I can't sleep: have you not in your shop the C. of the G.,[1] or some other book of devotion written by an R.P.J., [2] which you have not been able to sell, for long-kept remedies are often the best?' 'Sir,' replied the bookseller, 'I have the Holy Court of Father Caussin, [3] in six volumes, at your service; I will send it to you; and I hope you will be the better of it. If you would prefer the works of the reverend Father Rodrigo, a Spanish Jesuit, you need not want them. But, believe me, you had better stick to Father Caussin; I trust, with the help of God, that a single sentence of Father Caussin's will do you more good than a whole page of the C. of the G.' With that M. Anis left, and went to his shop to get the remedy. The Holy Court arrived; and the dust having been shaken off it, the son of the sick man, a schoolboy, began to read it: he was the first to feel its effects; at the second page, his utterance began to be almost inarticulate, and already the whole company was growing drowsy'; in a moment, everybody was snoring except the sick man, who, after having stood it a good while, was at last overcome, too."

"The physician arrived early next morning. 'Well,' he said, 'has my opiate been taken?' Nobody answered him: the sick man's wife, daughter, and little boy, radiant with joy, showed him Father Caussin. He asked what it was. They answered, 'Long life to Father Caussin; we must send him to be bound. Who would have said it? Who would have thought it? It is a miracle. Look, sir, look! Here is Father Caussin; it is this book which has given my father sleep.' And thereupon they explained the matter to him as it had happened."

"The physician was a skilful man, versed in the mysteries of the Cabala, and in the power of words and spirits. He was much struck, and, after deep thought, resolved to change his practice entirely. 'Here is indeed a notable fact!' said he. 'It is a new experience; and I must experiment further. And why should a spirit not be able to transmit to its work the same qualities which itself possesses? Do we not see it every day? At least it is well worth the trying. I am tired of the apothecaries; their syrups, their juleps, and all their galenical drugs destroy the health and the lives of their patients. Let us change the method, and try the power of the spirits.' With this idea, he drafted a new system of pharmacy, as you will see by the description which I am about to give you of the principal remedies which he employed."

"A Light Purgative"

"Take three leaves of Aristotle's logic in Greek; two leaves of a treatise on scholastic theology, the keener the better, as, for example, that of the subtle Scotus; four of Paracelsus; one of Avicenna; six of Averroes; three of Porphyry; as many of Plotinus, and as many of Jamblicus. Infuse the whole for twenty-four hours, and take four doses a day."

"A Stronger Purgative"

"Take ten A * * * of the C * * *, concerning the B * * * and the C * * * of the I * * *;[4] distil them in a water-bath; dilute a drop of the bitter and pungent product in a glass of common water; swallow the whole with confidence."

"An Emetic"

"Take six harangues; any dozen funeral orations, carefully excepting those of M. of N.; [5] a collection of new operas; fifty novels; thirty new memoirs. Put the whole in a large flask; leave it to settle for two days; then distil it on a sand-bath. And if all this should be insufficient, here is,

"Another More Powerful Emetic"

"Take a leaf of marbled paper which has served as cover to a collection of the pieces of the J.F., [6] infuse it for three minutes; warm a spoonful of the infusion, and drink it off."

"A Very Simple Cure for Asthma"

"Read all the works of the reverend Father Maimbourg, [7] formerly a Jesuit, taking care to pause only at the end of each sentence; and you will gradually find your power of breathing return to you so completely, that you will have no need to repeat the cure.

"An Antidote for the Itch, Rashes, Scaldhead, and Farcy"

"Take three of Aristotle's categories, two metaphysical degrees, one distinction, six lines of Chapelain, one phrase from the letters of the Abbe of Saint-Cyran; write them all on a piece of paper, fold it up, tie it to a ribbon, and carry it round your neck."

Miraculum chymicum, de violenta fermentatione, cum fumo, igne, et flamma.

"Misce Quesnellianam infusionem, cum infusione Lallemanianâ; fiat fermementatio cum magna vi, impetus et tonitru, acidio pugnantibus, et invicem penetrantibus alcalinos sales; fiet evaporation ardentium spiritium. Pone liquorem fermentatum in alembico; nihil inde extrahes, et nihil invenies, nisi caput mortuum."

"Lenitivum

"Recipe Molinae anodine chartas duas; Escobaris relaxativi paginas sex; Vasquii emollientis folium unum; infunde in aquae communis lib. iiij. Ad consumptionem dimidiae parties colentur et exprimantur; et, in expressione, dissolve Bauni detersive et Tamburini abluentis folia iij."

"Fiat clister."

"In chlorosim quam vulgus pallidos-colores, aut febrim amatoriam appellat "Recipe Aretini figures iiij.; R. Thomae Sanchii de matrimonies folia ij. Infuditur in aquae communis libras quinque. "Fiat ptisana aperiens.[8]

These are the drugs which our physician prescribed with remarkable success. 'He did not wish,' he said, 'lest he should kill his patients, to employ rare remedies, and such as are difficult to find-for example, a dedicatory epistle which had never made anybody yawn; too short a preface; a bishop's charge written by himself; and the work of a Jansenist despised by a Jansenist, or else admired by a Jesuit.' He held that remedies of that kind were only fit to maintain quackery, to which he had an insurmountable antipathy."

Letter 144

[1]*Usbek to Rica*

Some days ago I met in a country-house which I was visiting, two learned men who have a great reputation here. Their characters astonished me. The conversation of the first, justly estimated, reduced itself to this: "What I have said is true, because I have said it." The conversation of the second went the other way about: "What I have not said is not true, because I have not said it."

I liked the first pretty well; for it is not of the least consequence to me, however stiff in opinion a man may be but I cannot endure impertinence. The first defends his opinions; that is to say, his own property; the second attacks the opinions of others; that is to say, the property of the whole world.

Oh, my dear Rica,[2] how badly vanity serves those who have a larger share of it than is necessary for self-preservation! Such people wish to be admired by dint of offending. They wish to be superior, but they do not even attain to mediocrity.

Come hither to me, modest men, that I may embrace you! You are the charm, the delight of life. You think that you are nobodies; but I tell you that you possess the one thing needful. You think that no one is humiliated by you, and you humiliate the whole world. And when I compare you in my mind with those imperious people whom I see everywhere, I drag them from their judgment-seat, and throw them at your feet.

Paris, the 22nd of the moon of Chahban, 1720.

Letter 145

[1]*Usbek to * * ***

A MAN of genius is usually fastidious in society. He chooses few acquaintances; he finds the vast majority of people whom he is pleased to call bad company very tedious; and as he cannot altogether hide his disgust, he makes many enemies.

Sure of pleasing when he likes, he very often does not like.

He is much given to criticism, because he sees and feels more than others.

He almost always ruins his fortune, because his genius supplies him with a great variety of means for that purpose.

He fails in his undertakings because he attempts too much. His vision, which carries far, causes him to have in view objects which are too remote. It must also be remembered that, in projecting a scheme, he is less impressed by the difficulties which spring from it, than by the means of overcoming them, which he derives from his own resources.

He neglects minor details, although upon them the success of almost all great enterprises depends.

The mediocre man, on the other hand, tries to make use of everything, he is so well aware that he cannot afford to neglect trifles.

Universal approbation is very generally accorded to the mediocre man. Every one is delighted to give the latter praise, and enchanted to withhold it from the former. While envy expends itself on the one and nothing is forgiven him, everything is construed in the other's favour; vanity declares itself on his side.

But if so many disadvantages burden the man of genius, what is to be said of the hard lot of a scientific man?

I never think of it without recalling a letter written by a savant to one of his friends. Here it is:

"SIR, -I am a man whose nights are spent in studying through telescopes thirty feet long those great bodies which roll over our heads; and when I wish for relaxation, I take my little microscopes and examine a maggot or a mite.

"I am not rich, and I have only one room; I dare not even light a fire in it, because the unnatural warmth would cause the mercury to rise in my thermometer, which at the lowest, told me that my hands were freezing, I did not put myself about. And I have the consolation of knowing exactly the slightest changes in the weather for the whole of the past year.

"I have little intercourse with others; and among all the people whom I meet, I know no one. But there is a man at Stockholm, another at Leipsic, and another at London, whom I have never seen, and whom I shall doubtless never see, but with whom I keep up a correspondence so punctual, that I do not miss a single post.

"But although I know no one in my neighbourhood, my reputation here is so bad, that I shall sooner or later require to leave it. Five years ago I was grossly insulted by a woman for having dissected a dog which she pretended belonged to her. The wife of a butcher, who happened to be present, took her side. And, while the one abused me heartily, the other pelted me with stones, along with Dr. * * *, who was in my company, and who received such dreadful blows on the head, both back and front, that his mind was much shaken.

"Since that time, whenever a dog strays away from the street corner, it is at once taken for granted that he has passed through my hands. A decent citizen's wife, who had lost her pet dog, which she said she loved better than her children, came the other day and fainted in my room; not finding her dog, she summoned me before the magistrate. I believe I shall never be delivered from the persistent malice of these women, who, in shrieking tones, din me daily with the funeral oration of all the beasts that have died during the last six years. I am," etc.

All scientific men were formerly accused of magic. I am not surprised at it. Each one said to himself, "I have carried human capacity as far as it can go; and yet a certain savant has distanced me: beyond doubt he deals in sorcery."

Now that accusations of that kind have been discredited, another course has been taken; and the scientific man can hardly escape the reproach of ungodliness or of heresy. It is of little consequence that the people hold him innocent: the wound once made can never be quite closed again. It will always be a tender spot. An opponent will come thirty years after and say to him in an unassuming way, "God forbid that I should think you have been accused justly; but you were obliged to defend yourself." And thus his justification itself is turned against him.

If he writes a history, and shows himself of high intelligence and some share of righteousness, a thousand unjust accusations are brought against him. Some one will stir up the magistrate against him about an incident that took place ages ago, and if his pen is not to be bought they would have it restrained.

They are more fortunate, however, than those recreants who renounce their faith for trifling pension; who hardly make a single farthing by all their impostures; who overturn the constitution of the empire, diminish the rights of one state to increase those of another, give to princes what they have taken from the people, revive the obsolete rights, humour the passions which are in vogue in their time, and the favourite vices of the king; imposing upon posterity all the more infamously, that means are lacking to destroy their evidence.

But it is not enough that an author should have to endure all these insults; it is not enough that he should have been continually anxious about the success of his work. When it sees the light at last, that work, which has cost him so much, brings down upon him quarrels from all quarters. How can he avoid them? He holds an opinion, and maintains it in his writings, quite unaware that another man two hundred leagues away asserts the very reverse. There you have the way in which war arises.

But may he not hope to acquire some degree of fame? No; at the most he is only esteemed by those who have studied the same branch of science as he. The philosopher has a supreme contempt for the man whose head is stuffed with facts; and he in his turn is looked upon as a visionary by the possessor of a good memory.

As for those who profess haughty ignorance, they would have all mankind buried in the same oblivion as themselves.

When a man lacks a particular talent, he indemnifies himself by despising it: he removes the impediment between him and merit; and in that way finds himself on a level with those of whose works he formerly stood in awe.

Lastly, an author requires in pursuit of an equivocal reputation to abstain from all pleasure and sacrifice his health.

Paris, the 26th of the moon of Chahban, 1720.

Letter 146

[1]Usbek to Rhedi, at Venice

IT was long ago said that a minister cannot be great unless he is sincere.

A private person may avail himself of the obscurity in which he is placed; he discredits himself only in the opinion of a few, and the mask he wears deceives others; but a minister who steps aside from the straight path has a witness, a judge, in every subject of the state he governs.

Is it too daring to say that the greatest evil done by an unscrupulous minister is not the damage to the interests of his sovereign, not the ruin wrought among his people, but quite another thing, and in my opinion a thousand times more dangerous, namely the bad example which he sets?

You know that I have for a long time travelled in the Indies. There I beheld a nation, upright by nature, led away in an instant, from the lowest to the highest in the land, by the bad example of a minister; I beheld an entire race, in whom generosity, integrity, candour, and sincerity had always been regarded as natural qualities, become, in a flash, the most despicable of peoples; I beheld the contagion spread, sparing not even the healthiest members, and the most upright men act in the unworthiest manner, violating the first principles of justice, upon the vain pretext that injustice had been done to them.

They appealed to detestable laws, necessity, injustice and treachery, in support of the most iniquitous deeds.

I saw honesty banished from business, the holiest contracts become void, and all the laws of the family overturned. I saw miserly debtors, insolent in their poverty, unworthy instruments of the anger of the law and of the exigency of the time, make a pretence of payment, while they plunged a dagger into the bosom of their benefactors. I saw others, viler still, buy for the next to nothing, or rather gather from the ground oak leaves[2], and give them in exchange for the substance of widows and orphans.

I saw suddenly spring up in all hearts an insatiable thirst for riches. I saw men form in a moment a detestable conspiracy to acquire wealth, not by honest labour and liberal industry, but by the ruin of the sovereign, of the state, and of their fellow-citizens.

I saw a respectable citizen, in these disastrous times, never retire to rest without saying, "To-day I have ruined one family, to-morrow I shall ruin another."

"I am going," said another, "with a man in black who carries an inkhorn in his hand, and a pointed weapon[3] behind his ear, to assassinate all my creditors."

Another said, "I find that I am prospering: it is true that when I went three days ago to make a certain payment, I left a whole family in tears; that I have squandered the portions of two well-born girls; that I have deprived a boy of the means of education--his father will die of grief, the mother pines away broken-hearted: but I have only done what the law allows me."[4]

What crime can be greater than that which a minister commits when he corrupts the morals of a whole nation, debases the loftiest spirits, tarnishes the lustre of rank, obscures virtue itself, and levels the highest born with the most despised?

What will posterity say when it has to blush for the shame of its forefathers? What will the next generation say when it compares the iron age of earlier times with the age of gold which gave it birth? I doubt not that the nobles will remove from their genealogies a degree of nobility dishonouring to them, and leave the present generation in the oblivion it has so well deserved.

From Paris, the 11th of the moon of Rhamazan, 1720.

Letter 147

The Chief Eunuch to Usbek, at Paris

THINGS have come to such a pass here that it is not to be endured; your wives imagine that your departure exempts them from all restraint; there has been most atrocious behaviour: I myself tremble at the harrowing story I am about to tell.

Some days ago Zelis, on her way to the mosque, let her veil fall, and appeared before the people with her face almost wholly uncovered.

I found Zachi in bed with one of her maids, a thing absolutely forbidden by the laws of seraglio.

I intercepted, by the merest chance in the world, a letter which I send you: I have never been able to discover to whom it was sent.

Yesterday evening a young fellow was observed in the garden of the seraglio; he made his escape over the wall.

Add to this all that has not come to my knowledge; for you are certainly betrayed. I await your orders; and until the happy moment of their receipt, I shall be in a state of intolerable anxiety. But, if you do not leave all these women to my discretion, I will not be responsible for one of them, and will have news as heartrending to send you every day.

The Seraglio at Ispahan, the 1st of the moon of Rhegeb,1717.

Letter 148

Usbek to the Chief Eunuch, at the Seraglio at Ispahan

RECEIVE by this letter unlimited power over the whole seraglio; give your orders with as much authority as I do; let fear and terror accompany you; carry penance and chastisement from room to room; let dismay be upon all, and tears flow from every eye in your presence; examine the whole seraglio, beginning with the slaves; spare not my love: let all bow before your dreaded tribunal; bring to light the most hidden secrets; purify that infamous place, and restore banished virtue. For, from this moment, on your head shall be the slightest fault that may be committed. I imagine it was Zelis to whom the letter you intercepted was addressed: examine that matter with the eyes of the lynx.

* * *, *the 11th of the moon of Zilhage, 1718.*

Letter 149

Narsit to Usbek, at Paris

MAGNIFICENT lord, the cheif eunuch has just died: as I am the oldest of your slaves I have taken his place until you make known whom you select.

Two days after his death, one of your letters addressed to him was brought to me: I refrained from opening it, but covered it up respectfully,and locked it away, until you shall have informed me of your sacred pleasure.

Yesterday a slave came to me in the middle of the night, and told me that he had seen a young man in the seraglio: I rose, inquired into the matter, and found it had been a vision.

I kiss your feet, most noble lord; and beg you to confide in my zeal, my experience, and my old age.

The Seraglio at Ispahan, the 5th of the first moon of Gemmadi, 1718.

Letter 150

Usbek to Narsit, at the Seraglio at Ispahan

MISERABLE slave! you have in your hands letters which contain orders for prompt and strong measures; the least delay may reduce me to despair; and you remain inactive under an empty pretext!

Atrocious things are going on: perhaps the half of my slaves at this very moment merit death. With this I send you the letter which the chief eunuch wrote me before he died concerning these disorders. Had you opened the despatch addressed to him, you would have found bloody instructions. Read these instructions, and execute them, or you shall perish.

* * *, the 25th of the moon of Chalval, 1718.

Letter 151

Solim to Usbek, at Paris

WERE I to be silent any longer, I should be as guilty as the worst of the criminals in your seraglio.

I was the confidant of the chief eunuch, the most faithful of your slaves. When he felt himself near his end, he sent for me, and spoke to me as follows: "I am dying; but the only grief I have in leaving life, is that with my dying eyes I have seen the guilt of my master's wives. May Heaven preserve him from all the misery which I foresee! After my death, may my threatening shade appear to admonish these faithless ones of their duty, and to keep them still in awe! Here are the keys of those dreaded places; take them to the eldest of the black eunuchs. But if, after my death, he should prove a careless guardian, remember to let your master know." He expired in my arms with these words on his lips.

I know that he wrote you some time before his death about the conduct of your wives: there is in the seraglio a letter which would have carried terror to every bosom had it been opened. That which you wrote since has been intercepted three leagues from here. I know not how it is; but everything turns out badly. Meantime your wives do not maintain the least reserve: since the death of the chief eunuch, their licence knows no limit; Roxana alone abides by her duty, and preserves her modesty. Their morals grow more corrupt every day. The faces of your wives no longer exhibit that stern and noble virtue which reigned there formerly; the unusual gaiety which prevails is in my opinion an infallible sign of some uncustomary pleasure. In the smallest trifles, I notice that liberties are taken before unknown. Even among your slaves there prevails a certain disinclination to do their duty, and to obey rules, which surprises me; they are no longer inspired by that ardent zeal for your service, which seemed to animate the whole seraglio.

For the last eight days your wives have been seen in the country, at one of your most secluded seats. They say that the slave who has charge of it has been bribed; and that, on the day before your wives arrived, he concealed two men in a secret recess in the wall of the principal room, from which they came out at night, when we had retired. The old eunuch, who is at present our chief, is an imbecile, who can be made to believe anything.

I am possessed with a burning desire for vengeance on these traitors: and if Heaven, in your interest, ordains that you should think me capable of ruling, I promise you that, though your wives may not be virtuous, they shall at least be faithful.

The Seraglio at Ispahan, the 6th of the first moon of Rebiab, 1719.

Letter 152

Narsit to Usbek, at Paris

ROXANA and Zelis were anxious to go to the country; and I did not think it necessary to refuse them. Happy Usbek! The possessor of faithful wives, and ever watchful slaves; virtue seems to have made its home in the abode which I rule. Be assured that nothing shall happen of which you would not approve.

A misfortune has occurred which gives me great uneasiness. Some Armenian merchants, lately come to Ispahan, brought a letter of yours addressed to me; I sent a slave for it, but he was robbed on his return and the letter lost. Write me therefore at once; because I imagine that, at this juncture, you will have matters of importance to communicate to me.

The Seraglio at Fatme, the 6th of the first moon of Rebiab, 1719.

Letter 153

Usbek to Solim, at the Seraglio at Ispahan

I PLACE the sword in your hand. I entrust you with what is now to me the dearest thing in the world, my vengeance, to wit. In entering upon this new employment, banish all feeling, all pity. I have written to my wives to obey you implicitly; in their guilty confusion, they will sink down at your glance. I must owe to you my happiness and my peace of mind. Give me back my seraglio as I left it. Begin by purifying[1] it; exterminate the guilty, and make those quake with fear who are inclined to become so. What may you not expect from your master for such signal services? It only remains with yourself to obtain a position far above your present one, and above anything you have ever hoped for.

Paris, the 4th of the moon of Chabban, 1719.

Letter 154

Usbek to his Wives, at the Seraglio at Ispahan

MAY this letter fall among you like a thunderbolt from a stormy sky! Solim is your chief eunuch, not to guard you only, but to punish you. Let the whole seraglio humble itself before him. He is empowered to judge your past deeds; and in future he will subject you to a discipline so harsh, that, if you do not regret your virtue, you will certainly regret your liberty.

Paris, the 4th of the moon of Chabban, 1719.

Letter 155

Usbek to Nessir, at Ispahan

HAPPY is he, who estimating at its full value a life of ease and tranquility, makes his own family the centre of his thought, and knows no other land save that in which he was born!

I live in a barbarous country, surrounded by everything that offends me, and absent from all in which I am interested. A sombre melancholy holds me; I am dreadfully depressed: I feel as if I were about to be annihilated; and I only recover myself when some dismal jealousy awakes within me, and brings in its train fear, suspicion, hatred, and regret.

You understand me, Nessir; my heart is as open to you as your own. You would pity me, if you knew my deplorable condition. Sometimes I have to wait six whole months for news of the seraglio; I count every moment as it passes, prolonging them by my impatience; and when the expected moment is about to arrive, a sudden revolution takes place in my heart; my hand trembles to open a letter that may be fatal; the anxiety which caused my despair seems to me the happiest frame of mind in which I could be, and I dread to be forced from it by some stroke more cruel than a thousand deaths.

But, whatever reason I may have had to leave my country, and although I owe my life to my flight, I can no longer, Nessir, endure this dreadful exile. Should I not die all the same a prey to grief? I have pressed Rica a thousand times to leave this foreign land, but he always thwarts my purpose, and keeps me here under a thousand pretexts: he seems to have forgotten his country, or rather he seems to have forgotten me, he is so indifferent to my grief.

How wretched I am! I wish to see my country again, perhaps only to become more wretched. Ah! What shall I do there! I shall but hand my head to my enemies. That is not all: I shall enter the seraglio, where I must demand an account of the disastrous time of my absence; and should I find any criminals, what am I to do? And if the idea of it alone overcomes me at such a distance, how will it be when my presence brings it home to me? How shall it be, if I must see, if I must hear what I dare not imagine without a shudder? How shall it be, in short, if I myself must order the infliction of punishments, which shall be everlasting witnesses to my own vexation and despair?

I shall shut myself up within walls more terrible to me than to the women which they guard; I shall take with me all my suspicions; the eagerness of my wives will not remove them in the least; in my bed, in their arms, I shall only possess my anxiety: at a time so unsuitable for reflection, my jealousy will make occasions for it. Worthless scum of human kind, vile slaves whose hearts are for ever closed to all the feelings of love, you would no longer grumble at your condition, if you knew the misery of mine.

Paris, the 4th of the moon of Chabban, 1719.

Letter 156

Roxana to Usbek, at Paris

HORROR, darkness, and terror reign in the seraglio; a dreadful affliction is upon us; at every moment a tiger vents on us all his rage. He has tortured two white eunuchs, who have only confessed their innocence; he has sold part of our slaves, and forced us to share among us the services of those which remained. Zachi and Zelis have received in their chambers, in the darkness of the night, most unworthy treatment; the wretch has not feared to lay his sacrilegious hands upon them. He keeps us shut up each in her apartment; and although we are alone there, he forces us to wear our veils. We are no longer allowed to speak; to write would be a crime: we have no liberty except to weep.

A crowd of new eunuchs have entered the seraglio, and beset us night and day: our sleep is constantly interrupted by their real or feigned suspicions. What consoles me is, that all this cannot last for ever, and that my troubles will end with my life. And the end is not far distant, cruel Usbek: I will not give you time to put an end to all these outrages.

The Seraglio at Ispahan, the 2nd of the moon of Maharram, 1720.

Letter 157

[1]Zachi to Usbek, at Paris

OH, Heaven! A savage has outraged me even in the very manner of punishing me! He has inflicted upon me that chastisement, the first effect of which is to shock one's modesty; that most humiliating of chastisements, which takes one back to one's childhood.

My soul, at first overpowered by shame, recovered consciousness and began to be exasperated, when my cries resounded through the vaults of my apartments. They heard me asking mercy from the vilest of human beings, and trying to excite his pity, in proportion as he became inexorable.

Since that time his insolent and slavish mind dominates mine. His presence, his looks, his words, all horrible things, overwhelm me. When I am alone, I have at least the consolation of weeping; but when he appears before me, frenzy seizes me: I find myself impotent, and I sink into despair.

The tiger dares to tell me that you are the author of all these barbarities. He wishes to deprive me of my love, and even to desecrate the feelings of my heart. When he utters the name of him whom I love, I am unable to complain; I can only die.

I have endured your absence, and my love has been preserved by its own strength. The nights, the days, the moments were all dedicated to you. I was even proud of my love, and your made me respected here. But now … No, I can no longer bear the humiliation which has overtaken me. If I am innocent, return to love me; return, if I am guilty, that I may die at your feet.

The Seraglio at Ispahan, the 2nd of the moon of Maharram, 1720.

Letter 158

[1]Zelis to Usbek, at Paris

YOU are a thousand leagues from me, and yet you condemn me! A thousand leagues from me, and yet you punish me!

When a barbarous eunuch lays his vile hands upon me, it is by your order: it is the tyrant who outrages me, and not the instrument of his tyranny.

You may, if you choose, redouble your cruel treatment. My heart is at peace, since it can no longer love you. Your soul is debased, and you have become cruel. Rest assured that you are not beloved. Farewell.

The Seraglio at Ispahan, the 2nd of the moon of Maharram, 1720.

Solim to Usbek, at Paris

MAGNIFICENT lord, I lament for myself, and I lament for you: never did faithful servant sink into such an abyss of despair. Behold your misfortunes and mine; I write them with a trembling hand.

I swear, by all the prophets of heaven, that since you confided your wives to me, I have watched them night and day; that my anxiety has never left me for a single moment. When I assumed office I commenced with chastisement, which I have discontinued without relaxing my accustomed austerity.

But what am I saying? Why do I boast of fidelity which has been useless to you? Forget all my past services: look upon me as a traitor, and punish me for all the crimes which I have been unable to prevent. Roxana, the haughty Roxana – Oh, Heaven! In whom can we trust henceforth? You suspected Zelis, and never for a moment doubted Roxana; but her fierce virtue was a cruel imposture: it was the veil of her treachery. I surprised her in the arms of a young man, who, when he saw himself discovered, ran at me, and struck me twice with his dagger: the eunuchs came at the noise and surrounded him: he made a long defence, and wounded several of them; he wished even to re-enter the room to die, he said, in the presence of Roxana. But at last he yielded to numbers, and fell at our feet.

I know now, sublime lord, if I shall wait for your stern commands. You have placed your vengeance in my hands; and I ought not to defer it.

The Seraglio at Ispahan, the 8th of the first moon of Rebiab, 1720.

Letter 160

[1]*Solim to Usbek, at Paris*

I HAVE made up my mind: your misfortunes shall disappear; I am going to punish.

Already I feel a secret joy: my soul and yours will be appeased: we shall exterminate crime, and make innocence turn pale.

Oh, all you who seem made only to be unconscious of your own feelings, and to be indignant even at your own desires, everlasting slaves of shame and modesty, would that I could bring you in crowds into this unhappy seraglio, to astonish you with the torrent of blood I am about to shed!

The Seraglio at Ispahan, the 8th of the first moon of Rebiab, 1720.

Letter 161

Roxana to Usbek, at Paris

YES, I have deceived you; I have led away your eunuchs: I have made sport of your jealousy; and I have known how to turn your frightful seraglio into a place of pleasure and delight.

I am at the point of death; the poison courses through my veins: for what should I do here, since the only man who bound me to life is no more? I die; but my spirit shall not pass unaccompanied: I have dispatched before me those sacrilegious gaolers who spilt the sweetest blood in the world.

How could you think that I was such a weakling as to imagine there was nothing for me in the world but to worship your caprices; that while you indulged all your desires, you should have the right to thwart me in all mine? No: I have lived in slavery, and yet always retained my freedom: I have remodeled your laws upon those of nature; and my mind has always maintained its independence.

You ought to thank me, then, for the sacrifice I made you; for having sunk so low as to seem to be yours; for having, like a coward, hidden in my heart what I ought to have published to all the earth; finally, for having profaned virtue, by permitting my submission to your humours to be called by that name.

You were amazed never to find in me the transports of love: had you known me better you would have found all the violence of hate.

For a long time you have had the satisfaction of believing that you had conquered a heart like mine: now we are both delighted: you thought me deceived, and I have deceived you.

Doubtless such a letter as this you little expected to receive. Can it be possible that after having overwhelmed you with affliction I shall still force you to admire my courage? But all is ended now; the poison destroys me, my strength leaves me, my pen drops from my hand; even my hate grows weaker: I die.

The Seraglio at Ispahan, the 8th of the first moon of Rebiab, 1720.

John Davidson's Introduction

II

Letter XXXV.

III

Governor of Guienne, 1716-1719.
See p. 7 [Montesquieu's introduction].
So called because they wore a cap of the shape of a mortar, made of black velvet, ornamented with a gold band.

V

Letter LXXVIII.
Letter LXXXVI.
Letter LXXV.
Letter LXXXI.
Letter CXV.
Letters CIII., CIV.
Letter CXXII.

VI

"Pensées."

VIII

His "tranquil chaos" was what Carlyle admired most in Tennyson.
Garat, "Mémoires sur le Dix-huitième Siècle."
Sayoux, "Le Dix-huitième Siècle à l'Etranger."
Fr.Hardy, "Memoirs of Charlemont."

IX

Maupertuis, "Éloge de Montesquieu."
Garat, "Mémoires sur le Dix-huitième Siècle."
D'Alembert, "Éloge de Montesquieu."
"Pensées."
Laplace, "Pièces intéressantes et peu connues."
Ibid.
"Pensées."

Some Reflections on the Persian Letters

These reflections first appeared as an introduction to the quarto edition of the "Persian Letters" (1754), and have always been ascribed to Montesquieu himself.

A seraglio is a royal dwelling. Montesquieu used the world as if were synonymous with harem, the name of the portion of an oriental mansion in which the women are sequestered.

Probably an allusion to Lord Lyttleton's "Letters of Selim," publised in English in 1735, and shortly afterwards translated into French.

A reference to the "Lettres Turques" of Sainte-Foix, which in the edition of 1740 appeared collectively with the "Persian Letters."

At one time Montesquieu intended to remove what he called "certain juvenilia" from the "Persian Letters;" but the intention was never carried out.

Introduction

Some of these letters were added in the edition of 1754.

This lady has been identified as the author's wife.

Letters

Volume 1

Letter 1

Fatima, daughter of Mohammed, and wife of Ali--according to the Koran, one of the four perfect women.

More correctly, Safar, the second month of the Arabian year.

Letter 3

More correctly Muharram, the first month of the Persian year. Zachi's letter was, therefore, written about a month before the two that precede it.

Letter 5

Rabi means "the spring" in Persian. *Rabi-ul-awal*, "the first (month) of spring," is the third of the Arabian year.

Letter 6

The Persians generally belong to the sect of Shiites, who consider Abu Bekr, Omar, and Othman, the first three successors of Mohammed, as usurpers, and regard Ali, the cousin and son-in-law of the prophet as the first Iman, and equal to Mohammed. The Shiites also reject as unworthy of credit the Sonna, a collection of traditions which is the canon of the faith of the Sunites, the sect to which the Turks belong.

Letter 7

In Persia the women are confined much more closely than among the Turks or Indians.-- (M.)

Letter 8

The two *Gemmadis*, or *Gemalis*, are the fifth and sixth months of the Persian year. *Gemal-i-ul-awal* is the first of these.

Letter 9

This is the only letter *to* Ibbi, and there is only one *from* him, the XXXIX. He must not be confounded with Ibben, to whom many letters are addressed.

Revers in the original. M. Laboulaye asserts that Montesquieu is the only writer who uses *revers* in the sense of *revanche*; but Littré gives examples of a similar use of the word in Molière and Bossuet.
Letter 10

Montesquieu spells it "Mollaks." In Persia the mollah is a devotee; in Turkey, a judge.
Letter 11

"Essayer la mienne," a Gascon provincialism for "user," &c. the meaning is, therefore, as above, and not "to test mine."

Herodotus , Plutarch, Pomponius Mela, and Pliny the Elder, are the authorities for the Troglodites.

Contradictions of assertions in Pomponius Mela.

Gemal-i-ul-sani, the sixth month of the Persian year.
Letter 13

In Montesquieu's time it was not uncommon for parents of noble descent to compel their daughters to enter a convent in order that the eldest son might have greater means of display.
Letter 15

Letter XV. is the first of those added in the edition of 1754.
Letter 16

The three tombs are those of Fatima and two votaries of her family.

Zufagar, or Zoulfegar, the name of a double-bladed sword given by Mohammed to Ali. It was treasured for many years in the palace of the califs, until one of the successors of Abdoullah II. broke it by accident while hunting. A representation of this sword still appears on the flag of the Turkish navy.

The first twelve successors of Mohammed were the Imans, or holy men. To address any one as the "thirteenth Iman" is, therefore, a high compliment.

In the original, "as one distinguishes at daybreak the white thread from the black." According to the Mussulmans, day begins when there is light enough to make this distinction.
Letter 18

More correctly, Shaban, the eighth month of the Persian year.

Mohammedan tradition.-(M.)
Letter 19

That is to say, the new inventions of the European nations.

These are, apparently, the Knights of Malta.-(M.)
Letter 20

More correctly, Zilkaid, the eleventh month of the Persian year.
Letter 21

According to the persians there are a hundred thousand prophets. (See letter XLI.)
Letter 22

The second of those added in 1754.
Letter 23

The Persian women wear four.---(M.)
Letter 24

Louis XIV
The French kings regarded money as a mere symbol, the value of which they could raise or lower at their pleasure. "Kings treat men as they do pieces of money; they give them what value they choose, and people are forced to accept them according to their currency, and not according to their true worth."--LA ROCHEFOUCAULD.

An anachronism. The date of this letter is 1712, but the Bull Unigenitus, which, under the name of the "Constitution," troubled France during the greater part of the eighteenth century, was not issued til 1713.

Louis XIV, submitted the more readily because he required the Pope's aid to terminate the theological quarrels which had become so insufferable to him.

The Jansenists.
The Jesuits.
Rabi-ul-sani, the second month of spring, and fourth of the Persian year.
Letter 26

More correctly, Rejab, the seventh month of the Persian year.
Letter 27

Ispahan.--(M.)
Letter 28

"Come on, and let us get a seat on the theatre.--On the theatre, replied my Siamese; you're joking. We are not going to perform, we come to look on.--No matter, I said, let us go and loll there. We shall see nothing, and hear badly; but it is the most expensive, and consequently the most honourable place."--DUFRESNY'S *Amusements serieux et comiques*, chap. V.

More correctly, *Shawal*, the tenth month of the Persian year.
Letter 29

Lent.
Applied by Montesquieu's Persians to the friars, especially to the Jesuits.
A Rosary.
A scapulary.
The pilgrmage to Saint James of Compostella.
The Persians are the most tolerant of all the Mohammedans. -- (M.)
Letter 32

The almshouse of the "Quinze-Vingts," founded at Paris, in 1254, by Saint Louis, on his return from Palestine, for three hundred knights whose eyes had been put out by the Saracens
Letter 34

More correctly, Zil Haj, the last month of the Persian year.
Letter 35

The full title of the book to which Usbek alludes is, "Polygamia triumphatrix, id est discursus politicus de polygamia, auctore Theophilo Aletheo, cum notis Athanasii Vincentii, omnibus antipolygamis, ubique locorum, terrarum, insularum, pagorum, urbium, modeste et pie opposita." It was printed in Holland, probably in Amsterdam, although the name of a Swedish town appears on the title-page. Had it not suited Montesquieu's purpose to refer to it, the very name of the book would now be unknown except to a few specialists, as it is dull and uninteresting.
Letter 36

The Café Procope, a redezvous of the wits of the eighteenth century.
The quarrel regarding the relative merits of the ancients and the moderns, in which Homer was the chief subject of dispute.
The Latin of schools.
The Sorbonne and the University.
An allusion to a seminary of Irish priests instituted in 1677 by some refugees.
Letter 37

Louis XIV. Was then seventy-five years old, and had reigned for seventy.
When Louis XIV. Was in his sixteenth year, some courtiers discussed in his presence the absolute power of the Sultans, who dispose as they like of the goods and the lives of their subjects. "That is something like being a king," said the young monarch. Marshal d'Estrées, alarmed at the tendency revealed in the remark, rejoined, "But, sire, several of these emperors have been strangled even in my time."
Barbezieux, son of Louvois, Louis's youngest minister, held office at twenty-three, not eighteen; and he was dead in 1713.
Madame de Maintenon.
The Jansenists.
At Versailles.
The Shah of Persia.
Letter 38

Herodotus, iv. 110-147
Letter 39

A Hagi is a man who has made the pilgrimage to Mecca.-(M.)
Letter 42

A "sublime expression" which the reader is not spared.(See Introduction.)
Volume 2

Letter 45

In this letter Montesquieu was probably thinking of a physician named Boudin, who imagined that he had rediscovered the secrets of the alchemists. Saint-Simon has an admirable description of this man.

Nicholas Flamel, a citizen of Paris (1330-1418), was regarded as an alchemist by those who envied his great fortune. Raymond Lully, a Spanish savant (1235-1315), was considered, rightly or wrongly, one of the most famous alchemists.

Letter 46

A Jew.--(M.)
A Turk.--(M.)
An Armenian.--(M.)

Letter 47

Courouc (back! back!) is the cry of the eunuchs who accompany the women's litters.

Letter 48

Montesquieu describes himself in this passage.

Letter 51

These manners have changed. – (M.)
Peter the Great.

Letter 55

It was a rule of good society. "Most men understand that they should say very little about their wives; but few know that they should talk still less about themselves."--LA ROCHEFOUCAULD.

Letter 60

Voltaire, in his article on the Jews in the "Philosophical Dictionary," has reproduced this idea of Montesquieu's without acknowledging it.

Abu Bekr, father-in-law of Mohammed, was proclaimed Caliph on the death of the prophet, in 632. According to the Persians, this nomination was a usurpation of the rights of Ali, the cousin and son-in-law of Mohammed. (See Note, p. 20, Vol. i. [letter 6]).

Letter 63

Drawing-room we would say to-day. In the eighteenth century it was in their elegant cabinets de toilette that ladies received visitors.

Letter 67

Guebre, or infidel, the name applied to the fire-worshippers, descended from the immediate followers of Zoroaster. According to Dr. C. J. Wills, in his "Persia as It Is," there are only about 8000 Guebres left in Persia, and these are congregated at Yezd.

A fabulous Cambyses, father of Hystaspes, or Gustaspes, King of Persia, under whom Zoroaster lived. Cambyses, under the name of Hohoraspes, and his son are referred to further on in this letter.

The caste of hereditary priests under the Medes and Persians. Zoraster reformed their religious doctrines and ceremonies.

The ancient Bactra. The Arch-mage resided there till the followers of Zoroaster were overcome by the Caliphs.

A toman is equal to a little more than eighteen shillings.

Letter 69

Zeuxis, when he painted Helen for the Agrigentines.
This paragraph appeared first in the edition of 1754.

Letter 71

Moses.-Deuteronomy, ch. 22., 5. 13-21.
See Letter I., note 1.

Letter 72

Decisionnaire in the original, a word invented by Montesquieu to describe a man who lays down the law upon everything.
Tavernier (1605-1689) and Chardin (1643-1713), the Persian travelers from whose books Montesquieu derived his knowledge of Persia.

Letter 73

The dictionary of the Academy.
The dictionary of Furetière. The author was expelled from the Academy in 1685, because he was accused of having profited by the work of his fellow Academicians in the composition of the dictionary which bears his name.

Letter 75

:

"All we have gained then by our unbelief Is a life of doubt diversified by faith, For one of faith diversified by doubt: We called the chessboard white, --we call it black." --Browning.   The French colonies.
The Mohammedans had no wish to take Venice because they could not obtain water there suitable for their purifications. --(M.)

Letter 76

Cent millions de têtes in some editions. *Terres* seems preferable, however, as it is an anticlimax to proceed from all men to a hundred millions.

Letter 77

This letter was inserted in the edition of 1754 as a foil to that which precedes it.

Letter 78

Madame d'Aulnoy has a similar eulogy of spectacles in her "Voyage d'Espagne."
Jean de Castro.--(M.)
The exhibition of the foot, according to Madame d'Aulnoy's "Voyage d'Espagne," was regarded in Spain as being "*la dernière javeur.*"
"Don Quixote."
The Batuecas.--(M.) This is an invention of some wag whom Montesquieu seems to have taken seriously.

Letter 81

This letter contains much that Montesquieu developed afterwards in his "Esprit des Lois" In 1622.

Letter 82

The Huns.

Letter 86

This letter is a bold and generous protest against the revocation of the Edict of Nantes. The Parsees of Bombay are the descendants of the exiled Guebres.

Letter 87

According to a law derived from the Romans, in the southern provinces of France daughters could compel their fathers to dower them. (See Letter 125.)

Letter 90

This letter contains the germ of "principles of the three governments," a theory expounded by Montesquieu in the third book of "L'Esprit des Lois."

Letter 91

By an edict of Louis XIV. duelists incurred the penalty of death.

Letter 92

The fourth letter added in 1754.
The business-agent of a Persian provincial minister, in order to defray the expenses of a visit to France, pretended to be an ambassador. He was allowed to play the part for the king's amusement.

Letter 93

Louis XIV. died at Versailles on the 1st of September, 1715, in the seventy-seventh year of his age and the sixty-third of his reign.
The Duke of Orleans.
By an edict of 16th September, 1715, ratified in Parliament, the Regent revoked those articles of the decrees of 1667 and 1673 which took from Parliament the right of remonstrance.

Letter 94

A Mussulman living a conventual life.

Letter 102

The Bull *Unigenitus*, directed against the Jansenists. (See Letter XXIV.)

Letter 103

Philip-Augustus
He who was called the "old man of the mountains."

Letter 105

Charles I.
The New Testament.

Letter 107

Used by Montesquieu as inclusive of both the industrial and the fine arts

Letter 108

Louis XV., born 15th February, 1710.

Letter 109

The French journals of the eighteenth century contained nothing but notices of new books.

Letter 110

He means the dispute with Ramus.-(M.) Dr. Ramus (Pierre de la Ramée), Professor in the College Royal, wished to say *kiskis* and *kankam* instead of *quisquis* and *quanquam*. He was assassinated on the third day of the massacre of St. Bartholomew.

Philip III., King of Spain.

Letter 112

The fifth of the letters added in 1754.

Cardinal Mazarin, having occasion to use the phrase, "l'arrêt d'union," before the parliamentary deputies, pronounced it, "l'arrêt d'*ognon*," a slip of which the people made great fun.—(M.)

Letter 113

Some countries were, in Montesquieu's time, and are now, less populous than in their earlier history; but that the modern world contains fewer people than the antique one, is an assertion for which there is no proof.

In one sense true, as Cæsar's Gaul was covered with forests.

Letter 114

Mercury.

Letter 120

The heaven of the Chinese.

Letter 121

By an edict of Henry II., in 1556.

Letter 122

History proves the contrary.

Montesquieu did not foresee the "Negro question."

The author probably means the Isle of Bourbon.--(M.)

Not the only one; there is the method by which England has retained India.

Letter 124

Prince Eugene, who defeated the Turks at Peterwardein, took Belgrade in 1717, and concluded the advantageous peace of Passarowitz in 1718.

Letter 125

The sixth of the letters added in 1754.

Letter 126

Bonzes are the Buddhist priests of China, whom Montesquieu seems to have confounded with the Brahmins of India.

Letter 127

By the Great Mogul is here meant the King of Spain. His ambassador is the Prince of Cellamare, who was arrested and sent across the frontier for conspiring against the Regent with the Duke and Duchess of Maine.

The Duke of Maine.

Letter 128

Charles XII of Sweden.

Baron Gortz.

Letter 130

The Tuileries.

1717.

The Count of Lionne.

That is, to publish.

The Count of Lionne.

Letter 131

This letter contains the gist of the "Esprit des Lois."

Letter 132

The paper of the Bank having become worthless, the holders of bills had to pay their value in cash into the Treasury.

The depreciated paper retained in law its nominal value, so that a debtor could ruin his creditor by paying him in bank-bills.

Letter 135

Law, the banker.

Letter 137

Like Pascal, Montesquieu despised poetry, although he liked plays. Voltaire, having been taken to task concerning his attacks on Montesquieu, replied, "He is guilty of *lèse-poésie*."

M. Meyer, in his "Études de critique ancienne et moderne," detects here an allusion to Voltaire's "Henriade," the beginning of which was already circulating in manuscript. This is not impossible, as Montesquieu had no great regard for Voltaire.

Letter 138

The Duke of Noailles.

Law.

Rue Quincampoix, at that time the rendezvous of stockbrokers.

Letter 139

Ulrica-Eleonora, sister of Charles XII., elected Queen of Sweden by the people.
Frederic of Hesse-Cassel.

Letter 140

The Parliament, having opposed Law's system, was exiled to Pontoise by the Regent on the 21st of July, 1720.

Letter 142

The scotch financier, Law, of whose system this allegory is a satire.
France.
Louis XIV.
Le cours des actions, the price of shares.
It had been decreed that all specie should be taken to the Bank.
At the beginning of Law's "system," claims on the Bank were paid half in paper and half in cash.
A royal order, issued 20th June, 1720.
A decree of the 4th of July, 1720.
A decree of the 15th September, 1720.

Letter 143

"La Connaissance du Globe," according to the early editors.
Reverend pere Jesuite
A Jesuit, born at Troyes. He was the confessor of Louis XIII., and was exiled by Richelieu.
Ten Decrees (Arrets) of the Council, concerning the Bank and the Company of the Indies; or, according to the earlier editors, concerning the Bull and the Constitution of the Jesuits.
Flechier, Bishop of Nimes (Monsieur de Nimes).
The "Jeux Floraux," established in 1324 by the magistrates of Toulouse to revive the decaying art of the troubadours.
Louis Maimbourg, expelled from the company of Jesus in 1685 for having defended the libraries of the Gallican Church in his "traite historique de l'Englise de Rome."
"A marvel in chemistry, concerning a violent fermentation, accompanied with smoke, heat, and flame. *Mingle an infusion of Quesnel[9] with one of Lallemand;[10] let fermentation proceed with much violence, energy, and noise, as the acids fight together, and eat their way into each others alkaline salts;[11] the fiery spirits will thus evaporate. When fermentation is over, put the liquid in an alembic: you will get nothing out of it, and find nothing left in it, but a caput mortuum.-A Gentle Aperient. Take two papers of Molina as pain-killer; of Escobar, to keep the bowels open, take six pages; take of Vasquez, to keep the passage easy, one leaf; infuse in four pounds o f common water. When half has evaporated, strain and squeeze; and, while squeezing, dissolve in the mixture three leaves of Baun to act as detergent, and three of Tamburini [11] to wash away impurities. Make a clyster of the result.-A cure for chlorosis, vulgarly called the green-sickness,* or hot fit of love. *Take four plates from Aretinus; take of Thomas Sanchez' work on Marriage, two leaves. Infuse them in five pounds of common water, and you will have a pleasant aperient.*"

A Jansenist, and Great opponent of the Jesuits.

A Jesuit father.

A pun in the original; "sales" meaning also "witticisms."

Molina, Escobar, Vasquez, Bauni, and Tamburini were Jesuits who replied to the attacks of the Jansenists. Their names are frequently mentioned in Pascal's "Provincials." The name of Escobar makes at least one appearance in English literature:

"Now, they prick pins at a tissue
Fine as a skein of the casuist Escobar's
Worked on the bone of a lie."

Browning's Master Hugues of Saxe-Gotha. Vol. III **Letter 144**

The seventh letter added in 1754.

In the original "my dear Usbek," which is evidently a mistake.

Letter 145

The eighth letter added in 1754.

Letter 146

Another satire on the "system" of Law.

Paper money.

A pen.

That is, paid a debt in worthless paper.

Letter 153

Expier in the original. It is used again by Montesquieu in this unusual sense in "L'Esprit des Lois."

Letter 157

The ninth letter added in 1754.

Letter 158

The tenth of 1754.

Letter 160

The eleventh and last of the letters added in 1754.

Made in the USA
Columbia, SC
12 October 2023

24367638R00130